THE

DRAGON SPIRITS: BOOK 2

L.L. MACRAE

First published in Great Britain in 2023.

Cover by: Psycat Studios
Maps by: Domino44maps

Printed and bound by CPI Group (UK) Ltd, Croydon, CR0 4YY

www.llmacrae.com

For Pipkin,

Who brings so much joy, love, and happiness to my life.

And also lets me write all day.

ALSO BY L. L. MACRAE

DRAGON SPIRITS

NOVELS

The Iron Crown

The Shadow Gate

NOVELLAS

The Citrine Key

WORLD OF LINARIA

NOVELS

Moroda

Palom

Amarah

Isa

NOVELLAS

Rise of a Sky Pirate

ACKNOWLEDGMENTS

I cannot thank Olivia enough.

She has been instrumental in the building of this book—from its foundations right through to the finish line. With our weekly calls, late-night brainstorming, and her honesty when something wasn't working well, without her, this book would be a shadow of itself.

So much of what is good in *The Shadow Gate* comes from Olivia, and I am a better author—and person—because of her.

Thank you again to Eike W., my chief curse writer, who helped create so many of the mysterious and magical verses in this book.

My eternal gratitude goes out to Ian, Josephine, Laura, and Maxine, my unflappable beta readers, who gave me critique and confidence in equal measure, and have been stalwart guides during the writing process. Additional and particular thanks also goes to Iznib and Spectacle for stepping up to be last minute beta readers and taking on a mammoth reading task in not much time!

This team has helped shape the book, from cutting away the fat and adding in detail where needed, to influencing some of the better decisions and changes for both characters and plot. This book would not be what it is without them.

I would also like to thank a number of people for their unending support, assistance, and kind words. This includes all my fellow SPFBO7 Finalists, but especially, Kerstin, Tim, Clayton, Krystle, Taya, and Jen. It also includes several shining beacons in the indie fantasy community: Andrew, Craig, Dom, Esmay, Terry, Tufty, and countless others.

Their encouragement kept me going when the finish line seemed so very far away.

A final thank you goes to my incredible Egg and Tea Dragon patrons, Spectacle Cat, Lizz Turner, Becca Fowell, Lisa Woods, Kevin Hurley, Roondawg Valhalla, Andrew Burns, Zookie Cartoons, Dom McDermott, and Amy Tomlinson, whose support has directly contributed to the creation of this book.

To anyone who reads this, I am eternally grateful.

It would mean the world and more if you would be kind enough to review *The Shadow Gate*.

Polar Sea
Laseen Ocean
The Salt Sea
Foxmouth
Shrine of Toriaken
Nethal
Westbrook
Eastbrook
Horush
Porsenthia
Hillsbrin
Shrine of Miroth
Tonmouth
Northbourne
Marlrush Fortress
Southbourne
Port Frickley
The Spindle Woods
Spindleford
Shrine of Alnothen
Fellwood
Bragalia
Shrine of Chyram
Vaelar
Cliffton
Meadowhill
Olmir
Shrine of Yakris
Ordona
Hebstloch
Shrine of Neros
Segandis
Ballowtown
Ulbridge
Hogsbrooke
Saltash Forest
Isle of Salt
Domino44 Maps
Etrovia

REALM O
POLAR
Etrovia
FOXMOUTH
SHRINE OF TORIAKEN
NETHAL
WESTBROOK
EASTBROOK
HORUSH
HILLSBRIN
NORTHBOURNE
THE SALT SEA
SHRINE OF MIROTH
TONMOUTH
MARLRUSH FORTRESS
SHRINE OF ALNOTHEN
THE SPINDLE WOODS
SPINDLEFORD
FELLWOOD
SHRINE OF CHYRAM
VAELAR
CLIFFTON
MEADOWHILL
HERSTLOCH
SHRINE OF NEROS
SEGANDIS
HOGSBROOKE
SALTASH FOREST
BALLOWTOWN
ULBRIDGE
Isle of Salt
POLAR
DOMINO44 MAPS
TOWN/SETT
SHRINE

TASSAR
Meneos
MOONLIGHT PALACE
MA-RAI
WESTWICKS
CAPE GRULLON
SAFITI
BOL-RAI
ORT FRICKLEY
SHRINE OF YAKRIS
ORDONA
LORNRAI
THE ELMWOOD
Malbosh
TESRAI
CITY
LARGE CITY

SUMMARY OF THE IRON CROWN

Fenn, a young man with no memory of anything bar his own name, awakens in a bog on the Isle of Salt. He is immediately accosted by Hassen, the Dragon Spirit of Salt Ash Forest, who takes an interest in him. Hassen flies through Fenn, giving him a brief glimpse into the life energy of the forest and—unbeknownst to Fenn—bonds with him.

Fenn soon encounters Calidra and her partner, Jisyel, two residents of the island. Taking pity on his bedraggled state, they take him back to the inn owned by Jisyel's grandmother to rest. Calidra receives a letter from her estranged mother notifying her that her father—the Laird of a canton in Bragalia—has died, and she is being summoned for the funeral. She hasn't been home in seven years, blaming herself for her sister's death and ruined relationship with her mother—a response to the abuse she suffered at her mother's hand as a child. Used to running away, Calidra must now face her past.

Needing to cross from the Isle of Salt to Bragalia for the funeral, Calidra and Jisyel decide to take Fenn with them. If nothing else, the Queen's Inquisitors can deal with him. Jisyel, cursed by Hassen some time ago, also wants to use the travel opportunity to potentially find a way to remove it.

While resting at an inn in Bragalia, they encounter Torsten, the queen's Master Inquisitor. He tries to arrest Fenn, claiming there are many "lost souls" he has picked up recently, and with his lack of memory, Fenn could be one of them. However, he is thwarted at the last moment when the former Porsenthian General, Varlot, steps in to defend Fenn.

Things immediately escalate when a shadow-like creature attacks the town. Torsten, Varlot, and Calidra step in to fight it off, but Jisyel and Fenn are washed into the river during the scuffle. Torsten believes the creature to be one of the Myr's spirits—which should be impossible with the Iron Crown in power. He leaves town to investigate further, whilst Calidra and Varlot search for Jisyel and Fenn. On his way back to the capital city, Torsten stops at his hometown, Tonmouth, and visits the shrine of Miroth—the dragon spirit to whom he is bonded.

Miroth confirms the creature Torsten fought is one of the Myrish death spirits. It means the Myr are returning and Tassar is no longer safe. There is only one reason this could be happening, as he confirms with Queen Surayo on his return to the capital: one of the ancient and powerful Myrish artefacts—The Citrine Key—was *not* destroyed five years ago as had been promised.

Stranded with no supplies, Fenn and Jisyel turn to a nearby temple for help, and meet one of the priestesses, Selys. She has seen many people begging for aid recently, all of whom later died. As Fenn's symptoms are similar to these people, she states he has been touched by the Myr and will likely die soon. Only a powerful spirit can undo Fenn's curse—there is an ancient Myrish construct in the far north of Porsenthia, and this might be able to help him. In service to her own dragon spirit, Neros, Selys wishes to learn more about Fenn and the Myr, and agrees to lead them through the country.

Elsewhere, Calidra is beside herself with worry for Jisyel. Varlot convinces her to move on—she has a funeral to get to. Despite a successful career within the Porsenthian army and a charismatic charm that easily attracts people to him, Varlot is plagued by alcoholism, gambling debts, and a violent nature that bubbles just below the surface. Naturally suspicious—a survival instinct—Calidra has no choice but to work with Varlot, though she does not trust the man.

Begrudgingly, they make their way through Bragalia towards her hometown, Fellwood. On the way, they are attacked by another shadow-like creature, saved only by the arrival of an Olmese warrior on his war-griffin. Amsel, the warrior, confirms the Myr are returning and the warriors of Olmir are gathering to defend Tassar from their advance.

Amsel flies Calidra and Varlot to Fellwood, and Calidra makes it back in time for her father's funeral. Her terror of her mother, Furyn, gives way to an explosive reunion. It is fuelled by Furyn's refusal to support her search for Jisyel—whom Calidra dreads is drowned—as well as the revelation that Furyn had lied to her for years—Calidra's sister, Malora, is alive and living in northern Porsenthia.

Fenn, Jisyel, and Selys make their way to Fellwood. Along the way, Fenn sees more shadow-like creatures—his curse seemingly enabling him to observe spirits and magic of Myrish origin. After they all reunite, Furyn throws everyone out of Fellwood so she can focus on defending the canton from the encroaching Myr alongside a battalion of Olmese griffin riders.

Desperate to reach the Myrish construct before his time runs out, Fenn pushes north—from Bragalia into Porsenthia—led by Selys and aided by Varlot, though Calidra openly states she does not trust him. Having discovered her sister is alive, Calidra follows, along with Jisyel. They make their way through the Spindle Woods, home to an ancient dragon spirit, Alnothen, who appears and warns Varlot that he is not welcome.

Pressing on through the trees, Jisyel cuts her leg on a venomous plant known as Tanglethorn and subsequently collapses. After recuperating in a nearby village for a few hours, and so close to Alnothen's shrine, Jisyel begs to go there, as Alnothen might be powerful enough to lift the curse placed upon her by Hassen.

Although forbidden, Calidra implores Varlot to carry Jisyel through the trees to the shrine. Alnothen agrees to release Jisyel from her curse if she becomes one of her priestesses—forsaking all other things in life and devoting herself entirely to the spirit. Knowing what such a bond demands after seeing her sister beholden to a dragon spirit, Calidra begs Jisyel to refuse. Angered and further offended by Varlot's presence, Alnothen warns them off her domain.

As the group crosses the deadlands, Fenn is accosted by visions and memories of a great battle held there several years prior: the Myr against the forces of the Iron Crown. He sees Varlot and Torsten in the battlefield, along with the death and destruction left in the wake of the Myr.

Upon reaching Tonmouth, the group rests. Miroth is the

dragon spirit of a nearby lake, and Varlot confirms Torsten was born here. Having seen the Master Inquisitor behave erratically, it is suggested he might be bonded with the slowly dying spirit, and giving in to Miroth's whims. They send messages to their loved ones and board a ship that will take them the rest of the way.

Fenn, Varlot, and Selys disembark part-way through the journey, as the Myrish construct is in a cave in the Nethal mountains. Calidra and Jisyel remain onboard as it will sail around the mountains to Foxmouth—where Malora lives. As the group says their goodbyes, two Inquisitors meet them—ready to arrest Fenn. Varlot sent word of the Myr-touched, "lost soul," and is ready to claim his reward after betraying him. Selys fights off all three Inquisitors, then she and Fenn flee into the snowy mountains, though injured.

In Foxmouth, Malora's husband—and former thief—Apollo plays with their young daughter, Renys. This is cut short by the arrival of Inquisitor Nadja, who arrests Apollo for high treason and drags him away. Queen Surayo had commanded Apollo to destroy the Citrine Key in exchange for a full pardon five years prior. She believes he failed in that duty, otherwise the Myr would not be back. Apollo denies any wrongdoing, but is brought to the palace for questioning. At Apollo's request, Nadja sends a message to his wife informing her of his situation and likely imminent execution.

Torsten tortures Apollo for information using a Myrish spell made living. This creature absorbs memories, and he uses it to find out Apollo's truth. Although Apollo fights back, the creature learns what he did—and did not do—five years previously. Before Torsten learns this, the palace is attacked by the Myr.

Apollo manages to escape in the chaos, commandeering one of the Olmese war-griffins and flying away—but not before he steals the Myrish spell and dumps it in the Lasseen Ocean when they fly over it. Toriaken, Spirit of Iron, rises from the palace to defend the city against the Myr. In the wake of the enormous dragon, the griffin is blown off course, and Apollo crashes into the nearby woodland.

On the waters outside Foxmouth, Neros rises to face a Myrish attack on a second front. Boats capsize and people are flung into the sea—Calidra and Jisyel included. Calidra passes out after losing her strength in the water, but is pulled into a small fishing boat. Malora and others are scouring the wreckage, searching for survivors, and Calidra reunites with her sister. Jisyel was rescued earlier, and the three take refuge on a small, rocky island off the coast of Foxmouth, devastated by what has happened.

In the woodland outside the capital, Apollo sees one of the Myr devouring life energy from a tree, and flees. Inquisitors are hunting him down, and he is too weak after his torture to fight back. Before they can recapture him, a griffin swoops down to attack, and Apollo blacks out.

In the Nethal Mountains, Fenn reaches the Myrish construct, *Vermecio*, and it removes the excess Myrish magic from his body. He still has no memories, but with the curse nullified, he is no longer at risk of death. The construct promises to restore Fenn's memories if he restores its power. It needs a Myrish artefact to do so: the Citrine Key.

Neros reacts to the Myrish attacks—blessing Selys and sharing her power with the priestess. Overwhelmed by Neros's power, Selys collapses. Strengthened by the removal of his curse, Fenn carries her back down the mountain.

Unsure where to go, he makes his way towards the nearest town he can see. On the way, they cross paths with Inquisitors searching for Apollo—including Torsten.

Controlled by Miroth, Torsten attacks Fenn and Selys. No longer suppressed by Myrish magic, Hassen rises from Fenn and attacks. Though not a strong spirit, Hassen is more powerful than the slowly dying Miroth, and overpowers Torsten—proving Fenn's station as a priest of a dragon spirit.

Inquisitor Nadja apologises and they take Torsten away, allowing Fenn and Selys to travel unhindered to the nearby town of Westbrook. Many people caught in the Myrish attack on the capital are recovering here, Apollo included. Eager to help, Fenn distributes food among the injured. When he touches Apollo, he has another vision of what happened with the Citrine Key and Apollo through his connection with Myrish magic. Shocked, he begs Apollo to take him to the key. However, Apollo is distraught, having heard Foxmouth was destroyed by the Myr, and fears his wife and daughter are dead.

Nadja arrives in town, looking for Apollo. Upon finding him, she states her belief that he failed in his task with the Citrine Key and is therefore responsible for the new Myrish invasion. Apollo is shocked when the Inquisitor says she doesn't want to arrest him. Nadja wants him to fix his mistake, and will accompany him to the Citrine Key, making sure it is destroyed once and for all. She has taken a leave of absence to carry out the task, against Surayo's wishes that traitors to the crown must be executed.

Outside the building, Fenn and Selys spot Amsel and his griffin, Hailathlyl—who saved Apollo. Amsel was on his way to Foxmouth to see Malora to safety on behalf of Furyn Vantonen, when he and Hailathlyl happened upon Apollo in trouble and helped out. Apollo refuses to take them to the key until he knows Malora and Renys are safe. Nadja acquiesces. Though weak and injured, Apollo gets to his feet. Fenn, Selys, Apollo and Nadja climb on board the griffin, and Amsel flies them towards what's left of Foxmouth.

Meanwhile, Varlot arrives at the palace and seeks an audience with Torsten. He demands to be made an Inquisitor and his titles reinstated. In exchange, he will lead Torsten and the Iron Crown to Fenn.

PART I

Time has come to tear the veil,
When key and gate collide,
Our shadows cover land and sea,
Your forces stand allied.

Rolling darkness, spirits live,
Your people left to die,
And once we rend bone from flesh,
Dragons will ne'er again arise.

1
THE RUINS
FENN

Smoke rose in thick plumes on the horizon, choking the sky with ash.

Fenn and the others approached Foxmouth on griffin-back from the south, trepidation hanging heavy over them. The stench hit him soon after spotting what was left of the port town.

Charred flesh and melted stone.

It had been several days since the Myrish strike on Foxmouth, but the devastation remained as raw and violent as the attack itself. Debris littered the choppy waves, detritus strewn across the shingle beaches. People picked through it, several of them in blood-soaked rags, perhaps looking for loved ones. Signs of life. Others carried the injured or dead.

Fenn's stomach turned at the sight.

He'd never been here before—not that he could remember, at least. And yet he couldn't help but feel connected. Guilty. The Myr had attacked Foxmouth, and *he* was Myr-touched. Whatever was contributing to their return, he was part of it, whether he wanted to be or not.

Fenn couldn't stand the sight of the devastation and

turned his eyes towards the distant horizon, where the Lasseen Ocean stretched out as far as he could see. He needed to find the Citrine Key and return it to the Myrish construct deep in the Nethal Mountains. *Vermecio* awaited.

It was the only way he could restore his memories and find his family—if he had one.

Apollo, the only person who knew the key's location, had demanded to go home before he would help. Unfortunately, his home was a ruin.

Fenn tried to wet his lips—dry and chapped from the relentless wind—his gaze drifting down again. He didn't want to look at the destruction, but he couldn't help himself. They needed to help these people. 'Should we—'

'Don't.' Apollo cut him off, his jaw tight.

Fenn closed his mouth.

It was Apollo's home down there, buried somewhere under rubble. His family. Friends. Sadness and anger rolled off Apollo in waves, his shoulders hunching as they flew lower. Apollo had been a defeated man in a sick bed not so long ago. Fenn thought there'd been a spark in Apollo's eyes when he'd been dragged out by Nadja, but he was reverting back to that broken state.

Fenn turned to Selys, but the priestess's attention wasn't on him. The bandages around her shoulder were fraying at the edges, whipping around in the strong wind, but she didn't pay that any attention either.

Selys bowed her head, murmuring something under her breath too low for Fenn to catch. A prayer, perhaps? She was a priestess of Neros after all, and his first encounter with her had been while surrounded by death at her spirit's shrine.

It was fitting they were flying towards more of the same.

'You can do nothing for them. The strong have survived.' Hassen's voice sounded in his head and fire burned in his chest. Fenn suppressed a shudder. Since realising the dragon

had bonded with him, Hassen had been ever-present, like a splinter in his mind. He spoke when he wished and offered his own, unique perspective on the world and events.

Fenn wasn't sure he liked it, but if it hadn't been for Hassen, he would have succumbed to the Myrish curse he'd been afflicted with. Two spiritual powers vying for control, his body and mind their battleground. Since the excess Myrish magic had been purged—taking away his risk of death—Hassen's repressed power had flourished.

Fenn could still *feel* the Myr, though. A cold darkness, tiny next to Hassen's fire, but there all the same. It was difficult to tell them apart, and all he knew for certain was that his mind was not completely his own. Whispers echoed there, offering emotions or words.

Despite Hassen's help, Fenn wanted to block everything out. Wanted to be himself.

Hassen was, like most dragon spirits, prideful. He valued strength. He was also a trickster, and laughed at misfortune. Thankfully, he wasn't laughing now.

'Amsel. We need to land.' Apollo's words were clipped.

Fenn looked at the older man, gaze drawn to the pale scar curving down from the corner of his left eye to his mouth. Selys had explained it was the mark of a thief, carved into his face by one of the queen's Inquisitors.

Fenn didn't need to think hard about which Inquisitor had probably done that to Apollo.

Thankfully, Inquisitor Nadja was Torsten's complete opposite.

The five of them made a strange-looking group: a thief and an Inquisitor, a priestess of Neros, a priest of Hassen—both newly blessed, and an Olmese warrior riding the enormous war griffin, Hailathlyl.

At least he could introduce himself as one of Hassen's Blessed.

Anything was better than Myr-touched, lost soul, or cursed one. He'd grown to despise the fear and disgust with which people looked at him. Even those he'd considered friends. Calidra. Jisyel. They'd been mistrustful of him from the start.

Stomach queasy after the flight, Apollo's request to land couldn't have come soon enough. It would take him closer to the devastation, but at least he'd be on solid ground again.

One step closer to the key.

Hailalthlyl banked hard, descending on Foxmouth's main promenade where it jutted into the sea.

Fenn yelped, gripping the handrail of the seating platform.

A short way in front of him, near the griffin's head, Amsel laughed. 'You will not fall. You're like a child jumping at his own shadow, Fenn. I thought dragon priests were supposed to be fearless!'

Fenn tightened his grip. 'Never said I was scared!' Splashes of saltwater filled the air where the waves broke against wooden planks, cooling and stinging his cheeks as they swooped low.

'Neros.' Hassen hissed, acknowledging the presence of a larger, more powerful spirit.

Fenn dared not let go of the handrail to wipe his face, grunting when Hailathlyl's mismatched legs landed with a heavy thud. He clambered down the eleven-foot-tall griffin as quickly as he could, keen to get off before his knees buckled under him. His muscles were tight, his legs cramping, but being back on the ground was a relief.

Selys dismounted next, graceful despite her injured shoulder, and used the butt of her glaive as a walking stick.

Inquisitor Nadja helped Apollo down and onto the promenade. The pier creaked under their muddy boots, wet wood and slippery algae threatening to trip anyone not paying attention.

The tang of salt was thick in the air, every breath reminding him of Neros's presence. Heavy clouds pressed in, giving Foxmouth a sense of foreboding weight, and Fenn rubbed his arms.

'Hailathlyl and I will continue to scout from the sky. If Malora is here, we'll find her. Hailathlyl knows the scent of Furyn and Calidra. Malora will be similar. It is how we recognised you, after all, Apollo,' Amsel said. The griffin let out a trill of assent, fixing each of them with a quick glare from her bright orange eyes.

'Please, please find her,' Apollo said.

Amsel nudged Hailathlyl forward, and she leapt back into the air with a blast of her dark, feathered wings.

The sudden arrival and lift off had caused dozens of heads to glance up, and Fenn found a small but growing crowd staring at them. Before he could respond, several gazes landed on Apollo, and people let out whispered gasps. A few pointed towards him.

Apollo squared his jaw and immediately headed down the promenade towards the nearest of the ruined buildings, hobbling with every step.

'Apollo.' Nadja's command reverberated. 'Where are you going?'

'Home.'

'Amsel just said he'd scout from the sky. You're in no condition to be wandering around.'

Apollo's purposeful stride faltered. He stumbled, caught himself, then continued on.

Nadja considered the former thief for a moment, then followed with a resigned sigh, leaving Fenn and Selys alone with the churning sea at their backs.

More spray hit Fenn's cheek, cold and uncaring. Debris rolled along the ground, pushed by the chill wind. Directly ahead, stone and brick piles lay where buildings had stood only days previously. Bodies of the dead had been gathered and covered by blankets, clearly marked by the stench and swarms of flies.

The few people who had stopped, startled, at their arrival, mostly continued their business. A few shuffled after Apollo and Nadja, and those who remained shifted wood and stone, using wheelbarrows and baskets to carry away debris and clear pathways through the ruined town.

'Should we help them?' Fenn asked.

Selys sighed. 'We should.'

'But?'

'But Neros is angry. Distracted.' Selys turned to face the sea. Cold water lapped at the shingle beach running either side of where they stood, waves churning up froth.

It was hard to tell how much of the sky overhead was dark with smoke or gathering storm clouds. '*She* fought the Myr here. Drove them back. Yet…yet there is something else…' Selys crouched and dipped one hand into the saltwater, eyes closing in reverence. The green tattoo that swirled up her left arm flickered with light. 'The Myr's return is…'

Fenn crouched beside her and took a closer look at the sea. Several dead fish floated on the water's surface. Death followed the Myr wherever they went. It was no wonder everyone had been so afraid of him. Faint nausea crept along his gut. 'The Myr's return is what?'

He looked beyond the fish. The water was green and clear, long tendrils of seaweed waving underneath the surface in the current. Goosebumps rose along his skin as he stared towards the horizon. What little sunlight filtered through the smoke-filled, overcast sky glittered on the water like glass. The water swelled and receded, an ancient and terrible strength in every drop. He couldn't see Neros, not as a dragon, but Neros *was* the water.

It was a power that Selys could use.

'We *must* stop the Myr. Whatever happens, that is

irrefutable.' Selys leaned on her glaive, silk ribbons rippling in the wind.

'How?' Fenn wouldn't soon forget the Myrish spirits wandering Tassar, or how close he'd come to death due to their magic. It had only been through luck that he'd survived. Luck that Hassen had found him.

'Neros will guide me.' Selys spoke clearly, her voice as strong as her resolve. Her intricate tattoo in blue-green ink continued to shimmer where it swirled down her arm, then she pulled her hand from the water and the light faded. 'Her words aren't clear. But I feel what she feels. There is so much anger.'

'Hey! Priestess! Can you help? Some kids are trapped under the collapsed shop here. We can't get to them!'

Fenn stood up at the shout and spotted a woman in a brown shawl waving them over. She bled from a bandage around her leg, and her blonde hair was thick with dirt and dust.

'Duty calls.' Selys offered Fenn a smile, though it didn't reach her eyes, and approached the woman.

More fire burned in Fenn's chest. '*Weaklings.*'

'Maybe. But that doesn't mean we can't do *something*.' Fenn quietened his dragon spirit and followed Selys into what was left of the town, her words conflicting with his task.

If he didn't trust the Myr, he'd be lost forever.

He would do whatever it took to get his memories and family back. He had to.

Regardless of what happened, he had Hassen to help him fight the consequences.

FENN AND SELYS set to work moving rubble, clearing debris, and helping the injured wherever they could. They had no additional supplies to offer the people of Foxmouth, but the extra strength afforded to them by Hassen and Neros's blessings took the edge off the heavy lifting.

Several makeshift shelters had been constructed where an overhanging cliff provided cover from the Myrish attack. People congregated below the cliff, already working on reconstructing Foxmouth. Planks of usable wood had been gathered, along with whatever tools and materials could be salvaged.

Two Inquisitors stood in the centre of the square, directing people and organising the recovery effort. They stood out in their dark uniforms, longswords sheathed at their hips, silver dragon insignias gleaming.

Fenn wanted to run from them.

Torsten wanted him, and they'd fought not long ago. He imagined that man was the type to hold a grudge for decades. Hassen's blessing offered a small measure of comfort, as did travelling with Nadja, but nothing was certain. They gave the Inquisitors a wide berth and kept their efforts to the far wall.

By the time shadows lengthened with the setting sun, Nadja reappeared with a despondent Apollo.

'It's good of you to offer aid here,' Nadja said, noting what Fenn and Selys were doing. Despite having taken a leave of absence from the Inquisitors, she always spoke like one. 'I'm sure the Iron Crown will send more Inquisitors with resources soon enough. Eastbrook was attacked, too. Repair of the capital will no doubt take priority.'

Fenn grimaced through another stab of guilt. Somewhere else that had been attacked by the Myr. How many more people had died there?

He turned to Apollo, hoping for positive news, if not a distraction. 'Any luck?'

'Good news is my inn is standing. Well, three of the walls are. A chunk of roof caved in, but it's fixable.'

'That's great!'

Apollo shrugged. 'No sign of Mal and Ren. Part of the cliff collapsed. Too much rock down there to dig through, it'd take months.' He rubbed his bloodshot eyes. 'Could be there. Might not be. But I found this.' Apollo held up a dagger, a bright ogee pattern on its hilt. 'It's Mal's. I have one too. They match. Or, I *did* have it, before Torsten took it when he had me locked up.' He stared at Nadja, something dark in his gaze.

'Going around in circles looking won't help. We should rest while we can,' Selys suggested, breaking the tension. 'You've not long been walking, and I don't yet have full movement in my shoulder.'

'But they could be—'

'The priestess is right. It's already getting towards sunset. Let's chart a course to the key for now,' Nadja said, speaking gently but firmly.

At the key's mention, Fenn's stomach churned, fire roiling within him. It was more than a painful twinge, and he clutched his chest. 'Hassen, knock it off.'

'What?' Selys asked.

Fenn shook his head. 'N—Nothing! Just thinking out loud.'

'It will take some time to adjust to your blessing, Fenn. Better you don't fight it. Even I find Neros overwhelming.'

'I'll try.' He wondered how Selys could stand it. Having someone else in your head arguing all the time, and a chest that burned with fire every time the spirit was unhappy.

'Apollo? Apollo Tamlin!' A trio of people broke apart from the crowd and approached them, smiles wide. 'By the spirits, I never thought we'd see you again!'

'Heard old Torsten took your head!'

'You seen the state of your inn? Where we gonna spend our evenings now?'

'Just evenings? I've lost where I spend all day!

'State of the inn? Look at the state of *him*!'

They bustled around Fenn's group, ruffling Apollo's hair and thumping him on the back.

Apollo laughed, some of the weight he'd been carrying visibly lifting from his shoulders. He clasped the arm of the nearest—a thick-set man with an unkempt beard and piercing green eyes. 'My head? Hah! Torsten's got a better chance of becoming king than that happening.'

Fenn smirked at the blatant lie. The way he'd spoken about Torsten, Apollo had come very close to losing his head. But the clear affection they showed for each other made Fenn wonder whether he had such a tight-knit friendship group waiting for him. Would they gasp at the state of him? Would they be impressed by Hassen's blessing? Wonder where he'd been all these weeks?

'Incoming. Above you!'

Fenn flinched, jumping back at Hassen's hissed warning.

The shadow of a griffin passed overhead as Hailathlyl soared above, the wind from her passing causing the torches to violently flicker.

'Did you find her?' Apollo asked, limping forward before the griffin had even landed. The bearded man supported him, holding Apollo by the shoulder so he didn't fall.

Amsel patted Hailathlyl as the griffin touched the ground, but didn't dismount. 'No, and we circled Foxmouth three times. But we spotted a small island to the east, with a lighthouse? There were a few boats docked, so we flew across and asked around. Malora had been there, along with Renys. They'd been rescuing people caught up in the attack.'

'The lighthouse? Let's go!' Apollo reached out to clamber up, but Hailathlyl hissed angrily, halting him in his place. 'What?'

'She's gone.'

'Gone where?' Apollo clutched the leather straps of Hailathlyl's harness as if it gave him comfort. 'Why'd she leave? Surely it'd be safer here!'

'They didn't say why. But she left this morning.'

'What if she's heading to Eastbrook? Looking for me?'

Amsel straightened in his saddle, the griffin's straps and metal buckles clinking together. 'Hailathlyl and I are in service to Lady Vantonen. We *must* track down Malora, so we'll leave you here and head to Eastbrook.'

'Great. Help me up.' Apollo leaned over, but Amsel made no move to grab his hand.

'Apollo.' Nadja shifted her weight. 'Your wife is alive. You've had confirmation of that, which is what you wanted when we came here. Now, you must move on and focus on the key.'

'Will you stop going on about that damned key! Mal is a *day's* travel from here. Less on the back of that!' He jerked his thumb towards the war-griffin. 'Once we catch up to her, we'll talk about the key.'

'Apollo. We *must* find and destroy the Citrine Key. Everything else is irrelevant.'

He snorted. 'The key ain't near here. You have any idea where Paragos is?'

Fenn flinched as Hassen recoiled at the name, though he didn't recognise it.

Nadja frowned for a moment. 'Somewhere on the Meneos continent?'

'Exactly.'

Fenn had no idea where Meneos was, but the news only affected Nadja for a few moments. The Inquisitor approached Amsel, still sitting on Hailathlyl. 'Amsel, if you would fly us across the Lasseen Ocean to Meneos, you would be handsomely paid for your service.'

Amsel patted Hailathlyl. 'I'm sorry, Inquisitor, but I'm already in service.'

'The Iron Crown supersedes the authority of any Bragalian Laird.' Nadja's tone hardened.

The Olmese warrior shrugged. 'Sorry, Inquisitor, but I am

not beholden to your Iron Queen. I have a duty to Lady Vantonen, and we will deliver that swiftly. Come on Hailathlyl, we've deviated long enough.'

'Even if I wished to take you, the distance is too great for me to fly. We must aid Furyn's daughter,' said the griffin.

'Wait!' Apollo flailed with the straps. 'Take me with you! I need to find them!'

Hailathlyl snapped her beak and flexed one enormous, taloned foot towards Apollo.

'It's okay. They'll find Malora.' Fenn steadied Apollo by the shoulder. As much as he understood the desperation to find Malora and Renys, getting to the key was more important.

Apollo clutched tightly onto the harness, preventing Hailathlyl from taking off without knocking him down. 'I'm not going anywhere until I've seen Mal and Ren!'

'Apollo. How many times must I tell you? It *doesn't* matter!' Nadja snapped.

'Malora and Renys matter to me, thank you very much.'

Nadja scowled at him. 'If you don't destroy that key, you won't *have* a wife. *Nothing* will be left. Can't you see what the Myr are doing? Don't you remember what they did before?'

Apollo didn't reply, but he didn't budge either.

'Hailathlyl and I will find Malora and Renys. Don't worry, Apollo. We'll make sure they're safe. It's our duty. You must see to your own.' Amsel offered the group a salute, the golden torc around his arm glinting in the low light.

Apollo's friend gently pulled him away from the griffin. 'We'll get to work on *The Grumpy Fisherman*. Let the griffin search for Mal, yeah?'

'Safe travels.' Amsel turned Hailathlyl to face away from the market square, her orange eyes bright. She leapt into the air with a fierce shriek, and was soon lost in the inky blackness of the dusk sky.

Apollo slumped forward, all the fight fading from him.

'Spirits take me,' he swore. 'I suppose I have no choice but to go after this damned key?'

'I'm glad you're committed,' Nadja replied.

Apollo's glare refuted that, but he said nothing.

'How about a ship? Surely we can take one to cross the ocean?' Fenn suggested, trying to keep things moving.

'Excellent idea, Fenn. Let's go to the docks,' Nadja said, taking charge.

Apollo shook his head. 'Docks'll be closed. It's late. And I imagine half the boats here were damaged in the Myrish attack. Why don't we rest? We can—'

'With respect, Apollo. You can rest on the ship. Time is of the essence,' Nadja said, curt.

Apollo dismissed his friends—who kept offering to help him—and led Fenn, Nadja, and Selys to the docks. The former thief had not been wrong about the damage.

Fenn counted twelve ships, each large enough to carry fifty people or more, and not a single one looked seaworthy. Ripped sails and hulls with holes gouged in them spoke of the intense combat they had seen, and his heart sank.

'Looks like luck is not with us,' Selys muttered. The bandage around her shoulder had begun peeling away, and a thin stream of blood trickled down her arm.

'Don't give up so easily. There may be other ships.' Nadja gestured to the docks' far side.

Fenn's hope began to dwindle as they wandered past damaged ship after damaged ship. Choosing to sail from a town recently attacked by the Myr gave them few options.

He was about to say as much when a light across the ocean caught his eye. A large, three masted ship approached Foxmouth in the choppy surf, dark sails and banners boasting the Iron Crown's dragon insignia. Lanterns were fixed to each mast and along the railings. They'd been lit, and the ship appeared undamaged. 'Inquisitors?'

'Probably here to offer more help and provide resources,

as I suggested.' Nadja strolled down the crooked wooden steps to be the first to greet whomever disembarked first.

A dozen Inquisitors threw the gangplank to the dock and made their way down, each with a large sack over their shoulders. More people carrying supplies followed them—Fenn assumed in their employ. They moved with rigid uniformity, busy and bustling, and none of them spared them a glance.

'Welcome Inquisitor Deva.' Nadja approached the senior officer and nodded sharply. 'How long will you remain in Foxmouth?'

He shrugged, leaning against the side rail. His uniform was less than pristine, and his hair looked like it hadn't been combed in a while. 'As long as is needed, Nadja.' Fenn wondered why he'd omitted her title. 'Official schedule is three weeks, but we can request additional aid if required. Need to get Foxmouth restored as soon as possible. Ships need to be repaired and refitted as a matter of priority. The fleet will be important in the war.'

Fenn blinked, sure he'd misheard. He and Selys shared a worried glance.

Nadja stiffened. 'War?'

'Queen Surayo has declared the Porsenthian Empire is at war with the Myr once again. She wants these ships fighting fit before the next turn of the moon. You left at the right time, Nadja. You aren't gonna be on the front. Lucky.' Bitterness laced Inquisitor Deva's words.

Conversation broke out around Fenn, but he heard little of it. He swayed, Hassen's fury surging through him—his body a raging inferno. *'Spirits of death! We must burn them from Tassar! Every. Last. One!'*

Selys grabbed him by the elbow. 'Fenn? Breathe. Neros is angry, too.'

Nadja had maintained her composure despite the grim news. She cast her gaze over their group, then back to the

Inquisitor. 'If you're to be stationed here so long, I will need to use the ship.'

Inquisitor Deva shook his head as the last of his crew disembarked and made their way into Foxmouth. 'Afraid not, Nadja. The Iron Crown has declared a state of emergency. *Nothing* leaves the continent without Queen Surayo's leave.'

2
THE SISTER
CALIDRA

Seawater gently lapped at the wooden hull, rocking the small boat. Fish occasionally splashed on the surface, spraying Calidra with fine mist, but otherwise the water was quiet. More than that, it was solemn.

Even the few gulls gliding overhead didn't cry out.

To her right, the rocky coastline of Porsenthia provided an unending landmark. To her left, the open sea beckoned. Her stomach lurched with the boat and she shivered, fighting to keep her rising fear at bay.

Calidra didn't particularly care for spirits, but she had to thank Neros for keeping her sister safe through the chaos, whether by luck or design. It had been eight years since she'd last spoken to Malora, whom she'd thought dead, and seeing her alive and well—and with a young *daughter*—was surreal.

Malora had acted immediately during the attack, of course. She'd kept herself and Renys safe, and beyond that, had helped as many of the townsfolk as she could rescue in her little fishing boat. Calidra paled beside her sister's brighter flame.

Now, Malora was acting again—on a mission to Chyram's Shrine to beg for the return of her blessing. She'd staked everything on it. Chyram's blessing was the only thing she could think of to keep herself and her daughter safe with her husband gone and the Myr on the rise. Unfortunately, there was no guarantee the Spirit of Gold would entertain Malora's plea, fickle as spirits were.

Calidra understood Malora's determination, but disliked spirits' demands for subservience.

But the shrine was a long way off.

While it meant Malora had time to figure out how best to present her request, it was more time spent on the boat, and Calidra suppressed the urge to vomit. One more *day* on the boat was too much, and they had several more to go.

Her world had been utterly turned upside down. Her father had died, not that she'd been close to him even as a child. Her mother had destroyed any chance of rekindling their relationship. The sister whose death she'd blamed herself for was alive.

And now she was sitting on a boat sailing south, fighting to keep nausea down.

She'd never been good on water. Hated it to the point she'd kept herself trapped on the Isle of Salt for seven years. But at least she'd had Jisyel with her, so it hadn't *felt* like she'd been hiding.

Almost on cue, Jisyel offered her a smile. 'You doing okay?'

Another lurch and water splashed Calidra's face. She swallowed down bile. 'I'm fine.'

She grabbed Jisyel's hand and squeezed. She knew Jisyel wouldn't be able to feel the warmth of her hand or the softness of her skin, but she'd feel the pressure of her touch. It was all they could share.

Hassen's curse might have been amusing to the dragon, but it had defined Jisyel's life—*their lives*—ever since.

Jisyel's smile broadened, and Calidra ran her thumb over Jisyel's palm.

All along the water, debris floated by in various states of damage. It was hard to fathom how much of Foxmouth had been claimed by the sea following the Myrish strike—lost and floating on the water's surface. Malora and Renys had a few bags packed and stowed away on their boat, so they had no immediate worries regarding food or clothing, but it wasn't enough to last more than a handful of days.

She glanced at Malora, who had one hand on the tiller as she sat at the boat's stern, gently guiding their course. Malora's attention was half on where they were going and half on her daughter, who sat beside her, playing with an oyster shell and occasionally offering her own thoughts on where the boat should turn next.

Much as Calidra despised the water, Malora had always known best. Even in their youth, Malora had done things "right." *She* was the one helping their family, not Calidra, as their mother had so often reminded them. Malora had been blessed by the Spirit of Gold. Had elevated their family to rule a canton.

Calidra simply couldn't compete with her parents' favourite child.

She'd never fix things with her mother, but she wasn't going to give up on her sister, especially after Apollo had been taken away by Inquisitors—accused of crimes against Tassar and high treason to the Iron Crown.

If they were to have any chance of surviving the Myrish threat, they had to stick together. And Calidra wasn't going to lose Malora again. She was done running.

'Getting dark. Should we find somewhere to stop for the night?' Calidra asked, trying to spot a likely place along the stony shore. She certainly didn't relish the idea of sailing in darkness.

Malora adjusted the sail, the weakening breeze slowing their progress. 'We can keep going.' I want to reach a town before we rest. Northbourne is nearest.'

Jisyel frowned. 'Eastbrook is closer, isn't it?'

Calidra squeezed Jisyel's palm firmly, but wasn't sure if the other woman understood—or felt—her warning. Eastbrook was the capital of Porsenthia, where Apollo had been taken as a prisoner. She could understand why Malora wanted to steer clear of the palace. It could well be her husband's gravesite. 'Mal, we need time to set up camp. I'd rather not do it in pitch dark.'

Malora pulled Renys into a tight hug. The four-year old squirmed but didn't push away from her mother. Malora had always been one to hold her tongue when upset, preferring to act rather than speak as a way to relieve building tension.

Rock fell away into mud as the edge of a copse appeared a short way inland. Several willow trees grew near the edge, branches hanging low, leaves offering shelter on both land and water. 'How about there? We can get a fire going and cook some dinner. I know you want to reach Northbourne, but we've more chance of reaching it in one piece in daylight.' Calidra tried to reassure her sister.

Malora looked for a moment like she was going to argue, her lips pressing into a thin line that reminded Calidra of their mother whenever she was unhappy. Malora stared towards the setting sun for a long while. 'All right.'

Jisyel stood up at the suggestion and clapped her hands together. 'Food sounds good! Mal, you need any help bringing the boat in? I helped Gran manage the boats on the island, so I know what I'm doing!'

'I've got it under control, thank you, Jisyel. Ren, come out of the way, darling.' The breeze was barely strong enough to push the boat along, so Malora grabbed an oar to manually turn it towards shore.

Calidra hadn't expected to reconcile with her sister overnight, but their reunion was frostier than she would have liked. She kept quiet, not wanting to say the wrong thing and make it worse.

Jisyel wrapped an arm around Calidra's shoulders, steadying her as the boat wobbled in the shallows, more water splashing up the sides and setting her hair standing on end.

Malora glanced at her and smirked. 'Cal, it's not so bad. Stop fussing. Even Renys isn't worried and she's *four*!'

Renys giggled, her eyes shining with mirth, and waved at Calidra. 'It's fun, Cal!' She hopped from foot to foot, showing off how well she could balance.

Calidra couldn't stop shaking, but offered her niece a weak smile. How could she *not* love the bright-eyed child with her insatiable curiosity, boldness, and charm? Renys was the spitting image of Malora when she'd been the same age, save the hazel eyes and lighter skin she'd inherited from Apollo. Her dark, curly hair was already shoulder-length, and Calidra could imagine Furyn or her handmaidens desperately trying to tame and scent it with oils.

More than that, Renys was also the fiercely independent child *she* had been, once.

The child had her whole life ahead of her. Parents who loved her dearly.

Calidra's smile faded, replaced by something hollow. She wasn't envious of Renys. How could she be? The child was a handful of years into her life and had done nothing wrong. But Calidra was envious of what Renys's life was going to be.

What Malora's *had* been.

And what hers would never be.

As they made land, Jisyel kept Renys entertained while Calidra and Malora dragged the boat up the muddy shore. Once secure, Calidra went back to fetch their supplies which had been scattered haphazardly throughout the boat. For such a small vessel, it had a surprising number of nooks and crannies in which Renys hid and moved things. Calidra was grabbing the last jar of pickles from underneath one of the benches, when she spotted a wooden box.

Part of it was water damaged, the wood an unpleasant, mottled brown, but the silver hinges were free of rust. The ogee pattern carved into the box hinted it was Bragalian-made, and Calidra reached forward to pry it free of its hiding space. She had to dig her nails in, it was wedged so tightly. 'Mal?' Calidra asked, but her sister was too busy setting up a fire to respond.

She gave it another shove, and it came free in a cloud of dust and wood chips.

Now it wasn't half-hidden in the bowels of the boat, Calidra recognised what it was, and a pang of jealousy rippled through her.

Malora's sword.

One of the many treasures her sister had been afforded in her youth, and one that Calidra had desperately wanted. She'd been the one in the training yard with the household guard while Malora had explored Fellwood's streets with her band of thieves and petty criminals, hungry for her gold and attention. She'd lavished them with her blessing's golden touch and been the favourite of them, too. Everywhere Malora went, people loved and admired her. She helped people who needed it, regardless of who they were or where they were from.

But her powers hadn't come without consequences, and Calidra had been relieved when Chyram rescinded the blessing shortly after Malora turned twenty-three. Just over fifteen years of power removed overnight.

Calidra had hoped—naively, when she thought about it—she'd get her sister back once they were on equal footing again. In actuality, it meant those to whom Malora had promised gold came hunting, which often led to violence. Malora had called Calidra overbearing, ignorant, and selfish. Calidra had called her spoiled, entitled, and short-sighted.

Then, Apollo had whisked Malora away, and Calidra had never seen her again.

She'd always regretted their difficult youth and had blamed herself when she'd heard Malora had died. There had been so many lies, so many things twisted by her mother.

Calidra inspected the box, holding it carefully in both hands. Judging from the years of accumulated grime on the box and scabbard, it hadn't been used very much.

She traced the blade with her finger, wondering what she might have been like had she not been caged so and frightened like a dove. Would she have the free, adventurous spirit of Malora and Renys? Would she be quicker to see the good in people instead of suspicion of what they might do to hurt her?

Calidra shook her head. She didn't want to become entrenched in her thoughts again. Too repetitive. Too damaging. She was a master of self-sabotage.

Instead, she carried the box ashore and placed it on the edge of their makeshift camp. It would be useful on their journey, if nothing else. 'Mal, why don't you sit down and relax with Renys. We'll get some food going.'

Malora looked up and frowned. 'But—'

'You've been managing the boat all day. You need to rest.'

'I'd rather keep busy.'

Calidra's voice softened. 'I know. But you need to get to the shrine, right? You won't be able to speak with Chyram in any sort of presentable way if you exhaust yourself now.'

Malora chewed on her lip, gaze darting to Renys—who had planted herself on the damp grass and was amusing herself with some of the long willow leaves—then back to Calidra. 'But—'

'It'll be okay. Spend some time with your daughter. She'll need you.'

Tears filled Malora's eyes, but she blinked them away. 'Thank you.'

Calidra watched her sister crouch down beside Renys, their conversation too low for her to hear. Her heart swelled at seeing them alive and unhurt. Malora had a life and family away from their mother—everything Calidra had strived to have. She was happy for her sister and niece.

And if anyone or anything tried to harm them, she'd fight to her last breath.

❄

'Reminds me of home,' Malora said, sipping the steaming broth.

'Never could beat that Olmese spice blend.' Calidra blew on her spoon before taking another mouthful. Childhood comforts often settled her nerves. After the rocky journey on the boat, it was just what her stomach needed.

'Wish I could taste it.' Jisyel was no less bright and bubbly than usual, but Calidra heard the sorrow behind her words.

'It'll be the first thing I'll make for you once your curse is lifted.'

'Curse?' Renys asked, the child's abundant questions and chatter returning once her belly was full. 'Ma said that's… that's what spirits do to *bad* people!'

Malora's cheeks flushed and she froze mid-bite. 'Ren!'

'Yah, that's what you said happened to daddy's friend! And, and, and that you would do it to "people that had it coming to them" like Tors—'

'Ren, that's enough!' Malora coughed, dropping her bowl and grabbing her daughter around the middle.

Calidra couldn't help but laugh at Renys's free mouth, but her mirth disappeared when she realised Jisyel had hunkered into herself. 'Jisyel?'

'Spirits take me, Jisyel, I'm sorry! She's young, doesn't know what she's saying!' Malora apologised while Renys busied herself with her own bowl of broth, slurping loudly and smacking her lips.

'No, it's okay.' Jisyel stared at the ground and shook her

head. Her knuckles were white where she clutched the rim of her bowl.

'It isn't. It was rude, and—'

'Honestly, don't worry, Malora. I probably *was* being a nuisance as far as Hassen was concerned. Deserved everything I got.'

'Jisyel, you're silly and naive, and you may have *irritated* Hassen, but that doesn't mean you deserve to be cursed!' Calidra said, wishing Jisyel would believe her. She gently took the bowl from Jisyel's hand and kissed her cheek.

Once Renys was settled, Malora crossed their small camp and sat beside Jisyel on the log they were using as a seat. 'In the past, I may have said some things about a few people "deserving what they got." You know what children are like, parroting everything we say!' Malora looked over at Renys, who grinned at being mentioned. 'But sometimes we're just in the wrong place at the wrong time. It's no reflection on you if a spirit curses you.'

'I didn't respect him enough. Worship enough. And I lived in his forest!' Jisyel muttered.

'It isn't always about being faithful enough, Jisyel.' Malora took Jisyel's hands in her own. 'Sometimes they curse or bless us for no real reason. There's no meaning to it. Sometimes...sometimes it's just a bit shit.'

'Mal!' Calidra was surprised to hear her sister swear. Probably Apollo's influence—No. She caught herself before she thought too much like her mother. Calidra leaned into Jisyel, bumping their shoulders together. 'Don't blame yourself. Mal understands spirits more than anyone I know. If she says it wasn't your fault, I'd believe that.'

'Maybe. I always thought I wasn't good enough. He never touched Gran, did he?' Jisyel continued eating, and Calidra relaxed a little. 'She's more boisterous than I am.'

Malora shrugged. 'There isn't always a reason for a spirit

cursing or blessing us. Hassen is a trickster. He's fickle by nature. So are lots of the others.'

'Maybe...'

They lapsed into silence as they finished their broth. Calidra stole glances at Jisyel every other mouthful. Jisyel was always one to put on a brave face, but more cracks had appeared in recent months.

Calidra had always thought she was the one hiding from things that scared her. But she was realising more and more that Jisyel had been hiding, too.

'When we gonna see Daddy?' Renys asked, after they'd been staring at the campfire a while.

Calidra's stomach twisted at the question, but Malora took it in her stride. She pulled her daughter in close for another hug. 'I don't know, Ren. Lots of things have changed.'

'But I miss Daddy! I wanna play hiding!'

'I know, darling. He went away on a long trip. And we're on a trip too, aren't we?'

Renys yawned wide, her baby teeth standing out in pink gums. 'Wanna go home.'

'Soon, Renys.'

Calidra watched Malora rest her chin on her daughter's head, the flames reflected in her dark brown eyes. Tears threatened to spill, but her sister didn't let any fall. She glanced at Jisyel, who was equally captivated, lost in her own thoughts.

There was only the crackle of fire and the gentle lapping of the waves against the muddy shore for company. In the distance, insects began to chirp. Occasionally, one of the willow branches bent in the wind, leaves dragging against the muddy ground, and Calidra kept an eye on the edge of their camp. It would be easy for anyone to creep up on them using the shadows for cover. With the Myr attacking Foxmouth, who knew if any of those deathly creatures were nearby.

Malora had confirmed Neros drove them back, but Calidra was wary of lurking stragglers.

She thought about Malora's unused sword. About whether Apollo had fallen to Torsten's blade or if he'd managed to plead his innocence. Wondered whether their small group would even make it to Chyram's shrine, or if they were better off returning to the Isle of Salt.

'You two rest. I'll keep watch.' Calidra pulled a burning branch from the campfire and held it high above her head as she patrolled the perimeter. She kept one hand on her hunting knife as she swept the clearing, chasing away shadows with her light and ensuring she kept the campfire within earshot.

After some time, long enough that the fire burned low, Jisyel spoke, her words carrying through the darkness. 'Is Chyram powerful?'

'Strong enough,' Malora replied softly.

'Do you think…if you receive your blessing again…you'd be able to lift my curse?'

'Of course!' Malora didn't hesitate. 'I'd be glad to. Would make a change from people begging for gold coins!'

'I asked Alnothen, but she wanted my service. I considered it.'

Calidra lowered the torch as a startled hare darted away from the light.

Jisyel continued. 'I never thought I'd have the chance to lift the curse. I've been on the island all my life. Hassen is the only spirit there. So I jumped at Alnothen's offer.'

'But you're not one of her worshippers are you?'

'No. Calidra talked me out of it. Probably for the best…'

Malora didn't respond, and the crackle of their fire grew dim.

There were always consequences to a spirit's blessing. Calidra had seen that first-hand with Malora, let alone all the beggars at their doors, desperate for coin. All the attempted kidnappings and attacks on their home. The immediate hatred people had because someone *else* had been chosen. The snide remarks, the threats in the dark.

She had wanted to keep Jisyel safe from that.

Minutes passed, the silence so great she thought they had fallen asleep, when Malora spoke again in a voice so low it was barely above a whisper. 'Calidra knows nothing of spirits, really. But *I* do. I'll make sure your curse is removed. I swear it.'

Calidra flinched at her sister's words. Malora was probably right, but it still hurt.

'Thank you,' Jisyel said.

'It's the least I can do after you've come all this way with us. We should get some rest. Renys snores louder than Apollo when she's tired. If we don't sleep soon, she'll keep us up all night!'

They laughed, the sound echoing through the trees.

Calidra tried not to think of all the ways she'd held Jisyel back, and fought her own tears.

3
THE ESCAPE
FENN

'No. Absolutely not. We are *not* stealing a ship belonging to Queen Surayo!' Nadja was a mixture of aghast and pure anger.

'Then you're gonna have some trouble getting off the continent.' Apollo folded his arms and leaned against one of the posts that ran the length of the docks, heedless of the damp wood.

Fenn was sure Apollo's grin was more smug than usual.

The Queen's Inquisitors, and those in service to them, had disembarked and marched into town, returning to their ship several times to grab more supplies and haul them into Foxmouth.

Inquisitor Deva shouted orders from the dock before reboarding the ship, several rolled papers under one arm. He didn't spare Fenn or the others a glance as he disappeared into one of the cabins.

Nadja stared up at the ship, seemingly at a loss how to proceed. 'We *aren't* stealing it.'

Fenn couldn't blame her. All his earlier excitement at discovering Apollo's connection to the key had dissipated after they'd hit the roadblock. He'd been so certain they'd get the key within a few days, and his memory loss would finally come to an end.

He shifted from foot to foot. Without the key, he was nothing—a blank slate with no past and very little future. Fenn didn't want to break the law any more than Nadja did, but some things were more important than rules.

He also needed to get the key *before* Nadja and Apollo, and bring it back to *Vermecio*. Then, he'd be free, and they could do whatever they wanted with it.

Quite *how* he'd accomplish all that, he didn't know, but he'd figure things out when he got there. He'd already come this far with no real plan. Now he was a free man with a dragon spirit's blessing instead of locked up by Torsten—or killed by the power of the Myrish curse.

'Seeing as you got lines you won't cross, I guess we ain't going anywhere,' Apollo muttered.

Nadja's scowl deepened.

Fenn stepped between them. 'There has to be another way, right? Couldn't Neros help us, Selys? It *is* the Lasseen Ocean we need to cross, after all.'

Selys sighed. 'I'm blessed by the spirit. It doesn't mean I can make us walk across the ocean!'

'Shame,' Apollo said, in a voice that made it very clear he did *not* think it was a shame.

'Let me speak with Inquisitor Deva again,' Nadja said, her normally impeccable demeanour somewhat ruffled. 'I'm certain exceptions can be made for matters pertaining to the crown.'

'Oh, you Inquisitors *love* your exceptions.' Apollo snorted.

'Excuse me?'

He shrugged. 'Just saying that a piece of paper don't mean much if an Inquisitor looks at it.'

Nadja narrowed her eyes. 'This is *beyond* a wronged crime, Apollo. When will you understand what we face is greater than you and your family? Greater than any of us?'

Apollo shrugged again. 'I get it. It's important. But we need a ship to cross the ocean. You might have to forget you're an Inquisitor for a bit if you wanna do that.'

'I will *not* disregard the Iron Crown's law!'

Apollo laughed, humourless. 'Sorry, I thought you wanted to get this bloody key. Clearly you're not as committed as you make out.' He straightened, then winced at the motion, and gestured towards the town. 'Does that mean I can go and find my wife now?'

'No, you may not,' Nadja said through gritted teeth. 'You're making this harder than it needs to be, Apollo. I don't appreciate your cheek.'

'I'm trying to help you, you should be happy about that!'

Something dark flashed between the thief and the Inquisitor. Another hint of violence. It was gone before Fenn could say anything, but Hassen's discomfort flared within him, mirroring his emotions. He let out a shaky breath.

'Stay here. I'll be back shortly.' Brushing down her clothes, Nadja boarded the ship and strode to the cabin, knocking confidently.

Fenn backed away a few paces, keeping one eye on Apollo. It was almost night, and the cool evening air swept away some of his frustrations. Beside him, the waters of the Lasseen Ocean beat rhythmically against the shore. Salt was heavy in the air.

'What is a tree?'

Caught by surprise at Hassen's sudden words, Fenn glanced around in case anyone had seen him flinch. He rolled his shoulders and shook out his arms, wondering what the dragon was trying to get at this time. 'I don't know. Something growing?'

'Life.' The word reverberated through Fenn's body as the dragon spoke. Images flashed in his mind—the trees, flowers, and vines of Salt Ash Forest. *'It is what we are.'*

Fenn stared at the devastation the Myr had brought to

Foxmouth and beyond. So much life had been snuffed out. The people here hadn't stood a chance. He hoped Calidra and Jisyel hadn't been caught up in it. His throat tightened at the thought.

'The Myr are our opposite. Death. We are always opposed. We want to bathe the world in life. They wish to return it to something barren.'

'That Inquisitor did say we were at war,' Fenn said.

'These are treacherous times, Fenn.' Selys raised her glaive. 'Neros blessed me. She has never done so before. With *anyone*.' She glanced away from him and leaned her forehead on her glaive, eyes closed. 'I don't know how much longer I can stay here.'

'What do you mean? Are you sick?'

'I said before that Neros would guide me. I am her servant. I must obey her will. But her words are difficult to hear.'

Fenn faced her fully. He'd assumed Selys would help him get to grips with his blessing, teach him about the spirits and the Myr, and everything in between. If she was going to leave him to flounder about on his own, he was no better off than in Hassen's bog on the Isle of Salt. 'Is Neros telling you to do something now?'

'This war worries me. I left home and joined Neros's priesthood to get *away* from that life. It must be fate that war has followed me here.'

Fenn shook his head. 'The Myr caused this! Not you.'

'Oh, I don't blame myself. I just find it amusing that it follows me, no matter my path. Hah. Kaio was probably right.'

'Kaio?'

'My brother.' Selys stared at her glaive with something akin to reverence, her lip trembling.

Fenn leaned against a low stone wall that separated Foxmouth from the sea—one of the few structures near the coast still standing. 'You weren't always a priestess, were you? I remember Jisyel saying something about pi—' He caught himself before he said "pirates," realising a moment before that it was probably rude.

Selys rested her glaive against the wall. If she took offence, she didn't say anything. 'I was part of a warband. The Ioran warband. Our family headed it. We took what we wanted from wherever it was. Many people were hurt. Many died. Nothing was beyond our reach—villages, towns, cities. Even temples.'

He stared at her weapon, ribbons blowing in the sea breeze. The jade beads clinked together, sounding like tiny bells. 'That explains you wanting to get away from...' Fenn gestured vaguely towards the ruins of Foxmouth.

'Something like that. Funny. I'm trying to get away from my past. You're trying to run towards it. I wonder whether our gods plan this or they simply laugh at our struggles.'

A burst of heat in his chest—Hassen's amusement. 'Definitely laughing at us.' Fenn looked up to make sure Apollo hadn't wandered off.

Selys continued, 'Some people live for war. My brother is one of those people.'

'Seems like a lot of people are like that. Varlot, for one.' Fenn's thoughts soured when he remembered what the former Porsenthian General had done to him—tried to, anyway. He'd been skilled with an axe and confident in a fight. But he'd also *hungered* for it in a way that had put Fenn on edge.

At the time, he'd accepted Varlot's help. He'd had so few options.

But it had been a mistake that had come very close to costing him his life.

And that said nothing of Torsten, either. The man was a brute in every sense of the word, and just the thought of him gave Fenn chills. 'And some Inquisitors.'

Nadja, on the other hand, was altogether more human. She had a sense of humour. The capacity to listen, think, and negotiate.

Fenn added, 'But I suppose not all Inquisitors are like Torsten. Some are just following orders.'

'Not like Kaio. Once my brother realised he was bigger, stronger, and more vicious than those whose orders we followed? He no longer followed them. That's what life in Segandis is. Taking what you want when you want, until someone with bigger teeth comes along. I wanted my life to be *more* than that. To give something *back* to the world instead of only taking from it.' Her voice cracked and she cleared her throat. When she next spoke, her words were softer. 'There is a lot of pain in him. In us. Our past.'

It made Fenn wonder what *he* had given to the world. Once he had his memories back, he'd know.

Heavy boots aboard the ship caught his attention, and he looked up in time to see Inquisitors Nadja and Deva cross the deck towards them. They both peered over the railing, and Deva's lip curled like there was an unpleasant smell in his moustache.

'Ah, so it *is* true.' Inquisitor Deva sneered. 'I knew I should have taken a closer look at *you*.'

Hassen's fire raged, and Fenn's heart skipped a beat, his hand dropping to the sword at his waist. Then he realised the Inquisitor wasn't looking at him.

His attention was on Apollo.

'Torsten said something about Foxmouth being important. That the traitor to the crown might slink back here with his tail between his legs.' Deva pointed at Apollo. 'It's you, isn't it? The thief. Tamlin, yes? I see your scar.'

'Inquisitor Deva. He isn't for you. Apollo is with me.' Nadja's voice had darkened to a growl.

Deva looked Nadja up and down. 'I don't see you in uniform. And he isn't in irons. Are you turning traitor, too?'

She shifted her weight. 'Of course I'm not. I may be on leave, but I am still an Inquisitor. One who outranks you, Deva, as you seem to have forgotten.'

'I hardly think rank matters in this case. As you said, it *is* an exceptional circumstance.' Inquisitor Deva reached for the slender iron dagger at his belt.

Apollo backed away, hobbling every other step.

Selys raised her glaive, ready.

Nadja stepped in front of Deva and grabbed his arm. 'Hold, Inquisitor.'

The force of her command made Deva hesitate, his hand on the hilt of the dagger, half pulled free. 'What are you doing?' Deva stammered. 'Traitors to the crown must die! Don't you want revenge for your husba—'

'I said *hold*,' Nadja snarled. She stared him down. 'Gather your things and disembark at once. You're to help your squadron in Foxmouth. I will take command of this ship.'

'You'll do no such thing, Nadja! What are you, a thief, too?'

'Relinquish your command and I shan't inform Her Majesty that you obstructed me carrying out the Master Inquisitor's will.'

More movement caught Fenn's attention as a group of Deva's Inquisitors appeared on the far side of the docks, no doubt returning to obtain more supplies. Three of them carried torches high to ward off the darkness.

Deva laughed, regaining some of his composure. 'Nadja. Looks like your coup has fallen apart before it got off the ground! Help me with Apollo and I—'

'Step down, Inquisitor. That is an order.' Nadja left no room to argue, her sword drawn and raised. 'Apollo. Get on. Fenn, Selys, if you're coming with us, board the ship, too. We leave immediately.'

'You cannot be serious, Nadja!' Deva was almost frothing at the mouth.

Fenn hesitated. Something had snapped within Nadja, and he didn't know what.

'She has found more strength.' Fire surged in Fenn's chest, filling his limbs with strength. Unused to it, he stumbled onto the deck, tripped over Apollo's leg and rolled on board. He cracked the back of his head on the railing, stars filling his vision for a moment, before he pushed himself to his feet.

Nadja's sword was at Deva's throat a moment later. 'Now, you may leave quietly, or I'll throw you overboard once we set sail. Make your choice.'

Fenn could hardly believe Nadja.

'Far more to this Inquisitor than meets the eye,' Hassen hissed.

'Tell me about it!'

Nadja's arm did not waver, the tip of the blade a breath away from Deva's skin. 'This is beyond you, Deva. Any of us.'

'And here I thought you weren't interested in this sort of thing,' Apollo said. He hadn't bothered to stand up, and remained sitting on deck, his back against the railing.

Nadja didn't look at him. 'I concede that some rules must be bent. This act is to stop the war, which supersedes all else. I stand by my decisions.' Her gaze flickered to Fenn and Selys, then back to Deva, as he raised both hands and backed away. 'Selys Ioran. I believe you are the most skilled sailor among us. Would you get us underway?'

Selys nodded, disappearing along the deck.

'I can't believe what you're doing!' Deva spat.

'Now, Deva.' It didn't sound like Nadja had much patience left.

Inquisitor Deva curled his lip, then staggered onto the docks. 'You'll regret this, Nadja. Wait until I tell Torsten about this.'

'You may tell Torsten whatever you wish. My only authority is the queen.'

Fenn was sure he heard her voice waver slightly. Nothing

more was said between the two Inquisitors as the rest of Deva's group arrived, breathless.

At the same moment, the ship lurched forwards, foamy water splashing as the sails billowed out.

Immediately, Fenn felt the rolling sea underneath. His knees shook, and he took several deep breaths to steady himself. Whispers echoed in his mind, a churning cacophony of emotion that he did his best to ignore.

Something hissed alongside the whispers, but coupled with the unsteady waves and the flames constricting his chest, he couldn't make out the words. Fenn grasped the handrail and biting wind swept into his face. 'Hassen…?'

'The Citrine Key. Vermecio…'

4
THE PIRATE
KAIO

Blood filled Kaio's mouth, and he spat onto the varnished wooden planks underfoot, darkening them.

No teeth knocked out.

Good.

He staggered backwards, ears ringing from the blow, and regained his footing under the moving ship. As his vision refocused, Kaio searched for whoever had struck him.

Yaniv leered down. A wiry man, taller by a few inches, missing an eye but with more reach. He was in his fifties and every bit as strong as he'd been at half that age. He caressed his fist, his face more a grimace than a smirk. He wasn't happy about the punch, either.

Kaio wiped his mouth with the back of one hand, a smear of blood glistening on his skin. Overhead, the hot sun beat down on *Wolf's Grin*, and the ship rocked with the swell of the sea. 'Yaniv. You have ten seconds to explain that.' He was impressed he didn't slur his words, given his dizziness.

He'd been announcing a short extension of their voyage to a small island due east when the punch landed, and it had caught him off guard.

Yaniv rolled his fist in circles, fingers clutching his knuckles. 'Explain? *You're* the one who needs explaining, Kaio. You got us sailing into storms, abandoned hauls, and spirits know what else. This trip's done. We're going back to Segandis.'

Kaio narrowed his eyes. 'We'll go back when I'm damned good and ready to go back.'

'There's nothing out there, boy. Just rocks and shipwrecks. What, you looking for the bones of your family? Neros woulda taken 'em years ago.'

Kaio shifted his stance at the insult and bit down his urge to lash out. He *wasn't* that reckless youth anymore, and he wouldn't give Yaniv the satisfaction of seeing him lose his temper.

'Ioran's lost his touch,' someone bellowed. It earned several sniggers. 'Boy's got no bite.'

Kaio tried to focus on Ruka's advice about counting down his anger to avoid saying—or more likely doing—something he'd regret. But Ruka had studied in Olmir. She'd had to learn patience to better help those who were injured.

Counting down before he could react only ever made his blood boil instead of cooling it.

His first mate, Taran, had scouted something off the coast on their way back to Segandis, and Kaio trusted Taran with his life, let alone whatever items of interest he'd spotted. If the others couldn't see that, it wasn't down to him to change their minds.

Kaio took a step back and smirked at the man who'd struck him. 'You can always swim back to Segandis, Yaniv. I won't stop you.'

Yaniv bristled. 'You ain't no captain, Kaio.'

'No. That was my sister. But I *am* chief of this warband, so you do what I tell you on and off the ship. Or I'll take your other eye and put you back in line myself.' He had no problem following up his word—he'd never been one to make an idle threat—even though he knew Ruka and half the crew would be shaking their heads in disappointment at his recklessness.

The other half of the skeleton crew on *Wolf's Grin* probably echoed Yaniv's sentiment. Tension laced the air after the words, especially after their poor takings. It wouldn't surprise him if most of them were spoiling for a fight.

But the ship had brought him safely through more than one storm, and Kaio had every faith it would bring him through many more to come. After all, it had been the only one of the six sister ships to survive Neros's wrath, which brought it a small measure of luck as far as he was concerned.

Wolf's Sight.

Wolf's Skull.

Wolf's Foot.

Wolf's Fang.

Wolf's Gut.

All lost, along with their captains—his family. Nearly the entire Ioran warband felled in a single night.

Regardless of what anyone thought, he and *Grin would* come through this. 'I already told you—this is the last haul. We're heading back after. You getting itchy 'cause you have to wait two more days before you see Syras again?'

Kaio's anger had smoothed into deliberately aggravating Yaniv, and the jeers turned into chuckles. Three months was a long time for a man to be away from his wife.

Yaniv uncurled his fist, and for several long seconds, Kaio thought he was going to continue the brawl. Then the moment passed, Yaniv spat over the side of the ship and turned back to his duties, pride suitably knocked.

Kaio straightened as the handful of gathered crew flitted away. Ruka would be proud.

He hated diplomacy. So many subtle layers and posturing.

He watched the deck clear, wiped his mouth a second

time to make sure he wasn't still bleeding, and swore under his breath. He leaned on the railing of his sister's ship, watching his sister's crew move around. Despite growing up with these people, he'd never felt more distant from them.

Taran, Esto, and Ruka were the only three he could trust. Depend upon. No matter how well he could fight, no matter how much his reputation preceded him, the four of them weren't enough to hold his warband together, let alone the entire canton.

Kaio glared at the water.

It wasn't the Lasseen Ocean they sailed upon, but the Olmir Sea. Neros didn't lie in wait here, ready to capsize boats and drive storms across her waters.

But his anger remained nonetheless, dark and simmering. Mostly because Yaniv's jibe had struck true. Their last few courses hadn't thrown up much of value. Little money. Less treasure. And the last storm had damaged *Wolf's Grin* so badly they'd been stuck, listing at sea for the better part of a fortnight. He'd never known his run of luck to be so poor.

The wind changed, bringing with it the heavy scent of tobacco smoke. 'Keeping an eye out for pirates?' Taran slapped him on the back and leaned on the railing, cigarillo clenched between his teeth, a loop of knotted rope carried over one shoulder. He set to untangling the rope and glanced at Kaio, a grin plastered on his stubble-lined face. Shirtless, a fine sheen of sweat across his dark shoulders, Taran was as at home on the boat as Kaio.

Kaio shrugged. 'Just watching for the usual. Spirits. Myr.'

'Sshh, don't mention them!' Taran's easy humour was gone in an instant, rope clutched tightly, as if it would provide protection from the spirits of death.

Kaio snorted. 'You and your superstitions. What, you think saying their *name* will bring their wrath upon you?' He spun in a circle, arms held high. 'The Myr are back! Can you see me? Can you hear me? The Myr! Death itself! Come and kill me if you think you can!'

Several crew members chuckled as they walked past.

'Stop that!' Taran dropped the rope and grabbed Kaio's hands. 'It ain't their wrath I'm worried about. It's the *queen's*!'

Kaio pulled his hands away and leaned on the railing again. 'We're as far south in Bragalia as you can get. She ain't here.'

'No. But her Inquisitors are always spying. Not to mention that damned magic of hers. She can hear you *fart* in the wrong direction.'

'The queen has more important things to do than eavesdrop on *our* conversations.' Kaio's patience was waning, especially after Yaniv's strike. Yes, he'd heard the stories about the damned mage queen who ruled Porsenthia. People spoke about the Myr, or other treasonous words, and her Inquisitors swept in minutes later to throw you in irons. Her threads of magic spread across the entire continent, always listening, always watching. Farsight, it was called.

And of course, her Inquisitors could receive messages directly from her through their iron daggers. Nowhere in the Empire was safe from her senses.

It was all very impressive. Made everyone terrified of disobeying their conqueror queen. Terrified of her Inquisitors, and of Toriaken.

But Kaio didn't give two shits.

Supposedly she was of Bragalian blood, but she hadn't set foot in the country since she was a child. She was no queen of his, magic or no. Spirits or no.

As far as he was concerned, no one had the right to tell him what he could or couldn't say, and he told Taran as much. ''Sides, we ain't got a strip of iron on *Wolf's Grin*. She can't hear you.'

'Even so, best watch what you say. Sea can't keep you safe forever. Yaniv ain't the only one muttering, you know.' Taran sucked in a breath of smoke, then held the cigarillo loose between two fingers, tapping the ash overboard.

'Let 'em mutter.' Kaio scratched the back of his neck to hide his nerves. 'You sure about what you saw? Winds've changed the past few days.' Kaio trusted Taran, but if their run of poor luck continued, he was more likely to lose the ship than find anything of value.

They weren't going home completely empty-handed, but it was hardly an impressive haul for so long at sea. He wanted to try one last thing to boost his reputation and standing. Otherwise, the next of Yaniv's strikes might include a blade.

Taran released a mouthful of smoke and nodded, his warm, honey-brown eyes bright. He'd always claimed he had hawk's eyes, and was usually the first to spot anything of interest—trouble and treasure both. It'd be just his luck they'd find monsters on the island.

Kaio changed the subject. 'How's Esto?'

Taran screwed up his nose.

Kaio winced. 'That bad?'

'Let's just say I'm in no hurry to get back to Segandis.' He returned his cigarillo between his teeth and continued working on the rope. 'She locked me out the cabin. Had to sleep on deck in the pissing rain all night.'

Kaio chuckled, his gaze drawn to the blue-green water surrounding their ship, the coast of Segandis a dark line above the horizon. *Home*. Whatever that meant. A birthplace, perhaps, but his family was long gone. And there'd been more and more people crawling to Segandis before he'd set off on the latest voyage. Strangers running from something. Sometimes it was a concrete threat, like the Iron Queen or the Myr. Other times it was their past or crimes. Often, they wanted to join his warband for gold or glory, following its reputation rather than the reality of what it had become. Fractured and squabbling, like a group of childish brats. As chief of the warband, and de facto Laird of the canton, it fell to him to sort them out and give them a place in Segandis. It was a task he loathed. A sword or a ship and he was comfortable. Anything else just gave him a headache.

Something small and silent padded across the deck, tail straight up, whiskers twitching. The movement caught his attention, and he grinned.

'Oh no, not here!'

Kaio ignored Taran's complaint and leaned forward to scratch Fergus behind his good ear. The grey tabby's bad ear had been chewed to ribbons in a scrap with two other ship cats over a year ago, but Fergus had managed to chase them away with his dignity intact. Kaio always thought Fergus seemed proud of his war wounds, yowling and turning his head so his torn ear faced whoever had caught his attention. Fergus purred loudly at Kaio's touch and pressed into the fuss, orange eyes half-closing in pleasure.

Taran and Ruka often moaned about Fergus and the other cats on board the ship, stating their hair got everywhere and made them itch. Kaio argued that the ship remained mouse and rat-free, and Fergus shed less than they did.

At least his childhood friends kept their faith in him.

'No gift for me today?' Kaio asked, checking by the cat's paws in case he'd dropped something. Watching where you stepped on board a dark ship was a lesson Kaio had learned as a boy, though it hadn't been Fergus's catches back then.

Fergus pulled away after a minute and yawned, exposing sharp fangs to the sun, then sat down and set to cleaning his paws, the gentle rocking of the ship not bothering him in the slightest.

'You gotta ignore Yaniv,' Taran said, eying Fergus with distaste, his nose scrunched up.

'I do, for the most part. He'll pay for that punch, though.' Kaio pressed a hand to his jaw. It ached where the blow had landed, but he'd fallen harder before when drunk. It was the fact Yaniv had acted publicly that irritated him more than the punch itself.

'You don't have to go in knives ready every time you get challenged,' Taran said.

'What you want me to do? Ask 'em nicely to "please not do that 'cause it hurts my feelings"? Don't be an idiot, Taran.'

'Sometimes yes. You're chief. Gotta do more than just fight.'

Kaio rolled his eyes. His name commanded respect, even if his own grip of that respect was tenuous at best. Nothing had been the same since—

'There it is!' Taran called, pointing to a dark speck in the distance.

Kaio pulled the bronze scope from his waistband and brought it to his eye, following Taran's gesture. White froth topped the waves as they crashed against one of the many scattered islands off the coast of Segandis. Gulls swooped low, picking out the beached fish that were flung ashore by strong currents. Dark brown and black pebbles lined the edge of the island, worn smooth by centuries of seawater. Crabs scuttled up and down the rough coast, scavenging through the rocks in search of food. There was more debris amongst the wildlife, too—glass bottles, bits of a mast, and strips of fabric. 'Remind me again why we're going to *this* one?' Kaio lowered the scope and rubbed his face.

'You'll see when you get there.' Taran had that gleam in his eye. It always meant mischief, and often led them into trouble. He'd had that gleam since he was seven years old, and the ensuing decade and a half had done little to rid him of it.

Somewhere above them, *Wolf's Grin's* horn blew. Whoever was on scouting duty had spotted the island, too.

Fergus stopped cleaning and blinked slowly at him, the

sunlight turning his orange eyes golden. His good ear twitched, and he let out a lazy meow.

Esto marched over, her large straw hat keeping the sun and her hair out of her face. She was strongly built, with wide hips and a fairly slender waist. Kaio had always thought Taran lucky she gave him the time of day. Her cool green eyes passed over Taran, as if he wasn't there, and rested on Kaio. 'Close as we're gonna get to that island without risking the rocks, chief. You got a team in mind to explore it? We'll drop anchor.'

Kaio nodded. 'You have the ship, Esto. Taran and I will take a look ourselves. Keep Yaniv busy, will you?'

Esto tapped her hat to him in acknowledgement of the order, then strode across the deck, belt buckles jangling with every step.

Kaio stretched, joints popping in his shoulder. 'You ready to brave the unknown again?'

Taran grinned and flicked the almost finished cigarillo into the sea. It disappeared under the surf with a splash. 'I'm sure it'll be worth our while.'

5
THE TASK
TORSTEN

Eastbrook was a flurry of activity.

Conscription notices were being sent to all corners of Porsenthia and Bragalia, couriers leaving the iron fortress on horseback, by carriage, and on foot. Both countries were part of Queen Surayo's Empire, and both had a duty to fight in the new Myrish war.

Although Olmir was an ally of the Empire and had its own king, many of their warriors and war griffins had arrived to aid the Iron Crown of their own volition. It was an impressive sight, fifty or so of the enormous creatures flying in several formations above the castle towers, wingtip to wingtip. Each griffin held ten warriors, all battle-hardened and wearing golden torcs to signify their experience.

The majority of their forces remained in Olmir, to defend their borders against the rising Myrish threat. Although Olmir had only one known dragon spirit, the country rarely worried about invasions thanks to their war griffins. Even the Porsenthian Empire had not been able to claim it as their own territory, and Surayo had never attempted to conquer Olmir.

Torsten could see why.

War was the only reason he remained in his towers. Had Queen Surayo not made the declaration, he'd be scouring Foxmouth and the surrounding towns, looking for that spirits-damned thief, Apollo.

He could hardly believe the traitor had slipped through his fingers and taken Nestol. Quite what Apollo planned to do with the Myrish spell, Torsten couldn't say, but it was just another crime he needed to be punished for.

But it would not do to blindly run after the man.

He'd granted Nadja leave so she could track down Apollo without being caught up in Queen Surayo's war effort. He hadn't mentioned Nestol—no need for her to know about that—but once Apollo was back in his clutches, Torsten was sure he'd be able to unearth what had happened to the device.

But now, he had more pressing concerns.

Miroth had withdrawn into the recesses of his mind. A small flame, barely there. His spirit was weak, and Torsten needed to replenish what he'd used of Miroth's strength over the past few weeks.

Miroth always took priority, even in times of war.

Especially in times of war.

Torsten watched another formation of griffins from the window of his chamber, high in the palace's eastern tower. Sunlight glinted off their talons, and Torsten pressed a hand against the deep scar across his waist. That had been dealt by a griffin—a wild one he'd happened upon during a tour of Olmir. He'd never particularly warmed to griffins following that encounter.

He sipped from a goblet of wine and watched the winged creatures descend—the palette of their fur and feathers a rainbow under the sun—then land in the vast courtyards of the iron fortress.

'Master Inquisitor.'

Torsten turned at the sound of his title. His door was slightly ajar, a herald bowing low just outside.

'Her Majesty has summoned all Inquisitors currently in Eastbrook. She's to give an address.'

Torsten's hand dropped to the iron dagger at his belt, a shiver of metallic wind seeping through him for just a moment. The Queen's magic was potent, even when not called upon. 'Now?'

'Yes, Master Inquisitor.'

Torsten placed the half-finished goblet on the table. 'I'll be there presently. You may leave.'

As the herald left, Torsten pulled his cloak from the back of his chair and threw it around his shoulders. He took a moment to tighten it with the silver clasp at his collar, then strolled to the mirror in the corner of his room, checking the status of his uniform. The wounds on his face were far from healed, but there was nothing he could do about that. Damn that lost soul Fenn and his dragon spirit.

He should have killed the boy when he'd had the chance.

Torsten waited, glaring at his own reflection, but Miroth was silent, offering no criticism or judgement. The dragon spirit was too worn out.

Torsten smoothed his dark hair with one hand, adjusted the dragon insignia clasp, then left the tower and made his way down the winding stone steps.

His queen awaited.

Queen Surayo sat upon her throne, flames licking at her feet and hands, the smoky tendrils of Toriaken curled around her legs. He passed in and out of sight, his deep blue eyes as vast and empty as midnight. Surayo wore a diadem of iron upon her head, a ruby in the centre, the only mark of royalty upon her body. Sunlight drifted through the windows either side of the throne, filling the room with warmth.

She was motionless, save her fingers drumming on the heavy mahogany arms of her throne, polished nails painted grey. Fire flickered and danced with their movement, the dragon spirit and the queen as one.

A pair of the Iron Guard stood either side of her—tall, broad statues of solid iron armed with longswords and shields, inanimate save when Toriaken moved them. Bonded to the queen, the soldiers were not alive or dead, but bowed to her will. In all the generations since their creation, the Iron Guard had never been breached.

There were several others of the Iron Guard in the circular audience chamber, standing at attention against the walls. They'd always reminded Torsten of dragon teeth, and a chill ran down his spine at the sight. For all her flaws, Surayo was a force to be reckoned with. Especially bonded with the dragon spirit of iron.

More than two dozen Inquisitors were assembled before the queen, each attentively waiting for her to speak. Several nodded to him respectfully as he took his place near the front of the gathered Inquisitors, and he felt Nadja's absence keenly.

Behind him, the heavy oak doors to the room closed, the thud muffled by the plush, red carpet underfoot.

'It is no secret that the Myr are returning.' Surayo's voice cut through the air like a knife, quieting any chatter and pulling Torsten from his thoughts. 'I thought them gone, Toriaken and my magic enough to banish them from the Porsenthian Empire five years ago. You punished non-believers. Those who sought to undermine my victory, our peace, and spread dissent and lies.'

A murmur rippled through the crowd.

'Perhaps those who spread such talk knew something I

did not, for a traitor within my cities schemed to bring about our downfall. He *will* be brought to justice.'

Torsten clenched his jaw. Queen Surayo had yet to punish him for allowing Apollo to slip away, the damned thief. Then again, she was preoccupied with the Myr's resurgence. She'd be angry at him for hiding knowledge of that, too.

He thought back to the Myrish spirit he'd seen in Ballowtown all that time ago. Miroth had helped him defeat the creature, but Miroth's power couldn't be relied upon in all situations, weak as he was. If more of those Myrish spirits invaded, he wouldn't stand a chance.

'My attention remains on the new threat.' Queen Surayo's words pulled at Torsten's attention again. 'You will visit the cities and towns within the empire following the delivered conscription notices, and you will arrange new blood into our defences. There can be no chink in our armour. No weak link that can allow the Myr to gain a foothold here again. There is no more time for armistice. We will destroy these creatures *permanently* and vanquish them from our lands.' Queen Surayo spoke coldly, not once raising her voice.

Torsten admired her calm demeanour.

If a peace *he'd* purported to bring had been ruined, he'd be spitting flames.

'The Master Inquisitors will manage this effort. We'll have new recruits trained up with our most intense drills before they are sent out. They are not fodder to buy time or to be slaughtered. They will represent the Iron Crown in the coming battles, and I will not suffer defeats lightly. Until such time as this new wave can be sent out, our priority is to bolster Eastbrook's defences and open the city as a sanctuary, just like the temples. The Olmese will assist you in the defence effort. I will *not* stand for the Myr in Porsenthia nor Bragalia. Is everything clear?'

Assent muttered through the crowd. Torsten glanced left and right, picking out names and faces, already beginning to plan who he'd send where. He spotted a broad-shouldered man with a dark beard and bit back a surge of annoyance.

Varlot.

He'd swapped his heavy bearskin cloak for an Inquisitor's uniform and didn't look much better for it. The man commanded attention and respect in a fearless, primal sort of way. Torsten wasn't sure if he was sickened or proud at seeing him wear the uniform, the silver dragon insignia polished to a bright sheen.

He needed to keep an eye on him.

Or perhaps send him to the furthest corner of the empire.

'*Send your...enemies...away...*' Miroth whispered, his feeble voice breathless.

Torsten was inclined to agree. Somewhere in Bragalia, far to the south, where he wouldn't be a problem. He narrowed his eyes, thinking about the geography of the land.

Segandis.

Yes. The place was overrun with Bragalian warlords and pirates. The perfect testing ground for Varlot. If the brute wanted to bloody himself in an attempt to prove his loyalty, why not send him somewhere he could be useful, too?

Torsten himself would patrol the western coast of Porsenthia, which would allow him ample time to visit Miroth's temple and do what he could for his own spirit.

At the thought, Miroth filled him with warm fire—his adoration of being at the forefront of Torsten's priorities and attention.

Even weak as he was, the dragon spirit remained aware.

'Prepare to leave immediately. You are dismissed.'

'At once, your Highness.' As one, the Inquisitors clasped one hand across their chests, their other clutching iron daggers. A spike of Queen Surayo's magic filled the room, and the floor rumbled.

Torsten turned to leave with the others and stopped before he'd taken a single step. One of the queen's Iron

Guard had crossed the room to stand in front of him, halting him in place. It watched him with sightless eyes that sent a prickle of unease along his skin.

Torsten faced Queen Surayo, noting Varlot had been halted, too. He only saw the man out of the corner of his eye, but was glad he wasn't the only one facing the queen.

The other Inquisitors filed out of the audience chamber, talking amongst themselves and paying neither of them any attention. When the final few exited and the thud of the heavy door closing echoed a second time, the two Iron Guards that had stood before Torsten and Varlot marched back to their positions against the wall, heavy steps shaking the floor.

Torsten dropped to one knee before the queen, and he saw in his peripheral vision Varlot mirrored his action. 'My queen. I am humbly yours, to serve at your pleasure.' The words tasted strange on his tongue despite years of saying the phrase. Miroth hissed in disgust.

'Rise, Inquisitors.' Queen Surayo herself stood, leaving faint wisps of smoke trailing from her throne as Toriaken's fire disappeared. She walked to the vast window, the iron rings and bracelets adorning her fingers and coiling around her wrists clinking gently when she moved.

She held the room, commanding their silence and attention.

Much as it grated at Torsten, the queen wouldn't be hurried.

He was almost at the end of his patience when she spoke again.

'I have long wondered whether to speak of these things, but war is upon us again. I cannot leave it hidden any longer.' Queen Surayo held one hand in front of her face, bringing her fingers to her palm and seemingly inspecting her nails. 'My magic. Threads of farsight weave across the empire like a spider's web. It reacts to other powers, like the touch of the Myr.'

This, Torsten knew, though he couldn't say he fully understood how it worked.

'I see where their magic creeps. I feel their footsteps across my lands, like insects crawling on my skin. But the Myr are such fleeting creatures—so very different to the immortal dragon spirits. It is why they pour so much of their magic into artefacts. It gives them strength. Longevity. Locks their power here for a time far longer than their lifespans. This is why I have always sought to crush them,' she glanced at Torsten, 'or use them to my own ends.'

Torsten thought back to Nestol—originally one of the Myrish creations, warped by Queen Surayo's magic into something he could use to great effect.

'Despite my efforts, I feel more shifting powers in my empire each day. It *disgusts* me to feel their presence growing, tainting everything they touch.' She closed her eyes and took a breath, as if steeling herself for battle. 'There is another of their artefacts in my lands that I am now certain of.'

'What is it?' Varlot asked, leaning forward.

Torsten was about to chide him for speaking out of turn, but Surayo continued.

'I don't know what object it is. But it feels very much like the Citrine Key in age and power, and it wouldn't surprise me if it is similarly made. These are their creations from before the war. Perhaps they will come to nothing, perhaps not. But with the Myr on the rise again, I will take no chances. My farsight is unable to pinpoint an exact location. The tang of Myrish magic is not as precise as mine—but I am certain it is within Marlrush Fortress. I had for some time assumed the deadlands surrounding that place had arisen due to the death at the last battle there. Perhaps it is due to the lingering effect of that artefact.'

Torsten's stomach tightened. Marlrush brought back

many memories he'd rather forget. He tried to see whether Varlot responded to the queen's words, but he couldn't check without turning his head, and didn't wish to show Surayo such obvious disrespect.

'An artefact like a key? Don't sound worrying.' Varlot snorted and shifted his weight.

Queen Surayo's gaze darkened. 'Varlot, you wish to return to my good graces and become a full Inquisitor? This is my task for you. Find this Myrish artefact and bring it to me. Torsten, as you requested his return, you shall be responsible for him during this task.'

Torsten understood the truth of it. *He* had failed the queen, and it was as much a test for him as it was the disgraced Porsenthian General. Torsten bowed his head. 'Yes, your Highness.'

She stared at him, and for a long moment Torsten felt the white-hot breath of Toriaken's flames.

'I suggest you leave immediately. The longer this artefact is out there, the more powerful the Myr may become.'

Torsten bowed again, then retreated from the room without a look back.

The clock was ticking.

6
THE PROMISE
FENN

A cold wind knifed across the deck of the stolen Inquisitor ship. Dawn lit the horizon in swathes of gold, and Fenn turned towards the building warmth, savouring the sensation on his cheek. Waves of clear blue water stretched out in all directions as far as the eye could see. Funny, how quickly land had become a distant memory.

'Neros.' He wasn't sure if he'd spoken the word or Hassen had. He'd never realised how *vast* the body of water was. It seemed infinite. He couldn't fathom how the Myr had managed to cross Neros's domain to attack Foxmouth and Eastbrook without disintegrating.

Apollo slumped against the railing, turning his wife's knife over and over in his hand. He'd found a small bottle of rum so dark it was almost black and had downed most of it before they were out of Foxmouth harbour. Nadja and Selys spent most of their time in the captain's cabin or by the ship's wheel on the quarterdeck, and Fenn was happy to leave them to their business.

He clenched and unclenched his fists, feeling new strength ripple through his muscles, from shoulders to fingertips. Everything had happened so quickly—from being in the presence of *Vermecio*, to carrying Selys down the mountain, finding Apollo and learning of his connection to the Citrine Key, then the griffin-flight to Foxmouth.

It was the first time he'd been able to stop and just *breathe*.

'Fenn?' Selys called gently.

He whirled around to see her standing barely two paces from him, one hand on her hip, though she didn't carry her glaive. For all his increased strength and heightened senses, he'd had no idea she'd approached. 'Selys! You made me jump.'

'I apologise. I'm more at home on a ship than on land. Slip into old habits pretty quickly.'

'Habits of moving as quietly as a cat?'

'Quieter, if I can manage.' A grin shadowed across her face, then it was gone. 'I've been thinking, Fenn...well, speaking with Neros. A little. I only get flashes from her.'

Fenn grew serious at once. They were in Neros's domain. He needed to pay attention and be sure not to offend the dragon's priestess. He didn't think Selys *would* do anything, but if Neros was as opinionated as Hassen, who was to say the spirit wouldn't work through Selys if she had a mind to? 'What is it?'

'This key that you're after...'

Fenn's stomach knotted. He hoped he kept his face free of anything that might bely his warring emotions. 'The Citrine Key.'

'It's of Myrish origin. That's why *Vermecio* wants it.'

'To restore its power. Then, in return, it'll restore my memories.'

Selys frowned, and Fenn's stomach twisted again. He knew all of Tassar was at war with the Myr, knew that restoring one of their bastions of power would probably be considered treasonous as far as the Iron Queen was concerned. But what choice did he have? Inquisitors were already after his blood. He might as well do what he could to get his memories back and seek out his family.

Spirits knew how long he'd been away from them.

'Don't you think restoring power to the Myr is…a poor idea?' Selys glanced around, deer-like in her nervousness.

She was always so forthright, it was peculiar to see her stumbling over her words.

Fenn rubbed his chin, stubble rough against his palm. 'Well, it's not as if I haven't considered that. But what can I do? If I wander around as I am, Torsten or one of the other Inquisitors will have me locked up as a lost soul. They've already decided I'm committing treason against the Iron Crown just by being touched by the Myr. At least this way, I won't be lost anymore. I'll be able to go *home*.'

Home.

The idea of it filled him with such longing it was painful.

'And what if it tips the war in favour of the Myr? What if it brings destruction to all of Tassar?' Selys asked, speaking more confidently now, like her normal self.

He turned away, but she grabbed him by the arm and pulled him in to face her. 'Let go!'

Her grip was like a vice, no doubt some of Neros's strength infused into the movement. 'Fenn. This is serious. I haven't said anything until now because I haven't had a chance to. But you must understand, you and I are bonded to dragon spirits. Guardians of Tassar. If you mean to act against them—'

'I'm acting for *myself*! It's always been for myself. My family. My home. My life.' Fenn felt his voice rising and heart pounding, but couldn't stop it. He yanked his arm free, breaking her grip, and stepped away from her. The ship rocked underfoot, but he kept his balance. 'You tried to help me solve the riddle.'

Something flickered in her gaze that Fenn couldn't place. 'I know. I wanted to help you, Fenn. Wanted to see your curse lifted, your life saved. Wanted to see what the Myr were doing with these lost souls, and what changes it would bring to Tassar. It was knowledge that I sought. Knowledge that would help a greater purpose. But now Neros is here,' Selys tapped her chest with her middle finger, 'I see so much more. Understand things I hadn't been *aware* of.'

Fenn thought back to Hassen's description of trees and life and nodded to show his understanding.

Selys shifted her weight. 'Perhaps...perhaps this key is better off being destroyed, as Nadja and Apollo wish.'

'I have no problem with that. I'll even help them do it! *Once* I get my memories back.'

'Fenn. It might be a terrible thing to bring it to *Vermecio* first. Their artefacts are full of magic. They should be destroyed, not returned to the Myr. Haven't you heard what Inquisitor Nadja has been saying to Apollo? The consequences could be dire. He may not have a wife if the Myr win. *You* may not have a family.'

Emotions welled up in Fenn like an overflowing fountain. Anger and defiance, frustration and desperation. He wasn't stupid. He knew it might be a mistake, but he was certain with his newfound strength, he'd be able to weather any storm that broke. He wasn't the same lost soul who had woken up in Hassen's bog, even if that's all anyone saw when they looked at him. 'I'll know who my family is once the key is returned, and I'll protect them against the consequences. Whatever happens, I'll be able to fix it, Selys. Trust me on that.'

She went quiet for a moment, jaw working as if she was trying to figure out what to say. 'What if you're wrong? What if you can't?'

'Don't worry so much! However the Myr react, it can't be worse than what they're already doing. Death spirits on the move? I have Hassen. You have a dragon, too! I need my memories, and I need to find my family. I'll look after them. Whatever the Myr do, we'll manage.'

'Fenn, you're behaving like a child.'

Anger flared in Fenn's chest, bright and hot. 'Aren't you on my side?'

Selys's mouth fell open, shock etched on her face. 'I *am* on your side. That's why I'm pulling you up on this. This key is more than a way for you to obtain your memories. Why else would Surayo want it destroyed?'

Fenn turned away, out of reach in case she tried to grab him again. Everyone wanted him to stay exactly where he was—a lost puppy that did as it was told. No one seemed to understand he'd had his entire life ripped away from him.

If the Myr had taken it, the Myr would give it back.

What did it matter whether *Vermecio* had the key or not? Queen Surayo had Toriaken, Spirit of Iron. They'd defeated the Myr before. They'd do so again. He tried to think of a way to argue his case that she'd understand. 'Hassen picked me. Blessed *me*. I can't be that bad, can I?'

'Fenn, I know you're upset. But think about it. The Myr *attacked* you. Why help them?'

He had an answer, though he didn't like it very much. He was desperate. *Vermecio* had removed the abundant Myrish magic in his body and stopped him from dying. Had released Hassen. Had told him what to do next. It was more than what most people had said to him.

And those in authority wanted him locked up and probably beheaded. He was cornered, with no way out. He didn't trust the Myr, not after what he'd seen their death spirits do. But he had a chance to get back what he'd lost. He *had* to take it. 'Nadja can destroy the key once I'm done with it.'

Selys frowned. 'And if it cannot be undone once used? I don't agree with giving them access to that kind of power. Neither does Neros. Fenn, it could mean the war is—'

'I'm not here to start a war! I'm trying to stop being part of it.'

'War has *already* started. You heard the Inquisitors in Foxmouth.'

Fenn couldn't believe what she was saying. Again the sea swelled, and the ship lurched. He shook his head, his frustration spilling into something close to spite. 'Your spirit getting angry with me?'

Selys lifted her chin, assessing him with her cool gaze, blue eyes twinkling. 'If Neros was angry, Fenn, you would not survive it.' It didn't sound like a threat.

It sounded like a promise.

Fenn stared at her. Selys had been the only one who'd rooted for him since the moment they'd met. She'd told him of *Vermecio*. Had travelled with him up into the mountains. Defended him against Varlot and the other Inquisitors when they'd tried to arrest him. She'd been the only one who wasn't afraid of his taint. Had made him believe his life was worth living, worth saving.

And now…now…

'*Betrayal.*'

The word whispered in his ear, faint as shadow. But he heard it as clearly as if it had been shouted.

'Fenn. The world is more important than your family. Don't be selfish.'

He snorted. 'Easy for you to say when your family is already gone.' When he looked back at her, he knew he'd made a mistake.

Her mask of indifference slipped, her lip twitching. The early morning sun threw her face into sharp relief—the thin scar across her right eye, stark against her light brown skin. 'My opinion would be the same even if my family were still alive.' Selys's words were a deadly whisper. 'Do not assume things about me nor say anything that you might regret.' She considered him another moment before turning away, brushing her hand against the main mast as she passed it. She hopped up the stairs to the quarterdeck without a backwards glance.

Fenn was suddenly glad she wasn't holding her glaive. He knew what he'd said was rude and hurtful, and he regretted it. But the sting of betrayal lingered in his chest.

First Varlot, now Selys.

Admittedly it wasn't as overt as the former Porsenthian General, but her feelings were clear. She'd rather he gave up on fixing his life and instead continued to exist on the fringes of society, not knowing things, not understanding how Tassar worked.

What kind of life was that? And what did that say about his family? What if they were suffering? What if he had young children who needed him?

Selys hadn't said anything of the kind to Apollo, and he was also *putting his own family above the world*, as she called it. Fenn folded his arms and walked away, putting as much distance between the quarterdeck and himself as he could.

He'd just reached the railing when booted footsteps approached. He rolled his shoulders, bracing himself for another argument with Selys, when he realised it was Nadja. The lack of silent footsteps should have been a giveaway, and he mentally berated himself for the assumption. But the Inquisitor wasn't coming towards him.

'On your feet, Apollo. You are not allowed to die until you fix this mess.' Nadja turned his prone form over with the toe of her boot. 'I let you drink and sleep the night away, but morning is here, and it's time to work.'

Apollo grumbled in protest.

'Now, Apollo.'

Another grumble, then he staggered to his feet, grasping the side rail with both hands. His hair was a mess, sticking out at all angles, the strong wind not helping. Spray hit his face and he flinched. 'Not dead yet,' he muttered, taking a few unsteady steps backwards. He took a deep breath, then straightened up. Catching Fenn's gaze, he winked, then yawned.

Nadja let out an exasperated sigh, though she didn't scowl at him. 'There are maps in the captain's quarters. I want you to point out the last known location of the key. I also made up another vial of glinoc paste from the ship's supplies if your wounds require them.'

'Right now? Really?' Apollo covered his open mouth with one hand.

'Right now.'

Nadja remained in place, watching and waiting for Apollo to shuffle away. She glanced at Fenn while she waited, her gaze unreadable, and when Apollo finally managed to move, she followed at his heels.

Fenn felt an affinity with Apollo. Both displaced, both trying to do the best they could for their loved ones, both denied the ability to do so. Or at least, had their requests deeply frowned upon or constantly questioned.

He wanted to understand Selys, to not see her words for the betrayal they were, but the deep pain in his chest reminded him of what she said. *Don't get the key. Don't find your loved ones. Stay where you are, weak and lost and confused. That's better for the world. It doesn't matter if it's unfair so long as the rest of us are safe and happy.*

He was adding words and thoughts onto what the priestess had said, he knew, but they felt *right*.

There was no one he could trust but himself. Even Hassen acted to his own ends. He was just a pawn for the dragon, like he'd been a pawn for the Myr. Again, he clenched his fists. Felt his strength. He could trust in that, at least. Even if he had to drag the key back to *Vermecio* alone, he'd get it done.

He had to.

And he'd overcome whatever happened after.

Coming to a decision settled his brewing anger somewhat, and he shook out some of the tension in his body.

A chill spread across his skin, and for a moment he thought it was something to do with his shifting emotions. He blinked, realising the dawn glow had disappeared, and a thick cloud passed in front of the sun. He was about to dismiss it when he realised something was moving within the cloud. A black silhouette, like a shadow, quickly crossed the surface and disappeared. Far too swift to be any animal.

'Another…spirit?' Fenn muttered aloud, hoping it wasn't another Myrish creation.

In the silhouette's wake, more clouds formed, rolling and thickening with every heartbeat. Each cloud darkened, whipped up by strong winds, then plummeted towards the sea in a wide column that stretched across the horizon.

'Selys! Looks like there's a…a storm ahead!' Fenn called, unsure what kind of storm looked quite like that. Putting aside his feelings towards the priestess, he hurried up the steps to the quarterdeck, hammering on the captain's door as he passed it. The ship creaked underfoot, and sails that had been calm a few moments before now rippled loudly in the developing gusts.

It sent goosebumps up his exposed skin, and he skidded to a halt by the wheel, where Selys stared wide-eyed at the horizon. She strode away from the spoked wheel and peered across the churning sea, the waves swelling.

Fenn wobbled as the ship rose and fell under the increased movement, nausea beginning to rise.

More footsteps and Nadja appeared on the quarterdeck beside them, Apollo hobbling behind. Despite his injury and likely hangover, he was bright and alert, a fierceness to him that Fenn hadn't seen before.

'Strange for a storm to gather so quickly,' Apollo commented. He grabbed hold of the railing, knuckles white.

'Neros pissed off about something?' His jaw tightened, muscles twitching as he clenched his teeth.

'It isn't Neros,' Selys said, one hand resting on her chest. Any hint of their earlier disagreement had been wiped from her face—she was back to the warrior priestess she'd been before. Determined and calculating. 'It's one of the Archons.'

'One of the what?' Apollo asked, shivering in the wind.

'You are familiar with Paragos?' Selys didn't pull her gaze from the growing storm.

'Spirit of the Eternal Blizzard,' Apollo replied, more than a little bitterness in his voice.

'This one is of the same class. Spirits that have ascended beyond their domains. They can move and manifest where they choose.'

Dread built in Fenn's gut with every word she spoke. The flame in his chest, usually proud and blazing, shrank away, leaving him hollow and exposed.

Shards of black ice fell from the sky, a wave before the storm hit. They shattered on impact, littering the wooden deck in frozen mirrored fragments. Fenn stepped on one, crunching it under his boot. A hint of electricity charged through his foot for half a heartbeat.

Selys raised her glaive, silk ribbons flapping wildly in the raging wind, rain lashing her face, splintered with ice. 'It's Verkata, Spirit of the Eternal Storm.'

7
THE BONES
KAIO

They dropped anchor a short way from the small island. Kaio and Taran were the only two to disembark—Taran brought his ashwood bow, a handful of griffin-fletched arrows in a quiver over his shoulder.

Kaio kept his blade belted. He didn't need anything else.

Whatever Yaniv thought of him, Kaio at least trusted Esto. She would follow his command until the day she died, as would Taran and Ruka. With any luck, they'd influence more of the others, even after Yaniv's display.

He watched *Wolf's Grin* grow smaller as they rowed towards the beach, grateful at the physical activity to keep his mind clear. Each stroke emptied his mind of worries, sharpened it to focus on the next task. Rhythmic, methodical.

A ball of grey fluff slept soundly on the bench beside him. The rowboat had always been one of Fergus's favourite sleeping spots, and even being on the water didn't affect his daily nap. Kaio was used to the cat going wherever he wished, and allowed his gaze to linger on his ship while his mind filled with rowing.

All too soon, the rowboat hit the beach, and they dragged it out of the surf, senses alert for anyone—or anything—on the island that might be waiting to ambush unsuspecting visitors. Fergus blinked once at them, then yawned, stretched, and went back to sleep in the sunshine.

Kaio pushed all considerations of Yaniv's strike to the farthest reaches of his mind and followed Taran up the beach. Rocks and shells littered it, along with bits of dried seaweed and driftwood that had washed ashore, muddying the sand's colours.

He crouched by a particularly pretty white stone—he'd thought it an opal at first—then dismissed it as worthless and continued on. Whatever Taran had seen, it wasn't here. He supposed if it *had* been in full view, some other ship would have claimed it by now.

Taran made his way deeper onto the island, back straight and eyes narrowed, heedless of the crabs that nipped at his bare feet. Kaio followed, easily matching Taran's swift pace, though his boots offered more protection from curious claws.

White gulls took flight and shrieked in anger, disturbed from their afternoon rest by the two men. Kaio spared them a glance, mostly to make sure none decided to dive bomb the pair—they were known to be aggressive, especially around their nests—but they resettled on another part of the beach, feathers ruffled but no worse for wear.

The sun continued to beat down on them as they progressed, and Kaio had barely taken two dozen steps when he felt a sheen of sweat on his forehead and between his shoulder blades. Although the linen shirt he wore was loose, only the bottom two buttons done up, he was desperate for a cooling breeze on his exposed skin. Traipsing across terrain wasn't quite as easy as standing aboard *Wolf's Grin* as she cut through the surf.

Rocks became more frequent on the pale white sand, until they completely took over the ground. Slick with seaweed, Kaio stepped carefully as he followed Taran along a path only he could see. He didn't need to ask where they were going or how far until they got there, such was the trust he had in Taran.

And on the off chance Kaio fell behind, all he'd need to do was follow the smell of cigarillo smoke. He smirked at that and glanced over his shoulder to make sure *Wolf's Grin* was okay. The ship bobbed gently on the waves, black and gold sails glinting under the sun.

Satisfied, Kaio hurried after Taran.

At the edge of the beach, where it shifted into soil and grass amongst the rocks, an old statue jutted out of the ground. Its top-half was weathered by decades of wind and sea, now worn so smooth its original design had been lost. Kaio assumed it was of Queen Surayo, or perhaps one of the influential dragon spirits. Neros, more than likely. Wherever there was water, whispers of that spirit followed, even if they weren't upon the Lasseen Ocean.

It had always pissed him off. Treating Neros like she ruled all of Tassar.

As far as he was concerned, Neros only ever meant storms and death. Hardly worthy of worship.

A score of gulls huddled atop the statue, squawking at one another and repainting the worn stone in their own acidic white.

They walked in the shadow of the statue, up the grass and rough rock as the island terrain grew steep. Kaio counted the passing time by his heartbeat, and once he reached three hundred, a cave mouth opened up in the rock face before them. 'This the place you saw?'

Taran nodded, smoke from his cigarillo drifting up in thin streaks. He clenched it between his teeth and patted the rock face with one of his free hands. 'Seems solid enough. Must be in here.'

A low hiss emanated from within the tunnel, Kaio's

hackles rising instinctively. He grabbed the short, curved sword from his belt and held it close. 'Sure about this?'

'Well I *saw* something down here from a distance. Can't *hear* that far, can I? We backing down?' Taran's gaze was filled with mischief and curiosity. A child who'd never learned when to stop.

Kaio did *not* want to return to the ship empty-handed. He'd never live it down, and Yaniv would take it as more evidence he wasn't fit to lead the warband. 'What did you say was here?'

'Something interesting.'

'Taran. Knock off the riddle-speak.'

Taran chuckled, taking his cigarillo from his mouth and flicking ash onto the ground. 'Saw another boat unloading here four nights ago. Gotta be something interesting, right? What if it's Dalys and his lot? Hiding their latest haul? Was too dark to see their sails, so can't be sure who it was.'

Kaio wasn't above stealing from other pirates or warbands. It was how his own had strengthened over the years, after all. He'd just prefer to earn his own way, rather than through theft. The fact he'd outlived his family already made him a coward according to some. This wouldn't help that notion.

And that hiss unsettled him.

He peered into the depths, but couldn't make out any details no matter how much he squinted. 'What they unload? A damned cage of crocodiles?'

Taran grinned and shrugged. 'Your call, Kaio. Gotta say, I *am* curious what they've been up to here.'

Kaio squeezed the handle of his sword, the bone hilt worn from years of use, the blade notched in one spot but otherwise as sharp as it had ever been.

The island was a day and a half's sail from Segandis, right on his doorstep. If another warband wanted to use this island as a cache, he needed to know about it. They needed to pay their way, if he let them sail in his waters.

It was his by rights.

That's what the Ioran warband had always believed.

And he was no different, regardless of any perceived weaknesses.

'Guard up, then. And put that damned smoke away! We need to be sharp.'

Taran's grin didn't waver, his eyes twinkling. He flicked the cigarillo into one of the myriad rock pools surrounding the entrance, where it sputtered and fizzed before dying, and the two entered the cave.

IT DIDN'T TAKE LONG for Kaio's eyes to adjust to the gloom. The tunnel walls glistened with something wet and viscous, and he didn't touch it on the off-chance it wasn't seawater.

Taran had fallen back, allowing Kaio to lead the way. They were both blind in here, even with Taran boasting about his eyesight. Kaio wanted to make sure he was the first to spot whatever lurked in the cave depths—treasure or trouble.

Thankfully whatever hissed earlier had gone quiet. It could easily have been water pouring down through the cave's roof further in, or a large rock dislodged by water or waves.

No need to assume it was something with teeth.

They walked through the narrow tunnel, a shallow stream of water running along the centre of the cave floor. It came up to their ankles and marked their progress with loud, echoing splashes. More water dripped ahead, and Kaio narrowed his eyes, trying to block out the distraction in case it masked a more insidious—and dangerous—noise.

Underfoot, the soft, wet sand churned up, trying to suck

down their feet. Kaio grimaced, pulling his feet out aggressively every other step. A dozen paces later and he sank deeper—all the way to his knee.

'Kaio!' Taran grabbed him under the arms and hauled him up.

Kaio kicked out, shoving away great clumps of wet sand as Taran pulled him back, when his boot connected with something solid. He first thought it was a rock, but when he fell back, finally free of the hole, something pale white glinted in the gloom.

Taran crouched low. 'Just a bone.' He held it up for Kaio to see. It was small and thin, probably from one of the gulls.

'Guess this is the local wildlife's dining hall. Shame they're so messy.' Kaio brushed away the gloopy sand stuck to his leg as Taran threw the bone to the side of the tunnel.

They unearthed more small bones as they continued. A few poked out of the sand and water at first, then progressively more appeared, carpeting the ground. The tunnel sloped steeply downwards and widened into a cavernous chamber, more bone piles filling much of the space.

Behind them, the drip, drip, drip of falling water was a constant companion. Though Kaio knew exactly what it was, the noise set the hairs on the back of his neck standing up.

The smell of death permeated the place. Stagnant water. Rotted wood. He was used to such odours—and worse—but there was a stillness to the cavern. A sense of *wrongness* that he couldn't quite describe.

It seemed to pull the breath from him, though the discomforting sensation faded quickly.

They stopped where the tunnel opened up, the chamber illuminated by several shafts of sunlight streaming in from gaps in the ceiling. Large boulders littered the cavern, surrounded by a thin moat of seawater, fed by the trickle they'd walked through in the tunnel. All around the boulders, water shimmered gently in numerous rock pools. And nestled everywhere in between were more animal bones.

The salt tang of the ocean intensified, filling Kaio's nose with every breath, along with the fermented odour of rot and decay. 'Well? Where is it?' Kaio asked, unable to spot any likely looking chests of gold waiting to be plundered.

It was a good place to use as a cache, he agreed, but it didn't look like anyone had done so, regardless of what Taran had seen. More than likely predators had been hauling in their kills here for years and the only thing they could dig up would be half-rotted carcasses.

'Might be they buried it?' Taran muttered, strolling into the chamber, small bones crunching under his bare feet. He kicked a few away, the movement sharper than usual.

Kaio would normally have enjoyed Taran's frustration, but he was at the end of his patience with their bad luck. There was nothing here. He'd wasted his time and proven Yaniv right. He wasn't fit to lead if he couldn't make the right calls.

Oblivious to his frustrations, Taran called back to him, 'Come on.'

Kaio covered his nose with one hand, trying to stave off the rotting stench, and entered the cavern. He and Taran automatically split in different directions to cover more ground.

Footsteps stood out in the sand between the bones, a sign people *had* passed by recently, but nothing else looked to have been disturbed. A few bundles of rags sat against one of the boulders, some wooden bowls and cups next to them, but Kaio couldn't see any food residue.

Shadowed recesses within the irregular cave wall could certainly conceal items of value, but Kaio had expected something shiny to have given away its presence by now—gold coins, jewels, weapons, *something*. He grew more irritated the longer he had to search for apparently nothing.

Something crashed in the tunnel behind them.

Kaio whirled around, already in a crouch, blade up in a reverse grip, ready. He didn't need to see Taran to know he was prepared, too, hearing him notch an arrow.

Silently, they watched the mouth of the tunnel, and waited.

Seconds dragged past.

A minute.

'Watch my back,' Kaio ordered, keeping his voice as low as he could. He cautiously approached the tunnel, careful of making noise in the water, and peered down into the darkness. Twin pinpricks of light glinted at him, low to the ground.

Something whistled past his ear, and an arrow plunged into the gloom. It skittered off a rock and plopped into the water with a splash.

The pinpricks disappeared with a hiss, higher pitched than the one he'd heard earlier.

Kaio held out his hand. 'Wait, Taran!' He recognised that hiss. He took a few steps closer, leaving the chamber and re-entering the tunnel. Then, to his left, the light appeared again. Faintly orange. A disgruntled meow followed.

'Fergus?'

The grey cat padded towards him, pupils thin as slits, tail lashing. Kaio reached down and scooped him up, placing the cat on his shoulders. 'Thought you were having a nap in the sunshine!'

Taran lowered his bow with a shake of his head. 'Gonna kill me, that cat!'

Kaio laughed, tension easing away. At least there weren't any monsters down here after all.

'Spirit might be forming there soon.' Taran gestured to one of the larger rock pools with his toe, the water inside swirling, bubbles foaming furiously. 'Lots of pools here, people visiting. Creatures on the island.'

'I hope not.' Kaio could do without *another* dragon spirit close to Segandis, although if it was only just forming, it probably wouldn't be big enough to be a threat any time soon. 'Nothing else here, then? Nothing buried?'

Taran opened his mouth, then abruptly snapped it shut, his teeth clacking together.

Something wet crunched behind them, in the centre of the cavern.

Kaio winced and followed his first mate's gaze.

Beside one of the rock pools, bathed in shadow, a small, dark creature gnawed on one of the exposed bones. It stared up at them, eyes and body too dark to make out, as if its edges blurred. The creature was not much larger than Fergus, but it held Kaio's gaze with such terrifying strength that his entire body rooted to the spot.

Abruptly, the scent of decay and rot filled the air, stronger than before, like a warm breeze from a grave. It overwhelmed the mud and salt until there was nothing but the smell of death. It permeated the air, thick and heavy, settling on Kaio's body like a second skin. He fought the urge to retch.

Another arrow flew past his ear, plunging soundlessly into the centre of the shadowy creature.

It hissed.

Fergus hissed.

Shadows blossomed, filling the chamber in an explosion of darkness. Kaio covered his face with one arm, Fergus with the other, as a roaring wind blasted into him. He lunged forward, blade slashing as the creature approached him.

Another arrow punched into it, sending it lumbering to one side. It snarled again, a writhing mass of shadow, its domed skull unlike any creature Kaio had ever seen—of the sea or otherwise. With another hiss, it surged forward, the tiniest hint of sunlight glinting off its claws.

Fergus leapt off Kaio's shoulder.

The wind picked up with the creature's movements, and Kaio called after the cat, but his breath was taken by the gale. He sank his blade deep into the creature's flesh, though it felt hard as steel. There was no skin, blood, or bone in that mass of shadow. Despite that, it let out a piercing, inhuman cry.

The screech was deafening, the only thing he could hear beyond the wailing wind.

He twisted his blade and wrenched it free. He expected a spray of gore, but nothing other than shadow bubbled out. It stopped the creature's scream, and it staggered away.

Something grey streaked past his legs, and Kaio recognised it a moment before Fergus leapt, claws outstretched.

'Fergus!' Kaio screamed, though he could hardly hear his own voice.

The creature stumbled backwards, Fergus's claws gouging into it. It raised an arm and swiped at the cat, who somehow managed to dodge the blow, clinging onto its flesh with all four paws, ears back and hissing like something possessed.

As it brought its arm down for another strike, Kaio darted forward, plunging his blade into the meat of the creature's flesh a second time and grabbing Fergus with his other hand.

The cat spat, and Kaio pulled harder. 'Fergus! Let go!'

Kaio winced as the creature's claw slashed across his shoulder, sending him toppling over, Fergus clutched in one hand, his sword in the other.

Kaio tried to get to his feet, but he lost his balance, his legs numb and unable to bear his weight. Thick shadows filled his vision, a raging storm of dark mist. Only Fergus's orange eyes seemed to offer any light.

Another arrow slammed into the creature, and much of the shadow receded.

The stench of fermented meat filled the air. Kaio squeezed his eyes shut and turned his face away from the rancid odour. He crouched over Fergus and held his blade up, bracing for another strike, the cold water around his knees chilling him. He raked his blade blindly across the creature's body as another arrow found its mark, and finally, mercifully, the darkness receded.

Unbalanced, Kaio toppled to the ground, getting a face full of seawater and Fergus yowling in his ear. An overwhelming wave of nausea gripped him. Against his better sensibilities, Kaio vomited, his body lurching with each retch.

Fergus yowled again, more quietly this time, fur tickling Kaio's ear.

Dizzy and confused, Kaio shook his head, trying to gather his bearings. The rushing wind had faded, leaving only the faint stench of decay and shivers that racked his entire body. Every limb pricked with pain as sensation slowly returned.

He looked up to find the creature had disappeared, and pale sunlight filled the cave once more.

'It's okay. I vomited the first time, too.'

It wasn't Taran who had spoken.

Blinking, Kaio pushed himself to his feet and found himself staring down into the deep brown eyes of a woman he'd never met before. Limp, greasy black hair framed a face marred by burns. Her clothes were washed of so much colour she appeared to blend into one of the large boulders, half-in a rock pool. He'd dismissed her as nought but a bundle of rags at first glance.

She bowed her head to him. 'Thank you for chasing it off.'

He brought one hand to his temple and massaged it, trying to clear his head. 'What...what was that...?'

Her lips dropped into a frown. 'That...was one of the Myr.'

8
THE SWORD
CALIDRA

Calidra woke up groggy, her joints stiff and aching. Dawn barely coloured the horizon, and an owl hooted somewhere in the distance, far too dark to see. She'd not slept much—something had dug into her back all night, no matter how she'd twisted and turned—and her mind raced every time she closed her eyes.

Memories of being aboard the ship, Neros rising from the sea to fight the Myr, and finding her sister all came flooding back, alongside a faint sense of nausea. She worried she was doing the wrong thing by dragging herself and Jisyel deeper into Porsenthia and Bragalia, especially with the Myr on the attack.

But for all of Jisyel's happy exterior, she'd been discontent since Hassen had cursed her. She'd been so used to putting others before herself, she hadn't voiced her desire to leave and had probably resigned herself to her fate.

Jisyel wanted to lift her curse.

While Calidra was determined to help her sister regain her blessing—some small way of reconnecting or seeking forgiveness— she was going to help Jisyel, too.

Her mind was overactive, and she couldn't help but think

of all possible scenarios, trying to predict dangers so she could keep her loved ones safe. It was how she'd survived her mother's fury as a child. She'd constantly second-guess what response her mother wanted—or what would be less likely to lead to humiliation or punishment—and even after so many years, she couldn't stop the instinct. Not when every day had been walking along a knife's edge of fear.

Calidra worried about the Myr. Angry spirits. About Fenn and Selys after Varlot's betrayal. About destroying any chance of a reconciliation with her sister if she did or said the wrong thing.

And something else gnawed at her. Something deeper, that she had been afraid to face for years. Regardless of how she and her mother felt about each other, the Vantonen family ruled one of Bragalia's cantons. If her mother fell, or when she passed away, the only one left was her younger brother—a boy she hardly knew but who had such little combat and strategic experience that her father had hired the former Porsenthian General to personally tutor him.

And a weak Laird was easy prey for not just the Myr, but other Lairds within Bragalia eager to increase their own power.

She would have to return home if she didn't want what was left of her family to fall into ruin.

Malora wanted to regain her blessing and go after her husband, and Calidra doubted her sister had any intention of returning to Fellwood. But Malora was entitled to do what she thought was best for her family. Calidra didn't understand—much less approve—of going back to Chyram, but it was important to Malora, so she supported that.

Calidra sat up and took several deep breaths. Attempting to get back to sleep wasn't worth the effort. Instead, she got to her feet and dressed quickly despite the pre-dawn gloom. She checked on everyone and their belongings, the small weight of her hunting knife offering comfort. She glanced at the wooden box containing Malora's sword and wondered how *that* would feel in her hands.

It had been so long since she'd used a sword—eight years at least—that she wondered whether she'd forgotten how to hold it properly. Swords weren't much use on the Isle of Salt.

She hadn't taken formal training with the sword until her family had been elevated to Lairds. But every morning from sixteen years old until she'd left home at twenty-eight, Calidra had drilled with the household guard.

Most of those soldiers had been practising with swords since they were old enough to hold them.

She'd always had to catch up, so she'd trained twice as hard, pushing her body beyond exhaustion on multiple occasions, much to her mother's chagrin.

Calidra would never be as good as her sister.

But if she worked *harder*, her mother had to notice her. *Had* to approve.

While Jisyel, Malora, and Renys slept, Calidra made her way over to the box. Her fingers brushed the ornate silver hinges, felt the familiar pattern carved into the wood. She hesitated, considering whether or not to continue, but the doubt lasted only a moment. With a soft click, she unlocked the box, lifted the lid, and gazed upon the sheathed sword nestled on a bed of pale yellow silk. Emotions flooded her at the sight, emotions beyond the superficial pang of envy.

This was a link to her childhood. To what she tried to be.

Carefully, and with great reverence, Calidra lifted it from the box with both hands. She unsheathed the sword with a low whistle. The single-edged blade had a slight curve towards the tip, designed to be wielded with one hand. Its crossguard was elaborate, more ornate than was strictly necessary for a fighting weapon, but it had been designed for the daughter of a Laird, after all. One golden griffin and one golden dragon faced outwards, their claws up and wings crossed, the Vantonen coat of arms engraved between them.

The dragon had a sapphire for its eye, and the griffin an emerald. They were dull in the gloom, but Calidra had no doubt they'd blaze like fire in sunlight.

A smile stretched across her face. The sword was lighter than she thought it would be, and well-balanced when she tested the weight.

She moved into the training forms of her youth, slipping from each stance to the next fluidly. Defence. Aggression. Evasion. Parry. Counter. Kill. She was hardly aware of deciding how to move—her body's memory of the drills took over, and her mind slowly cleared of self-doubt and second-guessing.

There was only the sword.

Her arms grew heavy and her muscles burned with a pleasant warmth. She continued shifting through the stances, always keeping her feet moving, each step measured. The same rhythm, over and over, honing her body to the weapon, her breathing matching her movements. She pushed through the aches, only thinking of the next stance and the one after that.

Breathing deeply.

In and out.

In and out.

'You just can't help yourself.'

Calidra blinked, sweat dripping down her neck. The sun seemed incredibly bright all of a sudden. She glanced around, realising dawn had crept up and overtaken her without her realising. Malora watched her from the edge of camp, Renys by her side.

Calidra reddened. 'Mal!'

'I never gave the sword its due, did I? That was always you.' Mal smiled, though it didn't reach her eyes. 'Always trying to one-up me, weren't you?'

Embarrassed, Calidra lowered the weapon and strode towards the box. She didn't have an excuse for why she'd taken Malora's sword off the boat, let alone used it. She'd wanted to see if she still remembered her morning drills.

Mostly, she'd wanted to give herself a break from the chaos swirling around her mind.

Yes, there was a touch of jealousy there, too. But there always was between siblings.

Calidra sheathed the sword. 'I'm sorry, Mal. I didn't—'

'It's fine. I suppose it's better it had *some* use. You might as well hold onto it in case we get attacked, as you're so often warning us about threats.'

Malora's sharp tone belied her annoyance. Calidra considered returning the sword back to the box, anyway. Showing her sister that she didn't need it.

But she *wanted* it.

Calidra wavered, caught between two desires. Her own, and proving her sister wrong.

Renys had plucked a branch from the ground and was copying the last few stances Calidra had moved through, her face scrunched up in concentration, one arm held out for balance.

'Are you ready to go, or do you need to rest after your exercises?' Malora asked.

'I'm fine.' Calidra wiped her forehead with one arm. In truth, she could do with sitting down for a bit, and perhaps some food, but she didn't want to slow Malora's journey or upset her any more. She'd come along to help her sister and niece, to be there for them while their future was uncertain. Not to be looked after. 'Where's Jisyel?'

'She's getting the boat out and on the water. She *demanded* to do it herself,' Malora added quickly on seeing Calidra's wide eyes. 'We should be able to reach Northbourne today.'

Calidra grimaced—though she tried to hide it and hoped Malora didn't see. Another long day on the boat. If she thought about it, perhaps it was better she *didn't* eat breakfast.

Deciding practicality was better than being right, Calidra tied the sword to her hip and resealed the now empty box. She and Malora quickly packed up their small camp together —with Renys getting in the way more than assisting, though Calidra didn't mind—and headed down the muddy slope, where Jisyel waited with the boat. Sunlight glittered on the sea, making her dizzy as she approached.

She rested her hand on the sword hilt, mixed emotions coursing through her. She didn't like how valuable it obviously was—the gold glinted and drew attention to itself—but a sword was better than a hunting knife for keeping enemies away. She just wished she'd gained it without annoying her sister.

Calidra rinsed her face and neck with the water, the cooling touch a relief on her skin, before clambering aboard, her legs steadier than they'd been the day before.

'Never seen you look so happy!' Jisyel said once Calidra settled down beside her.

'Happy?' Calidra raised an eyebrow. She felt anything but.

'Well, no. That's the wrong word. You looked calm. Like nothing worried you for once. When you were doing those sword forms.'

Malora laughed. 'Nothing worrying Cal? That'll be a first. She's always stressed out about this or that. Ever since we were little.'

Jisyel kissed Calidra, one hand holding her cheek, thumb brushing her face. 'It was nice to see you with the sword. You really *did* look peaceful. I'm happy for you.'

Calidra nodded, some anxiety easing away at Jisyel's touch. She had been so focussed on the sword that she hadn't noticed the passage of time or the others getting up and ready. Perhaps she *had* been at peace. That was less embarrassing than simply dropping her guard. 'Do you have everything? Have you eaten?' Calidra checked Jisyel over for any bruises or scratches that might need tending.

Jisyel's curse, afflicted by Hassen, left her numb to all pleasure and pain. It had taken them a while to get some sort of system in place to cope with the loss of sensation, and the morning and evening checks were now part of their routine.

'Tried a pickle, wasn't a fan.'

'You should eat.' Calidra ran her hands down the back of Jisyel's head, fingers brushing out knots in her hair while she felt for bumps and cuts. Jisyel had no sense of taste, but she liked to act as if she did.

'I'm not hungry.'

Calidra frowned but didn't argue. In addition to numbness to most physical sensations—save pressure, though Jisyel had tripped over her feet several times during the first few months of her curse—she never felt hungry or tired, either.

It wasn't a fight worth having. Skipping the occasional meal wouldn't do much harm.

The boat lurched with a loud splash, and Calidra flinched. She shivered and took several steadying breaths, trying to return to that calm state of mind she'd been in while training with the sword.

Things *would* be okay.

They had to be.

'The boat is fun, Cal! I keep you safe!' Renys brandished the stick, eyes glinting in the sunlight as much as the water.

Calidra offered her niece a weak smile back, until the girl was satisfied and shuffled over to Malora.

'I wonder if Fenn made it to that construct,' Jisyel muttered.

'Fenn?' Malora asked, glancing over her shoulder to look at them while Renys leaned over the edge of the boat, one hand trailing the stick through the water.

Calidra stared at Malora. Perhaps becoming a mother had sharpened her hearing. Calidra didn't see anything wrong with letting her sister know, so she said, 'Young lad washed up on the island with us a while back. Had no memory.'

'Cursed?' Malora asked.

'We think so. By the Myr,' Jisyel added.

Calidra nudged Jisyel in the ribs, but her movement was either too slow or too weak for Jisyel to register because she continued.

'Met a priestess of Neros. Selys. She said he'd been Myr-touched. Lots of people had been. Inquisitors were calling them lost souls.'

Calidra saw Malora grimace at the mention of the Myr and grabbed Jisyel's hand to stop her talking. They'd been speaking so freely of Tassar's enemy that she'd half-forgotten most people in Porsenthia refused to even mention their name. Queen Surayo didn't look kindly on those who did—something about it sullying her victory over them five years prior. 'It's okay, Malora!'

'The Myr!' Renys gasped, pulling away from the sea, water dripping down her hand. Her bottom lip trembled, and she let out a whimper. She'd been so brave before, so fearless of the water, that Calidra couldn't stand to see Renys so afraid when the Myr had simply been mentioned.

'So *he* was responsible for what happened to Foxmouth?' Malora whirled around, their boat veering hard to the left with her movement.

'Mal!' Calidra grasped the edge of the boat.

Renys screamed as the boat jolted.

'Oh, Ren, I'm sorry!' Malora grabbed onto the tiller and corrected the rudder, the wood groaning under the strain. They faced towards open water as Malora wrestled with the current.

With their view of the sea unrestricted, Calidra sucked in a deep breath to control her bubbling fear. Ahead, in the far distance, a dark storm loomed over the water. Lightning crackled, blue light rippling through thick, black clouds. A wave of nausea washed over her at the sight, and she swallowed down bile.

She grabbed Jisyel's hand.

Malora regained control, turning the boat to hug the coastline once again. Calidra shuddered, but she could breathe freely now the intense fear had passed.

Renys sat beside her mother, leaning into her, bottom lip trembling. 'Don't like the Myr.'

'It *wasn't* Fenn who attacked Foxmouth,' Jisyel said once the silence grew, save Renys's snuffling. 'The Myr did that themselves. Fenn is a *good* person. He was just unlucky enough to be caught in the middle of it.'

'The Myr will do whatever they can to fight our spirits,' Malora said. She didn't look at them, her attention on comforting her daughter and the water ahead. 'Even using people—willing or not. That's what they *all* do. Spirits use us for their own ends, they always have.'

'But you *want* to see Chyram? You want to be used, too?' Jisyel gasped.

Malora shook her head. 'I want my blessing back. And then I'm going to save Apollo.'

'Mal…the letter said he'd been arrested for treason,' Calidra said, choosing her words carefully. 'Torsten was involved. Have you *met* Torsten?'

The boat rocked again as Malora twisted to face them. 'There's a chance he's been left imprisoned. Clearly the Iron Crown has bigger concerns now the Myr are attacking openly.' Her voice broke, and she cleared her throat.

'Is Chyram's blessing that great?' Jisyel asked.

Malora's gaze grew distant. 'Like you can't imagine.'

Calidra tried to reason with her sister. 'What are you going to do? Storm the castle? Even with Chyram's blessing, you can't hope to overcome the crown!'

Malora's gaze sharpened and she turned it on Calidra. 'I don't need to. Chyram is no match for Toriaken, true, but with his power, I'd be more than a match for any Inquisitor. Torsten or otherwise. And once I have my husband back, we're going into hiding. Waiting out this war. I'm going to keep my family safe, and that's all there is to it.'

Something in the way she spoke reminded Calidra of their mother. The sense of finality, and the danger of arguing. 'Where will you go? Back to Fellwood?'

Malora scowled. 'To *Mother*? Don't be ridiculous. I didn't even go back for the funeral.'

'Yes, I know. Mother was upset by that. She wanted to see you and meet Renys.' Calidra shivered. Thinking back to her return home was painful. 'Jisyel was missing. Mother didn't care. She was more interested in keeping up appearances than helping me and my partner.'

'Mother will never do anything to help anyone other than herself.' Malora squeezed Renys's shoulders as she spoke. 'Always taking what she can from those around her.'

Calidra found that shocking. Their parents had always helped Malora. Let her do as she wished, so long as it shone a favourable light upon their family. 'How can you say that? She did everything to help you.'

'That came with a lot of pressure, Calidra. It was hard for me, too.'

'Oh, producing gold on a whim must've been terrible for you. Running around town with your admirers. Must've been so *very* hard to deal with.' Calidra hated the coldness in her tone, but she couldn't help it. Malora had been spoiled and never understood how good she'd had things. It had always driven them apart in their youth, and she struggled to keep those long-buried emotions contained.

Again the boat lurched as Malora moved. She stood up, one hand on the tiller, the other on Renys's head. 'I had to perform. Like a dancing monkey. You could do anything.'

Calidra laughed at the absurdity of the statement. 'I was a *prisoner*, Mal. Kept in mother's cage.'

'I was the one imprisoned! You might have been scolded or hit from time to time, but you were free to do as you wished. I had to help those begging our family for gold.'

'Free? If only.' Calidra couldn't keep the bitterness from her voice. 'Everything I did was only ever compared to you. What was acceptable one day was wrong the next. I have a scar on the back of my legs from the buckle on her belt!'

Malora's voice wavered. 'Well, if you'd just done as you were told—'

'Mother wanted so much. Whatever I did would *never* be enough. I would never be able to make gold. When I inevitably failed her impossible tasks, I was beaten. Had food taken away. Berated in front of the guard, the servants. Father. Struck and slapped and told how useless and worthless I was. Whipped so I would *learn my place*.' Calidra shuddered as the memory of her mother's words filled her mind, but it was rising like a fountain. The desperation to be *seen* by her sister. For her to understand the pain.

'Cal, it can't...it can't have really been as bad as all that.'

Calidra pulled up the bottom of her breeches, showing where the pale scar marked her skin. 'She said *this* would help me remember her favourite tea was mint.'

Malora frowned, suddenly uneasy. 'But...but she always asked for rose blossom tea?'

Calidra laughed. 'I know. How was I supposed to realise she wanted mint that day, unless I was stupid? Or being deliberately difficult?'

Malora's defiance fell away, her shoulders dropping as the words sank in. She was quiet for several long moments. 'Why...why didn't you tell me what it was like?'

Calidra's anger faded after her outburst, at the sadness in her sister's words. She didn't know how to respond.

Jisyel squeezed Calidra's hands tighter than was necessary. 'I didn't know the funeral would be so awful. I...I always tried to convince you a relationship with your mother was worthwhile. I knew things were bad, but I couldn't imagine it. I don't remember my mother. It seemed silly to me that you'd walked away from yours. I was wrong.'

Calidra appreciated the gesture, ashamed her mother had shattered Jisyel's positivity. She looked at her niece, at her curly hair and unblemished skin, at the hope in her gaze despite the fear and uncertainty. Calidra sighed. 'You have eyes, Mal. And ears. You knew and pretended it wasn't happening. Or ignored it. Too busy with your thieving friends. Why else would I have left Fellwood and refused contact? Malora, I may be afraid of the Myr. Of war. Of losing Jisyel and my loved ones. But I swear by all the spirits in Tassar, Mother is the only thing I am truly *terrified* of. And it was that fear, that guilt, that obligation, that *shame*...that drove me back for the funeral.'

Calidra was shaking, though she was only dimly aware of it. 'The only good thing to come out of wandering back into that nest of fear was learning that you...that you were alive.'

She rested one hand on the sword at her hip and tried to ground herself. Count the waves as she had counted petals on the blooms in the flower gardens when she'd been a fear-stricken child, unable to do anything against the power of her mother's wrath.

She tried to fight the tears that burned the back of her eyes, the lump in her throat.

Again, the boat wobbled. Then, suddenly, Malora was there, arms wrapping around her shoulders.

'I'm sorry, Cal,' Malora whispered.

It wouldn't fix the gaping hole between them. Nowhere close. But it was a start.

As the sun rose and spread warmth across them, Calidra hugged her back.

9
THE FORTRESS
TORSTEN

Marlrush Fortress brought with it memories of war that Torsten would rather forget. Typical that Queen Surayo should send him here, of all places. He'd never tolerated failure and strove to bury those rare occurrences whenever they touched him.

Varlot travelled with him in the carriage, the other man's bulk taking up most of the space, making it seem too small, too uncomfortable. Varlot was a far cry from Nadja, whom he'd worked closely with for years, and respected. It was the only reason he'd accepted her request for leave—she was going to track down Apollo whilst everyone else prepared for the Myr.

The timing was terrible, but there was no one else he would trust with that task.

'Together again. Just like the old days,' Varlot muttered, his attention on the window. His voice was rougher than Torsten remembered, no doubt worn down by too much cheap wine.

Torsten folded his arms. In the *old days*, they were peers. Now, almost a decade later, they were worlds apart. Varlot had disgraced himself and been cast out of the Porsenthian army, while Torsten was one of the most powerful people in the empire—second only to the queen. 'How times have changed.'

Varlot smirked. 'You might be rounder in the gut, but you're the same annoying prick you've always been.'

Torsten did not rise to the bait.

Varlot had always been uncouth and brash. *He* was the one under review, at any rate. If he did not complete the task successfully, Queen Surayo would not make him an Inquisitor, and Varlot would be out of Torsten's hair once and for all.

That was one thorn Torsten was looking forward to being removed.

'I came to the palace because I had what you wanted. Fenn. That lost soul. If we spend too long out here, he'll be out of reach. If he hides, how am I supposed to lead you to him?' Varlot continued.

'That is not my concern. We obey Queen Surayo's commands, and this takes priority.'

Varlot snorted and shook his head.

All colour washed out of the landscape, a clear sign they were approaching Marlrush Fortress. Plants and vegetation were stripped of life for leagues surrounding the ruin, which gave the area its name: *deadlands*.

The Battle of Marlrush had in truth been a slaughter before Toriaken, Dragon Spirit of Iron, had arrived to burn away the Myrish forces. They'd lost thousands over those days of fighting, bodies piled so high they looked like hills, the ground saturated with so much blood and death that it had withered and cracked.

Torsten could smell the stench of death all these years later, as if he were standing in the thick of it, sword in hand, bleeding wounds littering his body. It festered like a plague no healer or mage could eradicate. Stories drifted from the area every so often—usually tales of corrupted spirits and wild magic. It was considered a cursed land by most. Though the Myr were gone, their dark influence remained. They were creatures of death, and their magic lingered here.

Having seen the things he had, Torsten believed the stories.

By the time they stopped and exited, Torsten was grateful for fresh air and open space. They hadn't spoken much during the journey from Eastbrook, which suited him well enough. Varlot had his own demons to fight, and the less Torsten heard of them, the better.

For his part, Torsten was desperate to return to Tonmouth and see his dragon spirit, Miroth. He had taken much of his power and would need to restore it, or at least show his face. The dragon was likely to feel slighted, otherwise. But before he could do that, he needed to see the fortress and weigh up the task his queen had set.

It had rained during the night, and a heavy mist rolled in over the deadlands like grey smoke. It smothered all noise, muffling footsteps and voices both, and was illuminated by pale morning sunlight. Torsten wondered if this was what the spirit world looked like.

'Crossed these plains not long ago.' Varlot hawked and spat, both hands on his hips as he surveyed the deadlands sprawling out ahead of them. 'Didn't wanna do it then. Don't wanna do it now.'

'You have no choice in the matter, Varlot, lest you abandon your desire to wear that uniform.' Even though Varlot wore the Inquisitor's uniform, Torsten could not bring himself to use the title.

Varlot grunted in acknowledgement, neither agreeing or disagreeing. He chewed on something that looked like a toothpick—made from a small bird's hollow claw. Varlot didn't look at him. He'd thrown his bearskin cloak over his shoulders, making his stance more impressive, and contemplated what lay ahead.

Torsten tried not to let Varlot's infallible confidence get to him. As far as he was concerned, Varlot was simply a grunt who had to follow his orders.

They'd travelled swiftly, without preamble or the usual caravan of carriages Torsten was used to. No trumpets, banners, heralds, or other fanfare. Aside from the carriage driver and four bay horses, they were alone. There wasn't even a page to fetch water or run errands.

Their carriage had stopped on the northern edge of the deadlands, a narrow stream trickling along the brown grassland. No doubt it was fed by the lake in Tonmouth, purified through its travel through the rocky landscape so it was drinkable. It disappeared where it entered the smoky deadlands, drying up as though it had never existed.

So close to his bonded spirit's domain, Torsten sensed tendrils of power just underfoot. They twisted and weaved, always searching for a way forward.

Few people knew of his bond with Miroth, and those who did likely laughed at him for it when his back was turned. Miroth was weak. Dying. No one in their right mind would bond with such a failing, fragile spirit.

To know that the Master Inquisitor, of all people, had bonded with Miroth would be a mark against his reputation. As much as it killed him to hide it, he made every effort to not alert others to his dragon's presence.

But he'd fed Miroth the tooth of a Myrish spirit, and there'd been enough magic in that to restore some of the dragon's strength. It wasn't the same as healing his domain, but it had helped Miroth regain his form, speak without needing to whisper, and appear as true and magnificently as he should. The dragon was his brother, and he owed every success in his life to him. Torsten would scour the length and breadth of Tassar if he had to—searching for more power to ensure the dragon did not fade. More than that, he hoped to boost his strength *beyond* what the lake would have given him, so Miroth would be shown the respect he rightfully deserved. One day, when Miroth was fully restored and the dragon's power made even the great Toriaken quail, Torsten would boast about it.

Each of the horses had been unhitched and were being watered, the portly driver keeping watch. The man was no Inquisitor—just a member of the palace stables; his allegiance indicated by a faded patch depicting the Porsenthian Empire's sigil on his upper arm—and paid them no attention as he looked after his animals. His scraggly beard was unkempt, his boots worn, and he thumbed through a deck of cards as he waited for his horses to finish eating.

Torsten unloaded his supplies from the carriage and secured his packs to his belt and shoulders. Then he addressed the man. 'Varlot and I will approach the fortress. Make camp here, including a large fire. Do *not* let it burn out under any circumstances. Even in the daytime, the spirits here can be vengeful. Do not leave those horses unattended, either. We may need to make a swift retreat.'

The carriage driver glanced up, his mouth hanging open as if surprised to be addressed. He did nothing for several seconds, after which he apparently realised a response was required, then nodded. 'Y—yes Inquisitor. Of course. I'll get a fire going right away, sir.'

Torsten didn't bother to correct him. As Master Inquisitor, he expected to be addressed as such, but the dim-witted driver seemed not to realise this or be aware of correct protocol, and Torsten had more pressing matters on his mind.

He ran a thumb along his sword, *Tinebás*, testing its edge. It meant *water's tooth* in the old tongue of the mages, a scripture still used in temples and shrines throughout Olmir and in some parts of the Porsenthian Empire. It was his direct connection to Miroth, or at least the spirit's power—but only in dire consequences. It even had a tiny spot of rust on the metal, where Miroth's lake domain had marked it.

Happy with his sword, Torsten sipped from his waterskin and turned in the direction of the fortress. It loomed ahead, rising above the rolling mists like an enormous, oppressive beast. Unease filled his guts at the sight, and Torsten shook it off, drawing strength and reassurance from the veins of water underground.

From Miroth.

He took a breath. 'Varlot. Ready?'

'NOTHING HERE NO MORE. No animals. Spirits. Nothing. It's not right. Not *natural*.' Varlot glanced around as he spoke, his words echoing faintly in the mist, which had not receded despite the morning wearing on.

They had long passed from the edge of Miroth's domain, and Torsten felt empty. There was no life here, no touch of the dragon spirits, the guardians of Tassar. He'd known to expect it, but it didn't make the experience any less jarring.

Death loomed here, and the deeper they walked into it, the closer they came to Marlrush Fortress—a mammoth collection of stone and twisted metal, melted together by Toriaken's flame.

Once it had been the household estate and lands of a noble family. During the war, it had been a bastion of the Porsenthian strength, nigh unbreachable, surrounded by walls of stone that soared almost sixty feet high.

Now, it was a cursed landmark that everyone with any sense avoided.

If there was a Myrish artefact anywhere in the Porsenthian Empire, Torsten had no doubt that it would be here.

Iron gates had once barred intruders from the fortress, however, during the battle of Marlrush, Toriaken had absorbed the metal to add to his strength, leaving the stone walls and pillars surprisingly bare. What metal was left in between each huge stone was a mixture of lesser compounds, much of which had long been burned and warped by dragonfire.

The air was thick and heavy with mist. Miroth did not like the power of this place—which was decidedly Myrish—and neither did Torsten, his breaths coming in shallow gasps. He carried a ring of keys to unlock doors within the fortress, though he doubted they would be needed, the structures were so brittle.

Even Varlot's bravado quietened as they entered the courtyard. Fountains lay empty, stone cracked and worn. Overgrown weeds had claimed most of the pathways, though dead stems and branches now crossed the stone slabs. Crawling ivy and plants which covered many of the exterior walls lay stripped of their leaves. It looked like brown, skeletal fingers covered the fortress, sprawling across every surface, trying to choke the stone. There was no comparison to the glory of the castle in Eastbrook, with its twisting spires of iron.

Despite the dead plants that clutched at the fortress, Torsten had enough familiarity with the place to lead them to the main entrance.

Or what was left of it.

A large part of one wall had collapsed, the wooden doors long since rotted away to damp splinters. Rainwater dripped along the gutters, pooling in stagnant puddles at the base of the walls. The grey stone seemed closer to black, whether from fire, water, or time, Torsten could not say. 'Stay sharp. There could be anything inside.'

'Queen likes to send you on dangerous jobs, don't she?' Varlot replied, drawing his enormous axe.

'This is beyond the normal requirements of an Inquisitor. This affects the fate of Tassar.' Torsten knew the inherent danger with the Myr. 'We must be ready for all eventualities.'

'Shame she didn't wanna hear about my knowledge of the Myr. Ties to Fenn, you know. Lad's in league with them.'

Torsten doubted the truth of Varlot's statement. He'd seen Fenn only a few days before. He'd considered him a lost soul, but Fenn had the blessing of a dragon spirit. Miroth abhorred the Myr, and Torsten couldn't think why any dragon would bless someone who worked for the death spirits.

Varlot, as was his way, was probably making up something to weasel his way back into power.

Torsten held his breath as they passed the threshold and into the large entrance hall. Although he expected spirits, they were greeted by more crumbling stone and derelict passages. Paintings and tapestries had fallen from the walls, shattered glass littering the floor. An elaborate red and gold carpet ran the length of the corridors, bunched up and stained by dirt and the blood of a thousand soldiers.

The fortress had been used to shelter from the waves of Myrish attacks. People had died here.

That death gave the Myr strength.

Torsten glanced through various doorways to different parts of the fortress—most were empty frames with no doors left—and tried to decide the best way to search. Remnants of the battle were strewn everywhere—broken weapons, abandoned armour, bundles of linen. Stains covered the carpet; most had seeped through to discolour the stone underneath.

Thankfully, there were no immediate signs of any Myr or their spirits, though their power festered here—even *he* could feel that. He waited, muscles tense, for several moments. But nothing immediately dangerous leapt out to attack them.

Without a direct threat, they could at least begin the task of securing the artefact.

'Place is worse than I remember.' Varlot picked at some of the peeling paint on the wall and inspected his fingernail.

'Varlot. The fortress is large and there are only two of us. Take the eastern wing, I shall take the west. Reconvene here with anything you find. We want to be back at camp before the sun sets, so I suggest you search quickly. Be wary of rotted floors, staircases, anything that might crumble as you search.' Torsten gestured to the large staircase that dominated the foyer. 'We can't cover too much ground, so we'll return here each day until we discover what Queen Surayo seeks. Clear?'

Varlot ran a hand thoughtfully across his beard, and Torsten had the distinct impression he was looking for a way to override those orders.

Before Varlot had the chance to contradict him, Torsten swung the large pack from his shoulder to the ground and crouched as he opened it. After rooting around, he pulled out two small necklaces, both with a ruby the size of his thumbnail clasped between iron jaws moulded to represent Toriaken. 'These will glow in the presence of anything Myrish. The stronger the glow, the more powerful the artefact. They use all manner of objects as vessels to store their magic in. Things you might ordinarily overlook.'

'Like what?'

'Keys,' Torsten replied, thinking immediately of the Citrine Key. He couldn't wait to get his hands back on Apollo for letting *that* artefact slip away. 'Bottles. Knives. Hairpins. Jewellery. Things that are small enough to carry. The more unassuming, the better.'

Varlot took the offered necklace, dwarfed in his enormous hands. His frown deepened.

Torsten wound his own necklace around his left wrist. As much as he loathed being in this sickly place, there would be powerful treasures here. Queen Surayo wanted only one object, and that was to be destroyed. This was the perfect opportunity to find magic to restore Miroth's power. With so many horses at camp, he could easily take one and travel back to Tonmouth alone, once he'd found something worthy of his dragon.

Torsten fought to keep the smirk from his face. It would not do to appear unprofessional, especially in front of Varlot. 'Any questions?'

Varlot shrugged out of his cloak and hung it upon the large, wooden bannister, a cloud of dust floating to the ground after being disturbed. He avoided several of the crumbling steps and cracked his knuckles. 'Thought your queen would have me doing some proper work. Put my skills to good use.'

'This *is* good use. Once you are an Inquisitor again, I'm sure you will have plenty of opportunities for work more… suited to your tastes.' Torsten knew the man's bloodlust often got the better of him. He was a brute, that was the short of it.

Queen Surayo rarely had places for brutes, but Torsten had no issues finding a use for Varlot among his ranks of Inquisitors. Right now, shoving him on the front lines against the Myr sounded good.

Varlot grunted again and turned away, his footsteps fading as he began to search the fortress.

Torsten watched him go, then raised his hand to touch the burn scar on his face. He'd caught Varlot staring but hadn't entertained an answer.

It was unlikely there'd be any intact mirrors in this place. He didn't want to see himself marked in such a way. The desire for revenge simmered. The gall of that lost soul who'd dared attack him with the flames of Hassen, the filthy trickster.

Deep in his soul, Miroth hissed, their emotions so strongly linked that the dragon could feel Torsten's hate, even during his slumber.

Torsten took several steadying breaths.

First, Miroth needed to be restored. The queen's artefact had to be destroyed.

Once that had been taken care of, he could finally pursue Apollo and Fenn.

10
THE ARCHON OF LIGHTNING
FENN

Powerful gusts buffeted the deck, sails flapping uselessly. The claws of Verkata's storm held the ship in place as if by anchor. Wood groaned under the unnatural strain, and lightning sheeted overhead, flashes of bright blue spearing dark clouds every few heartbeats.

Fenn squinted through the steel wind, arms wrapped around himself to protect his chest from the shards of icy hail that knifed everything in the path of the storm. The voices in his mind shrank away, Hassen or the Myr, he wasn't sure which. They feared this power.

Even Inquisitor Nadja, who'd hardly been ruffled throughout their journey, lingered by the door to the captain's cabin, unwilling to face the dragon's wrath.

Only Selys stood on deck, chin raised to the roaring thunder, unflinching.

Despite the mixed emotions Fenn felt towards the priestess following her betrayal, he didn't want to see her hurt. Standing before a powerful dragon spirit seemed a good way for that to happen. 'Selys! We should get under cover!'

The wind seemed to snatch his words, but Selys likely

would have ignored them even if she'd heard. She was following her own path.

Fenn knew it was the morning, but the black clouds were so heavy in the sky that he could have been convinced it was night. He grabbed hold of the mast with one hand, torn between his desire to take cover from the storm, and waiting to see what would happen with Selys and the dragon.

Apollo poked his head out of the cabin door, behind Nadja's shoulder. 'She's got guts, that one.'

'She may be able to secure our path forward. It was good of you to suggest they travel with us, Apollo,' Nadja replied, not taking her attention away from the priestess.

'If this dragon is anything like Paragos, we don't stand a chance. Hope you can swim, Inquisitor.'

Fenn shuffled towards the pair so they could hear him over the wind. 'Is the dragon likely to damage the ship?'

'Who knows what goes on in their minds,' Apollo replied flatly. 'Law unto themselves.'

'It may simply be passing over. I'm sure if it sought to attack us, we'd be dead already,' Nadja said.

'Hassen. Can't you do something?' Fenn asked aloud, but his dragon spirit had retreated so far away that he could barely feel the flame in his chest. For all he tried to do by himself, be they decisions or actions, Fenn was beginning to realise they were all pawns when it came to the dragon spirits.

He hated being caught in their snare.

Selys paced, her glaive pointed at the clouds overhead, heedless of the lightning which streaked down dangerously close to the ship every few seconds. Rain and icy hail pelted her, but she gave no indication of pain or irritation. 'Archon! Calm your fury!' Selys raised both hands, one clutching her glaive, the ribbons and beads waving wildly in the wind. The green and silver tattoos swirling up her left arm seemed to glow with every flash of lightning overhead. 'We mean you no harm.'

'Nadja, Apollo. Stay inside! We'll try and get us away!' Unable to cower any longer, Fenn rushed out to stand beside Selys. He didn't trust her, not after what she'd said, but unless they fled from this spirit, he'd have no chance of getting the key.

'We only wish to cross the Lasseen Ocean! Let us pass, Archon!' Fenn said, unsure how best to address the spirit but following Selys's lead.

For a moment it seemed as if the storm stilled. The rain ceased, and the wind died down.

Fenn didn't dare hope it was over as easily as that, and after only a few seconds, everything stirred up again. Electricity crackled in the air, sending goosebumps along his arms. Heat flared in his chest, but he heard no words of encouragement or support.

'What is the meaning of your passage through my domain?'

Fenn shuddered, dropping to his knees at the voice booming through the air like a thunderclap. He didn't need Selys to tell him it was Verkata speaking—the noise filled his chest and stole his breath. Only a dragon spirit could do that. He coughed, unable to take a deep breath, let alone speak.

Selys had managed to hold her ground, leaning on her glaive for support, though her injured arm trembled. 'We seek to destroy an artefact of Myrish origin. We fight for the same cause, Archon!'

The dark sky flickered again, then a fork of lightning pierced the cloud and plunged into the water at the ship's bow. A second fork snaked down, crackling through the air and landing behind the ship.

By the time Fenn managed to get back to his feet, countless forks surrounded them, the lightning fizzing and spitting with barely contained fury. The wind died down, and above them, the dragon appeared.

Verkata, Spirit of the Eternal Storm, slid from the clouds, each foot of his sinuous body the darkest purple. Gold and blue streaked through his scales, shimmering and pulsing, always shifting. His black wings dwarfed Hassen, even Alnothen, thin, membranous, and nearly transparent. Electricity crackled along his body, golden sparks darting off in all directions.

'Destroy an artefact?'

Fenn held his breath as the dragon opened its jaws to speak. He didn't want his chest constricted again, and he didn't want to say anything that might give his true purpose away. If the dragon learned he did not wish to destroy the key immediately—but *use* it—he had a feeling he wouldn't live to see another dawn.

'We are blessed by Neros and Hassen.' Selys bowed at the approaching dragon, then raised her chin again. More rain spattered her face, then the wind—stronger than ever—returned with a fury that shoved them both to their hands and knees.

Black frills speared off Verkata's head and cheeks, soft purple webbing between each horn flickering. Wisps of smoke streaked along the dragon's body where the rain touched his scales.

'He is touched by the Myr.'

Fenn thought his head was going to explode, the dragon's voice was so deep.

'He *was*, Archon. Now, he is free, and Hassen's Blessing rules!' Selys cried above the storm.

Fenn fought against the wind, the pressure, the force of the dragon. He would *not* be walked over, Archon or not. He twisted his face to look up, squinting through the wind and rain to stare into the dragon's golden eyes. So close to the bow of the ship, Verkata's head alone was bigger than the mainsail, and for a terrifying moment, Fenn thought the dragon would swallow the ship whole.

'Prove it.'

Fenn's heart skipped a beat.

How exactly was he supposed to—

Then he remembered calling upon Hassen's flames when Torsten had him cornered on the mountainside. That had been an easy motion. The dragon had simply been an extension of himself.

Although Verkata had given the command, the Archon did not relent his storm, and Fenn had to fight with every muscle of his newfound strength to get back to his feet and face the dragon.

'Hassen,' Fenn growled through clenched teeth. The dragon was inside him. Hassen *had* to hear his voice, no matter how strong Verkata's winds were.

But there was no response. He couldn't feel the fire in his chest, only the overwhelming storm of the Archon as it waited.

The dragon's body and tail rolled through the sky, surrounding the ship and making it list to one side with another groan of complaint. Coils of scaled muscle shimmered and disappeared, reappearing in multiple places at the same time, colours shifting from purple to black to gold. Fenn grew dizzy trying to keep his attention on where the dragon was, though Verkata's head and eyes hovered in place, motionless.

Watching him.

'Fenn! Show him!' Selys whispered, though her gaze did not leave Verkata.

'I'm trying!' Fenn whispered back, trying to remember how he'd summoned Hassen's power before. Was he supposed to draw his sword and show Verkata the fire? It would surely be snuffed out the moment the wind and rain touched it. Would it be enough?

'Try *harder*!' Selys's voice had gone up a notch.

'I don't know how! What do I do?' Fenn dared not look

away from the Archon and rested one hand on the hilt of his sword. 'Hassen isn't listening! I need time!'

'There is no time! You either learn this, or you're destroyed!'

Before Fenn could reply, another ripple of lightning forked from Verkata's body. *'Hassen! Weakling spirit of trees, plants, and poisonous thorns. Do you touch this one?'* Verkata bellowed.

Fenn staggered again, the force of the Archon's command felt like it could split him in two. It squeezed his chest, driving all the breath from his lungs. Every limb numbed in the pressure, the tips of his fingers tingling.

Something within his chest thrashed around. He sank to one knee, one hand clutching his tunic. He coughed, blood spraying the deck.

Verkata's presence alone was more than enough to kill, and terror gripped him.

'I see a trace of Hassen. And I see the Myr, though faint. Lingering in the deep places within you. Using you as their own artefact to move and influence our domains. Their presence is unforgivable.' Again, Verkata coiled around the ship, wings flapping and sending more gusts over them. The dragon let out a hiss as electricity built in the air, and he opened his jaws.

'Wait!' Fenn gasped.

Verkata spewed forth a plume of flame, lightning streaking through the fire, turning it blue and purple.

Fenn covered his face and hunkered down, desperately wishing he'd been able to find his family, to see them one last time, to create a new memory he'd be able to keep. Fire engulfed him. Electricity surged, a high-pitched wail screaming through the depths of his mind.

He lost all sensation. There was no searing pain before his inevitable incineration.

Fenn blinked and opened his eyes, expecting to be on the edge of the spirit world once more.

But he stood on the soaked deck, Selys several paces away, staring at him wide-eyed.

Fenn straightened to find his skin and clothes unburned. Green surrounded his vision, and he spun in place to find he was surrounded by the colour. It took several more seconds before the green receded, fading into his skin as if it had been part of him all along. As it shifted, he realised they were vines, leaves, ferns, and all manner of forest vegetation.

'You were always interesting. Standing up to dragons when you ought to show reverence. I wondered what you would do in the presence of an Archon. You never cease to disappoint.' Laughter accompanied Hassen's words, and Fenn wanted to throttle the trickster.

'You let me think I was about to die!' Fenn snapped.

More laughter. *'Of course not. A measure of my power is in you. I would not give that up willingly.'*

'Then why mock Verkata? He could burn us. All of us. *Alive!*'

A rumble of thunder from above turned Fenn's attention back to Verkata, who hovered above the ship, staring down at them with unreadable eyes. *'It is good you do not rely on your spirit for everything. Though I do not understand why Hassen permits what is left of the Myr within you. Such blasphemy. Death within life. But I care not for weakling spirits.'*

Fenn let out a shuddering breath. Perhaps today was not the day of his death. He still clutched his tunic, and wondered whether he would ever escape being called Myr-touched.

Verkata's attention had shifted to Selys. More thunder rumbled, and again the ship tilted.

Fenn had to shift his stance to avoid sliding backwards, though he had hardly any grip on the storm-ravaged deck.

'You carry the mark of the priestess,' Verkata said.

Selys touched her tattoo, the gesture calm, somehow intimate. She closed her eyes. 'I do. I have dedicated my life to following Neros, Spirit of the Lasseen Ocean.'

Verkata's front foot shot forward, each clawed digit surrounding Selys and pinning her to the deck in a strike so fast, Fenn could hardly follow it. *'Not* all *your life. I recognise your scent. Your warband blasphemes. Desecrates our shrines and temples. Your kin swore* against *the Guardians of Tassar.'*

Fenn darted forward. 'Let her go!'

Wind and hail blasted him back before he reached Selys. Though he fell heavily against the deck, again, there was no pain. He touched the back of his head where he'd collided with wood, but there was no blood, as he'd expected. 'Hassen?'

'I will protect you where I can, Fenn.' There was no trace of laughter, this time. *'Keep your pain numbed.'*

Fenn stood up, sure he was going to bruise, but able to ignore it. 'Selys!'

Verkata continued, *'I will not allow your ilk to roam free.'*

'I have no wish to fight you, Archon. But if you threaten me, I, too, will defend myself. Neros blessed me. *Chose* me. Our bond will keep you at bay!' The swirling green and silver tattoos on her arm flashed as she awoke Neros's power. Seawater churned around her, forming from thin air as the vines had formed from Fenn. A low rumble sounded from the rushing waters—Fenn was certain the noise came from Neros's jaws—then the force of water cascaded out and pushed Verkata's claws away from her body.

Selys stood tall and proud. She raised her glaive to the Archon's face. 'I am not your enemy. Whatever happened in my past is *over*. My future is only Neros and serving the dragon spirits.'

As she spoke, the tunnel of lightning surrounding the ship began to rise.

Fenn stumbled to the ship's railing and peered over in

time to see enormous waves swelling, pushing the lightning back in a roaring, foaming torrent.

Verkata snarled as Neros rose from the sea, her green scales glimmering in the reflected light of the storm. She bellowed a challenge, wings spreading across the width of the ship, defending it from Verkata's advance. Neros was enormous, far bigger than Alnothen, though Verkata held the size advantage. Fenn couldn't see the entirety of the Archon's body, so much of it disappeared and reappeared in the raging storm clouds above, but even to his untrained eye, he saw the difference in scale.

Yet Selys and Neros stood as one, facing the more powerful foe as if they had every likelihood of defeating it.

'Neros. How dare *you of all spirits bless this woman!'* A snap of lightning turned the sky brilliant white as Verkata snarled.

'She is in my service. Her debt is mine. And I will defend my own.'

Verkata let out a snarl of challenge.

Neros replied with an answering roar, and the ship trembled in their wake.

Caught between two enormous spirits, Fenn backed away. This wasn't his fight.

Apollo and Nadja stumbled towards him, and he turned to shake his head at them. 'Not hiding in the cabin waiting to be crushed by that!' Apollo said, mouth hanging open at the sight of the two dragons.

'We need to get out of here!' Fenn said, continuing to back away.

'There's nowhere to go!' Nadja replied. She'd drawn her sword, perhaps in desperation, but didn't raise it. 'We're on open water, in Neros's domain!'

Apollo gestured across the deck. 'I saw rowboats on the side of the ship. We get on them now, see if we can get far enough away before the battle—

Flames careened through the sky, turning it bright as midday. Heat seared the deck, blackening the wood in seconds. Again, Fenn was shielded from the worst of it by Hassen's protection, though the back of his arm ached where the fire was most intense.

The three of them sprinted away, avoiding debris where the ship's listing had shaken free barrels and crates. Everything trembled, and Fenn slipped on more than one occasion. The ship was slick with ice and rain, and it was hard to keep his footing.

With a deep groan, the ship lurched, and Apollo went flying. Fenn grabbed his arm, holding him on his feet. Even under attack, the strength from Hassen meant Apollo's weight hardly registered.

Lightning shot past him, crunching into the mast and splitting it clean in two. The scream of wood deafened Fenn, and he pressed both hands to his ears as the top third of the mast crashed to the deck, throwing splinters and shards of wood in all directions. Nadja winced, narrowly avoiding being crushed by the mast, her quick reflexes keeping her away from a grievous injury, or worse.

The tang of salt suddenly filled Fenn's nose, and he whirled around in time to see Selys raise her glaive. A waterfall of water burst from the tip and slammed into Verkata's eyes, forcing the Archon backwards.

Verkata responded with another thunderclap, the noise so intense it stunned the group. Fenn tripped again. He went down to his knees and only just managed to clutch onto the ship's rail to hold himself up. They were buffeted by the power, hardly able to keep on their feet. 'Hassen!' Fenn cried. Though he felt fire in his chest, there was nothing Hassen could do against the might of such formidable spirits.

'Appreciate the effort. But if Selys can't stop that thing, none of us can.' Apollo hauled Fenn to his feet, returning the favour from a few moments earlier.

They hadn't reached the boats, but they'd reached the ship's stern and were away from the thick of the fighting at the bow. With such violent movements, any steps they took were likely to put them on the floor again, so Fenn didn't risk trying.

He clenched his fists. They didn't deserve this. Not when they were on their way to get the key. It was his only chance of finding his family, and it was being taken away by an angry storm.

Credit to Selys, the priestess fought on. That almost certainly had more to do with Neros's power than any inner strength Selys had, but she held her own, despite being outmatched by the Archon.

Why Verkata was so angry at Selys, Fenn didn't understand. If they survived the encounter, he wanted to know exactly what Selys had done in her past.

The waves grew and the ship lurched more and more violently. It was all Fenn, Apollo, and Nadja could do to keep their footing. Fenn gritted his teeth and weathered the onslaught as best he could. Hassen kept most of the pain at bay, for which he was grateful, but it was too late to escape.

They had to ride the storm and hope they were all standing on the other side.

11
THE CASTAWAY
KAIO

The woman offered Kaio a faint smile, then her gaze drifted past him. 'Looks like your friend needs some help.'

Kaio turned, wincing slightly as the slash across his shoulder protested. Taran lay sprawled out on his back, an arm floating in one of the rock pools, his bow and arrows scattered. Fergus sniffed delicately at one of the arrows sticking out from the wet sand, his tail lashing.

Taran's chest rose and fell gently, which relieved Kaio more than he cared to admit. He made his way over to check nothing was broken. 'Taran? Taran, wake up.' Kaio nudged him with his boot, and Taran groaned.

'Wha?'

Kaio helped him sit up. 'Taran? You good?' He snapped his fingers several times in front of Taran's face, waiting for those keen eyes to refocus.

After a moment, Taran waved Kaio's hand away and, with great difficulty, got to his feet. 'I'm fine. I'm fine. Where's my stuff?'

Kaio gestured around. On seeing Taran feebly pat the ground in an attempt to collect his arrows, Kaio returned his attention to the bedraggled woman. 'That was close. Not seen the Myr here before. You were lucky.'

'They don't hurt me,' she replied.

'No? I thought they sucked the life from whatever they could find. Plants. Animals. People.'

She nodded, limp hair bobbing where it touched the water. 'I know. They've already taken from me. I don't think I'm of further value.'

Kaio narrowed his eyes. He'd never heard of the Myr letting someone go. It was always all or nothing, and part of why they were so feared. Myrish spirits were capable of all sorts of horrors, and seeing one meant your death—whether they killed you there and then or tricked you into some bargain you couldn't escape.

'Where'd she come from?' Taran lit a cigarillo, his fingers shaking. At Kaio's frown he said, 'Calms my nerves after what we went through. The *Myr*? The sea claim me, let me have this comfort.'

Kaio didn't argue. Not when they had bigger issues to worry about than being choked by smoke. Water continued to drip from the cavern's roof, the echoing noise sending goosebumps up his arms.

Who knew if the Myr would return with reinforcements.

'Looks like she hasn't eaten in a week.' Taran flicked the match onto the wet sand and released a mouthful of smoke.

Kaio glanced at her ragged body, the way her clothes hung off her petite frame. She wasn't from Segandis, that was for certain. Her skin was much too pale for anywhere in Bragalia or Olmir either, and her accent wasn't any of the Porsenthian dialects he knew. Her clothes were sodden and stained, discoloured by prolonged time in water, and ripped in several places. Hardly better than rags.

'Where are you from?' Kaio asked, tweaking Taran's words and addressing the woman directly.

She'd shrunk into herself while they'd been talking,

hunkering down by the boulder in the ankle-deep water that covered most of the cavern floor. 'Ma-Rai,' she answered in a meek voice. Whatever confidence she'd had a few minutes ago had fled.

Kaio crouched in front of her. He'd sailed around the continent of Etrovia more times than he could count, and prided himself on his geographical knowledge. But that wasn't a name he was familiar with. He glanced at Taran, who shrugged. 'That's nowhere in Bragalia I know of.'

'Bragalia?' She hugged herself. 'Where's that?'

'You're standing in it. This is an island off the southern coast of Bragalia. The nearest town is Segandis, where we're from.'

The woman frowned deeply, lines appearing on her forehead, twisting the burned skin on her face. 'I don't know about that...Ma-Rai is near a huge mountain range. Paragos rules there. Spirit of the Eternal Blizzard.'

'Blizzard? Sounds horrible,' Taran said.

She smiled thinly. 'There's snow all year round. It recedes a little in summer, for a few weeks.'

'Where do you know that snows all the time?' Taran asked, breathing out more smoke, his trembling coming to a stop.

'Nowhere I know. What country is Ma-Rai in?' Kaio asked.

'Malnova,' she replied without hesitation. She glanced between them, her eyes shifting from desperation to fear, and back again.

Kaio's stomach turned to ice. She was from far to the north-east of Etrovia. He'd visited one of the ports in Ulnoth once as a lad—another country on that distant, icy continent. It was a neighbour to Malnova. He remembered nothing but hating the cold and how long it had taken to get there and back.

How in all of Tassar had she managed to cross such a

huge swathe of ocean to end up on this spit of land? There'd been no shipwreck on the island. Driftwood, yes, but surely not enough to get her across such a distance.

Suspicion flared. Taran had been certain of seeing another ship here. She could be a spy sent by one of the other warbands looking to undermine his rule.

'It's so hot outside. I couldn't cope. I crept in here, in the cool. Hid.' She splashed her hands and feet in the water, shuddering where it touched her skin.

Now that he looked more closely, Kaio saw where her pale skin had caught the sun, patches of red and pink bright and sore on her arms. He tried a different approach. 'I'm Kaio. Kaio Ioran. I run the Ioran warband in Segandis.'

'Taran.' Taran tapped his forehead to her.

She froze when they gave her their names, eyes darting from side to side, her breathing coming in quick gasps. She clutched a small sack tight to her chest, its contents rattling around, sloshing in the water.

Kaio waited, expectant. He needed to ensure his crew were safe from all threats—other warbands, the Iron Queen, even the Myr. Whoever this woman was, she wasn't here by chance.

She blinked, her soft green eyes rimmed with red, and slowly regained her composure. 'My name is Evarine.'

'Are there any others with you?' Kaio glanced around, but it was just the three of them—plus Fergus. No sign of a shipwreck, no way for her to have arrived there that he could see.

'There were. But we were separated…' Evarine shivered.

'How?' Taran asked, tapping ash away. 'I saw a ship here a few nights ago. Were you with them?'

'They found me and the others on the water. Pulled us aboard.' Evarine's breathing grew laboured as she spoke. 'Took what we had of any worth, forced us to clean the ship. Repair it. Sew up fabric, that sort of thing. Whipped us if we didn't comply.' She trembled, but Kaio remained quiet, waiting for her to continue. 'I…I'm not sure how long we were there. Some of us jumped overboard, others were thrown into the sea. They…they dumped me here.' Tears filled her eyes.

Kaio glanced at Taran, then returned his attention to the woman. 'Whose ship was it? Do you remember the captain? Or the ship's colours? Was the Myr with them?'

She trembled again. 'I don't know.'

Kaio leaned closer. 'Think, Evarine. It's important!'

'I don't know! It was dark. We'd been at sea for weeks. Months. It's all blurred together.'

He didn't believe her. Though she seemed weak and clearly wasn't a threat to him or Taran at that moment, who knew what her relation was to the Myr or whichever ship had picked her up. He needed to question her more. But first, they needed to get out of the cave, where he was vulnerable.

Evarine looked up at him, tears streaking rivers through her dirty cheeks, her burned skin shining in the low light. 'Please. I know I've no right to ask for help, but I…I…' Her eyes lost focus and she slumped forward.

Kaio caught her before she fell into the water. 'Evarine? Evarine!' He shook her gently, but she had passed out.

Fergus approached, rubbing his head against her leg where she rested.

'We should get back to the ship. What if the Myr attacked after it fled here?' Taran muttered darkly.

'If it was stupid enough to attack *Wolf's Grin*, it'll learn why the ship has that name. But we should get back to Segandis. Three months is a long time to be away if the Myr are creeping around. Need to see the state of the town.' Kaio dismissed the notion the spirits of death could be in Bragalia. For all the Iron Queen's faults, she'd kept those creatures off her lands with savage aggression.

It had to be a one-off appearance, and he didn't dismiss

the coincidence of this woman having something to do with it.

'You gotta get Ruka to look at your shoulder, too,' Taran muttered.

Kaio ignored the pain, more interested in Evarine and the Myr on his doorstep.

'And her?' Taran asked, jerking a thumb to the foreign woman.

'I'm not leaving her here like this. We'll bring her back with us, where we can keep a better eye on her. Send out some patrols to scout other islands and see if we can pick up any of her companions. I want to know what she's doing so far from home, and what she has to do with the Myr.'

Kaio straightened up, lifting Evarine in both hands. She weighed hardly anything, and he wasn't sure she'd survive if she didn't get food and medicine soon. 'Lead the way, Taran. Need those keen eyes of yours to get back to the ship without any more ambushes.'

KAIO WEATHERED Yaniv's flat stare, grateful the man didn't voice his disapproval when he and Taran returned to *Wolf's Grin* with Evarine in tow. They were both worse for wear, with ripped clothing and wet hair, but Kaio clambered aboard as if nothing was wrong. He couldn't afford to show weakness or vulnerability, not when his role as chief was held in such a tenuous grip.

Esto reported all had been well during their absence, which reassured them both that the Myr hadn't attacked the ship. Kaio didn't tell Esto or the others about their encounter with the creature. They didn't need to know, not so close to home, not when patience and tempers were so frayed.

Kaio ordered their immediate return to Segandis, and his crew gave a barely concealed cheer.

It was perhaps that announcement which held Yaniv's tongue in check—he was getting what he wanted.

Evarine would be under Kaio's protection, even if anyone frowned at her presence. It was unlikely the crew cared about an additional passenger when she wouldn't be aboard long enough to affect their rations. He took her to the sick bay and let Ruka look over her. Esto gave Evarine a curious raised eyebrow, but said nothing as she whipped the crew into their positions and the anchor was raised.

Thankfully, their journey to Segandis was short and uneventful, *Wolf's Grin* cutting through clear water as easy as a knife through butter. The noise of the harbour washed over Kaio before he saw it, and he couldn't suppress a smile as the familiar sands of home greeted him.

A score of other boats, large and small, floated in the calm harbour waters. Half a dozen or so were already docked, people scrambling to load and unload their cargo, many carrying bags and crates, and shouting to each other. Kaio recognised most colours of the sails as residents of Segandis, several local—and not so local—merchants, and a few larger vessels that frequented the Bragalian coastline, bringing travellers and tourists alike.

There were no black and gold sails of the other Ioran ships.

Hadn't been for years.

Yet he felt their absence as keenly as the day they'd been destroyed by Neros's wrath.

Gulls and terns filled the air, white and grey streaks of feathers that swept down to grab morsels of food from anyone not paying enough attention to guard against their snapping beaks. He'd once seen a particularly large gull take an entire cooked chicken from an unsuspecting traveller too busy ridding a pebble from their sandal to realise they'd been under attack.

He smirked at the memory while Esto and the crew

brought *Wolf's Grin* into their usual dock. Before the anchor dropped for the second time in as many days, the wind shifted, and Kaio's skin prickled.

Something was amiss.

They'd been away on a three-month voyage. He expected things to have changed in that time. But coupled with the strange woman from a distant land and the sighting of the Myr, Kaio was more on edge than he would have been.

There were fewer uniforms—dockworkers that answered to him—for a start. Fewer traders hawking their wares. Fewer glints of silver and copper coins passed between hands.

And there was a bite in the air that hadn't been present before. Just like the Myr in the cave, it sent the hairs standing up on the back of his neck.

The energy shifted, as if a storm brewed just beyond the horizon.

His shoulder twinged where the Myr's claw had caught him. Taran was right, he really did need to get Ruka to have a look at it. Once she'd made sure Evarine wasn't at death's door.

'Chief Kaio! Chief Kaio! Welcome home! Want me to carry somethin' heavy for ya?' A boy ran along the wooden docks to the ship and held his hands out expectantly. Tesso was fifteen or sixteen, a young man by many standards, but small for his age, with skin as dark as his own. His strong jawline, a typical Bragalian feature, marked him as local, though Kaio didn't know his parents. Like many, Tesso had shown up on the beach one day looking for a place in the Ioran warband. Taken by his desire to be useful, Kaio had given him a black and gold uniform and sent him to work on the docks.

Tesso wanted to join Kaio on *Wolf's Grin*, however. Kaio had promised to get Taran to teach Tesso how to shoot a bow before he'd allow him on a voyage.

'You can help Esto with the bags. Not too much this time, but extra hands will help.'

Tesso grinned and scrambled aboard before Kaio had finished speaking.

'Great to be back, ain't it?' Taran stretched beside him, yawning widely, one gold tooth glinting in the sunshine. 'Need a good sleep after that trek.'

Kaio gave a noncommittal grunt and shouldered his own bag and Evarine's hemp sack. For all Taran's keen eyesight, he had no ability when it came to reading the room. Or in this case, the harbour. 'Let's get everything off the ship and get our heads down. Need you out again soon enough. Have Evarine brought to headquarters where she can rest. I'll see what I can learn from her once she's awake.'

He stood back as Esto, Yaniv, and the rest of the *Wolf's Grin* crew disembarked, bringing their hauls into Segandis. Their sacks of loot from countless raids were far lighter than he'd have liked, which contributed to the disgruntled mood. He'd already divided up each share, and though no one was happy with the total amount, no one openly challenged him. At least, they hadn't this time.

Kaio needed to rest and get the ship cleaned up and repaired. He wanted to figure out who Evarine was and what she was doing on his shores. But the duties of running a canton—and his absence for three months—was most pressing. There was only so much he could delegate to his lieutenants, and paperwork was the responsibility of a Laird he most despised.

He *knew* he wasn't a good leader. Far from it. But he refused to let the Ioran name and reputation fall into ruin, and he would die before anyone else took up the position of chief. He owed it to his family to continue their legacy.

He just needed a few long trips at sea each year to keep his sanity.

But if the Myr were skulking about, perhaps he'd returned to Segandis at the perfect time.

Beyond the harbour and white, sandy coastline, Segandis itself rose alongside verdant hills. Mostly made up of single or double storey buildings with square, flat rooftops, the city had been built out of white and cream stone. Wisteria climbed most walls, the lavender leaves visible for leagues. Many people turned their rooftops into balconies, water fountains and pools glistening in the sunlight.

It was a far cry from the spiralling buildings in other Bragalian towns, but every time Kaio saw the flat rooftops, it brought a strong sense of familiarity. Somewhere he was rooted.

The harbour was a near constant bustle of noise and motion. Most markets in Segandis were enormous and sprawling, but often people couldn't wait, and bought goods directly from the boats while they were being unloaded. Dockworkers and scribes who worked for the Ioran warband in a more official capacity—and managed paperwork—collected tithes from merchants and sailors bringing trade to the town. Kaio spotted their black and gold uniforms as he pushed through crowds of customers and tourists desperate for a glimpse at the famous *Wolf's Grin* now it had returned.

Tall coconut trees dotted the beaches, eventually giving way to wide-leaved ferns which Kaio walked past as he made his way along the familiar path towards the edge of the harbour, then under a grove of plum trees.

The noise and hubbub of the docks muffled immediately, and Kaio released a held breath. He checked his shoulder and grimaced at the blood trickling down his arm. It throbbed with a dull ache, but he'd endured worse.

After Neros's storm had taken his family and destroyed their ships, he'd half-crawled down the beach each morning and waded into the balmy waters. He'd stand in the waves for hours, willing them—praying for them—to take him, too.

There was no Dragon Spirit of the Olmir Sea, which Segandis rested against, but it hadn't stopped him trying in the depths of his grief.

Back then, a future of any kind had seemed pointless. What did it matter what he tried to do with his life if a spirit could take it all from him in the blink of an eye? He'd grown up in a world of taking from others and fighting them for the privilege. It was a harsh world, but one that he understood. One he thrived in.

Spirits, on the other hand, played by no rules but their own. They cared not for the pride or honour of people. For what was right or fair. For the legacies they built themselves. Spirits saw people only as pawns to use for their own twisted games, and Kaio refused to be part of any of it.

He pushed the memory away. He had to worry about his crew and the canton.

And Evarine wouldn't be much help to him if she died.

The sea was kept at bay by a gentle slope, and the constant sound of waves brought him comfort. By the time he reached his home—one of several long, sloping stone buildings on the edge of a grove of orange trees, several large tents set up in the clearing beside it for makeshift storage or sleeping—fatigue had reared its head, and he wanted nothing more than to bury himself in a pile of pillows.

A stack of letters awaited him, sealed and gathering dust, and he sighed. Though he was Chief of the Ioran warband, he was also the most powerful man in the canton. Everyone outside Segandis referred to him as Laird, though he'd never styled himself as such. It hadn't bothered him aside from having to swear fealty to the Iron Crown, along with paying an annual tithe. Much as he'd wanted to fight it, no one could stand against Toriaken.

It was why Bragalia, despite being ruled by Lairds across various cantons as they saw fit, was part of the Porsenthian Empire. Although he delegated the majority of his responsibilities, which left him free to sail *Wolf's Grin* and raid as he wished, there were some things he had to do himself as Laird.

Grudgingly, Kaio opened the nearest letter, scanned the first line, and dismissed the plea for financial aid from one of the weaker Lairds. He opened the second and dismissed it just as quickly. Perhaps if they didn't live in sprawling estates with crowds of staff and servants catering to their needs and pleasures, they wouldn't need to beg him for money.

They were Lairds. They could make their own coin.

Fergus meowed loudly as he padded inside, stretching in the shade of the building, toes extending and claws dragging against the cool, tiled floor. Kaio scratched the cat behind the ear, glad of the company.

'Chief Kaio?' Tesso poked his head through the open doorway. 'I brought you another bag of coffee beans. They're the ones from Olmir you said you liked! Ship came in two weeks ago with some, so thought I'd set some aside for you, and I got a great price on them too! Took me until—'

'Tesso. Knock it off, lad. Got a headache already without you yapping.'

Tesso grinned. 'Shall I get a pot brewed for you?'

Kaio sighed. 'Go on then. Then go bother Taran for more bow practice. Got Fergus following me enough without you being a second shadow.'

Tesso laughed and hurried in, and the rich scent of brewing coffee filled the air while Kaio thumbed through the remaining messages. He was hardly aware of the lad leaving, and by the time he'd drained his second cup, he noticed a pattern in the letters.

Lairds often begged aid, as did individuals, nobles and poorer families across the canton. However, these requests were all for money to garrison their lands or hire mercenaries. One message—from Furyn Vantonen no less—*demanded* he send a force of warriors to join Fellwood's town guard.

Though none explicitly stated *why* they wanted to bolster their defences so urgently, he understood the implications. They were bracing for the Myr's return.

Kaio sat in silence for a while, staring at his empty cup, trying to turn his attention from the sea to the land, and what the unsettling news meant for the warband's future. His first thought was to plan another three-month voyage, or one even longer. Keep to the waters and let Queen Surayo and her Inquisitors take on the Myr a second time.

It had nothing to do with him.

Why should he risk his people?

But he was no longer far removed from war, not if the Myr were skulking around the islands off the coast. It wouldn't be long before they came to Segandis, if they weren't already. He clenched the handle of his mug. These weren't enemies he could beat into submission. They were just as bad as the dragon spirits he detested. Playing their own game by their own rules while people were powerless against them.

His gaze fell on Evarine's sodden bag and, keen for a distraction from letters, he began sorting through the waterlogged contents to see what could be salvaged. He hung the clothing on a line to dry in the late afternoon sun. Although old, it was sturdy enough to survive.

Then, he sat outside and carefully went through the rest of it.

Ruka appeared from under one of the tent flaps as he was finishing, her dark hair tied back with a faded blue ribbon, her soft skin unblemished by the scars most of his warband carried. Her eyes were a dark brown that had always reminded him of melted chocolate. At Kaio's unvoiced question, she said, 'Evarine is sleeping, but she's very weak. I don't know what she's been through. Something traumatic if I had to guess. Only time will tell if she makes it. I left some figs for her—she needs to eat, and soon.'

Ruka dusted off her hands and rolled her sleeves down her arms.

He trusted Ruka's judgement as much as Taran and Esto, and nodded. The woman had grown up in Olmir, and though she had an odd way about her at times, her judgement had rarely been wrong.

Kaio was no stranger to death. Had seen it up close many times over the years, and if Evarine wasn't strong enough to make it, that was simply life. But he *was* interested in what she had to say about how she'd arrived on the island, and in the presence of the Myr, no less.

'Taran mentioned you were in a scrap on the island. You haven't said anything, but that patch of blood seeping through your sleeve says otherwise.' An amused grin played on Ruka's lips, dark eyes twinkling as much as Taran's.

Kaio grinned back. 'Appreciated, but unnecessary. It'll probably heal on its own.'

'Oh will it? I didn't realise you'd learned medicine with the Olmese monks, too. I must've missed that while you led us around in circles for three months.' Ruka folded her arms and shifted her weight.

'It'll be fine. I'll ask you to look if it gets worse. You need to rest, too,' Kaio replied, taking her advice and not rising to the bait.

Her grin faded, and she shook her head. 'Law unto yourself. If it was deep, it'll need stitching, you know that.'

'I know. I'm fine.'

She opened her mouth as if to argue more, then sighed. 'Fine. You know where I'll be when you find some common sense.'

Kaio watched her leave, heading towards her own apartments on the orange grove's other side.

He returned his attention to Evarine's bag, spilling the contents out on a strip of rough fabric so he could get a better look. A comb, one tooth broken. A stack of books and loose papers, most of their words washed away. A silver ring on a chain darkened by water. Two hand-axes, both sharp, their wooden handles worn. Four small, glass bottles, their contents long emptied. Three brass keys on a ring. Kindling, now useless after so long in the sea. Flint and a striking stone. A handful of copper coins stamped with an insignia he didn't recognise, one bent in half.

If she'd been telling the truth, whoever had picked her up had already taken anything of value. Most likely, these items were sentimental. He couldn't see any use for them.

Something bright flashed, catching his eye. It was a spiral shell that had been hidden by one of the papers. It looked like it was made from jade, and glittered with a light all its own.

Curious, he reached for it.

The moment his finger brushed the shell, shadows filled the clearing, surrounding him. He froze, shock rooting him to the spot. A dragon floated up from the ground, but even with its features obscured by shadow, he recognised the fins and wings of Neros. She writhed and twisted, a chain of shadow looped around her neck, anchoring her to the ground.

Hatred flooded him at the sight of Neros, and he stood up, drawing his blade in the same motion.

The shadow vanished, light birdsong drifting on the breeze.

Kaio frowned, wincing as his shoulder protested at the sudden movement.

He stared at the jade shell then rubbed his face. He needed sleep more than he realised if he was hallucinating.

But the vision unnerved him. Kaio walked over to the tent where Ruka had brought Evarine and peered inside. It took several moments for his eyes to adjust to the dark.

Evarine was bundled on a straw-stuffed mattress, a thin blanket covering her. She slept soundly, eyelids flickering as she dreamed. The burned skin on her face caught his attention, and he wondered whether it had been caused by a campfire gone rogue, or by dragonfire.

Perhaps she had encountered Neros's bad side, too.

'Evarine. Who are you…?'

The woman was a mystery. One he vowed to uncover.

12
THE STORM
FENN

Seawater cascaded across the deck and Fenn struggled to keep his footing. It was so dark due to Verkata's storm that he could hardly see where he was going, and he bashed his shin on a wooden crate.

He yelped, flinching at the pain, then slipped on the wet deck and crashed onto his back.

Fenn was exceedingly pleased the enormous dragon spirit terrorising their ship wasn't paying him the least bit of attention. He wasn't sure he could stand the embarrassment.

'*On your feet!*' the voice in his head snapped.

Fenn didn't need telling twice, flailing for the handrail and heaving himself up. If even Hassen wasn't laughing at his misfortune, his situation was more serious than he'd realised.

In front of him, through the sheeting rain, Verkata, Spirit of the Eternal Storm and Neros, Spirit of the Lasseen Ocean, snarled at one another. Lightning rippled through the air, illuminating every hailstone in flashes of bright white.

Neros lashed her tail over the ship as she avoided a strike from Verkata, seawater cascading from her barnacle-encrusted scales and flooding the deck in an immense wave.

Fenn gritted his teeth as the freezing water washed over

him. 'This storm is too much.' He had one eye closed, the other squinting against the relentless wind and hail.

'Imagine this, but your arse is half-frozen!' Apollo yelled above the wind. 'You got *that* to look forward to if you're desperate for this damned key! Paragos is *this* but a blizzard.'

Fenn's stomach turned at the words. Apollo had spoken about Paragos before, but now faced with an Archon, he wasn't sure he wanted to cross the path of another.

A deep bellow brought his attention back to the two dragon spirits. Neros surged forward, her wave lifting the ship and sending everything that wasn't nailed down careening into the air. Water crested the side rails and flooded the deck. It came up to Fenn's ankles. Kept rising. When it reached his knees, he grabbed hold of the mast—the one that hadn't been partly ripped away—and found Nadja there already. Apollo grabbed hold next to him as the water rose to his waist, soaking him to the bone.

Hassen did what he could to protect him from the worst of the cold. Though Fenn may not have felt the water, he'd be washed away along with anything else loose on the ship if he wasn't careful. 'We need to stop this!'

'If Neros doesn't drive Verkata off, we're dead anyway!' Apollo yelled back, one arm covering his face against the roaring wind.

Fenn hunkered down, braced against the wave as it receded, sucking them backwards. His grip slipped, fingernails digging into the wood. He just needed to hold on a few more seconds, until the wave passed.

The fire in his chest raged at Apollo's words. 'Hassen, you're nowhere near as strong as Neros. Don't be upset that you can't do anything here!' His chest tightened. True or not, the dragon's pride had been stung. Fenn felt it through their bond as clearly as if they were his own emotions.

'There's nothing we can do against an Archon,' Nadja

said. She let go of the mast as the wave disappeared, water sluicing down her legs. 'I would beg Toriaken's help—'

'Oh no, we don't need *another* dragon!' Apollo cut her off, stumbling away from the mast and coughing up water.

'I cannot call on him. I don't have my iron dagger.' Nadja glanced down at her belt, where an empty pouch filled with water. '*He* might have been able to fight Verkata. But we're on our own. There's no support from Queen Surayo or Toriaken.'

'Good. Queen'd be marching me back in irons the moment she got a sniff of me.' Apollo waded across the deck, each step slow, dragging through ankle-deep water. 'I came out here so I could get my family back. There's no spirit alive that'll keep me from them!' He pulled himself away, heading for the rowboats. 'Keep those dragons off this side of the ship. It'll give us a chance to get the boats onto the water!'

Overhead, the two dragons clashed, water and lightning raging together, thunder rippling around them. The ship shuddered, planks of wood peeling off the hull with a shriek.

'Nadja! You helping or not?' Apollo called over his shoulder.

The Inquisitor nodded. If she was uncomfortable with being ordered around by a thief, she didn't say anything about it. As far as Fenn was concerned, he could help Selys distract the dragons while Apollo and Nadja readied the boat for their escape.

The pair of them hurried off and Fenn took a deep breath to steady himself. Hassen did *not* wish to be seen as irrelevant. It didn't matter that Hassen was a tiny forest on the far side of the world, who had no hope of standing against an Archon. His pride would not let him be seen as inferior.

Fenn struggled to differentiate between his own and Hassen's thoughts, but the dragon's will was singularly-minded. He raced along the deck and raised his arm, the tip of his sword aimed at Verkata's nose.

If Apollo needed a distraction, Fenn was happy to oblige. It would keep Hassen's pride intact, too.

With a roar of fury, Fenn thrust his blade forward and fire plumed along the edge. It crossed the distance between himself and the dragon, buffeted by rain, hail, and wind, yet struck its target.

Verkata closed one eye as the flames licked his cheek, then looked down at them, almost as if he had forgotten they were there. '*You dare strike me, child?*' Verkata's tail lashed and a crack of thunder seemed to split the sky.

Fenn crumpled, but Hassen was bright and fierce, and through their bond, Fenn held his footing in the face of the dragon spirit. 'My flame is just as worthwhile as Neros!'

'*That may be. But this priestess does not worship Tassar's Guardians as she should. She and her family have defiled our name. That cannot stand.*' Verkata opened his jaws and unleashed a plume of fire at Selys—and the ship.

'*You have no right to judge when I have chosen to bless her! Cease this!*' Neros lunged forward to take the brunt of the flame and protect her blessed.

Fenn leapt to the side, barrelling into Selys and pulling them down to the deck as flames licked overhead.

By the time he looked up, both dragons were fighting again. The sea surged, rocking the ship violently from side to side. Waves swelled, drenching them to their waists, their chests. Fenn's heart leapt to his throat when his feet were lifted from the deck, and he thought he was about to be swept overboard.

Lightning crackled all around them, forks of electricity dancing through the sky with ear-splitting crashes.

As the wave receded, Neros rose higher, wings spread wide. Her flames filled the air, golden and blazing. She pushed Verkata backwards, blasting the wind and hail away in the same motion.

Fenn shielded his eyes from the bright fire, though its heat seared along his arms.

'*Apollo. Thief.*' Neros's voice rumbled around them, as powerful as the ocean waves.

Fenn blinked at the voice, his vision spotty.

'Neros?' Selys gasped.

Neros hung in the air, wings rippling, though her gaze was locked on the ship's far side, where Apollo sat in a rowboat he'd lowered to the water's surface. Verkata had been thrown so far backwards, his enormity no longer filled the sky.

Fenn breathed deeply in the window of calm. But why had Neros suddenly focussed on Apollo?

Neros flew through the air, though her bulk was so huge it took only a few seconds to reach Apollo. '*I taste the taint of Nestol. I see what Nestol sees. And I...I see* you.'

She struck forward, her head disappearing into the waves.

Fenn raced to the side, clutching the handrail as he peered over. He leaned so far forward that he almost tipped over. 'Apollo!'

In the storm's lull, he had a clear view of the water below. Apollo and Nadja floated on the surface, half a rowboat remaining, bitten clean in half by Neros. The two flailed, coughing and spluttering. Nadja grabbed onto the floating debris and pulled Apollo onto it beside her.

'I need to leave. This fight is my fault,' Selys whispered.

Fenn turned to the priestess. 'Leave?'

Despite the fractured light, he saw her bottom lip tremble. 'Neros cannot defeat Verkata. The ship and everything on it will be destroyed if the battle continues!' Selys turned away, using her glaive as a crutch. 'And she is full of such anger towards Apollo! It's...it's the only way.'

Panic welled at the thought of her gone. Everything was

suddenly too much, and emotions overwhelmed him. 'You *can't* leave! You said you'd help me understand Hassen! Being blessed! We need you to help get the key!' True, he was angry with her. Angry at how she'd treated him, how she thought of him. But she had knowledge and experience he was desperate for.

He got on well enough with Apollo and Nadja, but she was the closest thing to a friend he had. She'd been with him since his first encounter with a Myrish spirit, all the way to *Vermecio's* cave.

With her gone, he'd be adrift once again. Just like when he'd awoken on the Isle of Salt.

'You have me.'

Fenn ignored the dragon. 'You have to stay!' Desperation hitched his voice as he grabbed hold of her glaive in a feeble attempt to keep her from going away.

'Let go! You *want* the ship in splinters? Adrift at sea will be far worse than me leaving!' Selys kicked him squarely in the chest, the force of the blow sending him reeling.

Once more, the impact was numbed by Hassen's power, and though Fenn landed hard, he felt nothing.

Another wave rose, water spilling onto the deck. Fenn scrambled to his feet, saw blood trickling down his arm where he'd grazed it. There was no pain at least, and he pushed it out of his mind.

Neros surged from the sea, her wings a typhoon. Already, Verkata was approaching, a thunderous roar announcing his arrival. It wouldn't be long before the two dragon spirits filled the sky above them again.

Selys made her way to the side of the ship and looked over her shoulder at him. 'I'm sorry, Fenn. This is for the best. You may not understand it, but you don't have to. Just remember what I said. The Myr are the enemy. They always have been, and always will be. Remember that, and you'll do fine.'

'Wait! What about my bond with Hassen? You were going to help me understand it!' Fenn cried.

Selys stretched out her arms, greeting the next swell of Neros's wave.

When it receded, she was gone.

Fenn stood still, mouth half open, not quite able to believe what he'd just seen.

Thunder bellowed around them as Verkata snarled, turning his attention from Neros and the ship and casting his gaze out to sea.

The raging wind died abruptly with the dragon's focus gone. Fenn stared out but could not see Selys in the cold, dark water. He gripped the railing tightly. It had all happened so fast.

Apollo and Nadja climbed up the steps carved into the ship's side, drenched and struggling, but alive.

Fenn trembled.

Selys was blessed by Neros. Neros *was* the sea. She would be fine...at least, he hoped as much. But the sting of betrayal filled his mouth, tainting his thoughts. After how she had spoken to him, first belittling his dreams and now abandoning him to whatever fate he had, he could see why Verkata was so angry at the priestess.

He didn't know what she had done to offend such a mighty spirit, and the fact he would never know infuriated him.

Neros faded, diving back into the depths of the sea and shimmering with mist as she disappeared. Neros had her priestess. The dragon didn't care what happened to the ship.

The waves calmed along with the spirit's departure. Churning, frothing water gave way to a serene ocean. Overhead, Verkata turned, the thunderclouds and lightning flying through the air as the dragon's attention was pulled away. The icy hail disappeared along with the storm, and the raging winds softened with each passing second, until nothing but a gentle sea breeze blew across his face.

Stunned, Fenn stared into the distance, watching Verkata fade, the storm disappearing as the dragon chased his quarry. A few moments later, the sun crept into view.

Verkata's storm had been so intense, Fenn had almost forgotten what the sun felt like on his face. He shuddered at the warmth, realising his clothes were sodden. Water dripped down his back. Whatever protection Hassen had given him during the attack was fading, too, and he became acutely aware of how bruised, cold, wet, and utterly exhausted he was.

'Thank fuck for that.' Apollo leaned on the side rail and flicked water from his hair. 'Any longer and I was gonna puke my guts out.'

'Enough of that,' Nadja replied. She clutched one shoulder, but otherwise seemed unhurt.

Pain lanced down Fenn's arm, and he realised his shirt sleeve had been ripped off, the skin underneath grazed and bleeding from one of his numerous crashes to the deck. With sensation back, he realised how much the salt water burned the wound.

'Selys?' Nadja asked.

Fenn shook his head. 'She's gone.' He was shocked at how flat his voice was. Despite the raging emotions within, very little of it leaked into his tone.

Nadja was quiet for a moment. 'A shame. She'll be missed.'

Fenn shrugged, not quite sure why. 'Nothing stopping us from getting to the key, now?'

'You forgot about Paragos already?' Apollo asked.

'Paragos isn't here,' Fenn replied.

Apollo threw Fenn a gesture that appeared quite rude. Fenn put it down to Apollo's exhaustion.

'The path ahead seems clear, at least for now. We'll need to repair the ship as best we can.' Nadja looked around, inspecting the splintered wood and debris littering the deck. 'We sail slightly north of the rising sun, and we'll be there soon enough.'

Fenn watched her act, methodically working through the deck, fixing what she could and barking orders at himself and Apollo. He should have been glad. Excited, even. Yet something dark swirled through his mind, feeding his anger at Selys's betrayal.

Emotions continued to war within him.

His chest burned with an uninvited fire.

And Fenn could no longer tell which thoughts were his own.

13
THE FOREST
CALIDRA

Calidra raised one hand to shade her eyes from the sun as she scanned the dirt road. It was well-travelled and wide enough for four wagons to pass abreast, though a multitude of potholes had formed following recent rains, several large puddles dotting the way ahead. Jisyel, Malora, and Renys trailed behind, slowed by Renys's pace and her unwillingness to be carried.

After reaching Northbourne easily enough, their small group had helped fix a broken wheel on a merchant's wagon, and he'd taken them along with him to Southbourne, cutting their travelling time in half. Now they were back on foot, skirting around the edge of the Spindle Woods as they pushed further south, Bragalia so close that Calidra could smell the piney mountain air.

Renys struggled most of all with the journey. The girl had picked up a few cuts and bruises from clambering up the various rocks and low walls they'd encountered. Though her grip and footing had been sure—Malora explained she loved climbing trees with Apollo—a strong gust of wind just outside Southbourne had sent her tumbling down a hillside.

Credit to Renys, she hadn't so much as cried, even when

she'd seen her bloodied palms, skin scraped raw, but her adventurous spirit had been somewhat mollified since.

Jisyel, of course, felt nothing of the fatigue. Each morning and evening, Calidra checked Jisyel's feet for blisters and her clothes in case she'd been snagged by thorns. Even when Calidra could do nothing to alleviate her own tension and fatigue, she could at least be practical.

She had also continued her drills with the sword each morning, which had gone a long way to settling her mind. Now, it hung easily on her hip, as if it had always been there.

There had always been something comforting about the familiar.

Trees flanked them on their right as far as the eye could see—an endless wall of green, Alnothen somewhere within. Calidra daren't risk traversing those trees, not after Jisyel had refused Alnothen's bargain. Dragons often held grudges. To their left, the Olmir Bay glittered under the sun—her mother's homeland lay beyond those waters. They'd spotted a few griffins in the distance, but none had flown close to land.

The vast mountains loomed ahead, grey and white peaks puncturing the clouds, their tips hidden in white mist. Cliffton was on the other side—a town on the border of Porsenthia, Bragalia, and Olmir, and the final stop before the mountain trails to Chyram's Shrine.

Calidra's throat tightened at the thought.

It had been close to a decade since Malora had lost her powers, and Calidra wasn't convinced the Spirit of Gold would be willing to entertain her sister's plea. Dragon spirits were too fickle, and Chyram in particular was quick to be offended.

There had been Inquisitors along the roads, too. It was more than a show of strength—the queen was preparing to fight the Myr and bolstering her defences along main roads and trading routes. Though many people had tried to find out information about loved ones caught in Eastbrook or Foxmouth—Malora included—the Inquisitors had simply ushered people along.

Scores of people had been displaced in the wake of the Myrish attacks. Most fled south, heading for the mountain passes dividing Porsenthia and Bragalia, probably seeking out friends or relatives. The one shrine they'd passed on the road—dedicated to a small, river spirit she didn't know the name of—had been full of people desperate for food and shelter. Those people had eyed them hungrily, and Calidra had shown them her blade to warn them off before hurrying on.

A detachment from Eastbrook castle in uniforms reminiscent of Inquisitors had set up a checkpoint a short way ahead, halting people before they crossed the border into Bragalia. Calidra untwisted one of the straps on her sandals and took the opportunity to rest while the others caught up. She watched them for a while, noting they were more concerned with the few travellers crossing into Porsenthia, and seemed to wave through most people wanting to get into Bragalia. But their spears were always within grabbing distance, and they were more heavily armoured than she'd have expected them to be. Two Inquisitors were with them; noting down who was passing through and what they were carrying. An upturned crate had become a makeshift desk, lined with papers and ink splotches from the hasty setup. Several stacks of coins, weapons, and bags of supplies laid haphazardly around them, covered by a large fabric canvas. On one side, three rows of cages had been set up, each containing a red pigeon.

'More Inquisitors,' Malora muttered, coming to a halt beside Calidra, Renys holding onto Malora's thumb.

Calidra's heart went out to her niece. Her curly hair had lost its lustre, dirt and mud had smudged her clothes, and one of her boots had lost its sole. The girl picked at her boot, tip of her tongue poking out as she fiddled with it.

'Ren, leave it alone or you'll make it worse,' Malora chided gently.

It was a tough journey, especially when they pushed their pace so much, and the girl was much worse for wear than any of them.

'Let me help you with that, Renys.' Jisyel dropped to a crouch and took a closer look at the girl's boot. 'Thread is loose, see?' She shifted her position to pull the thread tight, when her foot slipped. She rolled to the side with a yelp, and Renys burst into laughter at the sight.

'Jisyel!' Malora offered her a hand up. 'Spirits take me, are you okay?'

'Well, if that tumble hurt, I didn't feel it at least. I didn't realise the ground sloped here, but it happened too fast for me to do anything.'

'It sounds difficult. I don't know what I'd do if Renys could fall out of a tree without hurting herself!'

'Yes! Need to climb up high!' Renys added, showing all her teeth in a wide grin.

'That *would* be dangerous.' Jisyel adjusted her boots and sighed. 'I can feel some things. Pressure, mostly. I remember once knocking my elbow so hard I couldn't feel my arm for hours. That's how it is all over.' She gestured up and down her body. 'There are a few plants in Hassen's forest that are poisonous. Numbs you. Too much of it and you can't move your fingers. I think that's why the curse is like that.'

Malora scratched her nose. 'I wonder what a curse from Chyram would be like. Wouldn't want to find out though!'

'There's movement up ahead,' Calidra called back to them, her focus on the checkpoint. One of the Inquisitors in an ill-fitting uniform rolled up a sheaf of paper tightly, no bigger than her smallest finger, and affixed it to the leg of one pigeon. She opened the cage door, and the bird leapt into the air with a flurry of red feathers.

Malora's gaze didn't leave the pigeon as it flew above them, heading towards the dark, stormy skies of the north. She wrapped her arms around herself. 'Apollo...'

Calidra had seen Malora re-reading the note from Inquisitor Nadja at night, when she thought no one was watching. Malora was brave. Determined. She had always been that way, and doubly so with trying to keep Renys's spirits up.

But Calidra knew she was terrified for Apollo. 'Mal...'

The two Inquisitors bundled up several confiscated items and headed away from the checkpoint, entering the woodland and speaking in low voices. The polished dragon insignias gleamed on their breastplates.

Malora turned away from the pigeon, now lost in the distant grey sky, and watched the Inquisitors. 'I wonder...I wonder if they're from the palace.'

Calidra followed her sister's line of thought and shook her head. 'Mal, we don't want to go in those trees.'

'I might find out more about Apollo and—'

'You want to stand in front of the queen's justice?' Calidra looked towards Jisyel for support.

Malora took a shuddering breath, tears in the corners of her eyes. She clutched onto Renys's hand tightly. 'It's been so long. What if they sent word? Foxmouth isn't there anymore. I might've missed some news.'

'That's Alnothen's domain. We don't want to go in there,' Jisyel said, a wobble in her voice belying her own anxiety.

Malora wavered, taking one step closer to the trees.

'Let's get through the checkpoint and into Bragalia. That was your plan all along, right?' Calidra tried to remind Malora of her goal. 'Apollo has been arrested. With tensions so high, what if they decide to arrest *you* for being associated with him?'

It wasn't something Calidra wanted to risk. She'd just found Jisyel and her sister again. 'We should keep moving. If we hurry, we'll reach the mountain passes by nightfall,' Calidra added, desperate to keep everyone on course. 'Mal, you said yourself you can't do much without your powers. The sooner we reach the shrine, the better.'

Calidra strode away, every step planted and confident.

When she didn't hear footsteps following, she whirled around.

Malora was closer to the forest than Jisyel, one hand holding Renys, the other resting on the trunk of the nearest tree.

'Mal!' Calidra called.

Malora wasn't listening. 'I'll be quick. I just need to know if he…if he…'

Jisyel put a hand on her shoulder. 'Please, Malora. Don't you remember what we told you about the Inquisitors? They attacked Fenn and Selys! Might take *us* in for our connection to lost souls! What would Apollo do?'

Malora shuddered. 'I'm sorry.' She picked up Renys and darted into the trees.

'Mal!' Calidra cried. She hesitated just long enough to glance at Jisyel. They both nodded, then were sprinting into the woodland after Malora.

Her sister was being foolish. Could be running straight into danger. But she would do the same if Jisyel had been taken from her.

Calidra kept Jisyel in sight as the pair of them ran side by side, keeping one eye on the forest floor for rocks and debris. Trees passed in a blur, thin branches and twigs whipping at her face. Even in her haste, she made sure to watch where she stepped, to ensure she didn't crush a plant and draw Alnothen's attention, and to keep Jisyel's footing secure.

By the time her thighs ached, she spotted her sister.

Malora stood a handful of paces away, Renys clutched to her chest with both hands.

They skidded to a halt. The trees were thinner here, more sunlight breaking through the canopy to light the way forward. Patches of shadow littered the forest floor, like puddles after a heavy rain. Each was oval, all plants and vegetation within the shadow sapped of life and colour. Larger ferns wilted—not brown as if in the coming winter, but curled up and dead, completely leached of life.

Calidra found it suddenly difficult to swallow. 'Jisyel…' She could hardly believe the Myr had been *here,* in the Spindle Woods. How could Alnothen have permitted it?

Did the Inquisitors know?

'Cal, I'm scared,' Jisyel whispered.

Calidra took Jisyel's hand in hers and they shuffled forward with tentative steps until they reached Malora and Renys. 'Mal. We need to get out of here,' she whispered through clenched teeth.

A score of Inquisitors filled the clearing, less than fifty paces away. It looked to have been a camp, embers of a large fire glowing brightly, boots removed and tents raised around the edges. The two Inquisitors they had followed had already joined their colleagues, laughing and joking, completely unaware of their presence.

Calidra nudged her sister, perhaps harder than she should have. 'Mal…we should go before we're spotted.'

Mal's jaw worked, tears trickling down her cheeks, though she didn't say anything for a long moment. 'I…I've been foolish.'

'It's okay. You saw a chance. You had to take it.' Malora needed time, but they hadn't much to spare. They'd seen signs of the Myr, and were less than a stone's throw from a group of Inquisitors who were unlikely to take their eavesdropping well. It was different to asking for the attention of a pair as they walked along.

Renys pulled away from Malora. 'Is daddy there?' Malora fumbled to keep her daughter in one place, but Renys was suddenly a tangle of limbs and she squirmed out of her mother's arms. Tumbling to the floor, she came up covered in dried leaf litter.

'Ren!'

Malora's cry caught the attention of several Inquisitors, who looked up. A handful of them approached, one drawing a sword. 'Who goes there?'

'No!' Malora scrambled after Renys, but her daughter slipped away, careening towards the Inquisitor's camp.

The forest trembled, and Calidra's worries shifted to something else: Alnothen. 'Oh no...'

'Renys!' Malora caught up with Renys and scooped her off the ground.

Everyone in the camp had their eyes on them.

'I warned you once. I will not warn you again. You are not welcome here.' Alnothen's voice echoed through the trees, a deep growl Calidra felt in her bones. It turned her insides to ice.

Before she could so much as blink, the world erupted in a wave of greens and browns. Alnothen's roar filled the air, so much fury in the noise, it rattled around her head, echoing over and over. All around her, foliage sprouted from the ground and shot into the air, filling the space with thick branches, leaves, and thorns in a matter of heartbeats.

The Inquisitors scattered as ferns and shrubbery sprouted up underneath their feet, shoving them backwards. A sapling burst from the ground, branches coiling up and spreading wide, blocking the Inquisitors' camp from view.

Malora leapt backwards as a fern shot up where she'd been standing a moment before. More plants sprouted and grew, thorns and nettles hissing with the dragon's anger.

'Get clear!' Malora ran up the slope, Renys held tightly.

Calidra and Jisyel spun on their heels as the existing trees groaned and twisted, fronds and branches reaching towards them like claws. Blossoms sprouted from branches, leaves spread wide, vines curled outwards, every plant stretching beyond its normal size.

Each new growth forced them back or to the side, and they leapt to avoid them. Nothing attacked them directly—even in her fury, Alnothen was a giver of life, not a taker of it—but the wall of impenetrable thorns and plants forced them away. It grew all around them, pushing them back to the edge of the trees, dozens springing up every few seconds.

Calidra hurried away, retracing her steps with Jisyel and Malora by her side.

Vines careened towards them like diving falcons, their thorny talons grazing clothes and nipping at their limbs, forcing them to dodge from side to side as the forest path rapidly shrank before them.

They ran, sprinting as more foliage leapt up from the ground, from above, from the sides.

Jisyel tripped and Calidra pulled her back to her feet before another fern exploded upwards.

When sunlight finally streamed in from the gap at the edge of the woodland, Calidra drew in a deep breath of relief, hardly daring to believe they'd escaped the dragon's wrath.

They collapsed to the ground as vines encircled the trees at the edge of the wood. The trees themselves stretched and swelled, trunks thickening into an impenetrable wall of bark and thorn-dotted leaves.

Panting heavily, Calidra sat up. Alnothen had closed her domain to them.

All because of one woman's refusal to obey her.

She turned to Jisyel, more pleased than ever that the woman had not given herself to the spirit. 'Are you okay?' She leaned against Jisyel.

'Fine...I think,' Jisyel replied, resting her head on Calidra's shoulder.

'Mal? Renys?' Calidra asked.

Her sister and niece cuddled each other. Renys was crying softly, and Malora held her against her chest, rocking gently where she sat, and whispering into her ear.

Calidra gingerly got to her feet and headed over to them. 'It's okay. We're okay.'

Renys snuffled and grasped for Calidra's outstretched hand.

'Hey! What happened to the Spindle Woods?'

Calidra turned at the shout to see others staring at the closed off trees, their mouths hanging open. There hadn't been more than a dozen people on the road, yet they all gathered to see what had caused the commotion.

'Is Alnothen dead?'

'She can't be! The trees are still standing!'

Calidra looked down the line of the trees, only to find the same blockade between every tree and plant as far as she could see.

Alnothen had cut off all access to the woodland.

14
THE ROT
TORSTEN

Dust choked the air.

Torsten stared out across the deadlands, lit by the pale morning sun. Clouds of grit and dirt rolled across the dry, cracked earth, tinging everything orange and brown. He leaned forward, elbows resting on his knees, and took a long swig from his leather canteen, wishing there was something stronger than water in it.

No one bothered to measure the extent of the deadlands anymore. At first count, it had been two leagues in all directions. Five years later, it was closer to six.

To the south, it was blocked by Alnothen, Dragon Spirit of the Spindle Woods.

To the north, Miroth's lake provided a barrier. Even should Miroth fall, Toriaken reigned supreme in the far north, vast where iron ore filled the Nethal Mountains and deep soil.

It could only creep west, where it would eventually be stopped by the Salt Sea, or east, where it had more ground to cover before reaching the Lasseen Ocean, and Neros.

If the Myr had their way, every spit of land would be dead and barren. All iotas of life sucked away. Not just Porsenthia, either. The entire Etrovian continent would be lost. Oceans and rivers would drain dry. Forests would wither. Everything would return to ash and dust, and only death would reign.

Torsten took another swig, swirling it around his mouth, before spitting out a glob of dusty water.

His lips were dry and chapped after several days in the stinking, festering pit of death, and he longed to be back with Miroth—to ensure his brother's survival and return to power.

He had always drawn strength from their bond—as Miroth had—but it had been hours since he'd last felt the dragon's presence. The fire that flickered in his chest was less an inferno and more a fading candle. Miroth had always been resilient, despite his small flame, but Torsten was beginning to worry.

He returned his canteen to his belt and turned to the array of Myrish artefacts he and Varlot had collected over the past few days. Any of them would help sustain his dragon's life and boost his power. But it was like trying to stop a burst dam.

Torsten needed to find a more permanent solution.

The artefacts had been arranged in order from most potent to least. He didn't know which of the artefacts was the one Queen Surayo specifically wanted, though common sense dictated he ought to bring them all to her.

But the one she wanted was comparable to the Citrine Key. The lesser artefacts would likely be of no interest to her. As far as he was concerned, it meant they were fair game.

He swept three of them into a small hessian bag. They were broken or damaged, their magic barely registering on the queen's device. Torsten couldn't fathom the need she would have of such things, which meant whatever power remained within them could go straight into Miroth.

Heavy boots on rotting floorboards caught Torsten's attention and he got to his feet as Varlot rounded the corner.

Varlot stood taller than him by almost a foot, and the bigger man always seemed to bear down on him. 'Shoulda known you'd be here. Lazing about enjoying the views while I'm in the dirt and grime doing all the work.'

'I'm accounting for what we've discovered. And remember, Varlot, I'm your superior. You'll address me as such.' Torsten's patience for the man's vulgar nature had worn thin in the days they'd spent together. Torsten wasn't sure how much longer he could stomach.

Something glittered in Varlot's eyes. 'Four days and that's all we have to show for it? Surely we coulda made more difference elsewhere. Caught deserters. Fought off the Myr.' Varlot spat.

It was both a disgusting and irritating habit, but no amount of sharp glares or sneers had dissuaded the man, so Torsten decided to simply ignore it. 'There is far more of the fortress yet to comb through. The basement levels and dungeons could take twice that time.'

'Why not send more of us?' Varlot picked up a broken bottle and frowned at the dusty glass.

'Our forces are better placed to defend against the Myr's resurgence while we deal with this delicate matter. Stop complaining for a moment and you'll learn something of how Queen Surayo's mind works.'

Varlot dropped the bottle none-too gently. It shattered on the stone floor. 'I don't care how the queen runs her empire. I have good information about a Myrish construct and instead she sends me here to shovel shit with you.'

'What Myrish construct?'

'In the Nethal Mountains. Torsten, don't you ever listen to a word I say?'

Irritation grew. He knew of the stories of those mountains. Nothing but children's fables to keep them from wandering up and getting lost. 'Whatever's up there is a ruin. Everyone knows that.'

'That's where Fenn was going. Queen needs to look at it. Might pick up his tracks or find out what the Myr are doing. If she's trying to get her defences together, I'd say that's important.'

'Sending Queen Surayo halfway across Porsenthia to "look at" a Myrish ruin is a waste of time and resources. We're doing good work here, Varlot.'

'Don't want good work. I want the respect I deserve. No chance I'll get that holed up in this fucking fortress with you.'

'Then follow orders and do as you're told. You'll get what you want, as sure as I will.'

'And what do *you* want?'

Torsten didn't reply, thinking of Miroth. He didn't relish the idea of leaving Varlot to his own devices, but he had no choice. Varlot could wait, and while he was stationed at the fortress in the middle of nowhere, he couldn't cause any trouble.

He looked back at the horizon, his will pulled towards Tonmouth's lake. 'You will spend today in the basement levels. I will report to Queen Surayo.'

'What?' Varlot's brow furrowed.

'I would not deign to insult Toriaken by speaking to him in this despicable place. Tonmouth is neutral ground, so I will conduct my report there, and return in a few days.'

'You're *leaving* me here in this place?' Varlot raised both hands to emphasise his point.

'Yes. And you will address me as *Master Inquisitor* henceforth. My next report ought to be better once we have cleared through more of the fortress. Work quickly, and you'll get your reward.'

Night chased Torsten when he arrived at Miroth's Shrine. The horse he'd taken, unused to such a gruelling pace, panted hard, muscles trembling as he dismounted.

Even at a shrine where few came to worship, the stable-hands carried out their duties loyally and without complaint, and one young lad took the horse away to be brushed down, fed, and watered. He also left his travelling supplies and iron dagger with the boy—save the hessian sack of Myrish artefacts—so he could better humble himself before his dragon.

The climb through the hills afforded him a clear view of the lake, but with darkness rolling in along with heavy clouds, he couldn't be sure of the state of the water.

Torsten continued up the stone steps towards the shrine itself. Several had cracked since his last visit, though that was likely due to weather rather than a sudden influx of visitors.

Before he was halfway up, a robed priest holding an oil lantern shuffled down to meet him. He wore a square cap atop his head, long blue tassels trailing down his back. Deep wrinkles lined his face and his hand trembled where he clutched the lantern. 'Master Inquisitor! Thank Miroth you're here!'

Torsten paused. Usually, he'd dismiss anyone who got in his way, especially when it came to the shrine. But something in the priest's fearful gaze made him hesitate.

'Lord Miroth is…not well.'

Torsten kept his voice calm. 'I am aware.'

'He has not been in the shrine for some days, staying within the waters of the lake.'

That was a worrying sign. Dragon spirits could become corporeal whenever they wished. If they were injured, they would return to their domain like a bear hibernating through the harshest winter. A piece of Miroth's soul was bound to the sword at the heart of his shrine—a failsafe that would keep the essence of the spirit alive should the worst ever happen to the lake.

Usually, Miroth crawled around that and conserved his energy within the shrine.

If he had retreated to the lake…

'I have prayed daily for his strength to return, but the lake cannot be purified. Please take this. The path is not used very often and there is a good deal of mud from the recent rains.' The priest held out the lantern for him.

Torsten took it, grateful. 'Do not lose faith.'

He knew Miroth had been struggling, but hadn't realised how bad the dragon was. It couldn't be the Myr. It was too soon, and Miroth was still a dragon spirit, no matter how weakened he may have been. Torsten was certain the priest would have mentioned the Myr if they had anything to do with Miroth's current state.

His brother had simply overexerted himself, that was all. Torsten had taken too much power, and Miroth had taken too much control.

They had been foolish, but it couldn't be worse than that.

It couldn't.

Torsten picked his way down the sloping path, using the lantern's soft, yellow light for guidance. In truth, he hadn't visited the lake itself for several years. There was no need when Miroth resided in the shrine.

Each step that brought him closer to the water filled his heart with more dread.

He sought inside himself. But the tell-tale flame that had been with him since he was a boy was not there, or it was so tiny that Torsten could not find it.

Crickets chirped in the thick grass surrounding the lake. Tiny fireflies fluttered about in lazy swarms, moving across the surface of the water, orange light glinting. Flowers that bloomed in the night opened their delicate lavender petals, drinking in the pale light of Tassar's broken moon.

There was life here, yet.

The salt had not destroyed the lake completely, and the

surrounding soil gave birth to plants, grasses, and shrubbery. Animals and insects had not yet left their home.

Miroth *had* to be alive.

Torsten came to a halt at the water's edge and gently set the lantern down on the muddy ground. The clicks, whistles, and calls of night creatures gave him hope, and he slowed his breathing to take in the sounds and smells of the lakeside.

Perhaps if it had been daytime, he might be able to recognise the rock beside which Miroth had first formed, where he'd first laid eyes on the fledgling spirit. But under cover of darkness, shadows grew great outside the halo of lantern light, and everything looked much the same.

'Lord Miroth…' Torsten whispered, crouching. He undid the buckles on his boots. The thick leather was usually polished to a fine sheen, but after his trek through the hillside, they were heavily caked in mud. Uniforms could be laundered and boots could be cleaned, and he ignored the quiet discomfort of seeing the sign of his station so dishevelled.

His socks came off next—bundling them up and pushing them into his boots to keep them dry if nothing else.

The legs of his breeches were well-fitted, designed not to wrinkle even after many days of wear, and the fabric was too tight for him to roll up much past his ankles. Unwilling to make himself completely vulnerable by stripping down to his smallclothes, Torsten waded into the water and gasped at the chill. He forced himself to keep moving. 'My Lord. I'm here.'

His words carried in the stillness of the night, all other sounds disappearing the moment the water splashed.

Thankfully, the lake was not deep near its edges, and Torsten waded in some distance before the level rose above his knees. He held the small bag up high, wondering if Miroth would be able to sense what he carried.

Waves rippled from his body in all directions. Miroth *had* to be aware of his presence. He was standing in the very centre of the dragon's domain. 'Miroth...?' Torsten dropped the formality as anxiety set in. He would wait as long as he needed to wait.

There was life here. Miroth had *not* faded.

Water dripped from his elbows, causing more ripples on the lake's surface. Slowly, the insect sounds returned. A shadow ghosted overhead—an owl, he realised at the last moment—and disappeared on the far side of the lake.

Still, he waited.

The chill began to set into his skin, and he fought to keep his teeth from chattering. He tasted salt on his lips—a reminder of what was slowly killing Miroth.

Torsten swallowed and turned, hoping he would see the dragon if he looked in the right place. It was foolish thinking, but he was growing steadily more desperate. Underfoot, the soft silt was decorated by hard rocks and slippery plants that held on to life as the water grew more toxic.

He took shallow breaths, forcing himself to remain calm, logical. Porsenthia's Master Inquisitor did *not* give up at the first hurdle. He would be patient. Controlled. He would assess the situation from multiple angles and figure out a way forward.

Torsten closed his eyes, once again searching for that flame. The fire that had been his companion. Confidant. Strength. For decades.

'Brother!' Torsten's cry burst from his throat—his own voice intertwined with Miroth's.

The dragon spirit erupted from the water in a cascade, letting out a low, keening wail that might have been a formidable growl once upon a time.

Torsten held back the desire to sink to his knees. He stood in the middle of the lake as Miroth coiled around him. Steam rose from his body, pluming up with every twist of muscle.

'I had...worried,' Torsten said, voice cracking.

Miroth stopped circling and came to rest several feet in front of Torsten. His finned tail lashed, rising and falling from the water in gentle undulations. The dragon watched Torsten with eyes of liquid silver, a gentle blue light emanating from his scales. *'I suffer.'*

Torsten bowed his head, showing the dragon as much reverence as he could without sinking deeper in the water. 'I know. I hardly feel you. I am…empty without your presence. Adrift.'

Smoke rose from Miroth's nostrils, and the dragon leaned forward, stretching his long neck until his head was level with Torsten.

When Torsten lifted his gaze, he was shocked to see the spirit so close. Torsten raised his free hand and rested it atop the dragon's head. Miroth did not share the might of Neros or Toriaken, but Torsten had never known a creature more magnificent. Miroth's head alone was the size of the horse Torsten had ridden here, and so close, his eyes seemed to bore into Torsten's soul.

'My only purpose is to strengthen you, so all of Tassar sees your greatness as I do.' Torsten shook with reverence, but he did nothing to hide it. Could do nothing.

Miroth did not reply, the edges of his scales fading in and out of sight. The dragon was using all of his strength simply to remain visible.

Without thinking, Torsten dropped to his knees—the lake water coming up to his chest. 'I have another gift for you, brother. Take it, and let its power be yours.'

He carefully brought his other hand towards Miroth's jaws. When the dragon obliged, opening his mouth, Torsten felt the wash of fire on Miroth's breath. Carefully, he placed the bag of Myrish artefacts on the dragon's tongue, then withdrew. 'Brother. I wish for more than to see you restored to glory. I wish for your magnificence to be seen and adored by those who would doubt it.'

Miroth held the bag in his mouth and stared at Torsten. Then, he closed his eyes, leaned back, and swallowed.

Fire blazed in Torsten's chest as the Myrish magic swept through Miroth. Every scale pulsed with blue light, and the water surrounding them rose up in a wave that towered above them.

Staggering to his feet, Torsten attempted to get to dry land, but he was caught in the maelstrom. He gasped for breath and covered his face as the water bubbled and frothed.

Miroth disappeared under water, light bursting from his scales so brightly that Torsten could not look directly upon him.

He collapsed.

TORSTEN DIDN'T KNOW how much time passed. It could have been seconds or hours, everything blurred together so strongly. When he came awake, he was sitting on the lakeshore, his uniform sopping wet, though he no longer felt cold.

Fire raged in his chest, warming every part of him, fingers to toes.

The oil lamp burned low beside his boots, and Miroth's light trickled out from the water, as though it were lit by a burning sun.

Of the dragon itself, Torsten felt nothing but relief. Miroth flew above the lake, his tail cutting lazily through the water underneath him. *'Brother. You shall always share in my glory.'*

Miroth's roar echoed across the water and surrounding hills. Goosebumps rose along Torsten's arms at the sound of it, and he wanted to do nothing more than prostrate himself before the god. But Miroth saw him as an equal, and equals did not bow to one another.

So he stood up, wincing at the few dull aches in his legs from riding so hard to reach Tonmouth quickly. Wind from Miroth's flapping wings washed over him, and Torsten breathed in deeply.

Then he frowned. He was not sure if it was his own tiredness or a trick of the frail oil lantern mixing with the light emanating from the spirit.

As he stared upon Miroth, he thought the dragon's scales were a few shades darker.

15
THE CHALLENGE
KAIO

More papers littered Kaio's desk than he knew what to do with. Put a sword in his hand and give him a target, and he was in his element. Ask him to manage the commerce, logistics, and supplies of a canton, and he was clutching at straws.

His brother had always been better at the finer aspect of ruling people. No one had ever questioned Skaru's orders, whereas Kaio was second guessed at every turn. Skaru simply had a gift for garnering support and getting people to listen.

After Neros had wiped out their family in one fell swoop, there'd been no one left with the Ioran name save himself and Selys. And she'd abandoned Segandis. Abandoned him.

He'd had no choice but to take up his brother's mantle. Their father, Dairo, might have sailed the flagship, but Skaru held the power. *He* had ruled the canton. Been the true Laird.

Kaio idly thumbed through a stack of unread papers, longingly thinking of being at sea.

Away from the headaches he couldn't fight his way through.

Other warbands circled Segandis like vultures, probing

him—the weakest son—for vulnerabilities. Demands for this or that. Renegotiating trade terms, borders, and boundaries.

Some had even come to petition at his door, and he'd turned them away. Didn't want to get overwhelmed. He'd shown them the sharp side of his blade and thrown back the insults hurled his way.

'Kaio, you have to deal with them sooner or later. Ignoring them will only make them angrier,' Esto said on the fifth morning since their return. She sat on the far side of his room, in the spot where sunlight drifted in through the window, Fergus on her lap, and offered advice on how best to respond to the letters and requests he'd received.

He'd checked on Evarine every morning for the past three days, but Ruka hadn't allowed him more than a glimpse of the woman. The healer confirmed Evarine was eating, but was too weak for any sort of interrogation. She promised to let him know when he could talk to her, so Kaio had begrudgingly left her to rest.

Taran had scoured the coast several times on a skiff while *Wolf's Grin* underwent repairs, but he hadn't been able to find anything to corroborate Evarine's story.

The lack of information didn't help Kaio's mood.

'I'm not ignoring them. I'm telling them to fuck off.' He sealed a letter he'd signed, confirming the number of residents in Segandis for Queen Surayo's Inquisitors. It was three months out of date—he was supposed to have sent it *before* his voyage—but struggled to muster the energy to care.

Esto's usual smile wasn't on her face. 'Skaru would have at least hosted a dinner for the other warband chiefs. Wining and dining them makes them more receptive to having their requests ignored than being told to *fuck off*.' She didn't speak with an ounce of humour.

'My way is faster. Saves money, too.' He tried to brush off the comparison to his dead brother, but his skin itched with annoyance. 'Not wasting my time on their pettiness.'

'You'll spend a lot more money replacing all the tithes they stop paying, or supplies they destroy.'

'They try that and they won't live long enough to regret it.' He stabbed the quill in its pot more vigorously than he'd intended, and ink splattered across the remaining papers.

Esto sighed. 'It isn't just the other chiefs you need to concern yourself with, Kaio. Yaniv's been stirring up trouble. Says he isn't being paid his fair share.'

'Share of *what*? He saw we brought back hardly anything!' Kaio was on his feet, voice raising.

'That's the problem. Another trip like that and we won't have enough to keep the ship in good order, let alone pay them. And that's before—'

'Yaniv can go fuck himself. What's he do other than complain, anyway?' It was a pointless argument, but Kaio was too worked up to care. Every letter reminded him of his failings, his lack of experience as a leader. Every complaint was a stark reminder of poor decisions, how he wasn't living up to the Ioran name or the glorious memory of his brother.

At this point, he almost wanted one of Taran's cigarillos to calm himself down.

'Well I can see you're in no mood for advice on diplomacy, so I'll leave you to deal with the rest of those.' Esto gestured vaguely towards the ink-splattered papers, and left the room with a huff, Fergus following.

Kaio sighed, sitting back in his chair, even the creaking wood irritating him. His gaze was drawn to the jade shell sitting on his desk. He'd taken it from Evarine's bag, mostly because it was a curiosity. It carried none of the wear of her other belongings and drank in sunlight. Every touch had given him a vision of Neros bathed in shadow, a chain around her neck.

He didn't know what it meant, but something about it called to him.

It was a symbol of the sea, and Neros specifically—the

thing that had taken his family from him and left him to run the canton alone.

Mages were uncommon, in fact the only one he really knew about was Queen Surayo herself. He didn't think Evarine carried any magic or blessings, so in addition to discovering what she had to do with the Myr, he wanted to know what the shell was, and how she'd come to be in possession of it.

If nothing else, the shell could be sold to the right bidder and boost his coffers.

Kaio glanced at another letter from the border checkpoints—more people wanting refuge in Segandis following the Myr's attacks in northern Porsenthia—and gave up with paperwork. He dragged his hands down his face, wishing he'd spent more time listening to his father and brother when they'd dealt with their responsibilities.

He threw the paper down and headed outside—and walked straight into Evarine, who'd been standing outside his door, petting Fergus. The woman seemed to have recovered well enough under Ruka's watchful eye, but was far from fighting fit.

'Oh, the minute I stop pestering Ruka to talk to you, you're up and about?' Kaio muttered, pride hurt from stumbling into her. His head pounded, and he just wanted the spray of the sea to soothe his soul, not deal with more complaints.

Admittedly, Evarine finally being awake was a good distraction from the endless tasks of being a Laird.

'I'm sorry if I've been any trouble. Ruka is very caring,' Evarine said. 'I wanted to talk to you as well.'

He pinched the bridge of his nose.

Many large tents were grouped under the orange trees in the clearing, several members of his warband milling around. Some sat on mats or cushions, leaning back and laughing.

Others sparred, the clink of blades scraping against each other as comforting as birdsong.

Kaio nodded. 'Walk with me.'

THE LIGHT of the low afternoon sun turned the colour of the sea to liquid gold, bright spots illuminated here and there. It was some distance to the main harbour—busy at all times of the day and night—but the cacophony of noise was lessened along the empty stretch of beach he and Evarine walked along.

Kaio wandered near the water's edge, allowing the waves to lap at his sandaled feet. Whatever ills occurred throughout Tassar, this point, at least, was peaceful. A far cry from the turmoil in his mind.

He'd only known Esto to speak the truth, no matter how harsh, and he half-expected Yaniv to mutiny any day now. He ran a hand down his face and wished he had more of his brother's tact.

'I'm glad you have a spare minute,' Evarine said, opening the conversation. Her confidence had grown with her recovery, and now she strolled along as if she were a part of his warband. 'You seem to turn everyone away. Even Taran.'

Kaio misstepped, recovering quickly. 'Didn't realise you were having me watched.'

'I was recovering, I'm not deaf. And you rule here. I have to watch you.'

'You're not a prisoner. You can leave whenever you want—not that Ruka thinks you're in any state to be going far. But I want answers first. What's your association with the Myr?'

'Nothing.'

Kaio narrowed his eyes. She'd answered too quickly for his liking, but it could have been nerves. He tried to remember Esto and Ruka's advice about being less rash. 'You sure about that? Not often people turn up in caves alongside those things.'

'My village was attacked by them. Is that what you wanted to know?'

'Why didn't they kill you?'

'Why do they do anything?' Evarine shrugged. 'I hope everyone back home is okay.'

'Ma-Rai?'

She nodded.

Kaio folded his arms and tried something different. 'And that jade shell you were carrying. Is that from Ma-Rai, too?'

She froze, her eyes going wide. 'You took it?'

'You going to give me answers? Or shall I assume you're a threat and drive you out of my canton?'

Evarine put one hand on her hip and stared at him with a ferocity he rarely saw. 'Okay. Fine. The shell is a Myrish artefact.'

Kaio hadn't expected that. He mulled it over, wondering what it was for. Something to do with Neros, if the vision was any clue. 'What are you doing with a Myrish artefact?'

'You have it now.'

He snorted. 'Sure. But what were you planning on doing with it? Taran's convinced you're in league with them. This doesn't really help.'

She slowed down, eyes darting to the side as if calculating something. 'I thought...maybe...'

'Spit it out.'

Evarine chewed on her thumbnail, her eyes clouding over. 'The Myr are overrunning my home. I've lost so much to them, to their corruption. Your queen fought them off here. Perhaps she can help.'

Kaio laughed. 'First, she isn't *my* queen. Second, there's not much chance of that.'

'Maybe she'd accept the shell as a gift? Get her to help? I... I want to go to Eastbrook.'

'Long walk. That direction.' He pointed with his thumb roughly north.

Evarine didn't respond.

Kaio paused and looked back at her, expecting some remark to his suggestion. But she stared at a spot on the beach several paces away.

His skin prickled. He followed her gaze and breathed in sharply.

Blood stained the sand, drying under the heavy Bragalian sun. The waves lapped at the beach as if reaching for a taste of the blood but too afraid to get close enough to take it.

'Is that a…is he okay?' Evarine's voice trembled.

Kaio stepped towards where the blood was thickest, seemingly appearing out of the sand itself. Steeling himself for what he was likely to find, he crouched and dug away at the soft sand with his hands.

It didn't take long to unearth the body buried underneath.

Tesso.

Given the depth of the gash across his throat, Kaio hoped he had been dead *before* he was buried. Kaio lifted Tesso's chin as best he could, inwardly grimacing at the squelch when unconnected sinew and muscle shifted. More blood leaked from the gash, slow and thick.

An apple had been shoved in Tesso's mouth, like he was a stuffed pig, but pushed in so forcefully it had dislocated his jaw. A thick line of bloodied spittle dribbled from his lips.

Behind him, Evarine retched, the wet sound compounding Kaio's own building nausea and rage.

The message was clear. Only one warband flew with apple red sails.

His pulse pounded in his ear. Someone had killed one of *his* people. Right under his nose.

And he would not stand for that.

Kaio gently pulled the apple from Tesso's mouth and stood up. Taran, Esto, and Ruka would tell him to think about things. To talk to his enemies, rather than attack first.

His family would have told him not to act rashly.

His brother would have some plan to retaliate without unnecessary bloodshed.

But none of those people were here. He only knew to fight back when threatened. And his blood boiled.

'Evarine. Fetch Taran, Ruka, and the others. Tell them to prepare for a proper send off.' Kaio strode away, all thoughts of the Myr pushed from his mind.

'Where are you going?'

'To avenge Tesso.'

'You walked in here with some swagger, I'll give you that. But you're going to regret it, boy.' Dalys smiled pleasantly at him.

Kaio didn't like that grin, or the smugness that came with it. He held Dalys's gaze while the other chief perched atop a throne of cushions, two of his lieutenants beside him. Another two flanked Kaio, the tips of their blades pressed against his lower back, ready to skewer him if he breathed the wrong way.

He ignored them all, his attention locked on Dalys's sweaty forehead.

Dalys was the leader of a small warband on the edge of Segandis, one who'd been a thorn in his family's side for over a decade. His brother, Skaru, had allowed them to remain part of their territory so long as they paid him thirty percent of their takings. They were mostly legitimate tradespeople, travelling to and from Olmir regularly, which made the arrangement profitable for the Ioran warband.

Taran even bought most of his bows and arrows from them.

Diplomacy was the preferred method for running the canton—according to everyone telling him what a poor job he was doing. But Kaio had long since advocated for cutting the snake's head off instead of keeping it around and hoping it wouldn't bite.

The murder of one of his own was the final straw. The fact it was Tesso made the sting particularly painful—the lad had done nothing wrong.

Dalys couldn't have expected trouble, otherwise he wouldn't have allowed Kaio into his territory alone. How could Dalys be so brazen to provoke him so openly? He wouldn't have dared to do that had Skaru or his father still been alive.

'I have something for you.' Kaio kept his tone as neutral as possible.

The lieutenants' gazes shifted uncomfortably to their chief, who inclined his head.

Kaio stepped forward, just in case either of the two men behind him were twitchy with their blades, reached into his pocket, and threw the mangled apple to the floor. The fruit rolled across the tent's floor before coming to a stop, blood from the apple's flesh staining the plush, Olmese rug in the middle of the room.

Kaio saw Dalys's throat bob as he swallowed. More sweat appeared on his brow. 'You wanted an answer from the Ioran warband? I'm here to answer it.'

'Kaio. You're young. Wet behind the ears. This isn't how negotiations begin. Perhaps if you'd responded to my written correspondence, you'd realise that.'

Kaio bristled.

'If Skaru were here, he'd know the proper way to approach any grievance is with a message the following day, and he'd know to send one of his—'

'Skaru isn't here.' Kaio didn't hide the bite in his voice. Even dead, his brother had more influence than he ever would. A shadow he could never escape. '*I'm* here now. I'm challenging you.' He drew his blade, surprised—and a little insulted—that Dalys's lieutenants hadn't even taken it from him on his arrival.

Duels were considered archaic, even among the most aggressive warbands. Technically, they were outlawed per the Iron Crown's law.

But ripping out the root of the problem was the fastest way to solve it.

Dalys blinked, as though he'd never been interrupted before and wasn't quite sure how to respond. 'Excuse me?'

'You heard. I'll fight you. Any of your lieutenants. Name your champion, and we'll end this *grievance* right now, the old-fashioned way.'

Dalys got to his slippered feet. The man spent more time sitting on cushions inside lavishly decorated tents than any hard work in the sun. 'Now see here, pup, this is *not* the way chiefs manage their business! We aren't savages!'

Kaio was unmoved. 'You're the one who murdered one of mine, and you call *me* savage? Name someone, or I'll kill you myself.'

Of course, the moment the words left his mouth, the two men either side of him pounced—grasping his arms. Kaio sidestepped their lunges, tripping the closer of the two. Quick as a flash, he parried the second lieutenant's blade and relieved him of his sword.

By the time the first had gathered his balance again, Kaio slashed into his hand, slicing two fingers clean off. The lieutenant's screams mingled with the blood spurting from his hand.

Kaio raised his bloodied sword towards Dalys. 'Name your champion.'

KAIO STOOD, waiting. All lean muscle and low stances, wolf-like and ready. The tension in the air had thickened, and he relished the sensation. *This* was what he lived for. *This* was what he understood.

It hadn't taken long for Taran and Ruka to arrive at Dalys's headquarters, along with a handful of others, including Yaniv and his coterie. Kaio wondered whether everyone was on his side or Yaniv's.

Half-wondered whether Yaniv had killed Tesso and put the blame on Dalys.

But it didn't matter now. His blood was up and he was going to get the fight he needed.

'Kaio! What is this?' Ruka hissed.

He didn't appreciate being undermined, though he was glad she kept her voice low so Dalys didn't hear.

Sweat rolled down his bare shoulders. Even with the sun approaching the horizon, Kaio longed for the spray of the sea. More than that, he longed to prove his strength to those who doubted him, and ensure his authority was not questioned.

Dalys's bare-chested champion stepped forward, a large axe held in both hands. Isiat, Kaio recalled his name. A circle of people surrounded them on the dusty ground, close to fifty paces across. What little grass grew so close to the coast was coarse and rough, more sand than green.

Isiat strode towards him, jeers pushing him on from Taran and the rest of Kaio's followers. Before he'd reached the middle of the circle, the axe-blade burst into flame.

'Oh, you have a spirit on your side? That the only way you can fight me?' Kaio snarled, infuriated by Isiat's cheating. Fighting someone who was bonded to a dragon was never easy, and most backed down from that challenge.

Isiat smirked, unmoved by the jibe. 'It is my power.' He was almost two heads taller than Kaio, far broader around the shoulders, chest, and belly.

What had the man done to get a dragon spirit's blessing? 'Power? Hmph. Some people will do anything for a taste.'

Kaio knew the rules of combat. Everyone in warbands the length and breadth of Bragalia did, even if duels were rarely carried out. However, Kaio had never really believed in them. *He* ran Segandis. *He* would implement the rules as he saw fit, not according to what their long-dead ancestors had decided upon however many generations ago.

He did not wait for the flag. Did not wait for them to cross arms.

He leapt forwards, curved sword held loose, his movements fluid.

Isiat braced, knuckles tightening on the axe's shaft. The crackling fire spat, shifting from warm orange to steely blue.

Kaio ignored the distraction. Isiat was his target, not whatever dragon spirit he'd made a deal with. He feinted left, then brought his sword up across the meat of Isiat's ribs.

Instead of plunging into soft flesh, his sword cracked as Isiat brought the shaft of his axe across his body, defending himself at the last moment. The shock of impact shook Kaio's arm, searing his wrist with a deep ache he gritted his teeth against. His shoulder flared with pain, the Myrish wound protesting.

Isiat surged forward, using his bigger size to force Kaio back a step. Water plumed from the blade, a shockingly cold burst that Kaio narrowly avoided. It coated the sand, compacting it.

Kaio shifted his stance, making sure he didn't lose his footing.

It seemed whatever dragon Isiat had the blessing of was a water spirit. Not that it would make a difference in the end.

Bending his knees, Kaio leaned forward, weathering the brunt of the strike following the water and slipping his blade in to slice a line of red against Isiat's bare skin. He grinned at drawing first blood.

Against a spirit-blessed opponent, no less.

Isiat grunted at the wound, but it hardly slowed him. He swung his axe low, water switching back to flames that reached hungrily toward him.

Kaio avoided the blade, but the fire singed the hairs on his arms. He hissed, pushing through the pain instead of leaping away, pressing his attack while he had momentum.

His aggression caught Isiat off balance, because he stumbled to block Kaio's next strike—aimed at the wrist. At the same time, Kaio kicked out, his booted foot connecting with Isiat's knee. It crunched.

Isiat fell forward, limp, a cry of agony on his lips.

He grabbed Isiat's head in both hands and brought his knee up forcefully. His knee connected with Isiat's nose, sending the bigger man hurtling to the sand in a daze. The axe fell from Isiat's grip and the flames extinguished.

'What's wrong? Can't fight without that spirit?' Kaio kicked the axe away. 'You need it because you're *weak*. Just like Dalys and the rest of you cowards.'

Isiat groaned, barely able to push himself upright. He spat a glob of blood at the ground by Kaio's feet.

Kaio shook his head. 'Pathetic.' His point had been made. There was no need to kill the man, but he wanted the lesson to be one they wouldn't forget.

With one swift movement, Kaio severed Isiat's left hand at the wrist. He braced for the burst of hot blood coating his arm, and tossed his sword away, where it landed point-down deep in the damp sand. The crowd erupted in a cheer.

Kaio glanced at Dalys, whose face had paled, tinged with green. It looked like the man had just come through the other side of a raging storm.

'We're done here. Taran. You can arrange our new cut from Dalys's coffers. We hold a funeral tonight for our own.'

Kaio swirled his cup, dark red liquid—almost black—sloshing inside, then drank to toast the passing of life to the spirit world. It was sweet and salty, like fruit gone bad in the sun. Several huge fires had been built right on the beach, surrounding the wake, the crackle and spit joining laughter and singing, the flames chasing away the darkness of night.

If he had his way, he'd never touch the drink again. The smell of it reminded him of having to drink cup after cup when his family had passed.

But it was traditional, respectful, and honoured the dead. And he owed Tesso that much.

The lad hadn't even gone on a voyage with them.

Kaio tried to bury his memories, and failings, as much as he could.

Evarine took her offered glass, head bowed low, and sipped. Credit to her, she hid her cough well. She'd approached him after the fight, no doubt wanting to ask about passage to Queen Surayo again, but had turned on her heel after taking one look at him. It suited him just fine. She wasn't going before she'd answered his questions to his satisfaction. She'd spent long enough resting. She could wait on him, now.

Kaio stared across those gathered, the strength of the Ioran warband stripped to a few score loyalists. He could count on one hand those he actually trusted. Taran. Esto. Ruka.

At the height of their strength, they had six ships, each carrying a crew of fifty. They had triple that number living in Segandis, and another thousand who roamed Bragalia, patrolling their borders and driving away any challengers. Not to mention countless others who swore fealty to the Ioran Laird.

Now they were a shadow of themselves. People had deserted the warband in their hundreds after Neros's storm. Defected to other warbands or left Bragalia altogether.

It was no wonder that maggot Dalys had tried to poke him.

Even *Wolf's Grin* was not fully garrisoned. They had grown weak under his watch. Instead of rising like a phoenix from the ashes of his family's deaths, they'd spiralled like a match fizzling out.

His rage simmered, bubbling beneath the surface. Despite his victory, the challenge to his leadership had wounded his pride. And the advice of his allies ate at him. What he'd done was reckless and foolhardy, but he hoped it was a strong enough signal to keep his enemies at arm's length.

Taran came to speak to him, though he barely heard his words. Kaio's mind was lost, wrapped up in layers of anger and paranoia. So much was out of his control, and the moment he shut down an issue, two more sprang up like weeds. Discontent had been sown, and betrayal grew.

Kaio drank deeply, trying to figure out how to stop being undermined by those who were supposed to follow him.

Suddenly, Taran gasped, dropping his cup.

Kaio glanced up.

A figure stood on the edge of their circle, glaive used as a walking stick, silk ribbons blowing in the breeze. Three jade beads clinked together, making toneless music that echoed across the sand.

She watched him with pale blue eyes that matched his own, and tilted her head. 'Well met, Chief.'

Kaio's mouth went dry.

16
THE SHADOW
CALIDRA

Calidra, Jisyel, Malora, and Renys kept their distance from the edge of the sealed Spindle Woods. Although plants and vines bridged the gap between the tree trunks, preventing anyone from entering or leaving, the foliage squirmed like it was continually tightening its grip. It shifted, blocking out all light.

Calidra didn't want to think about what would have happened if they'd offended another dragon spirit. Alnothen had always been a giver of life. She was known to be kind. Gentle.

Not all spirits were so forgiving.

'You really want to forsake your life again, Mal? Devote yourself to Chyram when they react like *that*?' She gestured, somewhat unnecessarily, towards the trees. 'What about Apollo? Renys?'

Malora rested her hand on Renys's head, absent-mindedly thumbing over her daughter's hair as she stared at the sealed forest. Sweat dripped down her collarbone. 'I will bargain.'

'Bargain?' Jisyel asked, her mouth hanging open.

Malora continued to stare at the trees. Her eyes watered,

though no tears fell. 'I need the strength to save my husband, to protect my daughter. If they are safe and well, Chyram can have me.'

Calidra took Jisyel's hand in her own, remembering the desperation she'd seen in her lover's eyes when they'd been before Alnothen. Calidra recalled her own desperation and terror that she had been about to lose Jisyel forever. 'You can't sacrifice yourself, Mal. It *isn't* worth it.'

At that, her sister finally looked at her. Malora's tears spilled and she smiled through them. It was a small, sad smile, one that meant multiple things that Calidra was too frustrated and scared to grasp. 'Calidra. I'm a mother. I sacrificed myself the moment Renys was born.' Malora stared down at her daughter, her smile broadening into something that could have banished all the darkness in the world. 'My life is for her.'

Calidra trembled. She'd been accepting of Malora's desire until now. Why *shouldn't* her sister have power? But she'd been so keen to help her, to mend the bridge between them, that she hadn't asked the obvious questions. Hadn't challenged Malora's thinking.

Had been too afraid to do that.

Alnothen's immediate, aggressive response reminded her why the dragons should be respected—perhaps feared—and ultimately left to their own devices.

She'd only just found out her sister was alive and couldn't bear to lose her. Not again. Not to a spirit so undeserving and unworthy of Malora's love. 'Mal…you don't even know if Apollo is still alive. You have Renys there, in your arms, right now. I think you're doing an amazing job of protecting her *without* Chyram's blessing. You saw her safely through the Myrish attack in Foxmouth!'

'Cal, I don't expect you to understand.'

Calidra quietened for a moment, trying to think as the gathered crowd thickened around them to stare at the sealed woodland. 'Dragons can also curse you. Jisyel is proof of that. And you did lose Chyram's favour, so—'

'Oi! You there! Step back from the trees!' a gruff voice barked in their direction.

Calidra whirled around in surprise. She'd been so intent on her sister she hadn't realised the officers approaching them alongside curious travellers. They wore navy uniforms highlighted in white, though the dragon insignia marking them under the service of Queen Surayo was bronze, rather than the silver of Inquisitors.

'I said step back!' He levelled his spear at them, its edge glinting in the sunlight. He was a broad man with a full beard and clear strength in his shoulders to wield his weapon. Three others flanked him, and suddenly their uniforms blocked her path. 'What did you do?'

'We didn't do anything!' Jisyel stood in front of Calidra, heedless of the spearpoint. 'It was Alnothen!'

'Inquisitors went into those trees. So did you. Now you're back out, they're still in there, and looks like they're trapped. So. I'll ask you again. *What* did you do?' He eyed them in disdain, gaze roaming each of the women, one at a time.

'We can't control a dragon. Even if one of us was bonded to her!' Malora pushed Renys behind her legs, out of the soldier's line of sight.

With nothing to answer that, he shook his head. 'You four travelling south? Where are your papers?'

'But we—we aren't even at the checkpoint yet!' Jisyel argued.

'If you aren't going into Bragalia, you'll come with us. If you are, you need to show me your papers.'

Calidra understood he was doing his job, that he was worried about the Myr and the effect they were having on the dragons, and his colleagues. She didn't think the Inquisitors would be hurt, but they were certainly trapped until such time as Alnothen decided otherwise.

But she didn't like his attitude, and wanted to reach for her sword's hilt.

Malora scowled and pulled her satchel from her shoulder. She opened the flap and rooted through it for several moments. Straightening up, she handed him two leafs of cream paper, signed and sealed with the dragon insignia of the Iron Crown.

He frowned as he scanned it, brows knitting together in either irritation or frustration once he'd read both papers. 'Malora Tamlin. Hmm. I know that name from somewhere...'

'I'm the daughter of Furyn Vantonen, one of Bragalia's Lairds.'

He didn't seem to hear her, throwing back the papers in her direction in disdain, then turned to Calidra and Jisyel. His small, beady eyes reminded Calidra of a small rodent. 'And you two? Come on, come on. Ain't got all day.'

Jisyel had been going through their own supplies with increasing fervour. 'They...they aren't here?'

Calidra crouched by Jisyel and helped her search. 'Are you sure?' She opened another compartment in their bag, pulling out a jar of Bragalian pickles to make more room. They'd stocked up on supplies in both Northbourne and Southbourne, and now carried more than when they'd left the Isle of Salt—that felt like a lifetime ago.

'Well?'

Malora shifted her weight. 'Does it matter? I told you, I'm the daughter of a Laird. This is my sister, Calidra, and her partner, Jisyel. We're travelling together. Would the daughter of a Laird keep the company of someone not permitted in her own country?' Her tone had sharpened, and she lost some of the Porsenthian lilt that had coloured her voice. She was back to being the favoured daughter, and all the power that came with it.

He faltered for a moment and squinted in the sunlight.

'We must've lost them on the boat after the attack! I'm sorry, Cal, I didn't think to look for them after everything that happened!' Jisyel hissed.

'It's fine, Jisyel! Not your fault. I didn't look either.'

He stamped the butt of his spear on the ground. 'I don't care who you are. No papers, no travelling into Bragalia.'

'Really? You're going to impede the travel of nobility?' Malora snapped.

'I'll do more than that, *daughter of a Laird*.' He sneered at her. 'We're at war. Anyone unregistered is to be arrested. There's too much chance of treachery during these uncertain times. Lost souls, spies, and traitors everywhere you look. Unless you want to join these two behind bars, I suggest you get back to your own country so we can deal with them.'

Jisyel marched forward, looking every inch like her grandmother—a woman who had no patience for anything she considered nonsense. 'You can't arrest us! We lost our papers during the Myr's attack! That's hardly our fault.'

'Well it's hardly my fault, either. You got thirty seconds. Otherwise we're putting you in irons.'

One of his colleagues pulled out the iron links from their belt.

As he reached to take one, he hesitated, eyes widening. 'Wait a minute. Tamlin. I *knew* I recognised that name!'

Malora wobbled, as if she wanted to take a step back but caught herself just before she moved.

'You're Apollo Tamlin's wife! *Yes*, Torsten said he had a young daughter too. That's her, ain't it? Hah. You *are* coming with us.' His eye glinted with something akin to malice.

Calidra drew her sword. 'This sword proves we are from Bragalia, that we are the Laird's daughters. That supersedes any other associations.'

'Not as far as the Master Inquisitor is concerned.' He laughed at them, a gruff noise that left him short of breath.

He fingered the shaft of his spear. 'Put that away before you hurt yourself.'

'Cal?' Jisyel whispered, reaching back to grab her hand.

Everything exploded into motion. The broad man swung his spear, sunlight catching the blade. Calidra shouldered Jisyel aside and slapped the spear away with her sword.

He had far more reach with that weapon, so she needed to be aggressive. She stepped forward, twice quickly, into his guard. She didn't want to injure the soldier, certainly not kill any of them—that would only lead to more trouble—but she needed to make it clear they weren't worth the effort of fighting.

She dragged the flat of her blade along the shaft of his spear, and he recoiled. Smashing the sword's pommel against his wrist was all it took for him to drop his weapon.

Calidra backed up towards Jisyel, Malora, and Renys, never taking her eyes off their aggressors, keeping her sword ready in her practised form. With no other weapons between them, they couldn't hope to fight them all and win.

'There is a war going on. The *Myr* are invading, and you're concerned about the wife of a former thief?' Malora spat at them. 'I wonder what Queen Surayo has to say about your conduct!'

The officers advanced, uncaring.

Calidra knew their type. They'd always go for the easy path, the one that would earn them the most money for the least amount of work, rather than the harder one that tackled the real wrongs in the world.

They needed to run. Make a break for the mountain paths.

Bragalia was part of the Porsenthian Empire, but it was governed by its own rules, with a different Laird in charge of each canton. The officers *could* follow them, but they wouldn't if it was too hard.

Renys cowered, clutching onto Malora's legs, too frightened for words.

Calidra gritted her teeth, half-wishing Malora *did* have Chyram's Blessing once again. She shook the thought from her mind almost as soon as she had it.

They didn't need a dragon on their side.

None of them did.

Calidra lowered her sword slightly. 'Step aside. Let us return to Bragalia, and we'll be out of your hair.'

'I'd be inclined to. But not after you trapped the Inquisitors in those trees.' He adjusted his grip on the spear, readying to attack again.

'You need to speak with Alnothen! We've done nothing wrong!' Jisyel tried again.

One officer glanced at the trees at Jisyel's words. His face paled.

A second looked at the same spot. His mouth fell open.

Calidra turned to look and gasped. Shadows darkened the bottoms of trees and plants, like water flowing along the ground. It seeped through the cracks between the trunks, hissing as the tendrils pushed their way out.

She jumped back, pulling Jisyel and Malora with her.

'What in Alnothen's name is *that*?' one of the officers cried.

Calidra knew what those shadows meant. They'd only ever meant one thing. Perhaps Alnothen's response to seal the forest hadn't been anything to do with them after all.

The realisation brought her relief and terror in equal parts. 'Run!'

They bolted, Malora grabbing Renys as they raced past the officers—their spears firmly locked on the encroaching darkness—and towards the border.

Calidra sheathed the sword as she ran, terror driving her onwards. The Myr.

Here.

'Keep running!' Jisyel yelled, urging them onwards.

Calidra glanced over her shoulder. Malora was only a few steps behind her, despite carrying her daughter. Fear and desire to protect gave her more speed than she would have thought possible.

Despite her curse affecting her footing, Jisyel kept up, too. Rocks dotted the path as they approached the border, where grass shifted into the mountain, and Porsenthia became Bragalia. Already, the ground was beginning to slope upwards, every stride taking more effort.

A cry of agony pierced the air.

Calidra didn't want to look. She didn't care about the officers, who'd only wanted to arrest them. Who cared nothing for their plights.

A second cry followed the first. Then a third.

Calidra couldn't ignore it. She stopped, panting heavily, and looked back.

The shadow touched one officer, holding him so high his feet no longer touched the ground. Black veins crept along his flesh as it drained his life.

The remaining soldiers waved their spears, punching into the additional shadows that burst from the Spindle Woods—or purged by Alnothen, more likely—and feasted upon the Porsenthian soldiers.

'Keep going! Don't stop!' Malora hissed as she ran past.

'Cal!' Jisyel hurtled into her, sending them both tumbling to the ground.

Calidra winced at the impact, her sandals slipping on the grass. Jisyel rolled down the incline, back towards the soldiers, the Myr, and the sealed forest.

Rubbing her head where she'd hit the ground hard, Calidra blinked away the water that filled her eyes, bright spots dancing in her vision. As her sight cleared, she saw the remaining soldiers sprinting away, heading north. Three of their colleagues were downed, lying on the ground, very still.

The shadow crawled towards them and Calidra's heart pounded. It wasn't one of the Myr, it was too big for that. It had to be one of their spirits.

She staggered to her feet and drew her sword again. 'Jisyel! Jisyel, get up!'

Jisyel groaned, pushing herself to her hands and knees. She managed to stand up, take a step, then slipped again on the unsteady ground.

Malora appeared in her periphery, one hand outstretched towards Jisyel.

'No, Mal! Get Ren to safety!' Calidra yelled, halting her sister in her tracks.

They locked eyes for a moment, then Malora was gone. There was no time for anything else.

Calidra looked back and flinched.

The shadow hissed, rolling towards Jisyel, clawed limbs churning up the grass and loose soil underneath. It was broad and flat, like some great animal had been squashed until it was a featureless mass. It put on a burst of speed, kicking up dust.

Calidra ran. Everything else disappeared.

'Jisyel!' Calidra cried. Her leg jarred with every step as she sprinted, desperate to cross the distance before the shadow reached Jisyel.

Jisyel's eyes were wide, rolling back in terror, a rabbit just before it was taken by the jaws of a wolf.

Calidra threw the sword mid-stride, using all her momentum to hurl it forwards. The blade careened towards Jisyel like a falcon, whistling in front of her face and blocking the shadow's approach for a heartbeat.

It was enough to snap Jisyel out of her trance. She fumbled to her feet, falling back twice before finally getting away.

The shadow writhed about, as if confused why its prey had moved. Then it lunged after Jisyel.

But Calidra had closed the gap. She skidded to a halt in front of the creature, fury in her eyes that it had dared attack Jisyel. Calidra pulled out her hunting knife, arms held wide to block the shadow's view of Jisyel and keep its attention fixed on herself.

'You. Will. *Not*. Touch. Her!'

The shadow creature made a noise Calidra had never heard before. A low, keening cry that set every hair standing up on end.

It devolved into a low hiss, then it surged towards her.

Calidra only knew darkness.

17
THE OUTPOST
FENN

Fenn had never been so cold before.

Ice filled his lungs with every breath, revitalising him. Pushing away fears and doubts.

The land that stretched before them seemed bleak—dark rock, blue-black and capped with thick layers of ice and snow. It filled the horizon. Even this part of the sea had darkened, looking like black ice as they churned through it.

All of the Lasseen Ocean was Neros. But Fenn couldn't sense her presence here. She was with Selys, wherever that was. Had been for days.

He licked his drying lips, breath misting in front of him as he looked upon the new continent. His fingers tingled with excitement. The Citrine Key was almost within touching distance.

'Finally made it.' Apollo patted him on the back. He'd found more supplies in the bowels of the ship, and they were all dressed as Inquisitors. Fenn was grateful for the gloves and thick cloaks, but he despised having to wear the symbol of the Iron Crown.

It reminded him of Torsten. Of everything that had been taken from him.

Apollo found the whole thing amusing, and paraded about the deck, giving orders and playing the part—evidently healed from his injuries. Nadja laughed, which Fenn found peculiar. He'd thought she'd take offence at the thief insulting everything she stood for.

Their ship listed dangerously to one side, and there had been several moments where Fenn had been sure they'd finish their journey in a rowboat. But luck had been with them, and the ship had completed the arduous journey across the sea.

Apollo appeared beside him, and they both stared over the railing. 'That's Gape Grullon. Hard port, not much happening there, but we can probably rustle up some supplies.'

Fenn gripped the rail tightly. Everything was so close now, nothing else seemed important.

'Good. We'll also have a ship readied for the return trip, so we aren't delayed,' Nadja said.

Fenn flinched. He hadn't realised she'd come up on his other side.

Apollo sighed. 'We need more than that. We gotta be prepared.'

'For what?' asked Nadja.

'For the worst.'

Fenn looked at him, but Apollo's attention was firmly locked on the port ahead, though he held Malora's dagger in his free hand. 'Apollo? I'm…I'm glad you didn't destroy the key.'

'What? Why?' Apollo blinked, eyes coming back into focus.

'Thanks to you, I have a chance to restore my memories and find my family.'

Apollo went quiet.

Nadja scowled. 'Are you so short-sighted, Fenn? Had

Apollo destroyed the key as ordered, the Myr wouldn't have returned to curse you in the first place!'

It was Fenn's turn to quieten. The flame in his chest had been erratic during the crossing. Sometimes he felt Hassen as clearly as if the dragon stood in front of him. Other times, it was like Hassen had hidden amongst weeds and thorns.

He pressed one hand to his chest, but there was no response. Fire flickered deep within, hidden within layers of himself.

Fenn wondered whether Hassen would stay with him once he had his memories back, or if he'd only been interested in his journey. 'I'm not sure I like this,' he whispered, more to himself.

Nadja, however, heard him. 'Because you're doing *something*. You're taking action. That always has consequences.' Though she spoke to Fenn, her gaze drifted back to Apollo.

Fenn shook his head, not trusting himself to respond.

Bells rang within Cape Grullon as their ship came into port, and Fenn let out a shaky breath.

It was time.

FENN DID as he was told, ordered about by both Nadja and the port workers of Cape Grullon.

This was not Porsenthia. There were no Inquisitors marshalling people around demanding papers and scowling down at him, no silver dragon insignia glinting in the pale sun. The sky was thick with grey clouds that threatened snow. Even now, a deep layer of it covered everything, from rooftops to people's hats, and Fenn was glad of the heavy cloak he wore. He could hardly feel his toes inside his boots, and wished Hassen's flame would return to warm him up.

People offered directions, pointed out shops where

various things could be purchased, and Nadja thanked them all with a graceful politeness that never seemed to leave her.

No one even stared at the thief's scar on Apollo's face.

Despite the cold and the discomfort, Fenn found himself smiling. It was *good* here. Better than Porsenthia's stuffy rules and regulations. Even if the cold was uncomfortable and made life difficult, the people were *free*.

He and Apollo followed Nadja as they visited several shops—not stalls like in the Bragalian marketplaces, but solid buildings of wood, each with fires burning in their hearths, bringing a sense of cosiness to each.

The coins here were different to the ones used in Porsenthia, but each vendor gratefully accepted Nadja's money, and she gave Fenn and Apollo several coins each so they could get their own supplies. Soon, they were bundled in thick furs, sturdy boots, and had plenty of long-lasting food packed away. Nadja also treated herself to a small, round iron kettle. 'I must report to Queen Surayo the moment we're successful. I don't have my dagger, so this will have to do. And it's a practical item.' She wrapped it carefully in linen, then added it to her bag of supplies, the fabric bulging. 'Is there anything else we need, Apollo? You're the one who's been here before.'

'Shouldn't we rest? Find a bed for the night?' Apollo suggested, yawning.

Nadja shook her head. 'There's enough light to travel. Every minute we spend waiting is another minute the Myr can press their attack. I'll not wait unless we have no choice.'

Apollo grumbled, but Fenn agreed with her. The sooner they moved, the better.

'Well I need to take care of some business first. Gonna be the last time we have any sort of comfort for a good long while,' Apollo said, disappearing to speak with the shopkeeper.

Fenn and Nadja waited near the front of the shop, staring

out the thick windows to the rest of Gape Grullon and the people bustling around outside, unaware a powerful Myrish artefact lay right on their doorstep.

The people here were all pale-skinned, so pale in some places Fenn half-thought they'd have transparent fingers. It was a far cry to those he'd met in Porsenthia and Bragalia, where most people were brown or bronzed. Of course, everyone here wore many layers, thick furs, and heavy boots, instead of the lightweight sandals in Bragalia. Most kept their heads down, intent on their own business, their breaths fogging the streets.

It took him far too long to feel Nadja staring at him, and Fenn stepped back from the window to look at the Inquisitor. Her eyes were dark brown and calculating, like she always knew what was going on but didn't talk about it. He struggled to hold her gaze for more than a few seconds, and looked away, coughing to cover his embarrassment. 'Everything okay, Nadja?'

She held the silence a while longer, deepening his discomfort. Then, she spoke. 'Fenn. Back in Westbrook, Apollo asked if I minded whether you travelled with us. As someone blessed by a dragon spirit, your strength is certainly useful. You might also be able to help when we encounter Paragos. But I *must* state that our goal is to destroy the key when we find it. There is nothing else more important. I hope you understand this.'

Fenn nodded. 'Of course I understand. And I would not stand in your way to do that.' He felt his ears redden, and was glad of the hat that covered them.

She cocked her head, eying him like a hawk, waiting for him to continue.

He licked his lips again, annoyed by their dryness. This was a conversation Selys had tried to have with him, and it hadn't gone well. He'd hoped that would be the end of it, but Nadja wasn't an Inquisitor for nothing. He hadn't had a chance to be alone with her to endure any of her questioning. But they were so close to the key now, he had to make his goals clear. Had to *make* her understand. 'I…I just need to use the key first.'

She recoiled. 'Excuse me?'

'That sounded worse than I meant. I…I *am* one of the lost souls Torsten was hunting down. The Myr cursed me somehow—I don't remember when or what they did to me. But this key will restore my memories. Once I have those back, once I know where I come from and where my family is, I'll be able to find them again. Then you can destroy the key.'

Nadja recovered quickly, and loomed over him. 'Fenn. You would *dare* stand in the way of the Iron Crown?'

Her words ignited the fire in his chest. It surged, bright and painful. '*You* would stand in the way of one blessed by a dragon spirit?'

She glared at him and slowly shook her head.

For the first time, Fenn realised the power he had running through his veins. Skilled and experienced as Nadja might have been, she could not hope to stand against Hassen if they came to blows. And if they wanted the best chance of crossing Paragos, they needed his help.

He had leverage. For the first time since the Isle of Salt.

'Fenn. Only Paragos can destroy this key. Or, I suppose one of the other two Archons, but they roam Tassar as they please. Paragos at least remains in one location. We'll feed the key to him, stop the Myr's resurgence, and I'll hear no more about it.'

Fenn glowered. How dare she stop him. How dare she know his plight, his loss, and dictate what he may or may not do. 'I will find myself. I *will* have my family back.'

'I'll not fight you, Fenn. Much like Apollo, your family does not matter if they are dead. This is the only way to prevent that. If you cannot see what we're working towards,

I cannot help you.' Her voice had dropped to a whisper, every bit as dangerous as if she'd drawn a sword and held it at his throat.

Dizziness wracked him. The fire in his chest flickered and disappeared, and he clutched the front of his cloak, fighting not to drop to his knees at the sudden chill that flooded his body.

'Fenn?' Nadja grabbed him by the shoulder, steadying him.

The fire returned a moment later and settled, burning in the background like an oil lamp. Fenn panted, wiping sweat from his brow. He had no idea where that outburst had come from or what was going on with his body, but the voice in his mind remained stubbornly silent.

Probably another of Hassen's tricks, just to make sure Fenn never forgot about the dragon.

He backed up, waving away Nadja's hand. 'I'm fine. It—it's fine.'

He sank onto the wooden bench pushed against the back of the shop, grateful to sit down and warm himself by the roaring hearth. If Apollo was right, they were in for a hard trek. Better to sit and rest while they had the chance—it wouldn't be long before Apollo returned and Nadja would force them towards Paragos.

As he caught his breath, he wondered whether he was doing the right thing. It was the first time he'd had a real doubt—even a tiny sliver of it—flashing at the edge of his resolve.

The fire in his chest flickered.

He pushed the doubt away.

Ignored Selys's voice in the back of his mind. Ignored what Nadja had just told him.

'Are you sure you're okay, Fenn?' Nadja sat down beside him, all emotions gone from her face save mild concern.

He nodded, not trusting his voice. Not trusting what he

felt. He didn't know if he was okay. The only thing he could do was push himself along the path he'd set himself.

Without that, he'd crumble.

The door to the shop opened and he glanced up as the small bell chimed. He winced. They'd only just sat down. If Apollo was back already—

It wasn't Apollo. Just another man wrapped in furs. This one had a red beard thicker than all the hair on Fenn's head, and he wore a heavy, oversized hat that covered both cheeks. He glanced at them briefly, then spoke to the vendor.

Fenn let out a breath and rubbed his forehead. He was falling apart, and they hadn't set foot in Paragos's domain yet. He was sure Hassen constantly laughed at him.

'...Fenn?'

Fenn glanced up at the sound of his name. Nadja hadn't spoken, and Apollo wasn't back yet.

'Is it really you? Fenn Ottan?' The man with the red beard stared at him like he had two heads, blue eyes twinkling with tears in the reflected fire light.

Nadja looked between Fenn and the man, one hand resting on the hilt of her sword.

'What? You...you know my name?' Fenn stood up, knees trembling. He wasn't entirely sure his legs could bear his own weight.

'I don't believe it! It *is* you! Paragos must finally be blessing us after all the bad luck! Spirits take me, I really thought we were going to be destroyed by all the corruption. There's hope for Ma-Rai yet!' Delight lit up the man's face and he crossed the shop to clasp Fenn's hands in his own. 'Thought you were for the spirit world, my friend. Look at you! Here! *Alive*!' He patted Fenn's body, as if making certain Fenn was truly there and not a figment of his imagination.

Fenn's mouth was too dry to say anything. He glanced at Nadja, lost.

She watched the interaction with the same cool, calculated gaze as always, though her lips turned up faintly at the corners in the beginnings of a smile.

The man stood back, still holding onto Fenn's shoulders, and beamed. His grip was warm even through his thick gloves. 'Perhaps now we'll have Evarine returned to us too.'

Fenn's chest and mind whirled, a cacophony of thoughts and fire and shadow, light and pain that pierced his head. He didn't realise he was crying until he felt the wetness on his cheeks.

Out of the whirling, spinning, confusing mass of darkness that threatened to smother him, a few words drifted into focus, barely more than a whisper. *'Betrayal. Tricks. Corruption.'*

tired gaze at always, though her lips turned up firmly at the corners in the beginnings of a smile.

The man stood back, still holding onto Ivan's shoulders, and beamed. His grip was warm even through his thick gloves. 'Perhaps now we'll have Eternal returned to us now.'

Ivan's chest and mind warmed, a cacophony of thoughts and fire and shadow, light and so much that he bowed his head. He didn't realise he was crying until he felt the wetness on his cheeks.

Out of the whirling, spinning, confusing mass of darkness that threatened to smother him, a few words rose and took form. Barely more than a whisper. *Relief. Just* [illegible]

PART II

Iron spirit, slave no more,
Break the immortal chain.
Eternal bond torn asunder,
Release from smothered pain.

Rotted darkness rise anew,
Sever bond and free domain.
The dragon's might cut away,
An ending cometh to your reign.

18
THE TAINT
APOLLO

Apollo had always found the deepest, most groundbreaking thoughts came to him whilst emptying his bowels. After all, there was nothing to do but sit, think, and wait for nature to take its course.

Having a half-frozen arse didn't help, but he would always take what quiet times he could get.

He could hardly believe he was back here. The frigid wasteland haunted his nightmares, when he remembered them. More recently, Torsten's torture of him with Nestol had taken over.

Of course, Nadja was responsible for dragging him here, the damned woman. She'd forced him up when he'd wanted to wallow, and all his old memories, fears, and wishes flooded back.

Paragos would kill him the moment he saw him. There was no question of that.

He was only here as a guide. He could point out the way to the Moonlight Palace, where the Citrine Key rested, and be done with it. Nadja and that half-crazed Fenn could go on their suicide mission if they wanted.

He'd done it once already, and had no desire to attempt it a second time.

And after escaping from Torsten's clutches, he wasn't going to allow a dragon to best him.

Nadja had already booked a return ship to Porsenthia. What was to stop him ducking away after pointing out the route, and sailing back? He had no idea where Mal and Ren were, but at least he'd be on the right bloody continent.

After all, it was easy to disappear in a blizzard.

FENN AND NADJA waited for him in the street outside the shop, a small crowd gathered around them.

Apollo hesitated, unsure whether he was about to walk into some trouble. He didn't remember much about the people here, save their hardiness to live on the fringes of a blizzard, where the ground was so cold and hard you could hardly grow anything. People like that often fought well. They didn't seem to feel as much pain as everyone else.

He lingered by the corner of the shop—the wood painted a striking red to be more easily seen during white-outs—and observed.

A tall man with a beard the colour of rust was talking animatedly to Fenn, though Apollo was too far away to make out distinct words. He didn't seem to be threatening, though Apollo thought it likely a punch from one of the guy's meaty fists would have him knocked out for half a day.

Nadja, however, stood as casually as the Inquisitor was able to stand. Arms folded—not on her sword—was the best sign there was no danger here. She laughed once.

Apollo's eyebrows rose at that.

With nothing to scare him off, and curious as always, he approached them, boots crunching in the snow that covered every street. 'What I miss?'

Fenn swivelled round, emotions warring on his face. Confusion seemed to dominate more than anything else, so Apollo patted him gently on the shoulder. 'You all right, Fenn?'

He didn't reply.

The russet-haired man stepped forward. 'All right? He's *alive*! I'm trying to come to terms with that! I remember when you helped move all my carrots indoors when I broke my leg. Remember that, Fenn? I couldn't walk and you were out there all day to make sure I didn't starve.'

Apollo glanced at him. 'You…know Fenn?'

'Lived next door to him for the past eight years! He helped build my house!'

'That right?' Apollo leaned back, surveying the situation. Fenn's demeanour didn't change, which was more concerning than curious. 'I'm Apollo.' He pulled one hand from the warmth of his pocket and held it out.

'Sanis.'

'This reunion is wonderful, of course, but we do have somewhere to be. Apollo?' Nadja began to walk away.

'You can't be leaving now?' Sanis said, his face falling. 'You've…you've only just got here!'

Fenn backed away, his gaze darting from Sanis to the distant mountains. 'I…I should…'

'You look like you've been to the spirit world and back, Fenn. Storm is coming in, too! Stay a while, eat, be comfortable!'

'I'm sorry, but we're on business of the Iron Crown. Fenn, you may of course stay with your kin, but Apollo and I must continue.'

'Where are you going in such a hurry?' Sanis asked.

'Date with Paragos.' Apollo let out a low whistle, wondering how Nadja would respond.

She halted in place. 'It is *confidential*, but of the greatest importance. Time is of the essence.'

Apollo grinned at her tone but didn't antagonise further.

Sanis shook his head. 'I don't know why you'd want to see Paragos, but it's a fair trek from here. You'd go past Ma-Rai, anyway. That's where we're from,' he gestured to himself and Fenn, 'Manori might be in a foul mood though. So you should travel with me. I have a carriage. Be faster than walking, too.'

'Manori?' Nadja asked.

'The spirit of the river here. He's...well, there's been a lot of corruption seeping into the land over the past few years. He makes travel...difficult. Even for such *important* envoys of Porsenthia.'

Apollo grinned at the sarcasm in Sanis's voice. He quite liked the man. 'That's generous of you, Sanis! Isn't that right, Nadja?'

She didn't bother to hide her scowl. 'Fine. As long as we get moving *now*.'

Sanis nodded, shifting the packages he carried under one arm and striding over to a small carriage beside a snowdrift. Two heavy draft horses waited patiently for him, and he loaded up quickly. 'Come up. Fenn, you have to tell me everything about what happened! We all thought you were lost.'

Apollo winked at Nadja. She might not have wanted to deal with Sanis, but now they didn't have to walk and their travel would be much quicker. 'After you, dear Inquisitor.' He bowed.

'I'm glad you're in such a good mood. Corrupted spirits are a problem, Apollo.'

The grin slipped from his face at her words. He recovered quickly, clambering up after Fenn and Nadja had seated themselves inside. It was cramped but comfortable, with well-worn seats that felt like they were stuffed with feathers. Perhaps if he ingratiated himself with Sanis, it would be another way off the continent.

It was always a good idea to make friends wherever the opportunity struck.

As Apollo settled in for the journey, Fenn caught his attention again. The lad seemed to have no recollection of Sanis, despite the other man being very familiar with him. Instead of excitement, Apollo saw doubt on Fenn's face. Fenn frowned more often than not, and replied with short, one-word answers.

Sanis didn't seem bothered by it, or he didn't notice, because he continued to talk and chatter away as if Fenn was a great conversationalist.

He looked at Nadja, and found she was watching Fenn, too.

Apollo felt sorry for him, just like he felt bad for all the other lost souls that had popped up in Porsenthia and Bragalia. He'd help anyone who needed it. Even if it wasn't in his power to do so, he had to try.

Nadja had blamed him for the lost soul who'd died outside Toriaken's shrine.

Guilt gnawed at him. At the possibility he was to blame for Fenn, too.

He grimaced. If he had any chance of getting back to Malora and Renys, he had to survive a few more dragon spirits.

❄

Fire in a land of snow would ordinarily bring welcome relief. Apollo held his joy back at the sight of it now. Fire meant dragons. And Sanis had warned them about Manori—a spirit slipping into corruption.

Of course, they had to follow the river from Gape Grullon to Ma-Rai, and then into the mountains Paragos reigned over.

There were no real seasons on this continent. It was

either cold or slightly less cold. Apparently, it was the less-cold season, and instead of being frozen solid, the river water gushed like a fountain. Chunks of ice floated atop the water, disappearing now and then with a deep splash that made him jump the first few times he heard it.

After hours of travel, Apollo hardly noticed it anymore.

A plume of fire was a different story, however, and he snapped to attention the moment he saw the colour.

Nadja, too, was awake and alert, scanning their surroundings for the cause of the flame.

'Careful. Manori's watching,' Sanis said. He slowed the horses, turning the constant rumble of the carriage into a bone-jarring stutter.

Apollo winced as the wheels rocked, wishing he had a thicker cushion to soften the bumps.

Out of the two windows either side of the carriage, the white landscape hardly seemed to shift. Save the gentle ebb and flow of the land and the occasional lone tree, there wasn't much to see aside from the river. It meandered gently, wide enough to make crossing difficult, but not as strong as the river that flowed from Toriaken's Shrine down to Eastbrook.

Something dark filled the window, then it was gone.

Sanis stopped the carriage, horses whickering nervously.

'What's going on? Why did we stop?' Fenn asked, his knuckles bone white.

'Better to let Manori pass. He doesn't see us anymore, not really. Better we blend in.'

'How does a horse-drawn carriage blend in with the snow?' Apollo asked, fear snaking through his guts.

'It's the movement he focuses on. He kills most things that move, and burns a lot of the rest.'

'That's reassuring.'

'Apollo. Quiet,' Nadja ordered. She'd drawn her sword, for all the good it would do against a dragon spirit.

Apollo hated being trapped in the carriage. What had for hours been a comfortable size suddenly seemed far too small. True, they couldn't be seen *through* the wooden walls and roof, but *he* couldn't see out either, and that set his nerves on edge. It reminded him of being trapped in his own mind, Nestol seeping through his memories and thoughts. Apollo shuddered, trying to rid himself of the crawling sensation on his skin.

He shifted, looking out the narrow windows on either side, scanning for movement, for signs the dragon had spotted them. But it was getting dark, and alongside a gentle snowfall, he wouldn't be able to see two steps from the carriage, let alone a dragon.

He held his breath.

More movement. Dark wings thrumming as something reptilian soared through the air, only to disappear into the river without so much as a splash.

Even the horses no longer whickered.

His heart pounded, every beat painful.

'Manori is gone.' Sanis gently urged the horses onwards, though they went at a faster pace than they had earlier.

Apollo let out a shuddering breath. 'Fucking hate dragons.'

'We'll be at Ma-Rai soon enough. Manori hasn't visited the town in a few months. Should be able to breathe easy then,' Sanis chuckled.

Apollo wasn't reassured.

MA-RAI WAS much as Apollo remembered it. Aside from the town being half the size it had been five years ago.

'Manori hurt us pretty bad earlier this year. Still recovering. Not enough of us to rebuild quickly, though I suppose the smaller we are, the less likely it is Manori will attack again.' Sanis stood beside his carriage, hands on his hips as he looked down at the small town nestled against a copse of trees, likely too small for any spirit to form.

It had taken a day and a half to reach Ma-Rai, and much of that had passed in a cold, dark blur, Apollo looking out the window for a corrupted dragon spirit every waking moment.

'Why'd Manori turn?' Apollo asked.

Sanis shrugged. 'Rot gets in 'em, I suppose. Or we didn't offer enough tithes. Didn't respect the river enough. Who knows. Sometimes they go bad, don't they? Or you not have corrupted spirits where you're from? Guess not, didn't your queen put a stop to all that?'

'It isn't unheard of. Very uncommon though,' Nadja replied, thoughtful.

Apollo did not allow himself to look at her while she spoke, his focus instead on what was left of the town. The buildings nearest the river bank were all missing—Apollo remembered having to squeeze against a wall to get past—now the gap was wide enough for ten or twelve carriages to ride abreast.

A small herd of large goats—or sheep, Apollo hadn't been great at telling them apart—with thick, woollen fur grazed nearby, digging up the snow with their cloven feet to find fresh shoots.

Fenn stared at the town he was purported to be from, his mouth hanging open, lost as a lamb.

'Welcome back Fenn.' Sanis threw an arm around Fenn's shoulders, his laughter loud and booming in the crisp air. 'I need to get the horses inside and rested up. Come by before you head off, and I'll make sure you have a hot meal. Just wait till I tell everyone!' Sanis strode down the incline, horses and carriage following. His laughter echoed long after he disappeared from view.

Smoke rose from many of the chimneys, and the streets had been mostly cleared of snow. People walked to and fro, much like in Gape Grullon, but without the fervour of the port. This was a gentler life.

'Fenn, this is your home. You don't need the key now, do you? You've found what you've been looking for,' Nadja said.

Fenn's hands trembled. 'It…it could be a trick. If the dragon spirit here is corrupted, the people could be, too. They're not…they're not to be…trusted.' He spoke haltingly, as if he didn't know whether or not to believe what he said.

Malora had told Apollo that Chyram spoke to her, in her mind, when she'd been bonded with the spirit. It had been something she'd simply grown used to during her years blessed by him. Fenn, no doubt, had Hassen's voice whispering in his ear, too.

Apollo's heart went out to the young man. Fenn didn't know a good thing when he had it. 'We need to pass by the town to reach the mountains. Why don't you have a nose about? See if you remember anything?'

'No! The only way my memories will come back is with the key! I could stare at my own mother in the face and not know who she was!' Fenn snapped, hands balled into fists.

Apollo took it in his stride. 'We could all do with a hot meal. Why don't we take Sanis up on his offer? Fenn, you don't have to stay here if you don't want to. But it might be best if you do.'

'I'm going after the key.' Fenn's voice dropped as he stared at the town, his eyes welling up at the sight. 'It's the only way. The *only* way…'

Apollo and Nadja shared a glance.

'If Manori comes back, we'll be in trouble. We have food already from Gape Grullon. If we ration it, we'll have plenty to get us to the key and back. Fenn, I can't stop you coming with us,' Nadja said, pulling up the fur-lined hood tightly round her face. 'But that key is going to be destroyed. You'll have to deal with that, so you should probably stay here and rekindle the friendships you have. Sanis didn't seem to mind your memory loss.'

'It doesn't matter if I don't remember!' Fenn shouted, his voice shaking.

'Fenn. Calm down,' Apollo used the same tone of voice when Renys was on the verge of a tantrum. 'We don't even have the key yet, and there's no guarantee we will.'

The trio turned away from Ma-Rai, their sights set on the mountains instead. As they began their slow trudge through the snowdrifts, the heavy clouds overhead released their bounty.

Fat snowflakes drifted down on the gentle breeze. They were pretty at first, melting quickly wherever they landed on Apollo's skin. Ahead, across the dark mountains, the blizzard swept in from the east.

Apollo shoved his nose into the fur lining his hood.

Paragos awaited.

19
THE BETRAYER
SELYS

Selys couldn't wipe the smile from her face.

Kaio hadn't changed in three years. He'd always hungered for a fight, whether one came or not. Taran looked to have grown up, but those quick eyes of his were the same as they'd always been. Esto, with her shrewd judgement and cunning, and Ruka, who was the softest touch in the warband, were all hallmarks of home. Family.

When she looked at Kaio, she realised she saw a bit of him in Fenn. That same youthful look, the same determination and naivety. She'd replaced her brother with Fenn without really noticing it—had found someone to guide and advise. Strange, how she'd always slipped into that role of older sister looking out for someone.

They all stared at her, many with suspicion.

Already, the lingering warmth of the Segandis heat was welcome, familiar. She'd missed her home more than she'd cared to give words to. Whatever changes had occurred while she'd been away did not matter.

Joy filled her heart.

She'd stumbled upon her kin in the middle of funeral

celebrations. She'd grown so used to Porsenthian rites—especially by the priests and priestesses of Neros—that it took her a good few seconds to recognise those in Bragalia. Several large platters of food had been grilled and laid out, people helping themselves to large chunks of meat, fruit, and vegetables. The marinade permeated the air and made her salivate.

But the true indicator of the funeral was the thick, sticky drink that toasted the passing of life. Served in brass cups brought out only for the occasion, she knew her timing was not the best.

Selys wasn't so brazen she'd take a cup and toast whomever had departed, but not drinking was a sign of disrespect—something she had no desire to bring to her brother and those of the Ioran warband. So she stepped into the circle, fire crackling around her, eyes following her every movement, until she stood before her brother.

He sat upon a wooden chair on a raised dais. Not quite a throne, but it might as well have been. Their oldest brother, Skaru, had sat there once. It was peculiar to see Kaio take that seat. It was too big for him, the wood seeming to swallow him up. But he sat on the chair as if he owned it, and that confidence kept him there, she had no doubt.

'Brother.' Selys knelt, her glaive held to the side, tip pointing down. Kneeling was a formal gesture, one rarely seen in Segandis, but pride was a delicate thing. Better to err on the side of caution than risk upsetting him.

When she stood, she found Kaio staring at her, disbelief in his narrowed eyes.

'May I drink?' Selys asked, gesturing to the barrel to her side, where several empty cups and two bottles sat waiting.

He inclined his head, the gesture subtle.

Selys took a cup, and filled it halfway. She raised it to him, another mark of respect, then drank, the familiar tastes awakening long-lost memories of Segandis.

Once people saw Kaio hadn't responded negatively to Selys's arrival, they continued with the wake—dancing and drinking, eating and playing music.

Selys took a breath to strengthen her resolve, then approached the dais. 'You look well?'

Kaio frowned at her. His gaze darted to the glaive she'd left on the sand. 'Why have you come back?'

'Do I need a reason to visit? Segandis is my home.'

'You haven't *visited* since the accident.' Every word he spoke was clipped. 'Since you left.'

'I grieved.'

'So did I. You should have been here.'

Selys turned away, didn't want him to see the hurt on her face. 'I *couldn't* stay here, surrounded by death and memories of loss. Can you blame me for that?'

'I *do* blame you for that!' Kaio straightened in his chair. 'You left me!'

'You're not a child Kaio. You might have been the youngest of us, but you're part of the Ioran family. You have all of our blood. What are you if not a survivor?'

Kaio's rage simmered and he took another sip from the cup he cradled in one hand. 'So why now? Done grieving? Done playing at priestess?' He eyed the tattoo along her left arm. 'I can burn that off.'

Selys rescinded all the warmth she'd offered, her tone cooling. 'The mark stays. I am blessed.'

Kaio, who had been drinking, sputtered at the revelation. 'You're *what*?' His words were so sharp that several people nearby looked up.

Selys knew what she had to say would hurt him more than any weapon could, more than any perceived abandonment. But she lived her own truth, and she would be honest with her brother. 'Yes. Neros has bonded with me.'

The cup fell from Kaio's hand, deep red liquid staining the wooden dais where it spilled.

Selys held his attention, unflinching.

Kaio's mouth worked, a few choked noises sputtering out. 'Y—You're lying.'

'Why would I?'

Kaio was on his feet a moment later. 'You mean to tell me that the foul creature who ripped apart our fleet, who killed our parents, our siblings, chose to bond with you?'

Selys nodded.

'And you *allowed* it?' Kaio's entire body shook. 'That *filth* is inside you? Listening to your thoughts? And you brought it back *here*?'

Others gathered around the dais, whispering.

Selys weathered their stares, her cheeks flushing. She needed to atone for her part in her family's savagery. For their disrespect towards the dragon spirits. And she needed to atone for leaving Kaio to shoulder the burden of ruling alone. 'I may have Neros, but I am still your sister.' She reached for him.

Kaio slapped her hand away, the strike stinging her skin. 'My sisters died in Neros's storm. My brothers and parents, too.'

Cold fury welled in her chest, driven by hurt. She hadn't wanted to leave him to manage the warband, of course not. But she hadn't been able to stay. She'd needed to get away, for her own well-being. Explaining that to Kaio would be futile, especially given his already fiery reaction to her return.

Much as she was desperate for him to understand—and if not understand, just *acknowledge* her hurt and accept how she had dealt with it—he was Kaio. And Kaio would not listen, not when he was like this.

She didn't reply immediately, instead focussing on her breathing so she wouldn't say something she came to regret. Something Kaio knew very little about. 'It's good to see you, Kaio. I'm glad you're well.'

Something went out of Kaio's eyes at that. He'd been gearing for a fight, had insulted her, expecting a retaliation. And she hadn't given it to him.

In the face of flat kindness, he didn't know how to react. Kaio stuttered, wobbling slightly like he was on board a ship during a storm. 'Drink…drink's getting to me,' he muttered darkly.

Selys allowed herself a smile. Whatever anger had taken over his heart, pushed him on, her baby brother was still somewhere deep inside. It gave her hope.

Kaio wobbled again, then grabbed the back of his chair to hold himself upright. 'I'm…I'm going…to bed.'

His eyes were red. Selys didn't know if it was a trick of the firelight or true. In spite of his vitriol, her heart went out to him. Just as it went out to their family who were no longer there.

Taran immediately stepped up, looping one of Kaio's arms around his shoulders. He gave her what could be described as an apologetic look, but that could easily have been a trick of the fire, too. Without a backwards glance, Taran supported Kaio down the dais and across the sand.

Many eyes returned to her, and whispers broke out.

With her brother gone, Selys could finally take in what was left of her crew. The fighters and sailors who'd been with her on countless voyages, whose lives she'd saved, and who had saved hers.

'Yaniv! How are you? How is Syras?' Selys leapt from the dais and was half-pulled into an embrace by more than a dozen hands.

'Selys!'

'I thought we'd never see you again!'

'Cleah said you were dead! I never believed them! Never!'

'The Ioran warband has hope again!'

If Selys had been close to tears before, they spilled over now, her cheeks stinging with a different kind of salt. Mixed with smoke from the numerous fires, it stung. She wiped her face, but more tears trickled down.

She'd left Segandis to grieve her heart being torn out. To cope with the unending, unyielding sorrow that threatened to swallow her up. She'd found a new purpose in the shrine, not that Kaio understood.

Neros had taken everything from her. And Neros would give her new life.

That was the idea that had driven her.

Then Fenn had appeared, and she'd learned of the Myr's resurgence. Verkata's storm had brought her role into sharp relief, and she'd realised she was running from her past. Searching for a peace that didn't exist.

Neros had bonded with her for a reason. Wanted her to act on the dragon's behalf.

And it had also returned her to her brother, the last of her blood family. She would fulfil Neros's wishes and gain the redemption she sought.

If she could turn Kaio away from his path of fury, he could be the greatest Ioran chief Segandis had ever known.

Another cup was pushed into her hands, so full the red liquid sloshing around spilled over the sides. Her mood turned sombre. 'Who was it?'

Yaniv was thinner than she remembered, but based on the strength of his hug, he was no worse for it. 'Tesso. One of the younger dock workers—wanted to apprentice under Taran. Another warband thought Kaio was vulnerable. Guess he was right.'

Selys did not miss the implication in those words.

Yaniv clicked his tongue. 'Fool boy makes fool decisions. Manages to keep his head above water, though. Just.'

'Fool decisions? Like what?'

'Picking up some castaway!' Another voice piped in—Jana, one of the younger members of the crew, she'd been little more than a child when Selys had left.

'Since when do we pick up castaways?' Selys couldn't fathom why Kaio would do such a thing.

'Dunno. She ain't from Bragalia or Olmir. Or even Porsenthia!' Jana said, taking another drink from her own cup. Given the heavy pink tinge to her eyes, she'd had at least two cups too many.

Her words gave Selys pause. 'She's from another continent? How did she get here?'

'One of her many mysteries,' Yaniv said with a snort.

Neros's flame in her chest surged and Selys's mind whirred. 'I should like to meet this castaway.'

'Her name's Evarine. Ruka's been keeping an eye on her. Been through some shit to do with the Myr. Kaio thinks she's important for something. I say just dump her in town and be done with her. We ain't a shrine.' Yaniv seemed to catch himself and stammered. 'N—Not that I mean anything *bad* by that, Selys, you understand. We just…we keep to our own, you know that.'

Already, Selys wondered why she had returned home now, of all times. She could have returned at any point in the last few years. She'd never felt that pull. Not until Neros blessed her. Not until Verkata reminded her of her sins and the sins of her family.

After she'd met a young man from a distant land who'd had a brush with the Myr.

'I understand,' Selys murmured, already walking away from the beach.

She needed to rest, and she needed to think. She rested her hand against her chest, where the flames of Neros filled her to the point she never thought she'd be cold again. She only heard flashes of the dragon spirit's voice, her power so enormous she could hardly bear it. So many of the dragon's instructions came in feelings and emotions.

But the spirit's voice, for once, was clear.

'You owe us.'

Whatever peace Selys chased once again seemed just out of reach.

20
THE DARKNESS
CALIDRA

Wind rushed around Calidra's face, stinging like a thousand pincers. She grimaced, pulling away from the pain, but something held her rooted in one spot.

With great effort, she opened her eyes. Her vision was blurry, eyes watering, and she blinked furiously to try and bring what she could see into focus.

But it didn't make sense.

Trying to wipe her eyes, Calidra grasped at the darkness smothering her.

Then she realised she had no hands.

No body.

No physical form.

Panic welled, fierce and biting.

She was lost in a sea of darkness and shadow. It filled her sight and mind in all directions, unrelenting pressure squeezing her awareness. The gusting wind that blasted around her was overwhelming, and she fought to be free of its grip. She wanted to cry, to call out for Jisyel. Malora. Renys.

Even the damned Porsenthian officers!

Anything but this darkness, this void of life and light.

'You are on the edge.' A cold voice cut through the darkness, and she halted her thrashing to listen.

'The edge of what?' Where her voice came from, she didn't know. The pressure that had been squeezing her dissipated, and she tried to move. It was difficult, without a body, sense of direction, or vision, but she fought all the same.

Jisyel was waiting. Malora and Renys, too. They *needed* her.

And she needed them.

'The edge of the spirit world.'

More panic flooded her. She became aware of her limbs. Her feet found something solid, and she kicked off it. She had to run. Had to get away. If that voice spoke true, the Myr had caught her, and was sucking the life from her body.

That *couldn't* happen.

'Dragons have caused you much pain. Why do you worship them?'

If Calidra could have scowled, she would have. 'I don't worship them!'

Something shifted in the darkness. A faint light appeared, turning pitch black into deepest grey. The movement was something she could focus on, so Calidra forced her way towards it.

'Why do you care for them?' The voice asked again, flat and monotone.

'I don't!' She was getting angry now. Good. Anger pushed her, drove her to get away. 'The Myr are attacking. I have to get to Jisyel!'

'We can stop the pain you feel from the dragons.'

Calidra hesitated for a moment, then dismissed it. 'I don't feel any pain.'

'Jisyel does. She suffers at the touch of a dragon's curse. Your sister suffers. You suffer.'

Calidra stopped fighting. 'Who are you?'

'Your dragons are worshipped as gods. You seek their strength to protect yourselves. But they see you as nothing but ants to be played with. Toyed with. And crushed when you no longer serve any purpose.'

Calidra pushed away again. She didn't know what this thing was, but she had a good idea. The attack. The darkness. The hatred towards dragons. 'Get away from me, you Myrish scum!'

Laughter, cold and grating, filled her ears. It echoed over and over, every reverberation louder than the one before. *'We can help you.'*

Calidra didn't entertain that ludicrous suggestion with a response. She wished she had her knife. Malora's sword. Anything to keep the oily touch of the Myr away from her.

The Myr tried again. *'Don't you want revenge for what they have done to you? Hassen. Alnothen. Forest spirits who have hurt you. Hurt your loved ones. Dragons who will never face justice.'*

Calidra admitted the thought of getting back at those spirits appealed. But it was the way of the world. Jisyel's curse *would* be lifted eventually, even if it took another dragon to do it.

'More than hurting those dragons...You would have strength. You could change the world as you see fit.'

'What makes you think I want that?' She continued looking for a way out of this bad dream. Light filtered in strange places, turning parts of her surroundings pale grey. Other parts of the void seemed to grow darker, deepening into pitch black. Something pushed her towards it, a gentle pressure on her back.

But she ignored that. She had been told what to do all her life. This Myr was not going to win.

'You are pawns in this world. Your life means nothing. The mark you leave upon Tassar will be forgotten in a generation. Your life is futile, a meaningless struggle while you try to survive, and

dragons use you as they wish. You do not want to stop that? To give your life purpose? To fight back against those who would hurt you? Use you? Demand reverence and give back naught in return?'

Calidra laughed. 'And you don't want anything in return either?'

'We would see the dragons destroyed. Their wrath smothered. Break the immortal chain. We would see their might cut away. Create new law.'

Calidra saw her hands now, balled into fists as she stumbled through the darkness. Goosebumps rose on her flesh as the creature spoke. As long as it was speaking, it wasn't hurting her.

The words sent chills along every bone in her body. 'They are givers of life.'

'And you must obey them. Would you not take our strength? Build a world you wish for. Where you are powerful and they are powerless.' It spat the last word, such venom in its tone that it made Calidra shudder.

Perhaps when she had been younger, she would have seen the glory in those words.

When she had nothing, could go nowhere, and everyone had turned against her. She would have wished her mother and the dragons were powerless.

Even now, some part of her *wanted* to take that strength. She wouldn't have to deal with checkpoint officers, Queen Surayo's Inquisitors, or worry about any dragon's sense of humour.

She could remove Jisyel's curse, instead of hoping for the charity and good will of others.

'One touch and that power is yours. That strength can never be taken from you. And it will destroy your enemies.'

Something cold followed her steps—a wraith of ice, its breath promising frostbite.

'Help us cripple the dragons. Neither you or we will be beholden to them any longer.'

'Hurt the dragon spirits?' It was ludicrous.

'We have artefacts. Magic powerful enough to sever the bond between the iron dragon and your queen. Cripple it. Such power could be in your hands.' The Myr reached towards her, icy claws cutting through the dark.

Calidra ran. It could not touch her.

She would not let it.

She daren't lash out. Daren't look back.

Calidra gulped down great lungfuls of air, fought against the pressure holding her, and ran towards the light.

CALIDRA SCREAMED.

'Cal! Cal, it's okay!' Jisyel held her as she sat up.

Calidra's breaths came in short, sharp bursts. Sweat dripped down her forehead, neck, chest. Her skin itched—burned—and she dragged her nails down her arms. 'Like insects! Crawling all over me!'

'What? There's nothing there, Cal! You're dreaming!' Jisyel said, leaning back slightly to check her over.

Calidra's breathing quickened even more. She couldn't stop it. Couldn't stop the tightness in her chest, like a fist of ice clutched her heart. The Myr had caught her! The Myr had caught her and now she was going to die!

'Cal, look at me. Cal!' Jisyel shuffled in front of Calidra, keeping both hands on her shoulders. 'Calidra. I'm here. I'm *right* here.' She squeezed her shoulders forcefully. 'Look at me. Breathe with me.'

Calidra heard Jisyel's voice, distant, as though she stood at the far end of a long tunnel. It was dark around them, but a rich, blue darkness of night. Pinpricks of light shimmered far overhead.

Stars?

She wasn't in that freezing void anymore. Was she?

'Cal, breathe with me.'

Pressure on her shoulders. Calidra wanted to tear her gaze from the sky, but she couldn't move her head. She counted the stars. One, two, three, four, five.

'Calidra. Please. Look at me,' Jisyel said.

Calidra lost track of her numbers. Spotted the broken moon just above the horizon as she slowly dragged her gaze down. Her breathing was so rapid it hurt. Tears fell freely down her cheeks, mixing with the snot dribbling from her nose. She wanted to wipe her face, but she couldn't. She couldn't. She *couldn't.*

Where was the Myr? Was it inside her? Was it outside? Dragons above, had it killed her? And Jisyel?

'Breathe in. With me.' Jisyel's voice was an anchor.

Calidra managed to turn her attention to Jisyel. She trembled, every muscle in her body shaking where she sat. But Jisyel was *there*. Solid and real and breathing.

'Breathe out. Come on, Calidra.' Another squeeze of the shoulder. It pinched.

Calidra couldn't stop hyperventilating. Couldn't stop the tears. Her hands were fists, nails digging into her skin, piercing her palms. The pain was horrible. She wanted to stop.

But that pain was another anchor.

'Breathe in. Breathe out. With me, Cal. I'm here. I'm here for you.'

Calidra nodded, a frantic movement. She had to show Jisyel she was there. That she understood.

Jisyel squeezed her shoulders with each breath in, then released.

Calidra closed her eyes, head lolling forward as she felt Jisyel's hands on her. Focussed on the sensation.

'Breathe in. Breathe out.'

Calidra breathed in with Jiyel. Exhaled with her.

Over and over again until she stopped shaking. Until her fingers pulled from her palms, and the tension in her muscles relaxed.

'In. Out. In. Out.'

She looked up at Jisyel to find her crying as well. 'J—Jisyel.'

'Cal…Oh, Cal!' Jisyel leaned forward, crushing Calidra in a hug as she buried her face in her shoulder. 'We thought you were gone!'

'The…Myr aren't…here?' Calidra asked, throat so raw it hurt to speak.

Jisyel shook her head, sobbing into her shoulder. 'They were, but you fought them off. You saved us from the attack.'

Calidra wrapped her arms around Jisyel's back, the two rocking in their hug. Her chest ached, and every swallow made her wince. She heard the crackle of a fire and looked towards the noise—her vision suddenly clear—taking in her surroundings.

Malora and Renys sat on the other side of the campfire, watching with wide eyes. Renys fiddled with the soles on her boots while staring over at Calidra and Jisyel, her bottom lip poking out.

'Mal?' Calidra gasped.

Malora's face was wet. 'I haven't seen you like that since… in a long time, Cal.' She rested a hand on Renys and gently stroked her daughter's hair. 'Are you okay?'

Calidra nodded. She wasn't okay, but she would be. And her sister looked worried enough without adding to it.

Jisyel pulled back from the hug, then pulled a linen kerchief from their bag and used it to wipe Calidra's cheeks and nose.

Calidra, who hated relying on others and wanted to prove she was capable by herself lest she was berated for needing help—or being stupid enough to need help—did not complain. She trusted Jisyel with her life, and was too tired to fight.

She trembled, but it had more to do with exhaustion rather than the intense anxiety that had her gripped. 'If Fenn went through that with the Myr…'

'What happened?'

'After the Myr attacked, it…I think it took me…to the spirit world. It spoke to me.'

'The Myr spoke to you?' Malora gasped. She'd pulled Renys into her lap, and her daughter had reached up to play with Malora's hair.

Jisyel finished cleaning Calidra and sat on her other side, keeping one arm around her shoulders.

Calidra fought another wave of tears as she recalled the creature of death and shadow. The intense cold and all-consuming darkness. The things it had said. Promised. What it wanted.

She clutched Jisyel's hand. 'I was too hard on Fenn. I hope…I hope he can forgive me.'

'What did the Myr say?' Malora asked from across the camp.

Jisyel pulled a blanket over Calidra's shoulder. 'Let's leave it for now. It's late. She's been through a lot.'

'Where are we?' Calidra asked. She didn't look around, didn't have the energy to do more than stare at the base of the fire, watching the logs crackle and spit. Her sword—though it was Malora's sword—lay beside the flames. She was glad to see they'd brought it. They wouldn't be completely defenceless.

'Just outside Cliffton,' Malora answered.

'We carried you most of the way. I was so afraid you'd…' Jisyel trailed off.

Calidra pulled Jisyel's hand to her lips and kissed the back of it. 'Thank you. For everything. I don't deserve you, Jisyel.'

Jisyel shook her head, a giggle bursting from her. 'Malora did most of the lifting, I just pointed out the way.'

Her laugh lit Calidra's heart on fire anew.

Jisyel turned Calidra's face to hers and kissed her through new tears. 'You're so silly, Cal. You've done plenty for me. Rest now. We'll be here.'

21
THE REPORT
TORSTEN

Torsten swirled his mug, staring into the golden liquid as if it held all the answers in the world. He'd commandeered a private room in the back of Tommouth's largest tavern, The Blue Dragon, and ordered its finest tea. The tavern had been named for Miroth—as most of the features and landmarks in the town had been—but it was part of the dragon's domain only in name.

The people here did not worship Miroth. Didn't particularly care for him.

Miroth was weak, after all.

Most pledged their allegiance to Toriaken, and made the trek north to his shrine at least twice a year. Although Torsten could understand supplication to the larger of two dragons—and Toriaken represented the queen herself, after all—he begrudged them for it. Miroth's forming had brought a flood of new people to the area. Industry and business had flourished. What had once been a small fishing village had swelled to a town worthy of its spot on the map.

Miroth had given so much to the people here.

Now he was dying, and these selfish people cared not one whit for that.

As Master Inquisitor, he was given more respect, but only because he carried the queen's word and held the threat of the iron dragon.

He'd been back in Tonmouth five days now. Desperate to keep Miroth alive, Torsten had requested the temple to be cleaned and repaired where necessary. And as he continued to feed Miroth artefacts, the dragon's weakness faded, attracting people to the temple.

It was a long process, but the first steps had been taken, and the rest would soon fall into place.

It also required most of his attention, so he'd left Varlot to continue searching through the fortress while he worked to help his brother. He could do nothing about the salinisation of the lake, but if he could bring more people to Tonmouth, more people to worship Miroth, that would help sustain him.

Torsten took a large gulp of his tea, crisp and acidic, a familiar warmth spreading along the back of his throat. It was good fruit, most likely from Nethal, where the cold sun lit the valleys all year round. He stared at his correspondence, as yet not returned from Varlot. He'd sent the man three letters, instructing him to bring his latest finds to Tonmouth so Torsten could assess what they'd discovered.

With Miroth in the state he was, Torsten had no intention of leaving Tonmouth, not until he was certain the dragon was at no more risk of fading.

He only hoped there was enough power in the artefacts he'd found to keep the dragon going.

Queen Surayo only wanted one. She wouldn't care about lesser magic. And if Miroth devoured the artefacts, he was also destroying them, too, which is what she ultimately wanted.

Torsten could see no flaw in his plan.

A knock on the door pulled his attention from a report on the state of repairs in Eastbrook, and he raised his head. 'Enter.'

The door opened with a creak. Torsten grimaced at the noise—the hinges needed oil—and a stocky woman entered, dark hair tied in a braid she rested over one shoulder. She carried a short sword at her hip, the scabbard faded and rough, and a stack of papers under one arm.

Ravona, part of the town guard, had always set her sights on bigger things. Torsten saw her gaze drawn to his uniform, to the burnished silver dragon insignia across his chest and upper arms. She frowned, though in truth Torsten had never seen another expression on her face, and did not take offence. Ravona halted a few paces from the edge of his table and crossed one arm over her chest in greeting. 'Master Inquisitor, I had hoped to speak with you.'

He drummed two fingers on the table, irritation beginning to form. She was speaking with him now. Why didn't people ever get to the point these days? He gestured for her to begin.

'We received our usual reports from the border checkpoints, sir. It is my job to be aware of matters near Bragalia, and forward important updates to the crown.'

Torsten gestured for her to continue. He didn't need a run down of her job description.

'Sir. There's been a…disturbance near Cliffton. Alnothen sealed off the Spindle Woods. Two Inquisitors are missing, and a squadron of the guard has been killed.'

His drumming stopped. 'Bragalian riff-raff hungry for blood? It'd be just like one of their Lairds to push into Porsenthia while our army is busy elsewhere.'

'No sir. It was…' Ravona licked her lips and glanced around the empty room, as if someone else might be eavesdropping. As if *he* was not the highest authority on the continent save the queen herself. 'It was the Myr.'

'I'll take that report.' He kept his voice neutral and extended a hand.

Ravona withdrew the stack of letters and thumbed through them, until she found the one in question.

'What are the rest of those?' Torsten asked. He didn't like being blind, even if Miroth took up most of his focus whilst he was here.

'Nothing to concern yourself with, sir. Requests from Eastbrook for ships to send people or supplies. The rest are movements of Bragalian pirate ships mostly. Dockworkers want to know if we're likely to be raided.'

'And are you?' Torsten raised an eyebrow.

'Are we what?'

'Likely to be raided? Lord Miroth protects you, or have you forgotten that?' Venom seeped into his voice at his dragon spirit's consistent dismissal. It was as if he never existed.

Ravona stuttered. 'Of—of course, sir. But their ships come from the Salt Sea, and…'

'And is Miroth not fierce in his devotion to you? In his desire to see this town and its people protected? He sacrifices himself in the hunting of these pirates. The salt weakens him, yet he persists. The cliffs crumble, and the Salt Sea enters the soil, mixing with the lake water. Yet he does not complain.'

'Yes, sir.'

Torsten wasn't aware when he'd stood up. He had one hand on the hilt of *Tinebás*, the blade pulled a handspan from the scabbard. He blinked, coming back to himself.

Miroth hadn't taken control, he didn't think…He'd just been overwhelmed by emotion.

Ravona backed away several paces.

Torsten exhaled sharply through his nose and released his grip on the sword, letting it fall back with a small clink. He straightened and ran a hand through his hair, realising he needed more oil for it, there were too many errant strands, and that made him look dishevelled. Like his emotions, they needed to be brought back into alignment.

Torsten cleared his throat. 'You're dismissed, Ravona.'

She left without another word, closing the door behind her.

The fire in his chest did not calm him as it usually did. It writhed and swirled, Miroth's emotions mixed. He felt what his dragon felt. Uncertainty dominated, punctuated with pain and fear.

Torsten whirled around with a roar and slammed his fist onto the heavy wooden table.

It didn't ease his frustration, and the ache now running through his fist only infuriated him more.

He sat heavily in the chair and thumbed through the report Ravona had brought. He needed to focus on work to keep his emotions suppressed.

She'd spoken truthfully, at least. Two Inquisitors. Five of the guard. Three horses. Seven red pigeons. All lost. Attached underneath the hastily scrawled report was a copy of the names passing through the checkpoint that day.

Only four had entered Porsenthia. But eighteen had travelled into Bragalia.

Cowards, all. Trying to escape the Myr's clutches instead of fighting with their queen.

The last two names on the list caught his eye, and his heart thumped.

Renys Tamlin, Foxmouth.

Malora Tamlin, Foxmouth.

Torsten read the report again, in its entirety, in case he'd missed something. The Myr had been sighted. Alnothen's forest had been sealed.

'And who brought the Myr, I wonder…?' Torsten whispered.

It was common knowledge that Apollo Tamlin was responsible for their resurgence. And this report, less than two days old depending on how quickly the pigeon had flown, meant Apollo's wife and daughter had survived the attack on Foxmouth. Were in Bragalia *right now*.

He pulled a map of the continent over, pushing his half-finished tea to one side, a sudden intensity and clarity filling his mind. Malora Tamlin. *Formerly Vantonen*.

Funny. He'd met the sister before, in Ballowtown.

If only he'd known then what he knew now.

Torsten would pay good money to see Apollo's head on a spike, and that damned thief had slipped through his fingers one time too many. He may not have known where Malora and Renys were going—though he'd put money on it being Fellwood, where the Vantonen family estate was—*they* were much closer to his grasp.

A sure way to lure out the reticent thief.

Heat surged in his chest.

He *couldn't* leave Miroth. Not in his current state. But he didn't know when he'd get a better opportunity to tie up that loose end.

Another knock on the door, insistent.

'What is it?' Torsten snapped.

The door burst open, and instead of Ravona, Varlot strode in on heavy boots. 'Am I not good enough to speak face to face anymore, *Master Inquisitor*?' The last two words dripped with sarcasm. His beard and hair were a tangled mess, laced through with travelling grime. Dust from the deadlands covered his uniform, shifting it from solid black to dirty beige. Something that looked suspiciously like dried blood coated the bottom of one boot, as if he'd stepped in something better avoided. His eyes were lidded, and a new scratch—possibly from a cat—crossed his chin, but he didn't sway.

He was sober, at least.

Torsten's lip curled at the sight of him. 'I've important business here—'

'More important than Queen Surayo's command? Than the Myr?' Spittle flew from Varlot's lips.

Torsten did not understand why the man was so enraged. 'What is the problem? Did you not find anything of value? I sent *three* letters. You didn't see fit to respond to a single one?'

Varlot folded his arms across his chest. 'You leave me in that spirits-damned place like some grunt? Nothing but orders sent my way?'

'What did you expect?'

'I'm an Inquisitor now, and—'

'*If* you pass this trial—'

'And I deserve the respect and treatment befitting my station!'

Torsten brushed down the arms of his own uniform, removing a piece of fluff he'd just noticed sitting in the crook of one elbow. 'Once you prove yourself, you'll find your station will be enhanced.'

Varlot glowered. Torsten wasn't sure whether the man would lash out in another fit of violence as he was prone to. Torsten was about to grab *Tinebás* when Varlot relented.

'Does this count as proving myself?' Varlot reached back through the door and dragged a heavy sack into the room, as equally covered in grime and dust as he was. It left a trail of dark mud on the floor.

Whatever was inside clinked together, a mixture of what sounded like metal and glass. Torsten was quite sure shadows flickered within the bag, dark strands licking up Varlot's arm like fire.

'While you were here doing whatever *important business* you had, and left me to fend for myself, I found the thing Queen Surayo wants. So I'm taking it to her now. You're lucky I thought to see you before I fucked off to do my own thing.'

Torsten was on his feet immediately. 'You have the artefact? Where?'

Varlot blocked the doorway with his bulk. 'What are you doing here, Torsten?'

'I told you before, I have business to attend to.'

'Been a while since my axe's been bloodied. No trouble where you're going?'

'You aren't needed.'

Something changed in Varlot. His eyes darkened, like a thundercloud had crossed his face. The muscles in his neck twinged. 'Why aren't I needed?'

Torsten raised his chin. Varlot was taller than he was, but Torsten had never been intimidated by someone simply for being bigger. He had Miroth. That made all the difference. 'Personal business does not always mean violence.'

'Then why am I here?' Varlot's roar shook the beams.

Torsten took one step back. 'You're here to follow orders. This is what you wanted.'

'You know damn well this ain't what I wanted!'

Torsten was unmoved. 'You wanted to be an Inquisitor. To have power. Respect. Control. These are the steps you must take to become that.'

'I was the Porsenthian *General*. The most decorated fighter since before Toriaken!'

'Afraid that doesn't mean very much as an Inquisitor. You cannot bully your way to the top.'

'Hah. You can talk.' Varlot jabbed a finger towards him. 'Everyone knows that's exactly what you are. If it weren't for me, you'd be left high and dry! I've been through shit, too, you pompous prick. It turned me into what I am.'

Torsten didn't hide his sneer. He'd let Varlot fester too long while he'd been distracted by Miroth, and he needed to shut him down before he grew out of control. 'And *what* are you?'

'Glorious! My reputation precedes me! Toughened my skin, hardened my heart. People fear to face me in combat!'

'No. It turned you into an insecure, manipulative, power-hungry bastard. There's *nothing* glorious about you.'

Varlot sputtered in the doorway, breath coming out in wheezes. He regained his composure, face darkening into a scowl. 'See? This is why you're fucking insufferable. But despite that, I'm always helping you out.' He gestured to the sack he'd brought in. 'You're too busy squirrelling away artefacts to notice. What you doing with them anyway?'

'That's none of your business,' Torsten repeated, shocked more than angry at the accusation. He was quite sure he'd been discreet, and berated himself for underestimating Varlot. He'd have to keep a closer eye on him. For a layabout drunk, the man had a keen eye.

Varlot snorted. 'Didn't expect an answer outta you. Selfish prick.'

'And it is exactly *that* kind of language that means you end up alone, doing "grunt" work.'

'Fine. Do whatever you want here. I'm going to the queen.'

'No. You wait for me. Then we'll go.'

'I did as I was asked. Now I'm going to get my reward. Don't think of cheating me out of that again, Torsten!' Varlot's voice had taken on an edge of violence. He shifted, one boot knocking into the sack, some of the contents spilling out on the floor.

There were so many to choose from, and several would have enough power for Miroth. He just needed to get a few more to him, then they could return to the queen.

Torsten caught the glint of yellow-gold before it was covered by the sack's material.

'I'm more decorated than you. Killed more Myr than you. Won more battles than you. People see me and rush over, thanking me for what I did. Begging me to marry their daughters, their sisters. What have *you* done for Porsenthia, eh? People see you and run away.'

Torsten ignored Varlot's speech about his own heroic deeds, his gaze drawn to the yellow artefact. It looked like an ordinary hairpin. Perhaps more ornate than usual, long and slender, pointed at the end. If he wasn't careful, it could be used as a knife. It had probably belonged to some noble child once, before the Myr turned it into one of their creations.

The hairpin glowed softly, as though a fire lit it from within. A yellow, glassy gemstone topped it, reminding him of topaz. A rare and beautiful jewel.

He could *feel* the power emanating from it.

It would be perfect for Miroth.

'Wait until tomorrow,' Torsten said, struggling to come up with a compelling reason that would stop Varlot from leaving immediately. 'You found the artefact? Surely that calls for a drink. There's another room in the inn. Have that. Celebrate tonight. We'll leave in the morning.'

Varlot's eyes gleamed. 'You want me to help you out? *Again?*'

'I want you to celebrate. My business will be done by the morning. We both get what we want.' Torsten reached into the purse on his belt and pulled out a handful of silver coins. 'Here. The crown will pay for your pleasure tonight.'

Varlot hesitated, shifting his weight from foot to foot. 'Saw a few sailors playing dice in the tavern. Guess I could join 'em for a few rounds. Lighten their pockets.' He grabbed the coins.

Torsten hardly heard him leave, all thoughts of Apollo, Malora, and Renys pushed from his mind in the face of the treasure, and the speed with which he needed to act.

He stared at the pin and whispered to himself, 'This will be strong enough to save him.'

22
THE BLIZZARD
APOLLO

If Apollo never saw snow again, it'd be too soon.

He'd had his fill of it the last time he'd travelled to this spirits-forsaken place.

He trudged along the road, snow up to his knees, and thought of his wife. Of Renys. The life he'd built for himself after enduring this place once before. Malora's knife was in his pocket, and he squeezed the hilt.

He was on the verge of losing everything.

Nadja seemed to be labouring under the delusion they'd survive the Archon. Their encounter with Verkata should have made the dragons' might starkly clear. *And* they'd had Neros to defend them.

Last time, he'd barely managed to escape Paragos and the Moonlight Palace with his life. And that had mostly been down to Yorik's sacrifice.

What could one thief, one Inquisitor, and one bonded to a weak forest spirit do against Paragos?

He gritted his teeth and shook his head, forcing the thought away. Nothing good ever came from dwelling on the what ifs and maybes. He would deal with whatever came towards him whenever it did so.

Which meant, for now, he focussed on the next step through the deepening snow, and how miserably cold he was.

Apollo didn't really understand the ins and outs of dragon spirits. That was Malora's specialty. But if there was corruption spreading through the land here, he wondered why Paragos had allowed it. Perhaps he couldn't stop it, for all his strength.

Perhaps he didn't care.

That was more likely, come to think of it.

'We're making good time,' Nadja said, as if she couldn't bear to have silence weigh down on them for more than a few minutes.

'Just wait until we reach the mountains. This bit is easy,' Apollo replied. Shades of white spread out ahead, snow and ice blanketing the landscape. Beside them, the river continued to rush by as they followed it uphill, its dark waters menacing.

Apollo tried not to look at the river. Every time he did, he almost walked towards it.

It would be a shame to come so far only to meet his end by plummeting into the freezing waters of a corrupted river spirit.

Every time there was more than a loud gurgle from the water, Fenn flinched, spinning around and looking for a threat like a startled rabbit. He'd grown twitchy ever since meeting Sanis. Apollo had thought Fenn half-crazed before, but had put that down to what he'd been through. The Myr's touch had to be hard on anyone. But now, he seemed gripped by levels of paranoia that went beyond trauma.

Sanis had definitely known Fenn. He'd put money on that. But Fenn's fears pushed him from a place of relative safety and deeper into danger. Apollo was fairly sure that if he didn't know who or where he was, given the choice between a warm bed by a fire and trudging into a blizzard, he'd take the sensible decision.

He'd noticed Nadja's gaze flicking to the young man more often, and wondered if she thought him dangerous. It made a nice change—not having an Inquisitor watch *him* like a hawk—but Apollo believed Fenn to be harmless. Muddled and afraid, and clearly desperate, but not a danger.

Not in the same way the spirits were.

Apollo kept an eye on Fenn as much as he could. He didn't want a second death in this frigid wasteland weighing on him.

There were no obvious signs of corruption in the landscape despite Sanis's warning. The few plants and trees they passed were all alive and healthy. There were no shadows creeping along the ground, the snow and ice was too enduring for that—probably Paragos's influence. But there was a bite in the air that went beyond cold.

Apollo slipped on a patch of ice, one arm dropping to the ground to catch himself before he crashed down. He let out a yelp of surprise, and when his hand connected with the ice, something dark crossed his vision. A crowd of shadowy people wandered past, wearing thick, fur-lined coats and hats. He couldn't make out their faces, and most had their backs to him as they trudged towards the river.

Some fell to their knees in supplication. Others pressed on, wading straight into the freezing waters, chunks of ice bumping into their legs.

Manori rose from the river. A small dragon by all accounts—about twice the size of Sanis's carriage—with scales of navy blue and black, and violet eyes. All his colour darkened and drained away in the space of a few heartbeats, leaving his eyes deathly white. Flames leapt from the dragon's jaws, burning the people in front of him alive.

They screamed, but no noise reached Apollo's ears.

'Apollo. Don't sit in the snow too long or you won't get up

again!' Nadja grabbed his free hand and heaved him up. 'Don't walk too close to the water, either.'

All the people and the dragon disappeared. He blinked, focussing on the Inquisitor, wondering what he'd just seen. A vision of some sort? They were the only people out here. It had been hours since they'd last passed by anyone.

He gulped down a large lungful of air. 'Nadja? Did you see anything?'

'See what?' Nadja asked.

'People? The dragon spirit?'

'Nothing. Is the weather getting to you? Giving you delusions?' Her tone was as cold as their surroundings.

Apollo brushed away the snow that had clumped around his boots and lower legs, and pushed himself to follow Nadja. 'It's a bad idea to be out here. Mark my words.' He passed Fenn, who stared at the spot Apollo had just collapsed in, though his eyes were glazed over.

Apollo massaged his temple. Was he going mad, too? Deluded, like Fenn? Yes, he was cold, but that wouldn't cause hallucinations, would it? He certainly hadn't seen anything like that the last time he'd been here.

Spirits take him, was he finally losing his mind?

'Memories overlay this area,' Fenn whispered.

'Memories?' Apollo repeated, the hairs on the back of his neck rising. He shuddered.

Why hadn't Nadja seen them, too?

He shortened his stride so he could keep moving while Fenn remained in earshot.

'The spirit is the connection to life here. The memories. Manori suffers.'

'Fenn, what are you talking about?' Nadja asked, whirling around. She grabbed the hilt of her sword, and Apollo wondered if the unflappable Inquisitor was actually unnerved.

Fenn wasn't looking at them. His attention remained on the spot, eyes unfocussed, lips moving, but no words came.

'Fenn?' Nadja called again, her voice sharper.

Fenn shook himself, rubbing his arms and hands. 'I'm coming.'

Apollo's concern for Fenn grew as he watched the young man hurry to catch up. He was speaking in riddles, and Apollo didn't know what it meant. Something to do with the dragon spirit affecting the land somehow. Because it was in pain.

He wished Malora was here to make sense of it all.

Snow fell in heavy clumps, muffling their footsteps. Apollo saw fewer and fewer memories as they drifted away from the river, and wondered if touching the ice, part of Manori's domain, was the reason *he* had seen ghosts of the past, and neither Fenn or Nadja had.

Trying to piece it together gave him a headache, so Apollo stopped thinking about it.

What the visions meant didn't matter. He just needed to focus on his next steps.

Apollo shivered. One foot in front of the other. Trudge. Trudge. Trudge. 'Won't be long now,' he muttered to himself.

Hours rolled by, gradually shifting into days.

They stopped for food, took turns keeping watch while the others slept, and continued on into the shapeless, frigid wilderness. If it weren't for the mountains as a clear landmark, Apollo worried they'd be lost out here until they died.

'How will we find the key in the snow?' Fenn asked one morning, sounding more in control of himself than he had since Foxmouth. He had flashes of competency, where he responded in a way that was to be expected. But the further they travelled, the more often his mind would wander, and his muttering would increase.

'Burying it out here would've made more sense. Definitely wouldn't be able to find it then,' Apollo replied. He wiped the ice freezing on his eyelashes, the air stinging his face. Every breath was beginning to grow shallow. 'It's in a building. Can't miss it.'

'Didn't realise people built things in the middle of Paragos's domain,' Nadja's attempt at humour fell short.

'It's called the Moonlight Palace,' Apollo said.

Nadja stopped mid-stride and whirled around to face him. 'That isn't real.'

A smile tugged at his lips. 'You'll see soon enough. It's every bit as horrible as you imagine. I left the key inside, in one of the lower halls.' Apollo closed his eyes, remembering the feel of the place, the pressure on his chest that forced the air from his lungs.

The Myrish spirit in the depths.

He wasn't looking forward to experiencing it a second time. He tried to push away the fear that kept creeping along his spine.

'Apollo. When were you going to disclose that information?'

Startled, Apollo stopped walking. 'What does it matter where it is?'

'All this time, I thought you didn't feed Paragos the key because you hid it somewhere then turned tail and fled. That's why you said it was lost. No threat. I thought we were going to a mountain cave or something. No wonder the Myr are back in Porsenthia and the local river spirit is corrupted! It's amazing half the people here aren't corrupted themselves!' Nadja pointed a gloved hand towards the dark waters that wound through the snow. 'You returned one of their strongest artefacts to a seat of their power!'

'To the…to the what? I know the palace was Myrish, but it's *ancient*. Something from a children's story?'

'Children's story or not, there are often lessons in them. You're a fool.'

'Perhaps if Queen Surayo hadn't barred all talk of the Myr

across Porsenthia, more people would know about it.' Heat and shame rose in his gut. So much could have been fixed if Queen Surayo trusted people with knowledge.

He could understand why she'd hidden it. No need to cause a panic for something that likely wasn't a threat. But it would have saved him a good deal of headache—and certainly a trip back here—if he'd known.

Apollo didn't know what to say. He prided himself on having a response to every situation, but this had him stumped. He'd known the palace was of Myrish origin. Yorik, the man who'd come with him on the mission, had been saved by one of the Myr. Had to bargain with it, and that had led him to the Moonlight Palace.

But the palace and the key were leagues away from Porsenthia. There had been no chance whatever influence they held would reach them across the ocean.

And it hadn't.

At first.

He stumbled, dread growing. It had taken five years to reach them, spending all that time festering, leaking its corrupting influence into the land and water here. Apollo looked at Fenn, at his lost gaze, his confusion. Remembered the man by Toriaken's temple, who'd died terrified and alone. Thought about what was coming to Porsenthia. Bragalia. Olmir.

To all the countries of the world.

This was only the beginning.

'Nadja, I…The key is *one* artefact. Surely it isn't enough to destroy Tassar. We're nearly there. Getting rid of the key will stop it, right?'

'Not being a mage nor familiar with Myrish magic, I *don't know*, Apollo.' Nadja's tone had shifted to iron. She was no longer someone who wanted to help Apollo correct a mistake. She was an Inquisitor again. 'This changes things. I knew the Myr were trying to resurge, but not to this degree.

I only hope they don't have any other artefacts as strong as the key.'

Apollo floundered for words. It was like his grandmother scolding him over what he'd thought was a small mistake, but turned out to have bigger consequences than he'd been aware of.

Fenn asked, in a weak voice, 'Can you explain the Moonlight Palace?'

The three of them continued on, increasing their pace. Apollo wasn't sure the Inquisitor would entertain the question, but Fenn didn't push.

Eventually Nadja said, 'The Myr represent death, where dragon spirits represent life. They take it. Dragons create it. But they *are* spirits, in the same way as dragons, and where dragons' powers come from their domains, the Myr do not have such a foothold in Tassar. So they pour their magic into artefacts that can last eternally, even if they themselves are vanquished.'

Apollo bowed his head as the wind picked up, blasting snow at them and turning each flake into a tiny needle that stung his face.

'Queen Surayo, in her wisdom, took many of these artefacts from the Myr during her war against them. She travelled to the distant continent of Malbosh, where the Myr have always been more prevalent. There are no dragon spirits in that place, nothing to oppose them. They have a fortress there, a bastion of power. Queen Surayo stormed the fortress, Toriaken and the Porsenthian army by her side, and laid waste to their creations.'

Apollo winced. While Surayo was out on her conquest, he had been robbing her palace in Eastbrook. Malora had debts. Had those after her blood. He'd been infatuated with her—still was—and had done the one thing he knew would help her: steal.

It had landed him in prison, a death sentence looming over him.

'Queen Surayo returned, victorious, having plundered their treasures and stolen what she could not burn. Some of their artefacts she twisted with her own magic, using them to the advantage of the Porsenthian Empire.'

He remembered one such artefact: Nestol. Torsten used it to torture people, and he'd managed to dump the thing in the Lasseen Ocean. Even now, he could remember Nestol's claws piercing his mind and body. He tensed.

Nadja continued, 'Most, she destroyed. But the Citrine Key was too powerful for even her magic. That is why she sent it to Paragos—only an Archon is capable of eviscerating an artefact of that power.'

Apollo focussed very hard on not slipping. Every word was a jab at his own failings, fears, and selfishness. But he hadn't wanted to die. Could he really be blamed for that?

'The Moonlight Palace is another fortress of the Myr. There are stories of a third, somewhere in the Nethal mountains of Porsenthia. Though if it exists, I doubt it's much more than a ruin. Queen Surayo did not know if the Moonlight Palace was a ruin, too, which is why she struck at the heart of the Myr. *She* drove them back. Drove death itself from our lands. And now I learn that for the past five years, an artefact capable of returning the Myr to their full strength has been sitting in a seat of their magical power because Apollo *did not do as he was told*.'

And there was the vitriol Apollo had come to expect from Inquisitors. He had no excuse for it.

But he was here, now. He *would* put things right.

A harsh cry rattled through the air, slicing through the wind and echoing around them. Apollo would never forget that sound as long as he lived—and it didn't seem like he had much time left.

Paragos was laughing.

Ice cold fear shot through his limbs, rooting him to the spot.

'What is that?' Nadja asked, her sword already drawn.

'Paragos. He…he knows we're here.' Apollo shivered, less to do with the cold and more with the terror that coursed through his veins. Since Nadja had found him in the sick bed, he'd been trying to get back to Malora and Renys. Yes, Nadja wanted him to correct a mistake he'd made five years ago, but his family had always been more important than that.

Would always be more important than that.

All his life, he'd run from danger and hidden until it had passed. He supposed it really was a matter of time before those mistakes caught up with him, no matter how many tricks he tried.

And this was one he couldn't escape.

Nadja had spoken true. As long as the key survived, the Myr's return was all but assured. And when they did return, *everything* would be lost—his family included. He didn't know what the key would do, but its presence had already had a marked effect on the spirits and people here. *If* he did this. *If* he finally faced his mistake…

Renys's face appeared in his mind, all wild curls and bright laughter. He *had* to do right by her. And that meant making sure the world she grew up in wasn't destroyed by shadow and death.

Apollo took a deep breath and felt stronger than he had for many days. It was strange. Once he'd made the decision, most of his fear left him. 'Nadja?'

'What?' The Inquisitor whirled around, streaks of white snow blowing in front of her face. She squinted at him through the biting wind. 'Apollo? What is it?'

He raised his chin. He couldn't see Paragos, not yet, but they were about to walk into the heart of the storm. There was no turning back now. 'When you get back to Porsenthia. When all this is done? Tell Mal I'm sorry. Tell her that I didn't try to run. That I did everything for her and Ren. And...and tell her I went out bravely.'

Apollo no longer hesitated. He pushed through the deepening snow, towards Paragos's waiting, icy jaws.

23
THE WOLF
SELYS

A cool breeze, so rare in Segandis, drifted in through the open window. It rippled the gossamer curtain and stirred Selys from sleep.

It took her a few moments to gather her bearings. She'd been travelling hard for so long that locations blurred together. But a few deep breaths and the smell of the sea reminded her where she was.

Selys got up, bare toes scrunching against the cold slate tiles underfoot. She strode to her window and peered out into the gloom. Dark waves lapped the sandy beach rhythmically. It was the Olmir Sea, rather than the Lasseen Ocean, but it reminded her of Neros's breath all the same, and she rested a hand against her chest, reassuring herself the dragon remained.

Before sunrise, when the world was still and quiet things ruled, had always been her favourite time. Before the heat of the day seared the ground, before voices and noise filled the air. This was the deep breathing of a world between life and death.

After washing and dressing, Selys stepped out onto the cool sand, bringing her glaive with her. She'd thought she would sleep poorly in the family home. Kaio stayed in his own wing, leaving the rest of the building empty. It was kept dusted and cleaned, but there was no *heart* left.

Yet, she'd slept as soundly as any other day over the past few weeks. Neros was all the comfort she needed. Neros also *wanted* her here, but the dragon's reasoning was unclear. Every time she tried to listen to Neros's voice, Selys was overwhelmed by fire.

There was still much she needed to learn.

Fergus slept atop a folded pile of clothes, and he watched her leave, eyes glinting in the early dawn.

The tall trees which surrounded the compound moved in the breeze, leaves rustling like a thousand hushed whispers. Selys passed under them and immediately walked through a pungent cloud of smoke. Suppressing a cough, she found Taran and Esto lounging beneath an orange tree, talking in low voices, cigarillos held between their fingers, an oil torch burning low between them.

Taran spotted her first and straightened up. 'Selys! Hah, if you'd told me I drank too much last night and imagined you'd come back, I'd have believed it.'

Selys inclined her head politely. 'I really *am* here. No alcohol-induced hallucination, I'm afraid.'

Taran's smirk broke into full laughter.

She laughed with him. 'It's good to see you both. It's been much too long. How's the ship?'

Their gazes drifted down to the swirling tattoo down her left arm. She'd worn a loose, sleeveless shirt to cope with the inevitable Bragalian heat, and though she didn't appreciate their looks, she was not ashamed of her priestess mark.

'*Wolf's Grin* keeps grinning. Needs a patch up but that's underway. Be a few more days until she's ready to sail again,' Taran replied.

'Kaio headed down to the water a while ago.' Esto jerked her chin towards the sound of the waves and took a long drag from her cigarillo, accurately guessing the reason for Selys's appearance. 'He stands there whenever he's stressed.'

Selys's laughter died. 'I suppose I'm the cause of his stress this morning?'

Esto exhaled the smoke through her nose. 'He's been stressed a while. Fight yesterday was probably good for him. You won't have helped, though.'

Selys appreciated the woman's bluntness. It was part of why she'd become a lieutenant. With Taran's skills and Esto's pragmatism, the pair had most likely been the reason Kaio had remained in one piece during her absence.

'Fight?'

'He challenged Dalys to a duel.'

Selys was incredulous. 'A *duel*? Why?'

Taran couldn't conceal his grimace. 'Tesso. It was his wake last night. Kaio found him dead and buried on the beach, an apple in his mouth.'

Selys couldn't believe it. Taran's version of the incident was different to Yaniv's. 'Dalys wouldn't be so bold, surely? Unless he's had a complete personality change since I was last here?'

'Kaio's been waiting for a chance to snap, truth be told. Act now, fuck the consequences. The usual. Ruka, Esto, and me try to talk sense into him. But you know what he's like when he gets an idea in his head. Not much can get him out of it.'

Selys massaged one temple. She had to speak to Kaio. Had to sort things out. There'd be a retaliation, that much was for certain. She might not have been part of the warband anymore, but she still cared for everyone in it.

She headed away from them, anxiety gnawing in her gut.

'I'd leave him be. He never talks to anyone when he's in that state,' Esto warned.

'He's my brother,' Selys replied simply, and continued towards the shore.

❄

Selys found Kaio easily enough. He stood in the surf, waves lapping at his knees, staring at the pale horizon.

His head turned at her approach, and she halted on the soft sand. She didn't want to crowd him or impose, so she waited for him to make the first move.

He was the one in charge now.

'You back for good?' Kaio asked when she didn't say anything, his voice flat. Whatever emotions he bottled up, she couldn't tell.

'For now,' Selys replied, honestly.

'Why now? Been three years. You didn't even write.'

Selys shifted her weight. 'I wrote. *You* stopped replying.'

'After you joined Neros's Shrine.'

She grimaced at his tone. She'd stood fearless in the face of an Archon, but hearing her brother's disappointment was crippling.

'How can you stomach having that…that *thing* in your head?' Kaio snarled, turning to face her.

'She is the spirit of the ocean, nothing more.'

'She ripped apart everything we had! She's the reason we're like…like…like *this*!' Kaio gestured angrily around them. 'You notice how few people there are? You know how many deserted us after the storm? After Neros killed our family?'

Grief surged through her chest at the pain in his words. At what she had to tell him. 'No, Kaio. *We* did this to ourselves. Don't blame Neros for trying to set us back on the path.'

'Don't you dare justify their murder. If Neros was another warband, we'd have retaliated. Annihilated them for striking at us. But it's a dragon so we can't do anything but accept it.'

'We *wouldn't* have been attacked by Neros had we not transgressed! Don't you see, Kaio? Not everything you do is *right.* That's like blaming Inquisitors if you get arrested in Porsenthian waters.'

He turned away from her again. Then, in a calmer voice, Kaio asked, 'Why did Neros bond with you in the first place?'

Selys had been asking herself that question ever since she'd realised she had the dragon's blessing. But Neros's strength was so overwhelming, she hadn't been able to get a concrete answer.

Neros *never* blessed her worshippers. She was unique among dragon spirits in that.

When she'd been on that freezing mountain with Fenn, she'd believed Neros had finally noticed her. Seen her dedication. Rewarded her loyalty. But Neros's words echoed in her mind, and Selys knew that wasn't true, as tempting as it was to believe she was special. 'I have a debt to pay. You do, too, Kaio. For what we did.'

Kaio snorted. 'Neros killed our family for what we did. That makes us even.'

Selys shook her head. 'No. I must atone. The Myr are on the rise, we *have* to do something about that.'

'Let Surayo do whatever she did before. Nothing to do with us.' Kaio shrugged.

'It's our world too. *We* transgressed. *We* must make it right.' Selys wished she could speak more clearly to Neros, like Fenn seemed to be able with Hassen.

More than the spirit confirming her debt, Selys had been pulled south. Neros *wanted* her here.

She could only assume she needed her brother to atone, too. Why else drive her back to Segandis?

Selys didn't tiptoe around the more urgent issue. 'Dalys might retaliate. Are you prepared for that? You say our numbers are down. What do we do if he attacks?'

'Dalys? I humiliated him.'

'Exactly. He's a proud man. Weaker than we are, true, but that doesn't mean he isn't dangerous.'

'I defeated his champion in a fair duel. Well. *Unfair*. The man was bonded to a dragon!' Kaio laughed. 'We'll destroy them all if he tries to come after us.'

'Is that your plan for everything that opposes you? Destroy them?'

Whatever lightness had come over Kaio disappeared. 'You have some nerve to say that.'

'Do I?'

'It's how the Ioaran warband has always run itself. We take what we want. We crush our enemies. The world is *ours*.'

'Kaio, there haven't been duels here for generations! Most Porsenthians think we're barbaric in Bragalia. Savages who have no ability to communicate in other ways. You aren't helping that thinking,' Selys said, irritation seeping into her voice.

'Why should I worry about what some Porsenthian thinks about me? I'll do whatever it takes for my freedom.'

Sadness crept into her heart at those words, some hers, some Neros's. It was a mantra she, too, had lived by for many years. 'Freedom? By fighting all the time? Sleeping with one eye open? Waiting for someone to retaliate after you walked over them?'

Kaio stared at her, incredulous. 'You want peace? Or do you want freedom?'

'Both.'

Kaio laughed, the sound cold. 'That's not the way the world works. Thought you'd know better.'

'I *do* know better, now.' Selys tapped her chest. 'There is so much more to this world than fighting, than war. Than saying what you want to whomever you want, and fuck the consequences.'

'Served us well enough.' Kaio folded his arms.

'Just because it worked before doesn't mean it's the best thing to do *now*. The world is changing, Kaio. We must change with it.' Their family's mindset of behaving as they wished had led to their deaths. Had turned Neros's wrath upon them. How could he not see that?

'Change?' He narrowed his eyes. 'By forsaking your family and joining with the creature that killed them?'

'I left to find meaning in meaningless loss. And I found it. You begrudge me for finding meaning in life, instead of just surviving through it?'

Kaio looked at her for a long time. He no longer seemed the youngest sibling, her baby brother, but a battle-hardened man who would not be swayed. Steel was back in his eyes. 'Selys. Do you want the truth? Or just meaning?'

When she said nothing, Kaio continued.

'Because the truth is—those dragons do *not* care about us. Never have. Never will. You find *meaning* in carrying their word? It's a lie.'

'Kaio, if you had felt the touch of Neros, or any spirit, you'd understand.'

'I understand enough from here. You're being used, Selys. And I am *not* a pawn in some dragon's game!' His voice rose, emotion fuelling his words. 'Peace or freedom. Surviving or living. These are the choices everyone must make.' Kaio stormed off, pausing only when he spotted the glaive she'd left on the sand.

Skaru's weapon.

They'd fished it from the wreckage after the storm. The only thing left of their eldest brother.

There was nothing but the waves to fill the gap between them, and silence grew heavy, the glaive glinting in the early morning sun.

Eventually he said, 'They call me the *Sea Wolf*. But wolves hunt in packs. And I'm always alone.'

That's what the Ioran warband had been called by their rivals. *The Sea Wolves*. Their fleet of six ships, each captained by one of the family. Their father, Dairo, had the flagship *Wolf's Sight*. Their mother, Zuela, had *Wolf's Foot,* the fastest of their fleet. Skaru, their eldest brother, captained *Wolf's Skull,* which held their fiercest fighters. Rowi, the middle brother, captained *Wolf's Gut,* with the biggest hold for loot and treasure. Josyin, Selys's only sister, had *Wolf's Fang,* the most heavily armed and armoured.

And Selys's own ship, *Wolf's Grin,* where Kaio ran as her first mate, was the scout. The decoy. The trap-setter. Always working with the others, but from a distance.

It was why *Wolf's Grin* had survived Neros's attack.

Why she and Kaio were the only survivors of their bloodline.

'I'm here,' Selys whispered.

Kaio looked at her. 'Are you? I can't welcome you back if you're just going to run off again.' He wasn't angry anymore. Something had broken in his voice, and he looked for all the world like that scared boy who'd just seen his family killed in front of him.

He'd only just seen his twentieth birthday, and was shouldering responsibilities those twice his age had to.

Selys ran over to him and wrapped her arms around her brother. 'I'm here,' she repeated.

Selys counted six heartbeats before Kaio returned the hug. She had everything she could possibly need with Neros by her side. But the hug reminded her there was another part of herself that had been adrift.

Now it, too, had returned.

Kaio's eyes, usually so full of steel, shone.

When they broke apart, sharp pain lanced through her belly, and Selys sank to one knee with a gasp of pain. Neros appeared behind her brother, but not as she knew the dragon spirit to look. Neros's scales were shadowed, wreathed in dark mist, a chain around her neck. An unspeakable darkness smothered the dragon and she stared at Selys for only a few seconds before she faded from sight with a soundless roar.

Fear flooded her—Neros had seen something. Felt something. Had been desperately trying to show Selys, but she hadn't understood. Fire surged in her chest and Selys looked at her hands and arms, where she'd touched Kaio.

Something dark had been in the Lasseen Ocean. An artefact of some sort. It had travelled south—to Segandis. This was why she'd been led back here. How she would atone.

This was what Neros wanted.

'Selys? What happened?' Kaio helped her stand.

'You…you've seen it. You've seen what Neros is searching for!'

He frowned, confusion plastered across his face.

'You've touched it! Where is it?' Selys prompted.

'Where is *what*?'

Emotions poured through her, Neros funnelling them. Elation. Anger. Fear. Desperation. 'The artefact! It's here somewhere. That must be…must be why Neros sent me here.' Selys fumbled her words, trying to keep her thoughts straight and piece together her spirit's calling in a way that made sense.

A frown swept across Kaio's features. 'Artefact? You're here to *steal* from me? What's the matter, your shrine low on donations?'

Selys shook her head, frantically trying to get him to understand. 'No, no! This is about more than treasure or the warband. This is bigger than the dragons themselves! I have to know what it is, Kaio!'

Neros's flame urged her on, a cacophony of words echoing in her mind. Too much for her to understand the details, but the desire was clear.

Neros wanted whatever Kaio had.

'Please. Brother. I'm *not* your enemy.'

He stared at her for a long moment, his eyes unreadable. Then he nodded. 'Fine. I'll show you. But you aren't taking anything of mine.' He headed back along the beach, his steps heavy.

Selys sighed, allowing the rhythmic waves to calm her chaotic emotions, her heart thumping heavily.

'Peace or freedom. Surviving or living. These are the choices everyone must make.' Kaio's words swirled in her mind. Neros's flame flared in her chest, urging her to follow her brother.

She had already made her choice. Now she had to serve her spirit.

24
THE SPIRIT OF GOLD
CALIDRA

With a clatter, the innkeeper dropped the plate in front of Calidra. She couldn't stop her stomach from growling at the sight and smell of it. Although she wasn't sure she could quite face eating after her encounter with the Myr, she knew she needed food.

'I know things have been hard. Eat, Cal. Please? It's good for you,' Malora said, genuine warmth in her smile.

Calidra inhaled the scent. Cliffton, on the border of three countries, enjoyed a fusion of several cultures and cuisines. The hollowed out loaf had been filled almost to overflowing with mutton and bean curry, rich with Olmese spices, and a thick, brown gravy. The base dish was Porsenthian—heavy and warming for cooler climates—but cooked with typically-Olmese seasonings and served in Bragalian bread, alongside a chunky, hot sauce made from chopped peppers, fruit, and spices that Calidra had used to top almost everything she'd eaten during her childhood. The *shonthal* condiment was never found in Porsenthia, and both she and Malora spooned a generous amount onto their portion.

Within minutes, the sauce had soaked into the white

bread, flavouring it and changing the texture. It was enough to make her salivate, and she dug in.

Renys ate ravenously, swinging her feet and bouncing them off the table leg. Even Calidra struggled to hold her decorum. After countless days on the road, being chased, and simply trying to survive, the lopsided, busy inn was practically a palace.

They'd been lucky to grab a seat—the inn was so full Calidra could hardly see the floor for people standing, tankards in hands. People bunched together, leaning against the walls and spooning broth into their mouths.

Malora had also emphasised the importance of being well-presented before they met Chyram, so they took advantage and enjoyed a bath and good food. The inn even offered cinnamon coffee, just as Calidra loved it, though Malora and Jisyel treated themselves to brown ale. Just the smell of coffee was enough to drive away much of the tension that had plagued her since their encounter with Alnothen and the Myr in the Spindle Woods.

Calidra leaned back in her chair, the wood creaking slightly. After washing the accumulated grime and travelling dust away, and with a full belly, it was hard to believe they were at war. She savoured their snatched pocket of normalcy, wishing it would last forever.

Across the table, Malora cupped her while she stared out the window, her gaze unfocussed. Renys smiled for the first time since they'd left the little fishing boat in Northbourne. She was comfortable in the tavern, despite the bustle and crowds, and Calidra remembered Malora and Apollo ran their own inn back in Foxmouth. It was probably the closest she'd felt to home since the Myr's attack.

There were several dovecotes in Cliffton, and Calidra wondered whether they ought to write to Bellandri. The last message they'd sent, from Tonmouth, had explained they were on their way to Foxmouth. Even on the remote Isle of Salt, news of the Myr's attack would have reached Jisyel's grandmother by now.

Malora had said she'd go straight to Eastbrook to look for Apollo once she had her blessing back.

Neither Calidra or Jisyel had said anything about that. Of course she supported her sister, but going to the Iron queen's castle to demand a prisoner back turned Calidra's stomach in knots.

And Chyram's Shrine was a stone's throw from Fellwood.

As much as Calidra dreaded the thought of seeing her mother again, she knew what the Myr could do. She could help Fellwood take a stand against the spirits of death.

Calidra had never thought of herself as a deserving ruler. Her mother had seen to that. But she wanted to protect the people she felt responsible for. So her heart was torn—stay with her sister and niece, or return home. She wanted to talk to Jisyel about it, to see where her head was. But the journey hadn't offered them any chance of a private conversation.

Though plans, fears, and ideas were never far from her own thoughts, there was no need to bring the mood down at the table by sharing her worries. Once Malora reached Chyram, once she had secured that first victory, and they'd reached their respective crossroads, they could discuss their next move.

Jisyel leaned on the table and let out a sigh. 'When we're done at the shrine, we need to come back here and eat that again. I can see how good it was by the looks on your faces!'

Calidra mirrored Jisyel's movement, resting on her elbow. She reached over and brushed a loose strand of hair behind Jisyel's ear. That had always tickled Jisyel, not that she felt it anymore because of Hassen's curse. She missed her lover's giggle. 'Absolutely. Whatever you want, we'll do.' It was silly and childish, because who was to say what they'd be able to do if the Myrish threat continued to grow. But she saw no harm in the promise.

Jisyel laced her fingers through Calidra's. 'I can't wait to feel *this* again.'

Calidra's heart fluttered. She hoped Jisyel wouldn't be disappointed.

'Laird wants the border fully garrisoned before the end of the day.'

Calidra looked up at the deep voice and quickly spotted a man on the table beside theirs. He had thick, dark hair, braided with gold thread, and was showing what looked like a map to his three companions. 'Got more griffins coming in this afternoon. Eyes in the sky will make sure we're not in danger while we finish setting up.'

Jisyel followed Calidra's gaze, then pulled her hand closer and kissed her fingers. 'Don't worry about that.'

Calidra chewed her bottom lip, her free hand resting on the hilt of her sword. Touching it brought comfort, grounding her. How could she *not* think about it? Danger lurked around every corner, and the people here were trying to protect themselves from the inevitable.

She abruptly became aware of the bustle within the tavern. What had until now been a distant hum that she could tune out suddenly washed over her with the force of a waterfall. It pressed in on all sides like a physical force. She gripped the hilt, squeezing her tension out. Her breathing quickened and she tried to steady it—without much success.

'Cal?' Malora's gaze was locked on her. 'Shall we get out of here? Get some fresh air?'

Calidra sat upright, heat creeping along her neck. She glanced around as pressure built in her belly again—that same cold fear as when the Myr had been upon her. It was too much, and she struggled to her feet. 'Let's do that.' Her heart pounded in the enclosed space, and her thoughts began to race again.

Their small group pushed their way out of the bustling inn, full of travellers, traders, and those simply trying to get away from danger, and stepped out into the warm Bragalian sun.

Immediately, Calidra's heartbeat slowed, and she could breathe deeply again.

'Are you okay, Cal? Does your tummy hurt 'cause you ate too fast?' Renys asked, pottering over to her and looking up. 'Daddy says that all the time.' The smile on her face suddenly faltered. 'Where's Daddy?'

Calidra crouched down and rested one hand on Renys's cheek. 'Sometimes my head hurts. Too much thinking.' She tapped Renys's forehead, and the girl giggled. 'But being outside and feeling the wind on my face helps. And being with family like you, too.' Calidra tapped her on the nose, and Renys reached up to tap Calidra's nose in the same way.

'Not far to go to the shrine.' Malora stretched her arms over her head. 'Walking off a meal that big will do us good. Ready?'

IT TOOK until just before sunset to reach the shrine. With full stomachs and the knowledge they were so close to journey's end, their pace was faster than ever—Calidra even enjoyed it. Jisyel skipped alongside Renys, though the girl often raced ahead and waited for them to catch up. When they did, she eagerly pointed out the rocks and plants she'd discovered.

Calidra had only visited Chyram's Shrine two or three times in her youth, and none of the well-worn paths were familiar. On their approach, they passed a few vendors selling from overturned barrels. Most of their wares were objects that had filled their home in Fellwood during their childhood. Golden pots, vases, and plaques were piled high, along with jewels and trinkets encrusted with gemstones.

Malora lingered for a closer look, though she didn't buy anything, even when Renys was taken by a small vase.

As they grew closer, more and more people littered the paths and surrounding plateaus. Dozens of tents, and a few more permanent structures, had been erected—it seemed like ten score people lived in the shadow of the shrine. Either Chyram's popularity had grown over the past decade, or people were flooding to any spirit they could, hoping for protection against the Myr.

Despite the burgeoning crowds, there didn't seem to be any priests or priestesses. It was a chaotic, unorganised mess. Smoke wafted through the air from campfires and cooking pots that had been haphazardly set up, and several washing lines had been strung between trees, clothes and strips of fabric hanging on them, dividing people into different sections. A few children played on the slopes, thin necklaces of gold jingling as they ran, matching their high-pitched laughter.

'This way.' Malora headed towards a branching path that stretched up a steep incline away from the noise.

'But the shrine is down there?' Jisyel pointed.

'I know. But Chyram is never in the shrine at this time. Sun's still up. He'll be basking. Trust me.' Malora marched along the path, renewed vigour in her stride.

Jisyel looked back at Calidra. 'So, should I ask her to remove Hassen's curse tonight or tomorrow?'

Calidra laughed.

Renys reached for Calidra. 'This way! Auntie Cal!'

Calidra leaned forward and took Renys's hand, allowing the girl to lead them after her mother, with Jisyel bringing up the rear. The path wound steeply uphill, twisting around rock formations until the main trail below was a distant memory, and not a whisper of the crowds reached them.

As they rounded a corner, Calidra staggered to a halt, her mouth falling open.

Chyram sat resplendent on the side of the mountain, low sunlight glinting off his golden scales, a throng of robed priests surrounding him. Each scale was rounded and smooth, making him seem far more lizard-like than any of the armoured dragons Calidra had seen before. Also unlike most dragons, predatory creatures that keenly observed their surroundings and hissed warnings, Chyram's eyes were closed as he basked.

Whether it was in the warmth of the sunlight or in the admiration of the people around him, she couldn't say. Occasionally his tail twitched, reminding her of a large cat more than the terrifying creatures she'd encountered.

Even Hassen had more bite than Chyram.

A sinuous stream of smoke trickled from one nostril, the only real sign that Chyram was indeed a dragon.

Instead of horns, a crest of long, black feathers protruded from the back of his head, nape of his neck, and his jaw, framing his golden face with a crown of dark points. He rumbled in aggrandised self-satisfaction, and the deep, guttural croaking shook the ground. Calidra's chest reverberated with it. The noise, if anything, reminded her even more of a cat purring.

Chyram carried himself with the arrogance of a preening peacock, and he'd hardly moved a muscle.

She chanced a look at Malora, who gazed up at him, eyes wet with tears.

Aside from Chyram's rumbling, those gathered spoke in hushed whispers. Calidra daren't step closer in case she broke whatever reverie was upon them. She tightened her grip on Renys's hand, and the girl quieted, hugging her leg.

Malora was not so hesitant. She hurried down the path, pebbles scuttling in her wake.

Calidra held her breath.

Several of the long feathers at the back of Chyram's head stiffened, and the dragon opened one lazy eye to stare upon them. Calidra was transfixed by the deep pool of green, rooted to the spot in the gaze of the divine.

'Chyram. Glorious and golden, holy one.' Malora sank to her knees, tears streaming down her cheeks. 'You ever were a wonder to behold.'

The dragon's feathers relaxed and he turned to face them, shifting his bulk and sending various worshippers fleeing so they were not crushed underfoot. Chyram's tail seemed shorter than most dragons, misshapen nuggets of gold running along the length of it. It left a gouge in the soft earth where he had been sitting moments before.

Still he did not speak.

'Allow us to behold your glory.'

Calidra's stomach turned at Malora's blatant flattery. She remembered little of the spirit, having only glimpsed him a few times before, and had no recollection of such sycophantic behaviour being a requirement.

She edged closer to Jisyel, holding Renys close, careful not to make any sudden movements. Though she wanted to ready her sword—a comfort more than anything else—she kept her hand firmly on Renys.

'Ah. The wanderer returns.' Chyram's voice was soft and melodious. It warmed the air as sure as if he'd breathed fire. He inhaled deeply, nostrils flaring. *'You have many scents on you. Hassen. Alnothen. A touch of Neros. The Myr.'* Chyram hissed the last word, sapping the warmth from his tone.

'It is why I have come to you. To beg your aid once more so that I might defend my daughter.' Malora rose to her feet and gestured for Renys.

Calidra hesitated, holding the child back, but Renys pulled away and tottered over to her mother, unafraid. 'Gold dragon! So pretty!' Renys pointed up at Chyram, a smile lighting her face.

Malora scooped her up and cuddled her.

'A child.'

Calidra sensed the danger, the subtle shift in Chyram's posture—a tension in his muscle, a constriction of the pupils. It was much like when her mother was about to explode in rage. Her heart began to pound, and she hoped the dragon couldn't hear it. 'Mal…' she whispered through gritted teeth.

Malora either didn't hear, or ignored her, because she continued. 'Renys is my love. I'll defend her until my final breath and beyond if the spirit world would allow it. Lord Chyram, I need your strength to fight the Myr, and any who would harm her.'

Smoke billowed from Chyram's nostrils and his mane of feathers straightened. *'I bonded with you once, Malora Vantonen. You were my love. I was yours. We coveted the gift we shared.'*

'I did. And I wish to have it returned.'

'You threw away my love. My gifts. My blessing.' Chyram had risen to his feet, talons of black digging into the rock, golden scales rippling in the sunlight. His wings half-unfurled, and suddenly the cat-like dragon was a predator looming over them. *'You looked upon me and saw no glory. You sought treasures and love elsewhere.'*

'Mal!' Calidra hurried forward and grabbed her sister's arm, but she fought to remain where she stood.

Malora had behaved towards this dragon in the same way she'd behaved when they were children. Spoiled, selfish, and entitled.

Calidra took a deep breath, wondering what the consequence was going to be.

Malora continued, 'I was young. Foolish. I now see that… that I am nothing without you.'

'I am that which people covet most.' More smoke, and the flicker of fire when Chyram opened his jaws to speak. *'Such demands. Where are your manners from before? You should be on*

your knees like these others. You should be begging forgiveness for throwing my blessing away.'

Malora stumbled. 'I…I am sorry for what I did, my Lord! I only wanted to *help* people with your gifts. But they hated it! Many were consumed by jealousy! They sought to hurt me!'

Chyram dragged a claw along the ground, gouging through the rock like it was made of softened butter. *'Then you should have stayed by my side. None could harm you under my protection.'*

And there it was. The complete devotion they wanted.

Hassen.

Alnothen.

Chyram.

They were all the same.

Calidra balled her hand, unsure whether the Myr's voice echoed in her mind, or if they were her own thoughts and realisations. This was why Malora had rescinded Chyram's blessing. Without it, she wasn't beholden to the dragon, and she was free to pursue a life with Apollo.

'Let me prove myself to you, Lord. Let me show you I am worthy of your bond!' Malora begged.

Chyram's snarl set Calidra's teeth on edge. They needed to get away. Now.

Malora fell to her knees. 'Please, Lord Chyram. We will all be destroyed by the Myr unless you bless me!'

'Then be destroyed by them. Let the darkness take you so you no longer sully the beauty here with your treachery.' Flames burst from his jaws as he spoke.

Calidra pulled hard, yanking Malora and Renys several steps away—a heartbeat later, Chyram's fire blasted where she'd been. 'Mal you never did see when things were turning against you! He's easier to read than Mother!'

'Holy one!' Malora cried, one arm covering her face, the

other clutching Renys tightly as her daughter screamed. 'If I have offended you, please forgive me!'

'Way past the forgiveness stage here!' Calidra wrapped another arm around Malora, shielding Renys from the dragonfire. 'We have to move!'

They ran from the temple, stumbling down the rocky slope, Chyram's fire chasing them away.

25
THE HAIRPIN
TORSTEN

Snarls rippled through the air, a low rumble that squeezed Torsten's chest and made it hard to breathe.

Queen Surayo stood on the far side of his tavern room, her form hidden by a veil of shadow. She bowed her head as if weeping, but Torsten couldn't hear anything from her. 'Your Majesty…?'

She did not respond.

Toriaken, faint as smoke on the wind, lay beside her, his tail curled around her legs. Though he was formed of dark shadow, he would recognise that dragon anywhere.

She reached for Toriaken, but he drifted away from her grasp, fading into nothing, leaving only the bowing queen. She pressed both hands to her chest, her mouth opening, but no sound came from her throat. Dark mist framed her body, shifting in a breeze that wasn't there.

The dragon did not return, no matter how long he waited.

Torsten flinched, dropping the topaz hairpin.

It crashed loudly on the flagstone floor, and he suddenly realised how deeply he was breathing. He hadn't realised he'd touched the artefact when the vision had overwhelmed him, and he sank back in his chair, chest heaving, sweat rolling down his forehead.

His uniform had rumpled during whatever fever dream he'd experienced, darkened across his chest and under his arms by sweat, and he shrugged out of his overtunic.

The Blue Dragon tavern was loud beyond his closed door, but conversations were muffled and indistinct. Judging by the light from the window, it was early evening. Birds were already singing to announce the setting sun. His mug of tea had long gone cold on the table, and a thin film had formed on the top.

Torsten's lip curled. Whatever trance the artefact had created, it had wasted time. He was supposed to have been to Miroth and back by now. Should have been resting so he and Varlot could leave for Eastbrook in the morning with the queen's treasure.

He clutched his head, groaning at the ache that pulsed incessantly behind his eyes. He dragged a hand through his hair, flicking away perspiration. His arm was numb, muscles twitching, like he'd just run halfway across town on an empty stomach. He'd touched many Myrish artefacts before, but none had had that sort of effect.

A *hairpin.*

Such an innocuous item. He'd been more concerned about cutting himself on the damned thing.

He'd fed Miroth a handful of weaker artefacts over the days he'd been in Tonmouth, and while the dragon could speak and fly freely, the flame within Torsten's chest remained fragile. A candle flickering instead of the inferno it could be.

Miroth was his *brother*.

More than a dragon who happened to live near his birthplace. He was Miroth's *only* blessed. The only one who'd been there when the spirit had formed, the only one who saw strength where others saw weakness. Other dragons bonded with dozens, if not hundreds of people. Some, like Miroth, were more choosy. It only cemented how valued their bond was.

Miroth had lent his fire to Torsten when he'd found him as a young, sickly boy. The dragon's power had flooded his limbs, even young as they both were, and Torsten had never fallen to illness again. His body had grown strong. He'd been able to fight back when he was bullied, and ensure no one harmed him again. That strength had given him renewed vigour for life. Pushed him to rise to the heights of Master Inquisitor.

Together, they'd achieved greatness.

Now Miroth's greatness was slipping, and it was down to Torsten to ensure that did not continue.

He'd been sure to lock the door to his room so Varlot or the innkeeper couldn't barge in. Given the state of the place, it was a decision he patted himself on the back for. He'd clearly been writhing around during the vision, papers scattered over the floor, a ceramic teapot knocked over, contents seeping into the thick rug under the table.

Torsten stripped off his shirt and strolled to the wash basin. After filling it with cold water, he dipped both hands in, relishing the chill. The mirror fixed to the wall was smeared and cracked in one corner. Unbecoming of Porsenthia's Master Inquisitor, but Tonmouth had never been a rich town. He'd need to get more coin put towards it. He'd started with the temple already, putting some of his own funds towards repairs. The town would have to wait, but it would follow.

He splashed water over his face and the back of his neck, trying to focus on the cold and rinsing the dirt from his skin.

He tried not to think of the strange vision of Queen

Surayo and Toriaken fading from her side. It made no sense, and he blamed it on his lack of sleep and stress over Miroth.

He was distracted. That always led to mistakes.

Torsten's gaze kept being drawn to the hairpin he'd left on the stone floor. It sat there, unassuming, yet pulling his attention like a moth to flame.

He searched for Miroth's fire in his chest, relieved when he felt it flicker. Simply knowing the dragon was there gave him enough comfort, enough willpower, to finish washing and dress in a clean uniform without going back to the pin.

Once presentable, he wrapped the topaz hairpin in a scrap of cloth—he didn't want to fall into that hallucination every time he touched the artefact—and left the room, sure to lock the door behind him. He jiggled the handle a few times to make absolutely certain the lock was in place, before he strode down the hall and across the sticky tavern floor.

Most of the tables were full of sailors and locals, and Torsten immediately spotted Varlot at one near the back of the room. He clutched a large tankard of ale, cards and dice splayed across the table.

Torsten caught Varlot's eye and nodded curtly, hoping the other man was too busy with his drinking and gambling to notice anything amiss. If he did realise something had happened, he didn't say anything, turning his attention back to those he drank with, his deep laugh booming across the tavern.

Torsten quickened his pace and exited the smoky room. The cool evening air was a welcome relief, and he took a few deep breaths before making his way through the familiar streets of Tonmouth towards Miroth's lake.

'I'm coming, brother.'

Miroth's flame, deep within Torsten's chest, grew as he left the town behind him and made his way up the hillside path towards the lake and shrine beyond.

Miroth's growing presence sparked hope. A few days prior, Miroth had been on the brink of fading. Now, after he'd consumed several Myrish artefacts and had some of his essence restored, he seemed stronger than he'd been in years.

The last of the sun's rays were warm and bright, streaks of red and pink colouring the sky like an errant paintbrush. Torsten gripped the cloth in his pocket. If he hadn't already touched the hairpin, he'd never have known it was one of the Myr's artefacts.

He just had to hope it would keep Miroth alive while he pursued Malora and Renys.

Torsten found Miroth resting alone on the far side of the lake, half his body submerged in the water. Torsten had tasked the few priests of the shrine with restoring many of the crumbling steps, sweeping empty chambers, and polishing the sword in Miroth's altar—making the shrine worthy of Miroth. Even though it had only been a handful of days, he was pleased to see a small crowd of people nearby.

So often on previous visits, Miroth had been completely alone.

'Brother. I feel your presence.' Miroth's voice was low and rumbling. He no longer spoke haltingly—not when he'd been fed so much magic—but he remained lethargic.

'My Lord.' Torsten dropped to one knee a few paces from the dragon's snout, boots squelching in the mud. When he rose, Miroth's eyes had opened, and the dragon peered down at him.

'There are many in the temple now. Such activity. Noise.'

'It is necessary, brother. A bright, clean temple will attract more people to worship you.'

'Am I not enough?'

'You are. But people are fickle and shallow. They will

overlook you for something brighter. So they must be told of your magnificence, and your shrine is the best way to do that. More priests and priestesses will help, too. They will show your glory among the people and spread word.'

Miroth grumbled, though Torsten wasn't sure if it was assent or dismissive. Emotions had blurred together recently, confusing his perception.

'I have brought you something, brother.' Torsten fished in his pocket and pulled out the cloth-wrapped pin. 'Another artefact. A powerful one.'

Miroth growled, but did not recoil. '*So much Myrish magic. I can take power from it, but it...is thick. Heavy.*'

'Until your lake is cleansed, there is no other way to prevent you from fading.'

'*The salt aches across my scales. Smothers my breath.*' Miroth turned his silvery gaze upon the lake water. On the opposite side, closer to the shrine, a small gathering of people worked to sweep and repair the gravel pathway.

Torsten felt the dragon's ache and winced. 'I know, brother. But we take what we want. We take from the weak. And the Myr *are* weak. It is only right we use their leavings.'

Miroth did not reply, but Torsten sensed the dragon's hesitance. 'I will *not* let you fade, my Lord.'

Smoke streamed from Miroth's nostrils, his blue scales darker than Torsten had ever seen them. The sun began to set, shadows lengthening.

'*There should be such strength in my claws that movement is effortless. There is not. And I am tired. I will take the Myr's power, brother. You have always been dear to me.*'

A wave of adoration washed through Torsten and he approached Miroth, wading into the water and resting his forehead against the tip of the dragon's snout. Miroth's scales were smooth and hard, burning hot to the touch. He was a spirit of water, but he was a dragon above all else, and fire prevailed.

Torsten closed his eyes, savouring the moment of connection. 'Here, brother. I must track down one of my enemies. This will see you restored until my return.'

Miroth hesitated a few moments longer, long enough that Torsten thought the dragon had reconsidered, then he snatched the hairpin in his jaws and swallowed.

'You're feeding artefacts to the lake dragon?' Varlot's shout cut through the air.

Torsten spun around, *Tinebás* drawn in one, swift movement. 'You have no business here, Varlot.'

'So much for following orders. You ignore what the queen told you to do because of *that*? It's fading away! Lake'll be dead in a few years! Why are you wasting your time?'

Fury like Torsten had never felt before filled him. 'I'll take your tongue!.' He rushed towards the man, hardly aware of his legs moving. He crossed the distance so quickly that Varlot had no time to draw his axe, turning to take the brunt of Torsten's strike on his pauldron. The metal struck with a clang, orange sparks shooting along the length of *Tinebás* as Torsten wrenched the sword back for a second attack.

Varlot was quicker to react, stepping out of range and pulling his great axe from the holster on his back. 'You'll regret that.'

Torsten stepped to the side, enough rationality to keep him on the defensive now Varlot had his weapon drawn. Bright fury reduced his vision to the man standing before him, the rest of the world disappearing into nothingness.

He held *Tinebás* ready to parry the inevitable strike. Widened his stance to bear the brunt of it. Varlot was strong, but Torsten knew he could take the brute as long as he kept his wits about him.

But the strike didn't come.

Varlot lowered his axe, mouth falling open as he stared at something behind Torsten.

Though he had it drilled into him to never turn your back on an enemy, Torsten couldn't help himself.

With his attention away from Varlot, he realised he could no longer feel Miroth's fire in his chest.

He was…empty.

Torsten turned around.

Miroth made a sound he had never heard before. A roar of pain and fury, delight and fear. He thrashed around the water's edge, rolling and tail lashing as his body pulsed with shadow, and *grew*. With every snarl, his limbs elongated, horns and fins lengthening. His small wings opened, the membranes stretched wide, dark veins rippling through his flesh.

He was already approaching Alnothen in size.

'Lord Miroth!' Torsten cried, but the dragon did not respond. He'd never seen Miroth with such strength. The artefact was like nothing else he'd seen.

'Now you've done it, Torsten.' Varlot laughed, though there was no mirth in the noise. 'Queen ain't gonna be pleased you fed her artefact to a spirit instead of giving it to her.'

'What?' Torsten rounded on Varlot, sword lancing towards him.

Varlot smacked it away with little effort. 'You're dead, Torsten. I win.'

Torsten faltered, struggling for words. 'You…you said you'd found the artefact she wanted! You were going to take it to her!'

'And get all her praise and reward for it. Now, I get to tell her you fucked up. I like that better, you know. I still get what I want, and you get knocked down.'

Miroth snarled again, pain lacing his cry, the sound sending ripples across the lake.

Varlot spat on the ground. 'If the dragon don't get you first, *she* will.' He sheathed his axe and backed off.

Miroth shot out a plume of fire, sending Torsten and Varlot diving in opposite directions. Varlot regained his footing quickly, turned, and raced away, heading in the direction of Tonmouth.

Torsten spared him a brief glance. The man could do what he liked. He'd deal with him later.

Miroth was all that mattered. The dragon plunged into the lake, water cascading up like a fountain.

'Brother!' Torsten ran to the water's edge. People were beginning to gather, some coming down from the temple, others cautiously making their way up from the town.

Torsten clutched his chest. 'Miroth? Miroth!' There was *nothing* inside him. No flame, no sense of the dragon. No voice. No emotion. No…

No strength.

Torsten's grip on his sword weakened, pain searing his wrist. He coughed, suddenly unable to breathe deeply and clearly. He dropped to his hands and knees, the muscles in his forearm losing their definition as he stared at them.

Before he could make sense of it, Miroth emerged from the lake with a beat of his wings.

Water cascaded down his body, and Torsten could hardly believe his eyes. Miroth rivalled Toriaken in size, now—the enormity of his form throwing the lake, the shrine, and half of Tonmouth into shadow. His scales were no longer the dusty blue of the lake water, but grey-black, pulsing with shadow. The dragon's eyes had shifted from silver to darkest grey.

Torsten's mouth fell open. He could hardly believe Miroth's new strength. Could hardly believe it had worked. 'Brother! Everyone will look upon your glory!'

Miroth let out a thunderous roar that shook Torsten to his bones. The lake water surged underneath the dragon and flooded their banks.

Flames leapt from Miroth's jaws, spewing indiscriminately below.

'No!' Torsten covered his face, the heat of the fire washing over him and burning nearby foliage. Vegetation immediately caught, spitting at the sudden, intense heat.

There was nothing in Torsten's chest. No flame. No blessing. No *bond.*

'Brother?' Desperation hitched his voice higher. He had no strength in his arms. Everything Miroth had given him... was gone.

Miroth did not respond. Did not seem to hear him. He flapped his wings to remain airborne, and with another sharp intake of breath, spewed more fire.

Torsten could do nothing but cower as heat seared his skin.

Fire unleashed, Miroth flew away from the lake with another deafening roar.

Torsten staggered to his feet, grass and shrubbery around him crackling with fire, and chased the dragon. Each step was like pushing through thick mud, his armour and cloak weighing him down. He slipped more than once, almost careening to the ground, only his momentum keeping him on both feet.

Screams filled the air, and he followed the sounds, barging past priests and townsfolk in his haste to catch up to Miroth. Many cowered beside trees or rocks, taking what cover they could find. Others stared open-mouthed at the streak of shadow that flew overhead.

Flashes of orange lit up the horizon as Miroth breathed fire down on everything in his path.

Torsten left the last of the onlookers behind, racing across burned grass and flaming shrubbery. He reached the top of a crest, panic fuelling him despite his body's abrupt weakness, and skidded to a halt.

He gasped for breath.

Miroth's scales were dull, dark smoke wreathing his legs and tail, illuminated only by the swathes of fire he unleashed upon the land below. The dragon flew chaotically, meandering north, then veering west, only to change course again.

'Lord...Lord Miroth...' Torsten slumped forward and watched Miroth soar into the distance. 'Brother.' Cold realisation set in.

Their bond had been severed.

26

THE ARCHON OF ICE

APOLLO

Apollo pressed his cheek into his thick, fur-lined hood, and pulled it as close around his face as the material allowed. Exposed on the mountainside, the wind cut through the air sharp as any blade. It stung his skin, but after so long out in the elements, most of his face was numb. He huddled down, teeth chattering, trying to focus on Nadja's words.

The Inquisitor had found shelter, though it was a loose definition of the term. They'd scraped out a shallow pit in the snow, beside the stump of a tree that had been dead for some time. At three feet tall and just as wide, it wasn't much protection against the relentless wind and snow, but it was better than nothing.

Fenn, poor lad, followed them without much thought, his gaze often distant.

At this point, they were too far into the mountains to leave him alone. And Nadja wouldn't lose time by taking him back to Ma-Rai. Apollo was sure Fenn would snap out of it, soon. He had to be in shock.

'What do you think, Apollo?'

He shook his head and blinked snowflakes from his eyelashes. 'I'm sorry. I wasn't listening. What did you say?'

Nadja scowled at him. 'We're on the cusp of another Archon and you're daydreaming?'

He shifted his weight, wincing as his knees cracked. 'Look, it's hard to focus when we're freezing our arses off.'

'The sooner we complete the task, the sooner we can get away.'

'Yes, yes, I know, I know.' Apollo shivered, sending the snow that had accumulated on his hunched shoulders falling to the ground. 'So what're we doing?'

Nadja sighed, rubbing her nose.

The gesture reminded him of Malora whenever she was annoyed with him. He'd give anything to see that look on Malora's face again.

He bit the inside of his cheek.

'Stealth is not an approach we can take. Not in Paragos's domain. We'll have to use aggression and speed. He'll expect us to flee. We'll need to use that to our advantage.'

Apollo nodded, understanding but not really acknowledging her words.

'I can see the tips of the palace spires from here. As long as at least one of us reaches it, they can grab the key. Paragos will destroy it and that will cripple the Myr. So we must split up, keep Paragos's attention on us.'

'You want us to…face Paragos. Keep his attention?'

'Exactly.'

'And assuming I'm not dead by then, we get into the palace and bring the key out?'

'Simple.'

Apollo shivered. 'Paragos wasn't interested in the key before. I don't know why he would be now.'

'The situation is different. The Myr are returning in full force. Paragos cannot stand for that. We'll make sure he destroys that key.' Nadja was more confident than Apollo had ever seen her. Or perhaps it was desperation.

The wind howled, driving more snow into the trio where they huddled. 'Simple,' Apollo repeated. When she said it like that, it seemed possible. Almost.

'Fenn?' Nadja asked their third companion.

Fenn nodded. 'I'm ready.'

Apollo doubted that. Lad didn't look like he was ready for anything other than a few weeks in bed, but he wasn't going to judge, and he wasn't going to deny him the chance to get what he wanted.

But if he wasn't careful, Paragos was going to swallow them whole. At least Hassen had helped Fenn when they'd encountered Verkata. Perhaps he'd do the same when confronted with Paragos, too.

Apollo rested a gloved hand on Fenn's shoulder. 'Keep it together, Fenn. We'll make it through this, yet.'

Fenn focussed his blue eyes on Apollo. They watered, but he wiped them and he nodded again, more definitively.

'Good lad.' Apollo patted his shoulder and straightened, trying not to groan as his legs protested.

'I would not send you in first. I'm here on business of the crown, and what we do here will keep the empire safe.' Nadja drew her sword. 'Stay behind me. Once Paragos has me in his sights, keep left and right. Hopefully one of you can slip past him.'

Apollo took a shaky breath and followed the Inquisitor into the blizzard.

'I WILL DEVOUR those who step into my domain.' Paragos's voice echoed through the biting wind and driving snow, freezing Apollo in his tracks more than the cold did.

He stood on the edge of the ice fields and stared out. They

were covered in snow thick enough to wade through. Some of it was compact and hard, easy to walk on, but drifts covered everything and he was just as likely to slip over as he was to sink up to his waist.

And Paragos watched everything.

He had no weapon save the Inquisitor sword, and that wouldn't be more than a toothpick to the dragon spirit.

The snowfall increased, reducing his vision to a few paces in front of him. Nadja soon disappeared, and he lost sight of Fenn a dozen steps later.

Paragos's growl filled the air and ice cold wind sapped his strength, but Apollo pushed through it. Though he could no longer see the Moonlight Palace, he knew it was straight ahead. He just needed to ensure he didn't get turned around in the driving snow. Getting lost in the dragon's blizzard and dying of exposure was just as likely as being eaten.

Something dark flashed in his periphery, but by the time he turned to look, it had been swallowed up by the snow. Probably Fenn walking.

Probably.

More laughter sounded, chilling him to the bone. For all of Paragos's anger, the dragon had a cruel sense of humour.

Apollo continued across the snowy fields, senses alert for sudden movement or flame. For anything that could kill him in a moment of distraction. Cautiously, he veered towards the left of where he'd last seen Nadja walk. There was always a chance Paragos was more interested in the newcomer and wouldn't notice him.

A tiny chance.

Insignificant really.

Paragos couldn't be reasoned with. He wouldn't bargain. Apollo's only way of ever getting himself out of trouble—by talking—was useless in this situation. He'd tried to talk to Paragos before, and very much doubted five years of time passing would warm the dragon to a conversation.

He muttered to himself under his breath, the crunch of his boots on snow his only companion, save the whistling wind. It was so cold he could barely feel his legs, each step planted out of habit rather than any real sensation of what was underfoot.

Every so often, he'd step deep, the snow coming up to his knees.

'Nadja? Fenn?' Apollo called out, only for his voice to be snatched by the wind.

Damned spirits and their tricks.

'*I remember you.*' Paragos's voice sounded from the snow.

Apollo flinched, but kept moving. It went against every instinct—to stop and hide if something hungry and with teeth watched you—but to stop would be death. It was too cold, the raging snows and freezing winds too capable of sapping his strength.

He forced himself onwards.

The snowy plains opened up in front of him, a sea of white. The last barrier between himself and the Moonlight Palace. Seeing it again, understanding more about what it was, threw shivers down Apollo's spine that had nothing to do with the blizzard.

The Myr. Where the seeds of corruption had sprouted.

Abruptly, the wind died, leaving only a gentle snowfall ahead of him.

Apollo stopped walking, knees bent slightly, ready to run. Bundled up in thick furs and boots, he didn't stand a chance of outrunning the dragon, but he was going to go down fighting if this was to be his end.

He drew the Inquisitor sword and held it loose by his side.

A spear of ice thick as his arm hurtled through the air towards him. Apollo leapt out of the way, just as it careened past and slammed into the ground barely a pace from where he'd been standing.

'No one may set foot here.' Paragos appeared in a blaze of white fire—a dragon of immeasurable size, the eternal blizzard made living.

Apollo leaned back as he stared up at the creature that dwarfed him. Silver-white, flecked with blue scales and dark, almost black streaks, Paragos seemed different than Apollo remembered. He'd been fighting for his life before, and hadn't studied the dragon in any great detail, but would put a good deal of money on Paragos's scales being far darker than before. The grey plates of horn running along his upper body were thick and twisted, like the gnarled roots of an ancient tree, and the dozens of gems encrusted on his lower body were grey instead of glittering blue.

Paragos walked towards him, a definite limp in his gait that hadn't been there before.

The ground trembled, snow and ice suddenly seeming less secure underfoot.

Was it the corruption that had affected the river spirit? Could an Archon be impacted, too?

His heart lifted. Perhaps they had a chance to get past him if Paragos was not fully himself.

Apollo took a breath, ready to say something to the dragon, when Paragos's pupils constricted, and fire licked his jaws. The dragon unleashed a column of fire directly at Apollo, his head low as he walked forwards, icy talons gripping onto the snow.

Apollo leapt forward and rolled to the ground just as the searing heat blasted overhead. He came to his feet somewhere underneath the dragon's belly, and glanced up at the gems above his head. Most were grey, but a few remained piercing, shining blue.

Before he could think any more on it, Paragos whirled around, claws raking the ground and sending cracks across the snow and ice.

Apollo narrowly avoided being shredded as easily as the

snow, diving to the side once again. He thrust his sword towards the dragon in desperation, the blade skittering harmlessly off Paragos's scales.

The dragon snarled, one foot slamming the sword into the snow, pinning it under his claws.

Apollo tried to wrench the weapon away from the dragon before realising his attempts were futile. Leaving the sword, he turned to run.

Paragos lashed his tail, quick as a flash. One of the spines struck Apollo across the side of his body, its tip slashing at his forehead. He cried out, thrown forward by the force of the blow, though he managed to stay on his feet. He didn't think, didn't look back, just ran straight ahead.

Every breath was shallow, but he *could* breathe.

Fenn stood motionless a short way ahead, staring at Paragos.

'Run, you idiot!' Apollo yelled, as the shaking ground underfoot told him Paragos was already on his tail. Another hiss, and Apollo dived to the side as more dragon-fire lanced the air. The flames crackled, as if it had bitten into something.

Apollo twisted to look behind him, mouth open as he saw the flames licking along several large, green vines. 'Fenn?'

The other man ran towards him, arms outstretched. His eyes were wide, but focussed. 'Apollo! Look out!' Fenn crashed into him, sending them both to the snow in a heap.

Another wash of fire, and suddenly Apollo and Fenn were covered by thick vines and foliage that had appeared out of the freezing snow around them, as if it had always been buried there.

'Fenn!' A maze of green surrounded them, impervious to Paragos's fire. Apollo could hardly believe it. 'Spirits take me, that was close.'

'It isn't over yet!' Fenn said.

'You okay?' Apollo asked, trying to look into Fenn's eyes.

Paragos roared, the ground shaking with the force of the dragon's breath. With a final snarl, he slashed down the foliage with his claws. Their tips ripped through the plants, sending leaves fluttering down past them, several vines snapping, but the structure held.

Apollo and Fenn crouched low, flattening themselves to the snow. Something warm trickled down his face, and Apollo realised he was bleeding.

Paragos's silhouette disappeared, and the foliage receded.

Freezing fog wreathed everything and Apollo couldn't see more than a few paces in any direction. Paragos roared and ice blasted out in a wide circle, spears as thick as Apollo's arm slicing through the air.

Apollo winced, bracing himself to be struck by ice, but nothing hit him.

The stillness lasted only a heartbeat, before the blizzard returned in full force, winds and snow blasting into them. 'Where's Nadja?' Apollo called through the wind.

'She said we should split up. That's the plan.'

'Fuck the plan. We don't keep together, we're all dead!'

Fenn's eyes darkened once again, shoulders slumping.

Apollo grabbed him by the shoulders and shook. 'Fenn? Snap out of it! What's wrong with you?'

But Fenn wasn't listening anymore. His eyes lost their focus, and he pulled away from Apollo. 'The Moonlight Palace.'

Apollo winced. Fenn reminded him of Yorik, who'd come with him to the palace five years ago, but hadn't left. More guilt washed over him, and he did nothing as Fenn stumbled away, swallowed up by the white winds.

He hobbled forward, following where he'd seen Fenn disappear, and keeping both eyes out for Paragos and Nadja. It was a mess. A foolish, stupid plan that was going to see them all killed.

Snow swallowed him on his next step and he sank down to his knees. He hauled himself up, now acutely aware of the bruising along the side of his body from the tail strike. Blood continued to stream down one side of his face, obscuring his vision in his right eye, and his breaths came shorter and shorter.

Damn that dragon!

He pushed onwards, the cold sapping the strength from his legs.

He slipped once.

Twice.

Forced himself to his feet again. Everything ached, and he wouldn't be surprised if he'd cracked a rib or two. There was no movement save the blinding white that filled his vision. No sign of Nadja or Paragos.

Or the palace, for that matter.

It had been just ahead…hadn't it?

More wind shrieked, rattling his head, disorienting him.

With a gasp of agony, he came to a stop. Tried to catch his breath. Tried to take just one more step…

Apollo sank down to the ground, pain surging across his arms and chest. Fuck. He almost wanted that freezing cold back to numb his limbs. Blood dripped down from his right eyebrow. When he wiped it away, he just smeared more of it down his face. It stung in the cold, the tiny drop of heat wrenched away.

'Mal…' Apollo whispered.

White filled the air around him, and spears of ice whistled past his head—Paragos attacking his companions or simply having fun now Apollo was on his knees. Just as he thought it, a blast of wind knocked him forward, face first into the crunching snow.

Something sharp dug into the side of his face, and he shoved himself up to his hands and knees, feeling more warmth trickle down his chin. He put his gloved hand to his mouth and it came away bright red.

Another freezing gust bit into the back of his head, claws of ice striking his neck and back.

He huddled into himself, protecting his face as much as he could. But every touch of ice drained his strength more and more, until it was all he could do to stay on his knees.

Bright orange light flickered off to his right, but it might as well have been back in Porsenthia. Right eye squinted shut, blood from the cut above his eye sheeting down, he tried to catch his breath.

Tried to will himself to stand again.

But his legs were numb. Or were they frozen to the ground?

He slumped again, too cold, too exhausted to even shiver.

Everything went white, and slowly began to fade into nothing. Ice crusted his eyelashes, and he could hardly keep his one good eye open.

Something gripped his arm, painfully squeezing. Paragos's jaws?

He couldn't see. No longer cared.

Nadja wrenched him upwards, hauling him to his feet. 'No. No. No! Now is *not* the time to lose your courage!'

Something awoke in him. Apollo grabbed hold of her, ice slippery under his boots. Dark spots filled his vision—Nadja was nothing more than a silhouette beside him, surrounded by white.

She released her grip, and his leg immediately gave way. He sank into the snow with a pained grunt.

'Apollo!' Nadja was frantic. She pulled him backwards and leapt away as a stream of flame cut a path across the snow.

The violence of the movement snapped him out of his reverie.

'Nadja? Where's the dragon?' His words came out as a cough, but it was enough to clear his head.

'You want to see your wife and daughter again? Get *up*!'

Apollo found grip, though his knees shook. He'd never been so cold in his life. He looked around, suddenly able to see more than just white. Something warm filled his mouth, and he spat blood onto the snow. The palace loomed closer than ever, spires of blue curling towards the sky. 'Paragos?'

'Everywhere. He's not able to aim his attacks, though. Who knows if the dragon is blind or disoriented, but we're lucky. Fenn's already inside. We need to *run*.'

Panic drove him. They sprinted for all they were worth, his breath coming in snatched gasps, legs pumping without thought. He didn't know where Paragos was, whether Fenn would beat them to the key, whether they'd all make it back to Porsenthia.

All he knew was he had to reach the palace.

Had to survive.

Apollo dived through the open door, crossing the threshold from Paragos's domain and into the Moonlight Palace for the second time in his life.

Fenn had left a trail of snowy footsteps along the floor.

Nadja barrelled into the side of him, both tumbling to the floor, Paragos's roars fading behind them.

Apollo laughed, panic more than humour driving it, but started to cough shortly after.

Nadja coughed, too, leaning on the enormous door frame for support.

He stumbled over her and glanced around. The Moonlight Palace had been full of magic the last time he was here —script written along the walls and floors that burst with light, voices chanting in ancient tongues.

But now, the building was dark and empty.

27
THE AMBUSH
SELYS

Selys's father had been a man of few words and quiet intensity. Whenever he entered a room, the energy shifted. He never needed to say a word, and people turned to him.

Skaru, her eldest brother, had been much the same.

Now Kaio lived in their shadow, and Selys saw so much of their brother and father in him—that same intensity. She was sure the respect would follow, given time.

Emotions washed over her, sudden and intense, and she wiped away the tears that came unbidden to her eyes. She thought she'd moved past the grief of losing her family.

Seeing her brother brought everything flooding back.

By the time she'd recovered herself, Selys realised she and Kaio weren't alone on the beach anymore.

Kaio had said they'd lost people, and it was to be expected that others might have joined the warband, too. But she didn't recognise any of the men surrounding them. They stood in a loose circle, keeping a good twenty paces' worth of distance.

She adjusted her grip on her glaive, but gave no outward sign of her surprise. A dozen of them had appeared. Two dozen. More coming all the time, from every direction.

Each one was armed to the teeth.

'Let's see what happens when Dairo's boy bites off more than he can chew. You wanted a duel, pup? Here you go.'

Selys whirled around at the voice and found Dalys standing between six of his lieutenants, each wielding blades of various lengths. They were broad and muscular, but didn't stand with any sort of discipline, nor did they hold their blades ready. Probably picked for how intimidating they looked rather than any real skill.

Her gaze roved across the others, gauging the measure of them. Dalys's band were merchant traders more than fighters. They certainly didn't have the bite of the Ioaran warband, no matter how much their numbers had been thinned.

'You're the one biting off more than you can chew, Dalys. Bit more than a duel, isn't it? You not know how to count to two?' Kaio replied.

Selys couldn't believe his arrogance, but she didn't want to undermine him in front of Dalys and those he had brought with him. Running the warband relied so much on posturing.

But she didn't like their odds. They were outnumbered fifteen, maybe twenty to one. And who knew if Dalys had roped in any of the other chiefs. Segandis was the biggest canton in Bragalia, and there were dozens of smaller warbands living within their territory. If they'd had enough of Kaio, they were in real trouble.

Worse, they were far enough down the beach that they were out of earshot of anyone back at the compound. She could run there to alert the others, but she wouldn't leave her brother to face Dalys and his followers alone.

Kaio strode towards Selys, and she kept her eyes on those behind him. Surrounded as they were, she didn't want Kaio's back to face anyone, so she automatically moved to cover him.

'You won't fight me yourself?' Kaio called towards Dalys.

The other chief laughed heartily. 'See, this is why you're a shite leader, Kaio. I got the best people to do things for me. Leaves me to get on with the business of running things. And I mean to start running Segandis'

Kaio's eyes widened. 'You're the one who wants to play by the rules. You can't just saunter down to my beach and—'

'You play by your own rules, Ioran. I can do the same,' Dalys snapped. 'Three years we've put up with you as Laird. Your brother ran things fair, like. Respectful. You've driven this canton into the ground, and you won't listen to reason. Yesterday's outburst proved you aren't fit to lead what's left of your family, let alone the canton. Time's up, boy. Welcome to your consequences.'

Though Selys didn't want to leave Kaio's back unguarded, she glanced over her shoulder in time to spot Dalys catch the attention of someone near the back of his group.

Acting on impulse, she grabbed Kaio by the shoulder and pulled him down to the sandy ground.

An arrow whistled overhead a heartbeat later, directly where he'd been standing.

'Close!' Kaio chuckled.

She wasn't in the mood for his jokes, and leapt up, glaive held defensively across her body. He'd brought this down on their heads and had the gall to laugh about it. 'Kaio!'

Directly ahead, three of Dalys's men charged forward. Selys narrowed her eyes, focussing on the immediate threat. There was no time to warn them of what she could do. They'd chosen the wrong people to attack.

Boots kicked up sand as they closed the gap, and Selys stood her ground, glaive at the ready. 'Neros…' she whispered. Fire filled her chest and spread along her arms until her fingers tingled.

The nearest enemy, a tall man wearing a strip of red fabric across his head and pale scars across both forearms, let out a bellow as he bore down on her. He held his short sword high, its edge gleaming.

Selys waited until he was within three paces of her, then brought her glaive around in an arcing strike. It cleaved him from collarbone to groin, the force of the blow knocking him to the side, where he collided with his comrade. The pair of them dropped to the ground, blood spilling from the wound she'd carved across his body.

It slowed the approach of the others, but not by much. If anything, it lit a fire in them—they raced forward as one, a surge of furious steel, and Selys had no other choice. 'Kaio. Stay back.'

'What?' He spun around, blood glistening on his blade from the two opponents he'd felled while she'd dealt with hers. They were surrounded. It was only a matter of time before they were overwhelmed.

'I will use Neros. It's the only way.'

'Fuck that! I can take them!' Kaio yelled, turning to meet the slash of another opponent—this man twice the width of him and holding a longsword in both hands. Kaio grunted, arms trembling as he matched him for strength, then kicked out to gain some distance. He followed it up with another slash, drawing a line of red across the man's upper arm.

'Kaio!' Selys cried, the only other warning she could give as Neros's power surged within her.

Fire erupted from her fingers, and she spun her glaive to send a plume of it careening through the air and straight into the line of Dalys's followers directly in front of her. The flames were so hot they scorched the sand, turning it vivid red, then black. It melted in the intensity, then a moment later, it shimmered as glass.

The confusion of the attack had its intended effect. People stopped in their tracks. Some because they'd dived out of the way, others stood wide-eyed and stared at the destruction Selys had left. She didn't give them time to regroup.

Taking her weapon in both hands, she widened her stance and waved her glaive in a slow sweep.

Water cascaded over them.

It wasn't just water as if it had been poured from a jug.

It wasn't even as ferocious as a waterfall.

It was the power of the ocean in that blow. Icy seawater churned and foamed with the fury of Neros and crashed into her enemies, blasting them away. Neros's roar ripped through every person the attack connected with, rocking the ground like a quake. Fruit from nearby trees fell, scattering on the beach along with several branches.

Selys straightened, glaive ready for another attack. Kaio stood beside her, silent for once.

Dalys had dropped to the ground, one arm wrapped around the nearest tree for support.

A quarter of the people he'd brought were on fire. Half were waterlogged and out of action. The rest hovered near Dalys, most clutching their weapons with white knuckles.

'Dalys. That was your warning.' Selys held her glaive out, blade pointing towards the other chief.

More movement in her peripheral vision caught her attention, and she glanced over to see Taran appear on the edge of the beach, his bow drawn and an arrow notched.

Others from the Ioran warband appeared behind him, bolstering their numbers.

Dalys took stock of the shifting odds, his frown growing. 'Wild pup has others to fight his battles too, it seems. Welcome back to Segandis, Selys.' There was nothing welcoming in his tone.

'It isn't welcome with you here. Get your injured and get off our land.' She kept her glaive held up, the surroundings and violence of Segandis easing her back into her old ways far more easily than she'd thought possible. Even Neros's flame seemed distant. 'Expect updated terms of your tithe and territory, Dalys.'

Whatever fight Dalys had left in him fled as Esto walked onto the beach and stood beside Selys and Kaio. Footsteps behind her confirmed they'd gained the advantage of numbers. Dalys swallowed, and gave the order to help the injured. With a final glare of contempt, he turned tail and left.

Selys spent a while watching the remainder of those hurt in the fight dragged away. When she turned around, Kaio was deep in conversation with Taran and Esto, and most of the others stole long glances at her, or at the streak of glass running along the sand.

Yaniv patted her on the back, and half a dozen of the warband surrounded her, heaping praise on her prowess in battle.

'Now we have *that* on our side, nothing can stand up to us!' Yaniv grinned broadly.

'Won't even be a fight no more!'

'We were slipping. Now, we're back!'

Selys smiled at their adoration, but she didn't want to take credit for the praise. Neros wasn't a power to be wielded lightly, nor for the wrong cause. But she didn't want to dampen their celebrations and didn't correct their dreams.

She extricated herself from them and made her way towards Kaio. 'Are you okay? Were you wounded?'

Kaio grabbed her by the arm and pulled her away from prying eyes and ears, his gaze dark. 'Why'd you do that? I had everything under control!'

Startled, Selys faltered. 'What? We were surrounded! There had to be at least three score of them!'

He shook his head. 'Now you waltz in and wave Skaru's weapon? Renegotiate our terms with other warbands? You want me to give you the Lairdship, too? Save you the effort?'

'What are you talking about? Kaio, you know I serve Neros. There's no room for anything else.'

He pressed his knuckles into his temples. 'Selys you're complicating things here. What's to stop Yaniv declaring for you, now? Look how they fawn over you! You've been back less than a day!'

Selys mirrored his stance, irritation prickling her thoughts. 'I was their captain for years. Don't begrudge that relationship. I'm not here to take anything from you. I'm here to serve Neros, that's it. While this mess is getting cleaned up,' she nodded towards the beach, 'you were going to show me that artefact.'

'If I show you it, will you fuck off?'

She held back her immediate reaction, which was to smack him. 'I'll do as Neros wishes. And if you were paying attention to that display, you won't fight me.'

It was harsh, but it seemed Kaio only learned things through bitter experience rather than being told. She didn't have the patience to deal with his tantrums or wait for him to be receptive to her requests.

He glared at her again, and she met it.

Neros could see through her eyes, too, and though it took longer than Selys would have thought, Kaio finally looked away from her dragon's stare.

He huffed and backed away from her. 'This way. I hope it's what you want.'

28
THE ATTACK
CALIDRA

'There is always space here for the faithful, *sigya*.' The old woman tightened the shawl around her neck—though it was surely too warm for the thin strip of fabric even so early in the morning—and held out a basket of food towards them.

Her face was the colour of teak, wrinkled and lined so deeply it was a wonder she had any skin left. Her eyes were the richest brown Calidra had ever seen, though one was somewhat milky. The creases of her face tightened into a smile as Calidra and Jisyel took their portions.

Calidra saw a few mint leaves between her teeth, chewed up and broken down.

'There is no charge. We loyal followers share in Chyram's glory and help one another.'

Malora bowed in gratitude, offering a thin smile in return.

It was a simple breakfast: thin flatbreads filled with yoghurt, tomatoes, olives, and mint sprigs, rolled into parcels for easier eating.

'Olives!' Renys took a huge bite out of her portion.

Calidra picked out the olives in her own breakfast and

gave them to Renys. While she liked them well enough, it was something small she could do for her niece.

Who knew when they'd have any better luck.

Renys wasn't affected by her mother's sadness. She happily told Calidra about how excited she was to sleep somewhere new, all the stories she was going to share with her father, and asked Calidra which stories she thought he might like the most.

The four of them had stayed on the mountainside, far away from the shrine and Chyram's gaze. The old woman was in charge of this section of tents and people, and made sure everyone had something to eat. She didn't dress in the robes of a priestess, just the worn and faded peasant garb of any local villager, although she wore a long chain of gold that clinked with every movement—a subtle sign of her allegiance.

Calidra sat beside Renys and Jisyel on a wide, flat rock, the smell of cooking thick in the air as dawn lit the eastern side of the mountains. It was already a bright morning, with clear blue skies overhead, and Bragalia clear to see for leagues below.

Despite Chyram's fury, Malora hadn't wanted to leave the shrine. So, exhausted, they'd rested in one of the many tents beside a young mother and her two infants, taking turns to help comfort them through the night in exchange for shelter.

Malora was working up the courage to approach Chyram a second time, and Calidra had given up trying to talk her out of it. Their childhood bickering was coming to the surface again, and Calidra wanted no part in that, though her sister's entitled behaviour was infuriating.

Most people gave anyone arguing a wide berth, but the old woman had appeared to offer them food, and the respite brought some peace. Calidra hoped it would give Malora some common sense, too.

Renys devoured the olives Calidra had given her and

began licking her fingers. She seemed happy enough now her immediate needs had been met, but Calidra wasn't sure how much longer the girl would stay like this. If Malora continued to ignore Chyram's wishes and aggravate the dragon, there was a chance he would drive them off the mountain entirely.

Or worse.

'You tell me to eat, Mal? That it's good for me. Now you've been told the same,' Calidra said, attempting some humour to diffuse the building tension.

Malora nodded absently and took a small bite from her rolled bread.

'You okay?' Calidra asked Jisyel.

Jisyel offered her a smile in response, but Calidra could tell she didn't mean it. Jisyel's attention kept being drawn to the people around them, and more often than not lingered on the path to the shrine itself.

'We'll get that curse removed. I promise.' Calidra hoped she wasn't too upset that Malora hadn't received her blessing. She needed to make sure Jisyel knew her needs were a priority and always would be.

'I'm fine,' Jisyel said, realising Calidra was staring at her, but she stood up and began to pace.

Calidra finished her breakfast and rubbed sleep from her eyes. She hadn't done her sword drills this morning—it hadn't felt right, and there were many people here that might react poorly to it.

She wanted to convince her sister to give up on Chyram. It was foolish, surely, to try her luck again. The dragon had wanted nothing to do with Malora the day before. Who was to say today would be any different?

'I thought dragon spirits didn't leave their domains?' Jisyel mused.

'A few can. Toriaken, but that's only because his domain is

so far-reaching. And the Archons of course,' Malora replied, dusting off her hands. 'Why?'

'Oh. Well, that isn't Toriaken. Is it one of the Archons?'

Malora almost bowled Calidra over in her haste to reach Jisyel. 'An Archon? *Here?*'

Calidra wandered over to Jisyel and Malora, curious to see for herself. There were several dragon spirits on this part of the mountain. Chyram was the most powerful and worshipped, of course, but there were river and forest spirits here, too. She doubted Jisyel would mistake one of those for an Archon.

From so high up, they had an excellent view of the rivers below, alongside the market town of Vaelar to the south, and Fellwood to the north-west. Forested mountains stretched around them for leagues.

A dragon with dark grey and black scales soared low, wings spread wide, approaching Fellwood from the north. It was huge, but the only dragon of that size was Alnothen, and this definitely wasn't her—certainly not after she'd sealed her forest. Calidra didn't recognise the beast, and that set a pang of worry rippling through her. With webbing between the dragon's fins and frills on its cheek, she would have said it was some sort of water spirit, but there were no rivers or lakes close by that looked like this dragon—the colouring was so unusual. Mountains bordered Fellwood to the north, and the dragon navigated the peaks, birds darting away with high-pitched squeals of fright.

Calidra frowned. As Malora had said, only Archons, or the most powerful dragon spirits could leave their domains. Who was this one, and where had it come from? 'What is going on?'

'I...I don't recognise it,' Malora said, the slightest wobble in her voice. 'I know *all* the spirits surrounding Fellwood. I've never seen this one before.'

'Is it an Archon?' Jisyel asked.

'No. It can't be. There's no fire surrounding it. No storm. It's the wrong colour. It's…it's all wrong.'

As she spoke, the dragon opened its jaws and spewed forth a stream of flame, burning the land below.

Jisyel clutched Calidra's hand, squeezing so tightly it hurt.

Calidra winced, but didn't pull away. 'What if it ends up in Fellwood?'

'Dragon?' Renys asked, pushing through their legs to get a better look. Malora reached down to hold Renys before she stumbled too near the edge of the cliff.

Everyone's attention was locked on the grey and black dragon. Calidra became aware of more people coming up to stand beside them. Fingers pointed towards the spirit. When it breathed fire again, they began to cry out in panic.

Calidra's breath caught. The dragon veered from side to side, flying erratically, but it was heading towards Fellwood. Her chest tightened at the terror of what would happen if it reached her hometown.

'Chyram will see I'm worthy again…' Malora whispered.

'What?' Jisyel asked.

'This dragon? If I can calm it? Stop it? That will prove I'm worthy of Chyram's blessing.'

'You're joking?' Calidra faced her sister.

Malora stared at the dragon spirit. 'I can do this. I *can*.'

Calidra grabbed Malora by the shoulders. 'You'll be putting yourself in danger if you go near it!'

'We're *already* in danger. I *need* my powers. This will show Chyram I'm worthy. That's all I can do. And Mother is there!'

Calidra and Jisyel caught each other's gazes.

'If it comes up here, we'll be sitting ducks,' Jisyel said, clutching her tunic in both hands. 'Should we ask Chyram for help?'

'Mother…' Calidra didn't want to think of her mother burned alive by a dragon spirit, but she wasn't about to throw herself in the path of the flames, either.

A hubbub of noise and movement erupted around them as more people flocked to the cliffside, staring at the dragon bearing down on the Laird's hometown. Others ran towards Chyram's shrine, screaming a warning.

'I have to do this.' Malora kissed Calidra on the cheek, then crouched to hug Renys tightly. 'Stay with your Aunt Cal, okay? I'll be back soon. I promise.'

Malora pushed her gently towards Calidra, her hand holding onto Renys's until the last possible moment, then she ran down the mountain.

'Malora!' Jisyel cried after her.

'Mama!' Renys wailed.

Calidra wasn't going to wait for her sister to be incinerated by a rampaging dragon, no matter how strongly she believed she could calm the spirit. She looked at Jisyel and took a breath.

'I'm coming with you,' Jisyel said, before Calidra could get a word out. 'Nowhere is safe. Not anymore. We stick together.'

Calidra wanted to argue, wanted to tell Jisyel that as of this moment, the mountainside was safer than Fellwood. But she wasn't going to take that choice from her. 'We stick together.' Calidra repeated. She lifted Renys to her chest, and they hurried after Malora as quickly as they could.

THICK SMOKE FILLED THE AIR, turning the sky black. Calidra led them down twisting paths, careful of loose rocks and pebbles that could easily lead to a turned ankle. Jisyel followed close behind, Malora a short distance ahead of them.

Several parts of the countryside were on fire, and heat seared Calidra's skin as a flame snapped up, licking along the branches of a tree unfortunate enough to be in its path. They passed several dead horses, burning fleshed smoking.

'Keep close!' Calidra called, one arm across her face to keep the smoke away as much as possible.

'Wanna go home!' Renys whimpered, alternating between sniffling and crying. 'Want Mama!'

'She's just ahead, Ren. We'll catch up soon.' Calidra tried to reassure her niece, but in truth, she was terrified for Malora and how she was behaving.

Already the Fellwood bell towers' sounded. A warning. An alarm. The heavy clanging echoed, vibrating in Calidra's chest as they tolled.

She'd developed a stitch in her side, but pushed through the discomfort. The wooden gates to Fellwood loomed ahead, and she saw the red haze of flames flickering up beyond those walls. Her breath shortened, and she clutched the hilt of her sword. There was nothing it would do against a spirit, but it gave her a measure of comfort she used to ground herself.

Her gaze darted to the sky every few seconds, terrified the dark dragon would swoop in to scorch them where they ran. In the occasional gaps between the black smoke, the sky remained purest blue. It only heightened her anxiety, that cold fear pushing her on towards her home.

Several people raced past them, away from Fellwood, their clothes singed.

'Run for your lives!'

'Get away from the town!'

They shoved past, heedless of anything in their way, and one knocked Jisyel to the ground. Calidra put Renys down gently, then helped Jisyel back to her feet.

Jisyel shook her head. 'Sorry, Cal. I'm just in the way.'

'No you're not! Don't say that!' Calidra reassured her.

Renys began to cry at a fresh graze down her elbow.

'Ren, it's okay.' Calidra crouched and kissed her niece's

elbow, trying desperately to hide her own fear and panic from the child. 'It's only a scratch, you'll be okay, won't you? You've been so brave already. Can you be brave a bit longer?'

Renys whimpered, rubbing her eyes and smearing tears and soot down her face.

'Your mum and dad are both very proud of you. I am, too.' She cupped her face with both hands, thumbs wiping away Renys's tears.

The world had been turned upside down and Calidra was amazed Renys had made it this far from home without much fuss. Bringing her into a town under attack wasn't wise, but they couldn't leave her outside, either.

Renys sniffled and nodded, one hand clutching the hem of her tunic.

A loud crack split the air, and part of the wooden wall surrounding Fellwood wrenched apart. Burning embers crackled, splinters thrown high, and it collapsed.

Malora, much closer to the wall than they were, darted in through the hole.

Calidra picked up Renys again and headed straight for the gap in the wall, closer than the town gates.

More people burst out, screaming in terror. Beyond the rush of bodies, a glint of armour shone in the town, along with shouted orders and frenzied commands. Flashes of colour darted between the dark smoke, some distance off the ground, coupled with a shriek that cut through the sky.

'Griffins!' Jisyel cried.

Calidra had forgotten there had been a contingent of Olmese griffin riders in her mother's service. The threat of the Myr had shifted dynamics, and several warriors had been stationed in Fellwood. If they were trained to fight the Myr, hopefully they'd be able to protect the townspeople from a dragon.

She caught glimpses of wings as they dived at the dragon spirit, pushing it away.

Calidra reached the broken wall and pushed through the gap, a scene of chaos greeting her. Several buildings stood aflame, many with rooftop infernos. A few posts had crashed to the ground, throwing splinters across the paved streets, charred debris smoking. Her stomach turned at the sight. Surely the mortared stone of the walls surrounding her family estate would not fall quickly—even to dragon-flame.

Guards and fighting men and women in the livery of the Vantonen family crest were out in force, weapons drawn, fear etched in their faces. But they stood firm, directing townspeople away from the inferno raging through Fellwood.

Calidra and Jisyel caught up to Malora, who stood just inside the town, staring up at the griffins and dragon filling the smoke-filled sky.

'Mama!' Renys reached for Malora.

'Darling, you have to be strong,' Malora said, though she kept her gaze on the sky.

'Let's get to the house!' Calidra said. It was the only place that would offer protection, and she needed to get Renys there, if nothing else. Malora nodded, and Calidra forced her way through the crowd, Jisyel right behind.

Screeches of griffins and the cries of guards pushed the townspeople out of direct danger, and soon they were surrounded only by the crackling of fire and wood, thick smoke obscuring streets and half a dozen buildings.

Something dark flashed overhead as the dragon swept into view for a heartbeat, disappearing again as a plume of smoke filled the sky. The threat of flames pushed Calidra on, through the stitch in her side and the ache in her legs.

'Take Ren to Mother. I will deal with the dragon,' Malora said.

'Wait!' Calidra cried, but it was too late. Malora darted down an alley and headed towards the town square, where the dragon was focussing its efforts.

Calidra stared after her, and tried to quieten Renys as she reached towards where her mother had disappeared.

Jisyel blocked their view. 'She'll be okay! We have to get out of the open!'

Renys continued to scream, scrambling in Calidra's arms and trying to get down to follow Malora. Calidra held her tight, trying to hush her niece to no avail, and pushed on.

There were more uniforms the closer they came to the family estate. Liveries of different colours blurred together—Vantonen family guard, town guard, even Inquisitors.

People shouted at her, but all Calidra could do was run. She *had* to keep Renys safe. Her surroundings were a cacophony of noise and colour, smoke and panic. It was overwhelming.

A man stood in front of her, blocking the street. 'Stop in the name of the Iron Crown!'

Calidra recognised the Inquisitor uniform, but fear pushed her on. 'Stand aside!'

The man drew a sword.

Calidra responded in kind. 'Out of my way! I'm Calidra Vantonen! I need to get to the estate!'

'You aren't going anywhere.'

His voice triggered a primal fear and Calidra skidded to a halt, Renys clutched in one arm, the sword in her other. She'd never forget that voice. The shock of it hardly seemed to register, not when Jisyel, Malora, and Renys were all in danger of being burned by the dragon. 'Torsten.'

'That's *Master* Inquisitor to you. Even if you *are* the daughter of a Laird.'

'Scary man!' Renys cried and pointed.

Torsten ignored Renys. 'I've had a barricade set up at the town gates. How rude of you to circumvent it by entering Fellwood through a hole in the wall.'

Calidra had no idea what he was talking about, and she had no desire to find out. 'I'm trying to get home, Master

Inquisitor.' Torsten's voice set her teeth on edge, and she was all too aware the dragon could attack this part of town at any moment. She hoped Malora was successful in her attempt to calm it—she had no idea if it was even possible.

His sneer didn't leave his face. 'I see you have Renys Tamlin there. Excellent. Now, where is Malora? She's under arrest.'

Calidra frowned, the absurdity of the question distracting her. 'Under arrest? What for?'

'If you do not tell me where she is, I will take the daughter to flush her out.'

'Don't you *dare* lay a finger on her!' Calidra gripped her sword so firmly it shook.

'Attack an Inquisitor and you'll be put to death. No need to arrest you, not when things can be settled here. I'll take the child, now.'

'Go away!' Renys screamed, flailing wildly and managing to leap out of Calidra's arms. She ran straight to Jisyel and grabbed her legs.

Torsten darted after her.

Calidra lunged, enjoying a moment of satisfaction as Torsten fumbled with his own sword to parry her strike.

'You are obstructing the queen's justice!'

'*Justice*? You want to arrest my sister, who has done nothing wrong! You're terrorising a four-year-old!' Calidra snarled back.

'Nothing wrong? She is married to a fugitive. A traitor to the crown, responsible for the Myr's resurgence!'

'She has done nothing!'

Torsten curled his lip. 'My word is law. Especially above the savages of Bragalia! Rule yourselves how you like, but *I* speak with Queen Surayo's voice.'

Calidra adjusted her footing, slipping into remembered forms as easily as breathing. She glared at Torsten. He looked thinner than she remembered, more gaunt somehow. It didn't matter. Despite who he was, despite his warnings, she would defend her family to her last breath.

Calidra thrust forward, and Torsten tried to meet her blade, but she forced him back. 'This is my hometown. Surayo isn't our queen.' It might have been a mistake, and was not strictly speaking true—they paid her fealty after all—but she would not be walked over by Torsten. Not when her sister and niece's lives were at stake.

Torsten lunged, his sword darting for Calidra's legs.

She stepped aside, caught his blade with her own, and deflected it. She didn't want to be too aggressive—only keep him away from Renys and Jisyel. 'You want Malora and Renys, you'll have to come back with a royal writ!'

'Insolent wretch!' Sweat trickled down one side of his face.

She lunged again, forcing him further away from Renys.

Another Inquisitor arrived through the smoke, but Calidra kept her focus on Torsten. 'Leave her be!'

'Do as you are told!' Torsten snarled, his voice rough.

Calidra brought her sword across his body, and he responded at the last moment, just managing to get his blade up to block hers. The swords clashed together, sparks thrown up where the metal dragged across each other. She stepped forward, overwhelming him with little effort. She pushed down, forcing his blade lower, more sparks glinting off their weapons.

'Stop this at once!' The second Inquisitor called, but she refused to let Torsten win. Not when she was clearly stronger than he was.

She drew back a moment and shifted her stance. 'I warned you, Torsten.' Calidra surged forward again, Torsten's eyes going wide.

Her sword connected with his again. She readied herself to press her attack, stepping forward and forcing him completely out of her way—

Pain shot through her leg and Calidra dropped to one knee with a cry.

'Cal!' Jisyel was beside her a moment later.

'I'm fine,' Calidra replied, automatically. But when she tried to stand, she found she had no strength in her legs. Darkness swam in front of her, smoke or the dragon, or something else, she couldn't tell.

She fought through it, tried to push herself up again, even as streaks of red flooded her vision.

But she couldn't.

Calidra looked down to see an arrow protruding from the meat of her left thigh. Blood stained her breeches, dripping down her leg and onto the paved street.

'I *told* you to halt!' The Inquisitor already had another arrow drawn.

Jisyel made to grab Renys, but the second Inquisitor loosed—it embedded itself between two stone pavings between them. A warning shot.

'No, don't!' Jisyel cried as Torsten strode over to them and grabbed Renys around the middle, hauling her off her feet.

'Torsten!' Calidra tried to get up again, but the arrow had done its job, and she couldn't stand.

'Be quiet, Vantonen, or I'll have my colleague take out your other leg,' Torsten hissed. His hair was loose, errant strands framing his face, and glared at them.

Another building burst into flame as Miroth flew overhead, turning on the wind and heading away from Fellwood.

Calidra flinched at the fire, more smoke filling the air in thick columns.

It obscured Renys's screams as Torsten and the other Inquisitors carried her away and out of sight.

29
THE PALACE
APOLLO

Apollo's eyelids fluttered open. Crumbs of ice that had been lodged between his lashes tumbled down his face, but most stuck to the crusted blood on his cheek.

He tried to move and immediately winced. Pain stabbed across his ribs, coupled with a deep ache in his legs, as though every bone in his body had been bruised. With another grunt of effort, he lifted his head from the marble floor and waited for the sudden dizziness to pass.

'I wasn't sure you'd wake,' Nadja said.

'You…waited fo' me…t'wake up?' Apollo struggled to form words, his speech slurred.

'You know where the key is.' Nadja stepped forward and offered her hand. With a heave, she pulled him to his feet.

His vision swam, and he took a few moments to catch his breath—and ensure he wasn't about to topple over. 'Fenn?'

'Not sure. Must be further inside the palace.'

Apollo nodded gently, not trusting himself to speak. He looked around, reorienting himself. Nausea churned in his gut alongside the stabbing pain, and he bent his knees slightly, steeling himself against the discomfort.

They stood in the vast entranceway of the Moonlight Palace. A Myrish construction of stone, marble, and what felt cold enough to be solid blocks of ice. Faint blue light emanated from the walls and floors, as if everything was bathed in perpetual moonlight. Animals and people were carved into the cornices of the room, their stony faces warped, most with too many limbs and several horns protruding from their skulls. Many had more than one pair of eyes, and they all seemed to watch him.

Apollo's throat went dry at the sight. He'd forgotten about those grotesque creatures, and it was every bit as unsettling as the last time he'd been here.

'Perhaps they're creatures from the spirit world,' Nadja said, following his gaze. 'Or animals native to Meneos?' She picked up the bag of supplies she'd been carrying since Cape Grullon, and pulled out a strip of linen. 'Let me help you.'

Apollo was about to dismiss her, then thought better of it.

She wrapped the fabric around his head, pulling it tight with deftness and efficiency. He winced at the pressure against his cuts and grazes.

Once done, Nadja strode away, her footsteps tapping on the silver-grey floor—a blend of stone and marble that reflected everything like a pool of crystal clear water. Black scrawling letters covered every inch of the floor and walls, and Apollo remembered them flashing with golden light when he'd walked across them before.

Now, they were silent.

Come to think of it, he could breathe easily, too. That was strange. He'd not soon forget his chest constricting with every breath the last time he'd been in this place.

Apollo said, 'We should find Fenn. He's not keen on us destroying the key.'

Nadja pressed her lips together, as though she was forcing herself not to frown.

'What's wrong? He say something?' His face and lips were

cold and cut up, but he could speak more like himself again. And he didn't feel like he was about to topple over, either.

'I was expecting this place to be worse. Didn't you say how awful it was here? That you couldn't breathe? I admit they,' Nadja gestured to the animal statues, 'are creepy. But it isn't so bad. Sounds to me like you were making it up to get out of returning here.'

Apollo didn't care for the accusation, but he didn't have the energy to argue back. 'You'll see.'

They walked along the entranceway, until it split into two corridors. Apollo stared down both directions, trying to remember the steps he'd taken before. There was no sign of Fenn, or anyone else, down here, and the emptiness set the hairs standing on the back of his neck. A chill wind blew from the left, and it snatched his breath away. 'Left.'

He led Nadja down the corridor, every step echoing more loudly than it had any right to. There were no windows to the outside, the only light coming from the softly glowing walls. He was no priest, but even he could feel the heavy magic of this place. It stuck to him like a second skin.

He'd been an idiot not to think of the consequences before.

The pathway did not deviate, though several doors lined the corridor, each closed and presumably locked. As they walked deeper through the palace, Apollo remembered more and more. One memory in particular suddenly floated to the top of his mind. 'Nadja…?' he whispered.

'What is it?' she whispered back.

'There's…well, there might be *something* here.'

'You mean other than the key?'

Apollo stopped a short distance away from a flight of stairs that led down into the dark. 'When I was here, something…took the key from me. One of the Myr, I think. Or one of their spirits. I didn't really hang around to find out exactly what it was. I recall she said something about guarding this place and its treasures…' He grimaced even as he spoke.

Nadja stared at him aghast for several long seconds. 'I shouldn't be surprised. I don't know why I assumed you had shared all the relevant information.' She drew her sword. 'This will have to do.'

Her frustration reminded him of Malora, and despite the danger, the exhaustion, and the fact they were walking towards one of the Myr—with Paragos waiting outside—Apollo laughed. Perhaps it was delirium, but he couldn't help himself, and the harder he tried to hold it in, the more it wanted to escape.

'Apollo? Apollo, will you shut up! It'll hear you!' Nadja hissed.

But he couldn't stop. He sank to his knees on the slippery floor, wrapped his arms around his waist, and allowed the snorting laughter to burst forth, tears streaming down his face.

Nadja grabbed him by the shoulders and heaved him up. 'Get hold of yourself, Apollo! This is no time to fall to pieces!'

He'd expected her to be angrier with him, but he only saw worry in her eyes.

It sobered him quickly, and he took a while to catch his breath—difficult when the pressure of the palace seemed to grow the closer they were to the staircase.

He was finally losing his mind, he was sure of it.

'Come on. Don't give up now, not when the key is so close. Think of your wife and daughter!'

Apollo shuddered as the fit of laughter passed. 'I'm sorry. I don't know what came over me.'

'Keep your head straight. Need your wits to be sharp.'

Apollo took an unsteady step forward, and once sure of his footing, continued towards the stairs. He peered down into the darkness, stomach tightening, threatening to bring up the rations they'd been eating. His breathing was shallower than normal.

Yorik had died down there.

The Grumpy Fisherman.

It had been five years, but everything came flooding back, as if it had only been yesterday. Yorik hadn't exactly been a friend. Even calling him an ally was a push. Yorik had been backed into a corner, accepted a Myrish bargain, and died for it. Spirits, but that was unfair. Yorik's sacrifice had allowed his escape. Malora's too. If not for Yorik, he wouldn't have had a life with her.

Emotions welled up, and Apollo's mouth ran dry.

This wasn't the time for memories. He was here for the future. He gritted his teeth and pushed on.

And though he couldn't see through the murk, it wouldn't surprise him if Fenn was already in the room at the bottom of the stairs.

Did he have the key? Was he talking to the Myrish spirit down there? Or was he to be devoured by the Myr, like a lamb brought to the slaughter?

Apollo wobbled on the top step, desperate to get as far away from this place as his legs would carry him. Even *his* insatiable curiosity wanted nothing to do with the cavernous hall down there.

Nadja rested a hand on his shoulder. 'I want you to fix what you started, Apollo. But I'm not going to force you. If the key is down there, I will retrieve it. You've brought us this far.'

His eyes burned at her words, threatening tears. He could hardly believe her lack of judgement, considering her job, considering everything he had put her through. No one gave him chances like that. Especially not Inquisitors. 'Nadja?'

She wasn't looking at him, her gaze on the dark stairway. 'I lost my husband in the war. Both of my sons. They were young, too young to fight, but they wanted to help.'

Apollo swallowed thickly. They'd spent weeks on the road together, and she'd shared not a single iota of her personal life.

'I should've known better. Fought harder to stop them, or protect them. But it didn't matter in the end. The Myr swept through our village and left only bones.'

'Nadja…'

She tore her gaze away from the darkness. 'We're fighting for the future. We always were. It isn't about honour. Medals. Prestige. It's about protecting our world. You'll be repenting for the rest of your life, whether that ends in the next few minutes, or whether you survive to be a grandfather.' Nadja made her way down the stairs and the darkness swallowed her.

Apollo lingered a moment longer, hardly able to process what she'd said, what she was doing. It was very likely that death waited for them at the bottom of that staircase. But so did the key.

If they could bring it back up, leave it in the open for Paragos to destroy, they had a chance to cut off the Myr's rising power.

Apollo took another breath, then followed Nadja into the dark.

NADJA WAITED at the bottom of the stairs and Apollo hurried to her side. A cold wind swirled in the dark hall, like the breath of some foul creature. Rolling darkness and stagnant air.

He shifted his weight and winced, trying to find a position to stand in that wasn't painful. Whatever the creature was down here, it had to know they'd entered the palace. It was only a matter of time before it struck.

'Fenn!' Nadja darted away, her footsteps muffled.

Apollo followed as quickly as he could, catching up with her after a handful of strides.

Fenn stood by one of the room's many pillars, eyes closed, both hands pressed against the stone surface. The lettering that had been scrawled along the floors and walls also crept up the pillar, but they glowed gold where Fenn touched them.

Voices filled the air, chanting just as they had five years ago.

Apollo's stomach turned.

Fenn joined the chant.

'UNDER THE MOON'S *broken light,*
Where the eternal blizzard blows,
A spirit roams every night,
In its frozen world of snow.

THE GUARDIAN OF A ROYAL SEAT,
Long-lost, long-dead, and forgotten,
Its power left incomplete,
A path to the spirit world begotten.'

APOLLO AND NADJA glanced at each other.

'Power left incomplete? Path to the spirit world?' Nadja hissed.

'I don't know,' Apollo replied.

Nadja adjusted her grip on her sword. 'Apollo, what if that explains what the Moonlight Palace is for. The creature you said was down here? That could be a guardian! And we're in the place where Paragos, the eternal blizzard, blows.'

'So—so they want to open a path to the spirit world?

What would that do?' Apollo asked.

'I don't know. But if its what the Myr want, it can't be good for us. Fenn? Fenn, come on, we need to get out.' Nadja shook him, but he didn't respond, simply stared up at the pillar and continued to chant.

'Fenn, snap out of it!' Apollo shoved Fenn more vigorously. 'This ain't the time for this!'

'It has been so long since I have fed on something fresh.'

Apollo's blood ran cold at the sound of a woman's voice. It crept along the hall like ice.

'Many years have passed. I have been diligent in my duties, and now I am tired. I am hungry. So very, very hungry...'

Apollo whirled around as the wind died down and the wall torches burst into flame. He squinted, covering his eyes against the sudden, painful light. The room was just as cavernous as he remembered, roughly square, the far wall so distant it was a smudge of blue. Pillars lined the room at regular intervals, more carvings depicted on each one—several were dragons, twisted and frail-looking.

'Fenn. Get away from that pillar!' Apollo said, backing away from the shadow that grew in the room's centre. Breathing became difficult, each breath shallower than the one before. 'Whatever power the palace had, it only seems to apply down here!'

Nadja didn't take her gaze off the centre. 'Look! The key!'

Apollo could hardly believe the thing they'd been searching for all this time was sitting in the middle of the floor. It *had* to be the same key as before, but it looked—*felt*—so different. Pale yellow light emanated from it, brighter than when Apollo had last seen it.

Had the magic of the palace gone into the key?

'Come on, Fenn!' Apollo tried again.

Fenn raised his gaze to look up at Apollo. The same distant stare was back, though his pupils trembled.

Apollo wondered whether the real Fenn was in there, somewhere, trying to get out.

'The key will…bring everything back to me…' Fenn stammered, somewhere between confusion and understanding. 'The Myr…said they would…they would…'

'Don't listen to the Myr, Fenn! You don't have to do what they say!'

Fenn shuddered, eyes widening. 'They…they want…they will…I *have* to…' He dissolved into muttered ramblings.

'As long as you have breath in your lungs, you have a choice!' Apollo couldn't tell if his words sunk in. Fenn's eyes glazed over, darkening.

'He cannot hear you. He listens only to my master.' A woman stepped out of the shadows, her slender form cloaked in dark mist. She watched them with four eyes—two appeared human-like, but the other two in the centre of her face were dark chips. Her dagger-like teeth flashed as she spoke. *'But you? You are food for me. I hunger.'*

'We're not food, sorry. We're just here to grab the key.' Apollo shuffled away.

She halted mid-step. *'You cannot touch it! It is mine to guard!'*

Nadja approached, every step planted and confident, the tip of her sword raised towards the woman. 'The Myr's return cannot be allowed. You are breaking the armistice. Queen Surayo will—'

'She is ours to kill! Her dragon, crippled! The sea, tamed! Our shadows will cover land and sea now the key is restored! We will have our retribution!' The creature lunged for Nadja with a shriek that sent goosebumps up Apollo's arms.

He wished he hadn't left his sword out on the ice fields.

Thin tendrils of dark smoke lanced out from the creature, striking at Nadja's arms and legs. The Inquisitor shifted her stance at the last moment, each strike gliding past her and punching into the air.

There was no time to waste. Leaving Fenn by the pillar, Apollo darted across the room towards the key.

Shadows burst from the creature, crossing the room in a heartbeat and sending Apollo careening away. '*You will not touch this.*' She sprang towards him, limbs elongating into one of the twisted carvings from the palace hallway, more smoke hissing out from her body. Her face twisted into something animalistic and wolfish, bone-like with a long muzzle and black gums.

Apollo skidded along the floor and slammed into one of the pillars, the impact knocking the breath from him. His body was already bruised from Paragos, and he was convinced that impact had knocked something loose inside him.

Stars danced in front of his eyes, and he shook his head to clear his vision. It was so hard to breathe now, he just wanted to lie down and rest. Just for a minute or two, then he'd be fine again.

Apollo shook his head more violently, ridding himself of the thought. He couldn't give up, not now. Nadja was right.

She fought the creature, keeping it at bay with well-timed slashes and knocking it backwards every handful of seconds.

But this was the creature's home. It drew power from here, and Nadja wouldn't last forever.

Apollo picked himself up, vision spotty, and stumbled forward, boots struggling for grip on the floor. Every breath was agony. He didn't even need to pay attention to where he was going, just needed to follow the gentle light of the key in order to reach it.

Fifty paces away.

Forty.

Thirty.

Nadja screamed.

Apollo looked over to see her pinned underneath the Myrish spirit, sword skidding away from her. She held two of its limbs in her hands, head turned away as it pressed its slavering jaws towards her face.

Strong and experienced as Nadja was, she wasn't stronger than the spirit. Apollo could see her arms trembling with the effort of holding it back, and it inched closer towards her flesh, fangs snapping at the air just above Nadja's cheek.

Nadja's grip slipped, and the spirit struck, biting down hard. Nadja managed to shift, so the spirit bit deep into her collar instead of her throat, but she screamed again as it tore a chunk of flesh from her.

'Nadja!' Apollo cried. There was no thought, no decision, only instinct. He sprinted for all he was worth, picking up Nadja's dropped sword mid-stride and plunging it into the spirit's body.

It shrieked and let out a blast of frigid wind that knocked him down, but he kicked out in the same movement, shoving the creature off Nadja and sending it rolling across the room.

'What are you doing? Get the key!' Nadja growled, one hand clutching her bleeding collar.

'On your feet, Inquisitor!'

Nadja pushed him away, then cried out in pain.

'Your leg!' He hadn't realised the spirit had gouged a wound across her shin, shredding her breeches in the process.

'It's not important. *I'm* not important! None of us are! Only the key!'

Apollo grabbed her again, adjusting his stance to take the weight of her leg so she wouldn't hurt herself more. 'I'm *not* leaving you. Not in my nature.'

Nadja winced, but didn't fight back. 'Your nature will get you killed.'

'Served me well enough so far.'

The spirit snarled and righted itself. Dark ichor poured from the wound Apollo had opened up on its side. It shambled forward on unsteady legs, blood smeared around its jaws, and loosed a guttural roar towards them.

'Apollo. Get the key and get out while you can! Don't worry about me!' Nadja hissed, sinking down.

'I'm not leaving you here to die!'

Bright yellow light filled the room, snuffing out the torches. Apollo looked towards the light and gasped—Fenn held the key in both hands. He stared down at it with reverence.

'Fenn?' Apollo called, but the man didn't reply.

Fenn closed his eyes and pressed the key to his cheek, caressing it. 'I can *see* it. I can see the path I have to take. My family, they're waiting for me...They're so close now!' When his eyes opened, they were no longer blue, but dark—filled with shadow.

He hissed out another chant, different from the one before, but no less terrifying.

'Time has come to tear the veil,
When key and gate collide,
Our shadows cover land and sea,
Your forces stand allied.

Rolling darkness, spirits live,
Your people left to die,
And once we rend bone from flesh,
Dragons will ne'er again arise.'

'What...what is he...' Nadja muttered, blood from her ripped collar seeping out between her fingers.

Apollo adjusted his hold on her to prevent her from collapsing to the ground, biting back his own gasp of pain.

They had to get out of there. Whatever the Myr were doing to Fenn, this palace was making everything worse. He was speaking in riddles, didn't look like himself, *sound* like himself.

The Myrish spirit ignored Fenn and stalked towards them with a low growl, claws clacking on the floor.

'Nadja, we have to move!'

'Fenn…' Nadja whispered, voice trembling.

Apollo followed her gaze. His mouth dropped open as Fenn's booted feet raced up the stairs and disappeared from view, leaving them behind.

'Now, I will feast upon your flesh.'

30
THE SHELL
SELYS

'This what your dragon wants, then?' Kaio leaned against the wall, one of Ruka's bandages wrapped around his shoulder. He'd come out of Dalys's ambush with surprisingly few injuries, only a handful of superficial cuts and bruises.

Selys found her gaze drawn to the jade shell on his desk. It glowed softly. Neros's flame flickered within her. 'Such a small, unassuming thing…'

Taran, Esto, Ruka, and Evarine stood in the room as well, forming a loose semi-circle around the desk. The first three, Selys could understand—they'd been Kaio's closest friends and most trusted allies since childhood—but the new woman threw her off, until Kaio had explained Evarine had been the one to bring the shell into Segandis.

He'd also explained she'd shown up in the middle of nowhere alongside one of the Myr.

There was a great deal that Selys wanted to know about her, and how she had come to have a Myrish artefact in her possession.

Kaio was suspicious by nature, but even in this case, she felt the same way.

She wondered if Neros was more interested in the woman or the shell she'd brought.

Fergus brushed past Kaio. When he didn't react, the cat tilted his head and showed off his ripped ear.

Ruka indulged Fergus with an ear scratch. 'Cats are more like griffins than you know.'

'I'd like to see Olmir one day. Sailed south of the country, but never docked,' Selys said. Her only experience of griffins was Hailathlyl, and the creature had been both competent and serious. She'd hate to be on the bad side of one.

But even thoughts of griffins wasn't enough to pull her attention away from the shell. Neros's thoughts and desires dominated, and Selys turned her gaze to her brother.

She rested her glaive against the wall. It had served her well for three years, but now she was back home, it seemed cumbersome. A reminder of the past. 'Neros is interested in a Myrish power she sensed. It was in the Lasseen Ocean, travelling south. When it left her waters, it disappeared from her sight.' Selys turned to Evarine. 'You travelled with this shell? This artefact?'

Evarine nodded.

'Why?' Kaio asked, tongue sharp as ever.

Evarine's gaze darted between them both. 'It's a gift for Queen Surayo.'

Selys frowned but didn't say anything.

Evarine continued, 'I tried to tell Chief Kaio. My home is overrun by the Myr. They're corrupting everything, even the local spirits. Queen Surayo vanquished the Myr here, once. We may not be part of the Porsenthian Empire, but we know of her victories. I thought...I thought she might help us defeat them.'

'And you wanted to buy her help with that?' Selys pointed at the shell.

'She has other artefacts. She's a mage. Why would she help us unless we gave something of great value to her?'

Esto tilted her head. 'How did you get it from the Myr in the first place? Not every day you see people wandering around with their trinkets.

Evarine's gaze dropped. She trembled. 'They raided us. Killed dozens of villagers. Took more of us away, even my husband…'

Selys narrowed her eyes. Evarine seemed good at avoiding the meat of the question.

'We followed them. Me and a few others. We were desperate! There was a scuffle by the coast. I don't remember the details. When I woke up, we were adrift at sea, beholden to the currents.'

'And you drifted all the way to Segandis, where you were picked up by a ship?' Taran asked, shuffling along the wall to keep his distance from Fergus.

Evarine sighed.

'A suspiciously impossible to remember ship,' Taran pressed.

She scowled. 'I'd like to see *you* remember details after fighting a group of the Myr! I was barely conscious for days. Didn't Ruka tell you how close to death I was?'

'Let's not throw accusations around,' Selys said, jumping in before any tensions grew. 'Evarine. I need you to think very hard about this. Do you know what that shell is? What it does? Anything at all about *how* you got it? These are tools of the Myr. They do not give them away willingly. And forgive me if I'm mistaken, but you don't look like much of a fighter.'

Evarine shook her head. 'I don't know. I can't remember!'

Her memory loss was reminiscent of those who'd been cursed by the Myr and later died. Selys had seen so many pass through her temple. Fenn, of course, had managed to avoid that fate due to Hassen's blessing. But this woman was neither bonded to a dragon or at death's door due to anything the Myr had done. Ruka had explained it was exhaustion and malnutrition affecting her more than anything else.

Selys reserved judgement.

They weren't getting the whole story, whether or not Evarine was deliberately missing out important details or simply couldn't remember them.

'This is a waste of time. We aren't getting anywhere here,' Esto said with a huff.

'May I?' Selys asked, giving in to her curiosity and crossing the room to Kaio's desk. Neros had guided her here for a reason. Given the dragon spirits' eternal war against the Myr, Selys could see no other cause for Neros's instruction than whatever this artefact was. She wanted to know how it tied to Evarine, but perhaps figuring out this artefact would be a good first step.

'It's worth a lot of money. You aren't taking it out of Segandis,' Kaio warned.

'I just want to look at it,' Selys replied. She couldn't believe he was behaving as though she was taking away his favourite toy.

If it wasn't for the faint glow from the object, Selys wouldn't have realised it was filled with the Myr's magic. She reached for the shell and gently wrapped her fingers around its cool surface. She didn't know what she expected to happen. There was no blast of shadow, no whispered voices in her ear. It appeared to be an ordinary shell.

Maybe some sort of guiding light if she—

Neros's flames filled her with such intensity she staggered backwards. *'Death!'*

Selys gasped at the word. Neros recoiled from the artefact, a hissed warning, fury at the Myr, and intense fear underlying every emotion.

'Selys!' Kaio grabbed her arm, steadying her.

She reached for him instinctively, the shell falling from

her hand. Before it could crash to the floor, Taran shot forward, snake-like, and caught it.

Neros recoiled again, roaring in fear, such terror pouring from the dragon it threatened to split her skull. 'Taran, don't touch it!' Selys screamed.

He looked at her, puzzled. 'I'm not doing anything?'

But Neros's panic would not be quelled, and the beast screamed. The tattoos on Selys's left arm glowed with furious light and columns of seawater burst from her skin, swirling around her body.

Kaio jumped back with a gasp, and Selys wrapped her arms around her head, sinking to her knees as the agony of Neros's power overwhelmed her. A dome of seawater encased her like a frothing barrier.

'Spirits take me, put the fucking shell down, Taran!' Kaio snapped.

Taran reacted as if he'd been whipped, darting back to the desk and dropping the shell beside a messy stack of papers.

The moment it was out of his hands, Neros receded. Selys took several deep breaths, the water fading along with the dragon's presence, though it had left a large puddle in the middle of the tiled floor.

'Are you okay, Selys?' Ruka asked, crouching beside her. She tilted her head up and checked each eye for several seconds. 'I'm afraid I've no experience with those who are spirit-blessed, but that didn't look like fun.'

'Whatever that shell is, Neros cannot bear anyone to touch it,' Selys gasped, trembling. She hobbled over to lean against the wall beside her glaive, hands on her thighs.

'Did you see Neros when you touched it?' Taran asked. He wasn't looking at her, but staring at a spot on the far side of the room. 'All...shadowy?'

Kaio's chin raised at Taran's words, his eyes narrowing.

'No. No, Neros is only inside.' Selys focussed on her breathing.

'Wait. I saw Neros too, when I touched the shell a few days ago. There was a chain of shadow around her neck,' Kaio said.

'That's just what I saw. Over there,' Taran pointed, 'where did you see her?'

'I was outside.'

'You're saying you *both* saw Neros. A shadowed version of the spirit?' Esto asked, stepping between them.

They nodded.

'Selys. You won't like what I'm about to suggest—'

'Do it.' Selys hadn't caught her breath back, but they needed to test it. She didn't doubt either Kaio or Taran's visions, but they needed to understand what they were working with. 'Brace yourself, Neros. You're stronger than whatever this is,' Selys whispered, then squeezed her eyes shut.

She kept them closed, but knew the moment Esto touched the shell.

Blinding fear. Fury. Fire. Water. Everything raged inside her like a maelstrom, and she was lost in the middle of it.

'It's over!' Esto said, jumping away from the desk. 'I saw her too.'

'So we got a shell that shows us a vision of Neros? But shadowed. What good is that for the Myr?' Kaio asked.

'Not just that. Neros has a *chain*.' Esto began pacing, one hand on her chin.

'Could it be some kinda weapon? Something to hurt Neros? She's pretty afraid of it, isn't she, Selys? Don't see why she would be unless it could hurt her somehow?' Taran asked.

'No doubt of that,' Selys replied.

'Selys?' Kaio asked, frowning not in anger, but in concern at her.

She was suddenly desperate for an ice-cold bath. Anything to wash away those awful sensations. She needed to get away from the shell and the enclosed space. 'I need some air.'

SELYS WALKED ALONG THE BEACH, away from the site of battle earlier, away from the hustle and bustle of the town. There had been a number of quiet groves she'd enjoyed when she'd lived here, and her feet brought her down familiar paths without her having to think about it.

What were the Myr doing? Planning some sort of attack alongside their resurgence? They were the dragon spirits' biggest enemy, everyone knew that. It would make sense they'd find some way to attack them, too. Given their propensity to put their magic in artefacts, it shouldn't have been surprising.

But Neros was one of the most powerful dragon spirits. Second only to Toriaken, aside from the Archons.

Was this artefact really so terrifying?

An echo of Neros's flames flickered deep within her.

'I guess it is a problem.' Selys slipped off her sandals and walked down to the shore, relishing the soft sand and smooth pebbles under her feet. She sat down, waves lapping at her bare feet, the wind in her hair. Neros was all she needed. But she'd missed this place.

Events and conversations swirled in her mind. The Jade Shell was a Myrish artefact. One Neros was terrified of. Fenn was looking for the Citrine Key, another Myrish artefact. Whatever the key opened, it would benefit the Myr in some way. Why else would they ask for it?

She stared at the horizon, the sea a line of azure blue. Fenn would be returning to *Vermecio* with the key—*if* he'd managed to get it. She picked up a pebble and rolled it around her palm.

Fergus appeared to her right, strolling down the beach, a

small rat clutched between his teeth. The tip of his tail bobbed from side to side with every step, and when he was a handful of paces from her, he laid down with his prize.

'Should've known you'd be down here.'

She twisted where she sat to see Kaio standing at the top of the slope.

'I'm a creature of habit, I suppose,' she said.

He strode towards her, sat down heavily, and scratched Fergus between his eyes. 'What the fuck are we getting ourselves involved in?'

'This is life, Kaio. Dragon spirits and the Myr are always going to be involved. There's no escaping it.'

He leaned forward and picked up a pebble. After a moment testing the feel of it, he skipped it along the surf. 'You doubting your dragon?'

'What makes you say that?'

'You always came and sat here when you were upset or figuring something out.' He threw another pebble. It skipped four times before disappearing below the waves.

Selys smiled thinly. 'I suppose things don't really change, do they?' She chose a stone of her own and threw it. It skipped five times.

Kaio grinned. 'Guess things are a bit bigger than I realised. I've never seen you like that.'

'I didn't realise myself until recently. I'm glad you understand, now.'

They skipped stones together for a while, content in each other's company despite their earlier animosity. The threat of the Myr had put to rest their doubts about each other, for the moment.

Eventually, Selys asked, 'What do keys open?'

'Locks?'

'On what?'

'Doors? Chests? Dungeon cells?' Kaio smirked.

Selys knew that. Those were the obvious answers. But

dread churned in her belly at hearing Kaio speak the words out loud. 'What do you think a Myrish key would open?'

He lowered his arm before he threw the next stone. 'You got another of their artefacts hidden away somewhere?'

Selys chewed the inside of her cheek. Fenn would probably be on the other continent by now. Would he have found the key? Was he on his way back with it? 'If something of theirs has been locked away…it should probably stay locked, shouldn't it?'

'Don't need to be a priest to see the truth in that.'

'If the Jade Shell is some sort of weapon, some sort of threat against Neros…'

What was the key going to do? Were there more of these artefacts?

'What is it?' Kaio asked.

'Something *that* powerful, like the shell? It's not as if the Myr can make an unlimited number of them, can they?' Selys voiced her thoughts.

'Who knows. I suppose having two or three strong weapons makes sense. Bit unruly to have more. Stretch yourself too thin, otherwise?'

Something heavy settled in the pit of her stomach. What in all of Tassar was going to happen if Fenn returned the Citrine Key to *Vermecio*? Her breathing quickened as fear grew, and she scrambled to her feet, kicking away sand. 'I…I have to stop him.'

Kaio was on his feet a heartbeat later. 'Stop who?'

'I have to go.'

'What? Selys? Where are you going? What's happening?'

She made to push past him, but he held her by the arm and forced her to stand still.

'Selys, don't you dare run off again! Tell me what's going on. If it's got you this scared, I need to know.'

'I'm such an idiot! I'm so stupid!' Selys wanted to hit herself for being so naive. 'He's after the Citrine Key.

Another Myrish artefact. Might be just as bad as the shell. Might be worse. I don't want to wait to find out.'

'Who's after what key? Selys, take a breath!'

Whatever happened, it would be bad.

She knew exactly where Fenn was going—she'd stood in that same cave. She'd heard *Vermecio* promise to restore his memories if he brought the key there. 'Fenn. He was Myr-touched but bonded to Hassen—a forest spirit. He's after another of the Myrish artefacts, thinks it'll restore his memory. Bring his family back.'

Kaio glanced away briefly. 'Well I know how that feels. Losing your family can make you desperate.'

Neros's flames roiled inside her, and she winced. 'If he's managed to get the key, I know exactly where he's going to take it. So I have to go there. Wait for him. If he turns up, I have to stop...whatever it is that key will unleash.'

Kaio shifted his grip from her arm to her hand, then clutched it tight. 'I'm with you, Selys.'

Selys squeezed his hand. There was no time to waste.

She was going to need her ship.

31
THE BARGAIN
APOLLO

Apollo hurled himself to the side as the Myrish creature's claw sliced the air where his head had been a moment before.

Sweat beaded down his neck despite the chill of the palace. It ran red where it mixed with his blood. His breaths came in short, wheezing gasps, and Nadja wasn't much better off.

They had one sword between them, and aside from a few wounds, they hadn't been able to slow the thing down, much less deal any real damage.

It laughed and darted after them in turn, toying with them. Despite the creature's insistence it was starving, it was whip-fast and stronger than he'd thought possible, and seemed to enjoy drawing out the fight.

He recalled—vaguely—that the last time he'd been in this forsaken place, he'd been able to escape this creature's clutches by getting back up the stairs. Even though the key it guarded was no longer there, he wondered if the same principle would apply a second time.

It wasn't as if they had many options.

Before he could do anything, it was upon him again.

Now it looked nothing like the shadowy woman from before. It was a feral, animalistic beast with dagger-like claws and fangs that looked sharp enough to bite him clean in two.

He kicked out, catching it on the side of the jaw and knocking it backwards. It flailed as it skidded away, one claw slicing him deep across the belly. It cut through his furs and undershirt and pierced skin. White hot pain seared across his middle and he clutched his stomach. When he looked down, crimson stained his hand.

Apollo darted out of the way as the creature righted itself and leapt for him again. The movement stung, but it didn't impair him.

It was something he could address later.

Nadja struck out with her sword, forcing the creature backwards. It had already been cut in a handful of places, though it wasn't slowed despite the amount of ichor leaking from its limbs.

'Not how you thought this'd end, is it?' Apollo asked, reverting to any slight humour to keep him going.

'Fenn still needs to get past Paragos! Have faith the Archon will stop him!'

Apollo laughed once, without mirth. 'So we hope we see a smear of blood on the snow out there? Hope Paragos finally got rid of that key?'

He conceded that Nadja might have a point. Though what it meant for their fates, he was less sure. Already the pain in his belly was growing, and his thighs were beginning to numb.

'*Paragos?*' Laughter filled the hall, bouncing off the stone floor and pillars. '*Perhaps before. But the key's power has been restored. The Moonlight Palace has seen to that. I have seen to that. Not even your Archon can destroy our greatest treasure now!*' The creature stalked towards them, head low, bloodied saliva dribbling down its jaws.

Apollo felt like he'd been struck by a bolt of lightning. 'He...he *can't* destroy it now?'

'I would let you go so you could see for yourself. But I hunger.' The creature lunged again, faster than Apollo could react. It barrelled into him, fangs and claws slashing. It ripped into his legs, tearing into his cloak and boots.

Nadja was on it a moment later, driving the sword deep into the creature's shoulder.

It screamed, pushing away from Apollo to attack Nadja with wide swipes of its claws.

Apollo was too stunned to think, and moved on instinct, rolling away from where the creature had caught him, one arm holding onto his middle. The stairs were closer now. If they could just get up them...

The clash of steel on fangs cut through the air, blood and ichor flying as Nadja and the creature battled one another. It was bigger than her, though, and for all her skill, it had her on the defensive.

She put herself between it and Apollo, sword darting in and out as she probed for weaknesses, slashing and cutting into its flesh every other strike.

With a roar, it pounced. Nadja brought up her sword, but it pushed past her guard through sheer force. It snapped at her face, and Nadja raised one arm to block. Its teeth caught her arm, between wrist and elbow.

'Nadja!' Apollo cried.

It bit down, and its fangs pierced flesh. Crunched through bone.

Nadja's scream went through him.

In one, violent movement, the Myrish creature ripped Nadja's forearm off. Blood sprayed from the wound and she dropped to her knees, her other hand grabbing hold of what was left below her elbow.

She howled, huddling over her injury, face pressed into the cold, stone floor.

Apollo ran towards her. He risked a glance backwards, grimacing at the sight of the creature chewing on Nadja's arm.

They weren't going to get a better chance than this.

'Come on, Inquisitor. Gotta get up.'

She groaned, but didn't move.

Apollo tried again. 'I know you're hurting. Spirits take me, I'm in pieces, too. But you *can't* quit!'

Nadja managed to get to one knee, then immediately slumped forward again, blood pooling around her.

'Nadja. I will *not* let you quit.' He grabbed her around the waist, looped her good arm over his shoulder, and heaved them both forward. One step. Then the next. He slipped on the puddle of blood, but pushed on.

The stairway was within reach, and the faint blue light coming from the floor above gave him renewed hope. 'We have to walk, Nadja. We *have* to!'

Her body shook, blood dripping down her side in thick, dark streaks.

Both of them stumbled forward, staggering into the stairway. Apollo smacked his shin on one of the stone steps and winced, but didn't let it slow him. He heaved Nadja up every step, the creature's snarls and chewing fading below them as they ascended.

By the time they reached the top, Nadja was in a bad way.

Apollo let go of her and unbuckled his belt, wrapping it tightly around Nadja's elbow, looping it through itself once, twice, three times. They'd worn a number of layers to brave the cold, and he pulled off one of his thicker shirts, folding it over itself and tying it around the stump of her arm.

Nadja whimpered and her teeth chattered, but she didn't complain. Didn't seem capable of speaking.

He wasn't entirely convinced the creature *wouldn't* follow them up, but he didn't want to take any chances. His hands and arms were slick with blood, and he wiped them as best he could on his breeches so he could get a better grip on her. 'We need to keep moving.'

'Can't...' Nadja gasped.

'You *must*.' Apollo forced them down the corridor, which hadn't seemed quite so far when they'd been walking down it before. Thankfully, breathing came easier up here, but they wouldn't be able to continue for long.

They reached the first door along the hallway, and Apollo grabbed the handle. To his surprise, it opened. 'In here.' He tried not to look at the very obvious trail of blood they had left behind.

Apollo pressed his shoulder against the door. It gave way with a grating screech where the stone ground against the floor. Gritting his teeth, he put his full weight against it and pulled himself and Nadja through.

With another grunt of effort, he shoved the door closed behind him. It was only then that he realised his stomach was white hot with searing pain. He'd left his own trail of blood, though it was thinner than Nadja's had been.

Already, the linen shirt around her arm was red, but no more blood seeped through. He was glad he'd remembered to tighten the wound with his belt.

'What...if it locks?' Nadja asked, her voice shaking.

'It was locked when I came here five years ago,' he replied, hobbling to the nearest wall and sliding down it with a gasp, 'whatever magic was in this place is gone now. Locks are gone, too.'

'She...she could find us!'

'I don't think she can leave that room.' It was a guess, and guesses usually led to things going wrong, but he didn't want to think about that. 'Besides, we have bigger things to worry about.'

Nadja slumped to the floor beside him. She pulled her bag from her hip and fumbled with the string that held it together.

'You need to rest,' he said.

She closed her eyes for a moment. 'I...am resting.'

'Rest harder.' He pulled the bag towards him. 'What're you looking for? I'll do it.'

There wasn't much light in the palace as it was, and with the door to the room closed, it was hard to see beyond the murky shadows, but the faint blue light emanating from the walls helped. Apollo thought there would be linen for bandages, glinoc paste, anything to help with their injuries inside.

When he pulled out the iron kettle, Nadja nodded.

His breath caught. 'You ain't about to make tea, are you?'

She didn't reply, wincing as she pushed the bag out of the way with one foot and gestured for him to lay the kettle on the stone floor in front of her. 'We're lucky...the power here is gone. I can use this...to contact...Queen Surayo.'

'Nadja!' Apollo reached for the kettle with the intention of shoving it away, but he found he had no strength left and instead feebly fumbled towards it.

'I'm going to...request help. And...I need to tell her...the key... is gone.'

Apollo shook his head, the earlier fit of desperate laughter threatening to return. 'Help? No help here. We're in the middle of nowhere. There's...there's an Archon outside. Queen's leagues away. *Days* away...' His voice broke as the truth of his words hit.

He wasn't getting out of this alive. Neither of them were.

All their efforts had been for nothing. He'd had one chance and one chance only to destroy the key and prevent the Myr's rise. And he'd wasted it. To make matters worse, his second chance had been a lie. Now, he was going to die on the edge of the world and it would all be for nothing. He hung his head, unable to bear the shame of even facing the queen. He was going to die here. Just like Yorik. Five years late, but Torsten would get what he wanted. So would the queen.

'This isn't...the same as my dagger. Might...take a while.' Nadja's breaths were growing ragged, her neck and collar a mess of mangled flesh and blood, but she remained resolute. She kept her good hand on the kettle and stared down at it with the intensity of a hawk.

Apollo turned away, focussed mostly on trying not to whimper like a kicked dog. Pain was good. It meant he was alive. But the longer he sat there, the more numb and cold his legs went, and that scared him.

'Ah, look who has finally appeared after her adventures!'

Apollo would never forget that voice. He glanced over to see an apparition of Torsten standing in the middle of the room. He was well-lit, and appeared to be in some sort of stone fortress. Someone, it looked like a child, crouched on the floor by his feet, playing in the dirt.

'Torsten? Please...please get a message—'

'Torsten!' Apollo leaned towards the vision. He tried to stand, but his legs wouldn't obey. He couldn't believe what he was seeing. The child was Renys. Was he delirious?

'Daddy!' Renys cried out.

His heart skipped a beat. Renys reached for him with both hands, dirt in her hair and tears in her eyes. Torsten rested one hand on her shoulder, preventing her from running away.

'What the fuck are you doing, Torsten?' Apollo roared, fury granting him strength.

'Ah, it *is* the elusive thief. Funny how luck can change,' Torsten said, his usual sneer plastered across his face. He seemed more unhinged than ever before—his shirt dishevelled, a smear of dark soot down one cheek, he even hunched forward, as if putting all his weight on both legs was difficult. 'I knew I'd find you eventually. Nadja, you are commendable.'

'Daddy! Where's Mama?'

Spirits take him, her voice broke his heart. 'Where are you keeping her? Where's Malora? What have you done to them?'

'Now, now. You are in no position to be demanding anything, Apollo. Renys, as you can see, is quite safe. She's been traipsing around the country, but I've put a stop to that.'

Apollo shook with fury. Nadja said something, but he couldn't hear her words, he was so focussed on the image of Torsten with his daughter. 'Don't you dare hurt her. Don't you fucking dare!'

Torsten's smile broadened, loose hair framing his eyebrows. 'Inquisitor Nadja. I'm glad your time away has borne fruit. Apollo. Your daughter is in Marlrush Fortress. Turn yourself in for your just punishments, and I'll let her go.'

'Torsten! We're in Meneos! The chances of getting back… to Porsenthia are slim at best! We're both…wounded! Fenn took the key!' Nadja cried.

'Oh dear, tut tut tut. Won't be much chance of Renys going free then, will there?'

'I wanna go to Daddy!' Tears streamed down Renys's face.

'Renys! You don't let that bastard scare you, you hear me?' Apollo's throat was raw, but he didn't care. He shouted, 'Torsten! You harm a single hair on her head, and I'll—'

'I suggest you return to Eastbrook if you want to prevent that.'

Apollo slammed his fist into the wall. 'I swear to all the spirits, to all the Myr, that I will get you for what you've done!'

Torsten's smug expression didn't falter. 'Come now, Apollo. There's no need for this. Do as I ask and everything will be made right.'

Apollo let out a cry of anguish. He couldn't reach through the image and pull his daughter into his arms. Couldn't comfort her, let her know she was safe. Kiss away her tears.

More blood trickled from the wound across his belly, and everything below his navel was numb.

'Torsten. Please…send word to…the queen,' Nadja tried again, gasps punctuating her words.

'Ren…' Apollo slumped forward and fought to keep his eyes open. 'Ren, you have…you have to fight him…you have to stay…strong…' He coughed, bright red droplets marring the blue-grey floor.

'Apollo!' Nadja reached for him.

He had no strength left, not after that outburst.

He thought of Malora and Renys. Everything he had done to keep them safe.

Even though he'd failed, he had no regrets for trying to put things right.

'Mal…Ren…'

Apollo closed his eyes and a wave of cold smothered him.

PART III

Ocean waters vast and deep,
None stand against her roar.
Split the tides and turn them in,
Towards our march of war.

Reaping darkness tame the seas,
Buried deep on distant shores.
Rising waters fall from grace,
Corrupt her power, create new law.

32
THE LIE
FENN

Sunlight streamed down from above, almost blinding after so long in the dark palace. Fenn raised one hand to cover his eyes, trying to make sense of what he could see. Hadn't something been here before?

He stepped onto the crisp, fresh snow, the Moonlight Palace at his back, vast icy fields ahead of him. Yes. Something *had* been here.

Something large, that had blocked out the sun and brought icy winds and freezing snow.

It was gone now.

'It is afraid of you. What you carry,' said the voice in his mind. It obscured most thought, focussed his efforts onto what he needed to do next. Where he needed to go.

'Why is it afraid?' Fenn asked, his breath misting in the air. He was glad he wore gloves, though he couldn't quite recall where they'd come from. Hadn't others been with him, too? He was sure he'd had companions. A woman. And a man. She'd scowled a lot. He'd had a scar on his face.

'They left you.'

Fenn held onto the key in his pocket, drawing comfort from it.

They had left him. Whoever his companions had been, they weren't here now. They'd abandoned him in the cold.

They didn't matter.

'You must keep going. It is a long trek to Vermecio. Then you'll find your family.'

Fenn's worries and confusion faded, replaced by a single, straightforward goal.

He needed to get back to *Vermecio*.

That was all that mattered.

He was grateful for the help. If it wasn't for Hassen, he would have died long ago. His bond had strengthened over the past few days, it seemed. The arguing voices and mixed emotions had faded into something much more solid, and he'd latched onto that. Everything was easier when he just listened. Concentrating. Walking. Even dealing with the dangers that plagued his journey.

He didn't need to second-guess himself, or bemoan his lack of understanding and knowledge.

Not when he could just follow the path laid out before him.

The flames in his chest were much lessened, too, which helped. It was barely an ember, and he hardly noticed it. There were no more headaches, no more twinges of pain every time he disagreed with the voices. And what did it matter if he was confused from time to time? *Vermecio* was going to restore all his memories, then everything would make sense.

He recalled Selys's words, and the warning that came with them. He didn't know what the Citrine Key would do once *Vermecio* had it, but whatever happened, he had Hassen. The dragon would keep him safe.

He'd already looked after him this far.

Fenn walked slowly, trying to find his footing in the icy terrain. Something flashed in his mind's eye—there had been a blizzard here. 'Paragos...?'

'A dragon spirit. It isn't here.'

Fenn frowned, suddenly aware he was walking across the empty field. Confusion filled him. When had he stepped outside again? Hadn't he been walking down endless hallways of stone and marble? And the Spirit of the Eternal Blizzard ruled here. Where was it now? 'Why isn't Paragos here? Didn't the dragon live in these mountains?'

A hint of frustration swirled in his mind. *'It doesn't matter. The dragon spirit is weakened.'*

Fenn didn't argue. Didn't want the headache and pain that came with it.

'You will see people again soon. They will lie to you, like they did before.'

Fenn shuddered. Everyone was out to get him. Trying to get him involved in their own struggles while ignoring his. 'I wish they didn't.'

'It will not be long before you have your memories back. Then you may go where you wish.'

Everything reduced down to that one thought—finding his family. On what he would say. He'd explain how hard he'd been trying to get back to them, and for how long. He'd crossed continents. Oceans.

Another memory flickered across his mind—a small light in the growing darkness. A man who'd said he knew Fenn. Knew his family. Sanis. He hadn't seemed so bad. Hadn't demanded anything of him.

Fenn raised his face to the clear sky, the cool wind on his skin offering a hint of clarity. Snow crackled under his feet, every step a satisfying crunch. The darkness shifted slightly. Maybe he could speak to Sanis and find out more about—

'Sanis does not care for you. Otherwise he would be with you now. And where is he?'

'But…but he knew me?'

'Another trick people use for their own gain. It is a trap to return you to Ma-Rai and keep you from returning to Vermecio.'

Fenn began to hunker into himself. 'Another trap?'

'You do not need Sanis. Nor any of them. You are doing well with me, aren't you?'

Fenn nodded, and the cool darkness pressed in around his mind again, obscuring questions, worries, and confusion. He had the key, now. Finally! After no help from anyone else.

And yet he couldn't completely take solace in the words. Something kept flickering in the back of his mind—a silver butterfly desperate to be noticed. A light that pierced the dark fog.

Sanis had mentioned someone else...

Fenn stopped walking, squeezing his eyes shut as he tried to think through the confusion muddling his thoughts. A name floated to the surface. 'Evarine.'

'Lies!'

The name was snatched away, melding back into the fog. Darkness blossomed, pushing away other thoughts and questions. It smothered every last trickle of light, every last worry.

Fenn lowered his head and began to walk forward, without quite being aware of moving his feet.

Crunch, crunch, crunch. The rhythmic sound brought him comfort.

Hassen was right. Since waking up on the Isle of Salt, people had done nothing but lie to him. He could only count in himself.

Fenn tried to reach for Hassen's flames, but felt nothing in his chest. It didn't matter. He heard the voice. His next steps were clear.

That was all that mattered.

33
THE REUNION
CALIDRA

Silence fell upon the town.

Calidra stared at the blackened remains of buildings, animals, and people unable to get out of the dragon's way quickly enough. The smell was nauseating.

Something cold touched her cheek, breaking her out of her reverie. She touched a finger to her face, and it came away ashen grey. Flakes of soot floated down from the overcast sky—ashfall, rather than snow—which started to cover the town in grey and white.

Adrenaline faded out of her, turning her bright, burning anger and driving panic into something hollow. The pain in her thigh pulsed, and she became acutely aware of the hot blood leaking from her wound.

It wasn't enough to tear her attention away from the damage wrought, or the street she'd seen Torsten disappear down with Renys in tow. No matter how hard she stared at it, he wasn't coming back.

Malora hadn't reappeared, either, not that she had the strength to look for her sister.

'Cal. You have to get up.' Jisyel crouched by her side.

The wind changed, and something rolled out from a nearby alley, coming to a rest beside the puddle of blood Calidra had created. She looked down and realised it was a mango. Fruit trees lined many streets in Fellwood—people helped themselves to mangoes, peaches, and whatever else was in season—this mango had probably been knocked off its tree. It left a trail of glistening pulp on the paved street, and Calidra wondered if the tree it came from was still standing.

'Please, Cal.' Jisyel pulled on her arm. 'We need to get that arrow out!'

'Renys… ' Calidra whispered, her voice broken. 'He took her. Jisyel, he *took* her!'

Tears leaked from the corners of Jisyel's eyes. 'I know. We'll get her back. But *you* need help! Isn't your family home close? I don't remember the way there.'

Calidra wanted to collapse and let the darkness take her. What was the point in fighting anymore? After Torsten had…If anything happened to Renys, she'd never forgive herself.

Malora would never forgive her.

'I can't walk.' Her gaze dropped to the fallen mango, its flesh bruised, juice running from dents in its side. She felt as broken as the fruit.

'I'm here.' Jisyel looped one of her arms underneath Calidra's and pulled her up. 'It was hard for me to walk, too, remember? I'll help you.'

Calidra cried, though her tears had less to do with the pain of her leg and more from her love for Jisyel. Together, they hobbled away, picking a path through the smoking debris.

The drapes were drawn across every window on the sprawling estate, keeping both sunlight and the sight of destruction out of view. It was a sign of mourning for those lost, though Calidra couldn't help but be glad her mother wouldn't see her coming in such a state.

Stone encircled the main house, outbuildings, and gardens. Given the rising smoke, it was clear even the gardens hadn't escaped the dragon's wrath. The gates to the compound were unguarded, and Calidra limped into the atrium. Most tiles were in good repair, though a few were cracked.

'All I can do is gather a force to follow Torsten,' Calidra muttered. She'd ruined everything. If only she'd been stronger. Faster. Made better choices. 'I'm sure Mother will listen to me this time.' Her mother was unlikely to help her, not after she'd thrown her out of Fellwood.

But Malora was her favourite daughter, and Renys was her only grandchild.

That was an entirely different thing.

Calidra held onto that thread of hope, used it to drag herself through the compound, hobbling past flowered archways and verandas towards the main building where she hoped her mother would be.

Before she was halfway there, a tall, broad man in full armour crossed her path. He wore the colours of the Vantonen house, along with the family crest emblazoned on his breastplate—three white feathers tipped with gold. He looked at her for a moment, then frowned. 'Miss Vantonen? You're injured!'

Calidra tried to catch her breath and ended up coughing. She recognised him despite the soot that smeared his face. His skin was more deeply tanned than when she'd last seen him—no doubt a result of spending a good deal of time outside under the Bragalian sun. 'Commander Sekano? Where's my mother?'

His gaze darted to Jisyel, lingered on her a moment, then returned to Calidra. 'The Lady Vantonen is in her rooms. She has a burn on her arm from the wayward flames. I'm sure her medic can look at you as well—but she is in town at the moment, assisting where she can. We can send a message and retrieve her.' He gestured to the arrow protruding from Calidra's leg.

Calidra's relationship with her mother was strained at the best of times, but she didn't wish any ill on her, and the knowledge she hadn't been seriously hurt was more of a relief than she cared to admit.

'Let's get you inside,' Jisyel said.

Something darted around the corner, and it took Calidra a moment to realise it was one of her mother's griffins—Siranna. She had golden claws and sleek purple feathers that shifted into smooth fur, though it was somewhat ruffled. Ash coloured the griffin's left side, leaving streaks of white through her rich fur. Even Siranna's bejewelled collar had lost its glimmer, and she let out an indignant shriek as she raced past them, wings pumping to add height to each bound.

'Allow me.' Commander Sekano carefully picked up Calidra in both hands and strode away. She held onto his shoulder to steady herself. Being carried like a child was an indignity she normally wouldn't have suffered, but she had no choice. She couldn't walk, and her mother would have bigger concerns than the state of her arrival.

The beauty of the compound threw the destruction of Fellwood into stark contrast. Potted plants in heavy ceramic vases lined walkways, and draping leaves framed with delicate flowers comprised the archways between buildings and the courtyard. Most of the stonework seemed undamaged, and only the faint waft of burning vegetation from the distant flower garden showcased the attack.

She grimaced at the pain in her leg and looked over Sekano's shoulder to catch Jisyel's eye.

Jisyel smiled back, though her own gaze dropped immediately after.

'Malora...is in town,' Calidra said, abruptly realising just how exhausted she was.

'I'll inform Lady Vantonen,' Sekano replied. He sounded tired, and Calidra wondered how much of the devastation he'd seen. 'We've been rallying our troops, sending those we can spare into Fellwood to help.'

'You need to tell her...that Renys...Torsten has her!'

'Renys...?

Calidra gritted her teeth. 'Malora's daughter.'

Sekano immediately straightened up. 'The Master Inquisitor has her?'

Calidra nodded, unable to say anything else. Limp in the commander's arms, drowsiness threatened to overwhelm her.

Two war griffins, their riders saddled, stood at attention outside the large double doors leading into Furyn's personal residence. Both griffins were twice as tall as Calidra, and wore thick, leather armour that stretched out from their harnesses to cover their chests and underbellies. Their gleaming orange eyes were locked on the skies, their muscles tensed, ready to spring into action the moment the command was issued. Both creatures turned their heads to face Sekano, Calidra, and Jisyel as they approached, and one of them let out a warning hiss.

'At ease. This is Calidra Vantonen and her partner. She needs a medic,' Sekano said.

At his words, the griffins returned their attention skywards.

'Lady Vantonen has said no one is to disturb her,' warned one of the riders, an older warrior, bald save for a well-trimmed beard, with two long scars across his cheek. His thick, Olmese accent made it difficult for Calidra to understand him—especially in her exhausted state.

'She'll want to be disturbed for this. Do you have any griffins off duty, Captain Aetei? Can we send out a scout?' Sekano asked.

'What for?' Aetei asked, both his and his griffin's gazes locked on Sekano. 'We are tasked with guarding Lady Vantonen and the canton, not trivial scouting missions.'

Calidra shrank below their intense stare, fear filling her, but Sekano was unfazed.

'Your support is required in this. The scout is to follow Master Inquisitor Torsten. I have reason to believe he has something of ours. Something very precious.'

Aetei turned to his companion astride the other griffin, and they spoke quickly to each other in Olmese. Calidra couldn't follow what was being said, not that she understood more than a handful of words in the language anyway.

'I'll have someone in the air imminently,' Aetei said.

'Excellent. I'll return to my patrol once I've seen to these two. Malora Tamlin, formerly Vantonen, is also in Fellwood. Permit her entry when she comes here,' Sekano said.

Aetei's grey and white griffin let out a sharp trill that could have been surprise or anger—Calidra wasn't very good with reading griffins' body language—and was immeasurably glad that Sekano took them inside straight after.

She trailed her hand back, reaching for Jisyel as Sekano stepped into the villa. Several servants darted around, their sandals tapping on tiled floors. Most carried baskets of linens, cloth, water, cleaning supplies, medicine, and glass jars of food.

A liveried member of the Vantonen Household Guard ordered people around with short, barked commands, counting baskets and requesting more of this or less of that. It had to be the beginning of the relief effort within Fellwood. As Laird, her mother had a responsibility for people in the canton. It meant she had to act whenever disaster struck.

The Porsenthian Inquisitors had a similar job.

And yet, Torsten had left once he'd taken Renys. He had no inclination to help the townsfolk, that much was clear. He was an arse, but she didn't understand why he was shirking his duties. Surely a dragon spirit gone rogue and attacking a town was of greater importance than the family of a thief on the loose?

Sekano adjusted his grip, knocking the arrow protruding from her thigh, and Calidra screamed.

'Apologies, Miss Vantonen. Can you stand to address Lady Vantonen?' Sekano asked.

Calidra wiped the sweat from her brow, pushing hair out of her eyes. 'I…can stand.'

Jisyel was by her side a heartbeat later, and Calidra leaned on her as Commander Sekano knocked once on the door and strode in without waiting for a reply.

Calidra and Jisyel hobbled after him into the dimly-lit room.

The heavy scent of jasmine incense filled the air, turning every breath thick. Drapes covered the windows, letting in only the tiniest crack of pale sunlight. Oil lamps burned low in sconces along the richly tapestried walls, and another lamp rested beside the table where Furyn currently sat, a large book held in one hand. Neat bandages covered her right arm from wrist to shoulder. She stared at the pages through a pair of seeing eye glasses on a thin golden chain, and lowered it at their approach.

There were no servants here. No guards. Not even her handmaiden, Quillaja.

Siranna sat in the corner of the room, licking the feathers around her talons, much like a cat would clean its front paws. She paid them no attention.

Calidra took a breath, wobbled on her feet, and inclined

her head in greeting. 'Mother.' She was proud that her voice didn't tremble.

Furyn looked over the edge of the book she was reading, and took in Calidra's appearance with a quick, sweeping gaze. 'You're bleeding on the floor.'

Calidra tensed her jaw, half to cope with the pain throbbing through her, half to stop herself from saying something she'd regret. 'It isn't...on purpose.'

'Get yourself cleaned up. The washroom is free.' Furyn turned back to her book and rested her glasses on the bridge of her nose.

'M—Mother. If you hadn't...noticed...There is an arrow...in my leg!'

Furyn lay the book flat on the table. 'A rogue dragon spirit attacked Fellwood, if you hadn't noticed. I'm trying to discover a way to defend against it should it return. Torsten and some of his Inquisitors arrived earlier today and set up a barricade. Apparently he was after Malora, but wouldn't listen when I said I hadn't seen her in years. His contingent didn't bother to help with the dragon. Are you going to?'

Calidra tried to take a step forward, but she couldn't put any weight on her leg, and instead grabbed the other edge of the table to support herself. She didn't care she'd left an ashen smear on the expensive wood, or blood on the floorboards. But her mother's words about Torsten looking for Malora matched what he'd told her. What she'd fought him for. 'Malora...is with me, too.'

This, Furyn did react to. Her nostrils flared slightly. 'I don't see her here?'

'She's in town, helping people.'

'Of course she is. She cannot stop herself.' Furyn chuckled.

Calidra's fingers trembled where they gripped the table. 'She had her daughter with her, too. Renys. Torsten...he...he...'

Furyn raised one eyebrow, the only sign of her growing impatience.

Siranna trotted over, her back the height of the table, her feathered tail swishing gently. She let out a low cry. Furyn dropped one hand to the griffin's head, scratching the smooth fur between Siranna's eyes.

Sekano stepped forward, one hand clasped across his chest. 'The Master Inquisitor has taken Renys. I've arranged for one of the Olmese riders to scout from the air. It must be a misunderstanding.'

The heavy, rich atmosphere disappeared in the blink of an eye. It was as if icy water had been poured down Calidra's back.

'Malora returned to Fellwood with my granddaughter. And now Renys has been taken? Do I understand correctly?' Furyn asked.

Calidra trembled. 'Renys was with me. But, Torsten—'

'This is Fellwood. *We* rule here. Not him. I told him he had no business in my canton.'

Calidra swayed, nausea bubbling in her stomach. 'I couldn't...couldn't do anything...He shot me! He was going to shoot Jisyel, too!'

Furyn's dark eyes flicked to Jisyel and narrowed. 'So *she's* the cause of it.'

'No!' Calidra stood across Jisyel, balancing on one leg, the other limp.

'No? So you *let* him take Renys? Why did you do that?'

Calidra glanced up. 'What choice did I have?'

'Even in a crisis, you act like an idiot! I thought you were raised better,' Furyn's voice rose with her anger. 'Get into that washroom and clean yourself up. Sekano, send for my medic to come here and deal with her leg.'

Siranna snapped her beak with a hiss and jumped away from Furyn's voice, talons clicking on the wooden floor.

Tears fell, unbidden, hot and burning. Calidra and Jisyel

stumbled away, towards the adjoining room. She *hated* herself. If only she'd been better. More like Malora. Everything would have been easier.

Before they reached the washroom, footsteps pounded along the floor. Calidra glanced up, her heart sinking even more as Malora entered the study in a rush. Her braided hair had come loose, her face flushed.

She nodded first to Commander Sekano, then to Furyn. 'Mother. It...it has been too long.'

'Malora.' Furyn rose to her feet, arms partially extended—the closest she'd ever come to reaching for a hug.

Malora stepped into her mother's embrace. 'Life has been very busy. I should have visited you sooner. Especially...after father...'

'You had many priorities,' Furyn replied, smoothing Malora's hair.

Malora glanced at the floor, mouth falling open when she saw the trail of blood. 'Cal? Cal you're hurt!'

'It's nothing,' Calidra muttered, rooted to the spot in terror. 'Medic'll be here soon.'

'The dragon has gone now. I think it ran out of buildings to burn. I couldn't even get close to it! But I need to find out why it attacked, then I'm sure it can be stopped.' Malora looked around the room. 'Where's Ren? Is she sleeping?'

Calidra's stomach dropped. 'No, she...she...'

They locked eyes, Malora's faint smile slowly dropping. 'Calidra. Where is my daughter?'

Crippling shame filled Calidra from head to toe. She was a child again, wilting under her mother's wrath and blame. 'She...there was...On the way here, we...Torsten caught up with us before we got here.'

Malora's eyes widened.

Calidra couldn't hide from the pain that was about to fall. If Furyn told Malora, she'd twist the words somehow. Make everything a thousand times worse. So she braced herself and took a deep breath. 'He wanted to arrest you to get to Apollo. You weren't there, so out of spite, he took her.'

Seconds passed as the weight of the words settled.

Calidra didn't dare breathe.

Then, the scream Malora unleashed cut through her like a knife. And Calidra wished the Inquisitor's arrow had hit her in the chest instead.

34
THE SEARCH

TORSTEN

Torsten rested his head in his hands, his skin sagging where he'd lost the definition in his muscle. If the lack of fire in his chest wasn't a clear enough indication his bond with Miroth had been severed, the return of his ailments had sealed the deal.

He'd been born into a dirt-poor family. His father worked in the palace as a steward, and was away for months at a time, leaving his mother to raise his younger siblings—twins—alone. He'd always been left to his own devices, malnourished and often ill, and it had turned the bullying eyes of other village children towards him. He'd been much smaller than most others his age—and a few younger—and his mother had always fussed over him.

He'd always hated it.

Being stared at. Pitied.

Miroth had put a stop to that suffering, and given him both physical and mental strength that he'd relied on for well over three decades.

And it was all gone. Snatched away in a heartbeat.

Because of Varlot.

The dark thought consumed him, even as he gathered his

breath after returning to Marlrush Fortress. Varlot's pettiness and desire to be seen as the hero in all situations extended to humiliating Torsten in front of the queen, and destroying his bond with his brother.

That man was going to pay for what he'd done.

Even in chaos, Torsten had found a way forward. A way to start fixing things. He'd rushed south to Fellwood, hoping Malora Tamlin was there, as he'd predicted. If he could use her to bring Apollo in, Queen Surayo might forgive him for losing the artefact she'd wanted.

He'd set up barricades. Spoken to Furyn Vantonen. The damned Bragalian woman hadn't helped him at all, and he'd been forced to wait like a common guard.

Then Miroth had struck.

Torsten hadn't thought he'd see the dragon again, let alone so soon. Yet Miroth's path of destruction did not falter.

The silver lining had been capturing Renys Tamlin. He'd have preferred Malora, but he'd run out of options, especially with Furyn's daughter so skilled with a sword.

He formed a fist. Squeezed. Torsten let out a gasp. It took all his effort to ball his hands, yet there was no strength in it.

So he turned his attention to the next thing he *could* do: finding a way to fix his bond with Miroth. Dozens of Myrish artefacts lay dormant in the depths of the fortress. One had severed his bond. He was certain if he looked hard enough, he'd find something to repair it.

'Daddy!' Renys's voice echoed from the other room, accompanied by a sob.

Torsten didn't bother looking up from his makeshift desk. The girl was irritating beyond belief, and he'd been glad he'd requested a squadron of Inquisitors to join him at the fortress—better to get them now, while he had the chance—so they could deal with her while he searched for solutions.

Varlot would arrive at Eastbrook before too long, and he

didn't know what Queen Surayo would do to him for failing in his quest. He had to control the damage caused by that drunken buffoon while he could.

That being said, Miroth devouring the artefact Surayo wanted had caused their bond to sever. He assumed the same could have happened to Toriaken. That would have decimated the Porsenthian Empire's defences as far as the Myr's resurgence was concerned.

No iron dragon meant no Iron Crown.

Perhaps Queen Surayo would see that. And together with Apollo's daughter, it would guarantee his survival. Maybe even his rank. Perhaps he'd avoid being brandished a traitor and instead be praised for averting disaster.

Queen Surayo had always been short-sighted. But he would do what he could to shine a more favourable light on himself.

Realisation dawned on him. His body was weak, but for the first time in as long as he could remember, his mind was sharp. Whole. And totally his.

Miroth had taken control of him several times, mostly when emotions ran high. But there was no fear of that, now. His brother's presence had been a crutch—one he'd relied on for decades. It had also muddled his mind and made strategic thinking trickier than it needed to be.

The thought made his emptiness all the greater.

Dragon spirits used people. Of course they did. If they weren't cursing those who crossed them, they bestowed blessings. Torsten had never seen the downside to that partnership before. He'd been feeble and weak, and because of Miroth, he was one of the most powerful people in the Porsenthian Empire.

Miroth had been able to leave his lake. See Porsenthia, Bragalia, and Olmir, through Torsten's eyes. It was all Miroth desired. Knowledge. Influence. For people to see him as glorious as he saw himself, and Torsten had never regretted that.

But now, with the dragon gone, he could look back on that bond with clarity, and see it for what it was—his time as a pawn.

Just like he was a pawn of Queen Surayo.

'Sir? Renys Tamlin will not be comforted.'

Torsten wearily raised his head to see who'd spoken to him. There were three Inquisitors stationed at the fortress, along with a handful of guards, and all their faces blurred together. Coupled with a bone-deep exhaustion, he wasn't sure he could bear another conversation. 'Just do what you can. She's a child. What comforts could she possibly need? Make sure she's fed and throw in an extra blanket.'

The Inquisitor, Halios, Torsten thought his name was, decided against arguing and simply bowed and exited the room.

He missed Nadja. Even Sarron.

Torsten rolled his sleeves down to cover his thinning arms. Travelling so quickly from Tonmouth to Fellwood and back to Marlrush Fortress had exhausted him more than he ever thought possible. He was quite sure he'd sleep through until winter if he rested now.

His head throbbed, pressure building behind his eyes. Torsten winced, fighting against the urge to give in to his weakness. Miroth needed him. Even if he had strength to rival any other spirit, the dragon was still his brother.

Renys's crying resounded through the stone walls. Torsten ignored it and continued his search through empty rooms and halls for anything that might help restore his bond. He considered contacting priests and priestesses of other spirits in case they held knowledge that would aid him, but didn't want to reveal his weakness. He was vulnerable, and people usually took advantage of that.

He had to sort this mess out on his own.

Varlot had left the fortress in disarray—furniture, papers, empty bottles, and other debris littered most floors, and Torsten and the others had needed to spend half a day clearing out the mess before he could get to work.

Thankfully, the fortress was not short on rooms that were habitable, and Renys had been placed in one of the studies on the second floor—high up enough she couldn't escape out a window, and not too far away that he couldn't reach her if Apollo made contact again.

Torsten hoped Malora would turn up as well. Outside of Fellwood, he had more power than she did—and not only would he be able to arrest her, but Renys would have her mother back.

That would shut the child up.

Torsten massaged his temple, trying to rid himself of the ache in his head, exacerbated by Renys's constant wailing, and walked into the next room, ready to begin his search anew.

He had no interest in harming an innocent child—though her crying was sorely testing that—but Apollo *thought* he would. That threat was all he needed.

Minutes slipped past, pouring into hours. Light faded away as the sun set, and Torsten kept searching. There were dozens of artefacts here, each barely registering any magic. He knew he was searching blindly, knew he didn't have the first idea of what any artefact would do, but he couldn't stand idly by, waiting for Varlot to turn his queen against him.

He clutched his chest, searching for the tell-tale flame of his brother.

But Miroth was not there, and his body was cold and empty.

Bright sunlight woke Torsten from an uneasy sleep. He sat up in his bunk with a wince, sheets bundled up by his feet. Usually he was awake at dawn, if not before.

He glanced at the window, dust motes floating in the shaft of light. It was closer to midday than dawn. Though there were no trees or plants surrounding the fortress, no birdsong or insects, the sun was a clear indicator of the time of day, and he reprimanded himself for being so slovenly.

His lower back ached and he pressed his knuckles into it to try and ease the pain. When he moved, he spotted something glinting in the corner of his eye, and looked across to see a small breakfast platter resting on his table. A large glass decanter held a pale yellow liquid—citrus juice of some sort, he guessed from the smell—along with three thick slices of bread, and what appeared to be cold sausage and tomatoes.

Torsten looked at his door, which remained closed. How dare they enter his room without explicit permission!

He stood up and immediately collapsed to one knee. He flailed blindly, trying to grab something to keep him on his feet. His hand hit the wooden platter, spilling the contents over himself. The decanter sailed overhead and smashed on the floor, spilling shards of glass and juice across his rug.

Within moments, footsteps pounded outside. 'Master Inquisitor!' The brass door handle rattled.

'I'm fine!' Torsten barked, wiping a smear of juice off his cheek as he finally caught his balance and pulled himself to standing. 'Get back to your posts!'

Torsten didn't move until he heard their footsteps fading down the corridor, after which he proceeded to clean up the mess and change the sheets of his sopping wet bunk. He shook his head at his feebleness, and desperately missed Miroth.

He breathed in deeply, waiting for the pain of his exertion to subside. It didn't, but several minutes gathering his breath on his hands and knees had allowed him to get used to it.

He dressed in a fresh uniform, exited his room, and locked it. He carefully chose a path that would not bring him near any of the people in the fortress. Thankfully, neither leg gave out as he continued his search, this time focussing on rooms he'd not visited during his time here with Varlot.

It was a desperate search, but he was desperate.

Hours ticked past. His hunger grew, but he pushed it aside. Eating could wait.

He'd already wasted half the morning abed, and he would not waste another minute if he could help it.

Torsten buried himself in room after room, sorting through piles of discarded supplies, broken furniture, ruined armour and weaponry. He picked up more than a few cuts as he rummaged around feverishly, fingers running red by late afternoon, but his hands were numb to it.

He had to find an answer.

His life depended on it.

The ground trembled, dust sifting to the floor. Loose objects rolled off shelves and tables with a clatter. Anything made of glass shattered. Torsten steadied himself against the nearest wall, heart pounding. Had Miroth come to burn the fortress? Were the Myr launching an attack?

When the shaking subsided, Torsten pushed along the wall to the nearest window, and peered out onto the dry, barren, deadlands. He waited, breath held, searching for any flicker of movement.

Something grey streaked across his vision, blocking the window—the entire wall—for several long seconds and bathing the fortress in shadow.

Torsten knew what it was. It could only be one thing.

He froze as Toriaken's bulk encircled the fortress, enormous wings blocking out the sky. Scales of iron grazed against the stone, sending more crumbling chunks to the ground, enormous clouds of dust thrown up by the might of his passing.

Two Inquisitors burst into the room. 'Master Inquisitor!'

'I can see the dragon,' Torsten muttered, not turning away from the window.

Toriaken landed, his talons gouging into the dry land like paper, though his wings remained extended in a show of force.

Torsten allowed a smile to creep on his face—a hint of pride that Queen Surayo sent her dragon directly. There was no simple message through the iron dagger. He was worth more than that.

Of course, Toriaken could roast him where he stood. But he couldn't imagine Surayo ordering that without dragging him back to the palace first.

'Shouldn't we greet Lord Toriaken?' one of the Inquisitors asked, taking a tentative step into the debris-strewn room.

Torsten sighed and turned to face the pair. 'We'd better. Everyone we can spare outside, now. Leave a single guard by the prisoner's door.'

They bowed and left, footsteps hurrying away.

Torsten found a mirror on the wall, broken and cracked in several places, but wide enough he could see his face. His skin was sallow and thin, his eyes sunken, but there was nothing to be done about that. With great difficulty, he bandaged his bleeding hands, wincing as the rough linen pressed against his wounds. It would not do to appear before the queen—or her dragon—injured. Regardless of what mistakes he'd made, he would not lower his standards.

He wished he'd had more time to search. Another full day, at least, and he mentally berated himself for missing the morning.

Smoothing his hair and uniform as best he could, he exited the room and made his way down the wide staircase to the entrance foyer.

All three Inquisitors and five of the six guards stood at attention at the bottom of the stairs, their uniforms pressed and as gleaming as they could be in a dusty fortress. Torsten halted and nodded for them to lead him out. He didn't want them to see his limp. He counted ten heartbeats before he followed them through the main door, bracing himself to address the dragon.

The air was still, devoid of life or wind, which made Torsten's shuddering breaths all the more apparent. In the barren, brown landscape of dust and rock, the grey dragon stood out. The tip of his tail curled around the fortress, trapping them in coils of iron. Toriaken's head dwarfed Miroth's, although Miroth's new size would certainly give the iron dragon pause.

Torsten looked up at Toriaken, breathing quickening at the smoke drifting lazily from the dragon's nose and the intense heat from his breath. Thick horns protruded from Toriaken's head and jaws, a solid mass of iron that could carve out deep rents in the earth as easily as any of his talons.

The Inquisitors and guards of the fortress had formed a line, and he followed their lead, walking past their bowed heads while he kept his chin raised. Every step was painful, all of his focus on not losing his footing. Something that had come to him as easily as breathing now took so much effort, and walking was even more difficult under the scrutiny of a dragon.

Finally, after what felt like an eternity, he reached the end of the line, where Toriaken waited.

Torsten dropped to one knee, ever respectful, though his mind whirled in chaotic confusion punctuated with fear. 'My queen. You honour me with your dragon's presence.'

Toriaken stared at him, seemed to see right through to all the fear and chaos in his mind, and Torsten could not hold his gaze. He looked away, shame-faced, cheeks burning.

The dragon let out a snarl that Torsten felt in his chest, then opened his flaming jaws. Queen Surayo's voice echoed from the spirit's throat. 'Torsten. You will gather your men and return to Eastbrook at once.'

35
THE GATHERING
SELYS

Wolf's Grin bobbed lightly on the surf, pulling occasionally against the ropes mooring her to shore, as if she itched to set sail.

Selys ran a hand along the rail, varnished wood faded but sturdy under her fingers.

Kaio had taken good care of her ship.

Although she supposed it was no longer *her* ship.

Kaio refused to leave the Jade Shell in Segandis, which she understood. Anyone determined enough could steal it, smuggle it, use it. But it meant he brought it with him, and every time she saw a flash of jade, she and Neros bristled.

The small crew bustled around her, carrying supplies and weapons aboard, each sinking into their roles with ease. They hadn't taken their full strength—they daren't leave Segandis unguarded, especially with tensions so frayed—but she kept out of their way. Above them, gulls soared on the wind, crying out to one another, readying themselves to grab the fish that would be displaced in the ship's wake.

Fergus strolled past, tail held high, the tip twitching. She smiled at the grey tabby, who roamed where he wished and chose only a select few for company.

'He only sails when Kaio does,' Taran said, his arrival preceded by a trail of cigarillo smoke. 'Anyone else goes out, and he just sleeps.'

'Kaio has some loyal followers.' Selys crouched to run her fingers along the cat's back. Fergus purred appreciatively. 'Even on four legs.'

'A shame he don't care for all of them. Would save the headache.' Taran folded his arms and leaned on the railing beside her, watching as the rest of the crew prepared the ship for its next voyage.

Selys shook her head. 'Kaio cares. He's just too proud to admit it out loud. Even to me. I think my display with Neros was enough to keep any scavengers clear. The warbands have always lived with temporary truces. This should keep things quiet, at least while we're away. No headache for now.'

'You reckon?' Taran raised an eyebrow. 'You should see how he spoke to Yaniv. Thought there was a mutiny brewing to be honest. You've seemed to calm 'em down for now.'

'At least Kaio can see the bigger picture. He understands the threat of the Myr. Understands we need to take a stand against them.'

'Does he?' Taran blew smoke over his shoulder where the wind snatched it away. It curled and thinned as it faded across the balmy waters.

Fire burned hot within Selys's chest at the mention of the Myr, and she resisted the urge to grimace. She was growing more accustomed to Neros's presence as the days went on, but the spirit's power overwhelmed her more often than not. 'Even if Kaio is helping me for his own reasons, the effect remains the same. He'll stand with me against the Myr. That's all the dragon spirits want. I can't ask more than that from him.'

Taran grunted, apparently more interested in his cigarillo than discussing the Myr.

Selys didn't mind. Her brother was hot-headed and

impulsive, but he was maturing. Slowly. He'd do the right thing, she was certain of it.

He'd already agreed to sail with her to the Nethal Mountains, where *Vermecio's* cave lay. That was worlds apart from his blind hatred when she had first returned. She supposed seeing Neros's abject terror of the Jade Shell and the realisation it was a Myr weapon had gone some way to convince him of her plight.

He would of course be prone to tantrums and arguments, but it was progress.

Selys closed her eyes, picturing the cave. She'd been injured and weak the last time she'd been there. Neros had chosen that moment to bestow her blessing, and she'd passed out. If she'd had her wits about her, perhaps she could have done something about Fenn. Realised the danger the Citrine Key would have put them all in.

Something.

Skaru would have known what to do. He always did.

Her eyes burned at the memory of her brother. She'd pushed the pain of losing her family away, which was easy enough to do when you moved to a temple and had to devote your life to a dragon spirit. Being back in Segandis brought back the complicated feelings she'd tried to hide, and even with Neros's comforting presence, it hurt.

'Skaru. If only you were here,' Selys whispered. Another burst of fire filled her, and she grimaced. Though she couldn't make out what Neros said to her, she felt the dragon's anger at the thought of her family. 'He was…a good leader. Everyone listened to him. We never had any trouble with other warbands. None that we needed to shed blood over, at least. Everyone had their patch of territory, Inquisitors never bothered us. Happier times.'

Esto crossed the wide gangplank, a hessian sack held easily over one shoulder. It bulged with its contents, and she gently lowered it against the mast. 'Barrels of water over there.' She pointed, addressing the rest of the crew.

Taran leaned back on the rail, tilting his head up to the clear, blue sky, cigarillo clenched between his teeth. 'Skaru? He was an arse though, wasn't he?'

Selys mentally berated herself for speaking her mind so loudly. She hadn't intended for anyone to overhear her muttering. 'What?'

Taran shrugged. 'Kaio's one of us. Skaru never was. Looked down on us a lot. And spirits save you if you crossed him.'

Selys blinked, taken aback by Taran's description. She hadn't considered his thoughts—or any of the crews' for that matter. She just wished Skaru was back to lead them. He always knew what to do in a situation, always seemed to be one step ahead of everyone around them.

And yet Taran seemed happy enough with Kaio.

Perhaps she didn't know her brothers as well as she thought.

Esto approached, waving her hat in front of her face to disperse the cigarillo smoke. 'The difference between Skaru and Kaio? Skaru took responsibility for *everyone*. Kaio picks and chooses. He needs to learn it's *all* his responsibility now.'

'He needs to grow up?' Selys asked. Taran and Esto were certainly the ship's eyes and ears.

'In essence.'

'Can you blame him? He was seventeen when…' Selys swallowed, not wanting to put words to the event, not when Neros was part of her now. 'When…Neros killed our family. I was only twenty-four. Three years isn't anywhere near long enough to grieve that *and* take on such a responsibility without making a few mistakes.' Her gaze fell, guilt flaring. She'd left him to cope alone, while she'd sought solace at the temple of the spirit who'd put them in that situation.

'Selys. We need to look ahead.' Esto lifted Selys's chin

with a finger. 'What happened to the strength of the Ioran warband, hmm? You were always our fierce fighter. Don't lose that now. Don't give in to any doubts.'

Selys pulled back, allowing herself a brief smile. She and Kaio were both trying to do the best they could. Trying to respect their dead family. Dwelling on the past didn't help that goal. 'You're right. Skaru wouldn't forgive all this moping, would he?'

'Exactly. No use thinking about it now.'

Selys turned her attention to more practical matters. 'Is the ship ready?'

Esto glanced along the deck, eyes darting from one crewmate to the next. 'Won't be long now.'

Kaio strode aboard, and Fergus immediately trotted over to him. Evarine followed Kaio, a shawl across her shoulders to protect her skin against the harsh Bragalian sun.

'You sure you want her here? Yaniv or someone else could keep an eye on her if you leave her in Segandis,' Taran asked.

'I'd rather keep an eye on her myself. She took the shell from the Myr and carried it into Segandis. She's important, whether she knows it or not,' Selys said.

'You reckon she's hiding something?'

'I think she knows more than she realises. When I lived at Neros's Shrine, we had a number of people coming to us, begging for help. They had no memories of themselves, their families, or the world. We called them "lost souls".'

'Sounds shit.'

'Even worse when you realise they'd die, one by one. All except Fenn.' She thought back to her travelling companion. He'd been an ally, once. She hoped he still was. 'Hassen blessed him, which saved his life, even if it didn't restore his memories.'

'So what was wrong with them?' Esto asked.

'Myr-touched.'

'And she had a Myrish artefact. A weapon.' Esto shared a glance with Taran.

'I wish Kaio would leave the shell in Segandis. But if it's here, at least I know it can't be used.' Selys shuddered, Neros's fear echoing within her.

But Esto was right. They had to look ahead. 'Can you get Kaio and Evarine? I'll meet you in the captain's quarters to check our course.'

❄

SELYS STOOD at the large table that dominated the captain's quarters. The large room was sparsely furnished with a handful of stools, scopes, compasses, and a large map of the Etrovian continent carved into the wooden table.

She'd sailed the Salt Sea a few times, but there wasn't much to pick at, save Tonmouth, and that town had never been a rich one. Her stomach tightened as she thought of her past life. How many towns they'd raided. Statues they'd pulled down. Shrines they'd desecrated.

It didn't take long for the others to join her. Thankfully, Taran had put out his cigarillo so she didn't have to peer at the map through smoke.

She'd expected Kaio to fight with her over orders, but he'd slipped back into his first mate position as easily as putting on an old boot. While things were working, she had no desire to question him and worsen it.

Once they were all inside, she glanced at the door, and Esto closed it, plunging them into semi-darkness—the only light coming from a small, circular window at the back of the room.

Selys looked at each of them in turn, and drew strength from Neros to steady her breathing. 'We sail for northern Porsenthia. The Nethal Mountains, named for the mining town at its base on the western side. There is a cave in the mountains where a Myrish construct, called *Vermecio,* awaits. This is our goal.'

They each nodded in turn, aside from Evarine, who looked like she might faint at any moment.

Selys continued on. 'As you know, the Jade Shell is a Myrish weapon. Someone I know may well be going to that cave with a second weapon, and he means to use it there. What the effect will be, I do not know. But if it's anything like the shell, it will be bad for Tassar. Speed is of the essence, so I apologise for not explaining the matter until we are already away.'

'Why would this guy use it?' Esto asked.

'He lost his memories after being cursed by the Myr. This, *Vermecio,* in the cave, has promised to restore them.'

Evarine stiffened.

Selys turned to her, one eyebrow raised. When she didn't say anything, Selys asked the gathered group, 'Any questions?'

'We killing this guy?' Kaio had pulled out his blade and was idly scratching the side of his nose with the tip of it.

It was a question Selys had ignored whenever it had floated up in her own mind. 'I hope it won't come to that. But we *cannot* allow that artefact to be used.'

'This man? He is…a…friend of yours?' Evarine asked, hesitant.

Selys nodded. 'We are acquainted.'

'And you said he's Myr-touched?'

'Indeed. Many people were. Most have died. The Queen's Inquisitors were rounding them up in Porsenthia and Bragalia.' Selys pointed to the two countries on the map.

Evarine stepped forward and stared at it, gripping the table with both hands.

The map depicted the continent of Etrovia in relief, with countries marked out in faded colours, mountain ranges and rivers carved in exquisite detail. Evarine traced her hand over the country borders, lingering on Segandis and the sea they were to cross. 'What if he...what if he's one of the others? Taken from Ma-Rai?'

Selys inclined her head. 'It's possible. We don't know where the lost souls came from. As far as I understand, this man was alone when he "woke up," and many other lost souls were grouped together.'

Evarine stared down. She didn't blink, almost as if by looking hard enough at it, she'd find the answers she sought.

Taran stood beside Evarine and pointed at Segandis. 'Myr are already being sighted in Bragalia. What if Ma-Rai was just the first wave? Then they crept back into Etrovia and started worming their way through villages?'

Selys rubbed one eye. 'I cannot claim to understand the tactics of the Myr. Who knows what they did, or why. All we can do is stop their weapons from being used, and hope Queen Surayo takes care of the rest.'

Taran held up one of his griffin-fletched arrows, sighting it. 'Well, if the Myr are trying to take over, killing the people they curse isn't gonna help 'em, is it?'

'They kill everyone they touch,' Selys said, growing tired.

'Didn't kill her.' Taran pointed the arrow-tip at Evarine.

All eyes fell on Evarine, who hadn't torn her attention away from the map.

Kaio narrowed his eyes, blade held loose in one hand. 'You ain't telling us the entire truth, are you, Evarine?'

She didn't reply.

'Evarine.' Kaio said, more loudly. 'You need to tell me everything you know.'

She closed her eyes and let out a sigh. 'I've already told you what I know.'

'Not good enough. Too many holes in this story of yours.'

Evarine looked up at him and shook her head. 'You took the shell from me. You're taking me on a voyage. What more do you want?'

Selys ran a finger along the Nethal Mountains, thinking. Evarine wasn't telling them everything, but she was right—Kaio held all the power. Whatever she was trying to do, she was at Kaio's mercy.

'How long till we get there?' Esto asked, turning everyone's attention back to the map.

'Two or three days, depending on the wind. But I hope it's a wasted journey. If Fenn turns up, it'll be complicated. If he doesn't make it…well, Paragos will have done our job for us.'

Evarine let out a gasp, her entire body going rigid.

'Evarine?' Kaio asked, nudging her shoulder with the flat of his blade.

'Fenn…?' Evarine whispered.

'A Myr-touched man from a village half a world away. A Myr-touched woman turning up in the middle of nowhere. Seems too much of a coincidence to be unrelated, doesn't it?' Esto scratched the back of her head.

Selys shouldn't have been surprised. 'You know someone called Fenn?'

'My husband was taken by the Myr. One of several from Ma-Rai. He…His name is Fenn.' Evarine trembled. Her knuckles whitened where she gripped the table. 'I…I thought I'd lost you.'

36
THE RACE
FENN

The ship Nadja had booked their return passage on could not be crewed by one person, so no matter how much Fenn had pleaded, the portmasters at Cape Grullon refused to allow him aboard.

Disheartened but determined, Fenn had begged a young sailor called Kesi to help him back to Porsenthia.

Kesi was hard on his luck and owned a smaller vessel. Fenn offered the last of his share of Nadja's money, and it had been enough to persuade him. Kesi was a young man with a wispy beard and cheeks red from cold and salt, short but stocky, and eyes that constantly smiled. His boat, a fishing trawler about fifty feet long, was painted a vivid shade of red. The brass wheel was chipped, but both masts looked sturdy enough, with no fraying or damage to the sails that Fenn could see.

At a quarter of the size of the Inquisitor's ship, it wasn't impressive, but it didn't have to be. It simply had to get him across the expanse of the Lasseen Ocean.

Thankfully, Kesi was keen to earn his coin, so the duo were underway quickly enough.

'You're from Ma-Rai, right?' Kesi asked, less than an hour into their journey. The coast of Meneos hadn't yet disappeared from view, and Kesi seemed unable to let silence last for long.

'Ma-Rai?' Fenn asked, attention pulled away from the horizon.

'Yeah, you all have that same nose, don't you? Is Manori still causing trouble up there? Truth be told, we were afraid he might've come down to Gape Grullon. His river flows right past us.'

Fenn didn't say anything, something about Kesi's words making him uncomfortable, but he couldn't put his finger on what.

'I s'pose there's more of us on the coast than in Ma-Rai. That's gotta help, right? Not as easy to pick off. Oh, sorry! Didn't mean nothin' by that!'

Fenn glanced away, unsure what to say. Kesi was the second person confident he was from Ma-Rai, but all he heard were the whispers in his mind warning him of treachery.

He couldn't trust anything people said. Not these strangers. Not the Inquisitors. Not even Selys.

Her betrayal hurt more than the others.

The boat rocked, jostled by the rough waves of the sea so far north. Fenn wondered if Neros knew he crossed her waters, or if he needed to touch the water for the spirit to be aware.

Perhaps Neros was too busy with Selys to give thought to anything else.

He shoved his hand in the pocket of his cloak, partly to keep his fingers warm, but mostly to reassure himself the Citrine Key was still there. Even sitting in his pocket, he could feel the magic pulsing within.

It had the power to restore his memories. He was so close now, he could taste it.

'Of course, I'm only out here 'cause my ma has no one left. Brothers went away. Both ended up in Westwicks. Less fishing but more farming. Easier life up there, strange as it sounds. Further away from Paragos too, so it's not so cold, either,' Kesi continued, oblivious to Fenn's indifference. 'Her eyes aren't good for much these days, so I gotta help her out. She weren't keen on me taking this trip, but gotta say that gold'll help out. Might get us through 'til next season, if I'm honest. She always says—'

Fenn tuned him out. Kesi seemed happy enough to chatter even without a second participant in the conversation.

'Everyone has been using you. Calidra. Jisyel. Selys. The Inquisitor. This one will be no different. Use him instead. He will get you closer to Vermecio.'

Fenn nodded absently. He wondered if Hassen had always spoken so much, or if he simply hadn't paid as much attention before. But the spirit's excitement for returning to *Vermecio* matched his own, and Fenn appreciated that.

Hassen was the only one on his side.

And if Selys's worries came to pass? If something terrible happened after *Vermecio* had the key? Hassen would help him get through the danger there, too.

It was easy. Simple. Why didn't anyone understand that?

'Fenn? Fenn, you hear me?'

Fenn shuddered as Kesi called him. He faced the sailor. 'Sorry, Kesi. What did you say?'

'I asked if anything's in the water? Rudder's not turning like it should. Sometimes there's old netting left floating.'

Fenn strode to the railing and peered overboard. Foamy water churned below, but he couldn't see anything that might've caught the ship. He was about to say as such when a pang of anxiety rippled through him.

Perhaps they had been caught—but not by a net. 'You ever see Neros?'

Kesi's eyes widened and he shifted his hold on the brass wheel. 'From a distance. Once. I...Do you think it's her?'

Fenn frowned at the churning waters. 'It might be.'

Thankfully, there was no sign of Verkata this time. Selys had said the Archons could wander Tassar as they wished, so Verkata was probably off causing a storm somewhere else. That was one thing to be grateful for.

'The key holds power. Not even Paragos can match it. Neros stands no chance.'

Fenn took comfort from the voice in his mind. It hadn't steered him wrong before. But even with the reassuring words, facing Neros was not something Fenn looked forward to. He licked his lips—chapped and dry in the cold wind—and braced himself.

'Fenn? If Neros attacks, we—we're sunk!' Kesi called, voice trembling.

'It'll be okay. Stay on course,' Fenn called back, hoping Hassen was right.

Dizziness washed over him, and he gripped the handrail tightly. The sudden waves of nausea and confusion had become more frequent, and he'd always lost chunks of time whenever they hit him. Probably some lingering part of the Myrish curse.

Fenn fought to stay conscious, but could already feel his shoulders slumping, his vision glazing.

The whispers in his mind hissed—words or noises in a language Fenn didn't understand. But the darkness was comforting. It wrapped around his mind like a blanket.

It would be okay.

The spirit would keep him safe.

It had so far. There was no reason to believe it would stop now.

'Fenn!'

He stirred. Something was calling him. Some*one*. It sounded like Hassen, but...but it couldn't be.

'Fenn!'

There was no fire accompanying the words. No sarcastic comment or mockery.

No.

Everything else was lies and treachery.

More darkness smothered him, slowing his breath, calming his worries.

'What's wrong with you? Fenn?' Kesi called, sounding clearer, but distant. Muffled.

Fenn tried to speak, but the words wouldn't form.

Something vivid green and blue appeared ahead of the boat. Water crashed and an almighty roar shook the air, but the darkness blocked most of it out.

He didn't need Hassen's vines anymore, either. Not when he had the darkness. Not when he had the key. Fenn clutched it—the one action he was aware of—and warmth spread through his fingers when they wrapped around the metal. Golden light surrounded him the moment he touched it—a barrier of flickering magic that expanded to encompass the entire boat.

Neros—for the enormous shape in front of the boat could be nothing else—screamed her fury at the light.

Fenn bowed his head, barely able to see more than the conflicting colours of green and blue of Neros against the golden light of the key. Something that sounded like wind rushed around him, drowning out other noise. He couldn't hear the boat, the crashing waves, even Kesi's frantic calls.

Smothering everything was the shadowy, misty darkness, like a blanket.

It was all Fenn knew, as he drifted in and out of consciousness.

WHEN FENN NEXT CAME AWARE, the key's golden light had disappeared, and dark clouds filled the sky from horizon to horizon.

He blinked, a sudden coldness taking over his body.

Neros hovered some distance off the port side, watching the boat with deep green eyes. The spirit was so enormous that even from afar, she seemed to loom over them. But she did nothing aside from float on the surface, her tail and rear legs disappearing below the water, sending up huge waves.

Fenn shivered and drew his fur-lined cloak more tightly around his neck to stave off the chill. 'Kesi? How...how long until we reach Porsenthia?' Fenn asked, his attention on Neros in case the spirit tried to attack.

When there was no response from the usually vocal man, Fenn turned towards the wheel.

Kesi backed away, one hand clutching a small knife with more nicks in its edge than the key, and pointed at Fenn. 'W—what are you?'

Fenn shook his head, coming back to himself. The wind seemed to hit him for the first time, and he winced as he regained control and balance, blinking rapidly. He didn't know what had happened—he thought Neros had approached the ship. Then the key had glowed and...darkness.

Kesi grabbed the wheel and the boat lurched.

Fenn braced himself against the main mast. 'What's wrong? Neros isn't after the boat?'

'Whole *ocean's* running from you!'

Dazed, Fenn looked out to the water, gasping as the waves indeed seemed to be fleeing from their boat in enormous ripples. 'I did that?' His legs threatened to buckle under him.

'Neros fears you. As Paragos does. The key you carry is more valuable than you can understand.'

Fenn tried to wet his lips again. Tried to figure out what it all meant. But his head pounded, and he wanted nothing more than to lie down and sleep. Everything would be over soon. Then things would make sense.

'Neros…she's been watching us for about two hours now,' Kesi said, eying Fenn with caution.

He staggered. Two hours had passed? It only felt like a few minutes at most. 'But she hasn't attacked?'

'Not since you did…whatever you did with that light! I've never seen a spirit driven away like that! Never! You a mage? Didn't know they had mages in Ma-Rai. Thought they were all from—'

'I'm not a mage,' Fenn cut in. Kesi seemed as eager to talk when he was scared as when he was in a pleasant mood. It wasn't helping his headache. 'I need to get to Porsenthia. Soon.'

'If Neros doesn't bother us, it'll be at least another day before we see the coast.'

So close now. A matter of days, then everything would be put right. It was his only thread of hope, and he clutched it as tightly as he could.

The sea continued to churn, the boat lurching this way and that as it cut across the dark, foaming waters. Fenn kept his attention on Neros, and the dragon spirit eyed their passage. Seaweed trailed from her claws and barnacles clustered across her chest, but aside from her wings, the dragon hardly moved.

Creeping dread pushed Fenn away from the rail, but the moment he stepped back, Neros opened her jaws.

He froze, expecting to see flames between her fangs.

But the spirit spoke. '*Please, Fenn. Remember what I told you. The Myr are our enemy!*' Selys's voice echoed from the dragon's throat. It was so unexpected, he didn't know how to respond.

'I know where you're going. I know you want to get your memories back and learn who you are, find your family. But you can't! Not at the risk of everyone alive in Tassar! Please, Fenn. Don't take the Citrine Key to Vermecio!'

'Selys?' Fenn whispered.

'Betrayer. They will never understand.'

Fenn nodded slowly, in agreement with the voice in his mind. Selys had her own goals. She didn't care about him. After he'd carried her down the mountain and made sure she received help. She'd turned her back on him.

'Kesi, can this boat go any faster?'

'Not without a strong wind. Be too unstable then, to be honest.'

Fenn glared at the dragon. Then his scowl shifted into a smile.

Hassen was right. Neros was afraid of him. The dragon couldn't bully her way to get what she wanted, so she played up to his softer side with Selys.

He laughed at the audacity of it, the hollow noise swallowed in the sea breeze. *He* had the advantage. He wasn't going to hand the key over just because they realised they couldn't fight him. Fenn folded his arms. There was no point in responding to Neros. Everything was trickery and manipulation, and it was all to benefit the spirits.

There was no reason he needed to care.

So he turned away from the dragon and pretended she was a bit of debris floating on the surface of the water. The smile felt *right* on his face. He was doing what was necessary, and nothing could stop him.

Fenn strode towards the wheel. 'Sorry if I scared you, Kesi. But I'll make sure Neros doesn't bother you, so don't worry about sailing cautiously. I need to get to Porsenthia as quickly as possible. You can do that for me, can't you?'

Kesi's face was redder than usual, his cheeks puffy. A bead

of sweat lined his forehead, eyes darting to the nearby dragon, then back to Fenn. 'Y—yeah. I can do that.'

Kesi was afraid.

Fenn found it peculiar. A young sailor and a dragon spirit, both afraid of a man with nothing.

He chuckled. 'That's good. Why don't you share a story of the sea? To pass the time.'

37
THE BLESSED
CALIDRA

Calidra ran. She ran without feeling the ground below her feet. Without any idea of how far or fast she was going. There was only shadowy mist, and the desperate need to get out of it.

It wouldn't be long before the voice returned.

The Myr.

She ran for all she was worth, but the smothering darkness did not relent.

'The dragon of gold laughed at you.'

Calidra stopped. There was no point in wearing herself out trying to escape. 'Why won't you leave me alone!'

'Yet you worship them. For nothing. No gain. They can take away their blessing if they are displeased.'

Calidra looked around, trying to find a light, a way out. But there was nothing.

'A bargain with us is for life. We understand you have your own nature. Desires. This should not be punished.'

A chill spread down her back, and Calidra whirled around to see one of the Myr standing less than two paces away. It stared at her with amber eyes, its domed skull giving the creature a hunched appearance. Its body seemed shapeless, formed of the void they stood in.

She didn't want to look at it. 'What do you want? I told you I'm not interested in anything you have!'

The Myr laughed, a whispering hiss that made her shudder. *'We caught you by Alnothen's forest. We can speak to you when you are susceptible.'*

She rolled her eyes. 'So I have to deal with you every time I fall asleep?'

'We could leave you be. If you help us.'

'I'm *not* helping you!'

More laughter.

'Just leave me alone! You're wasting your time!' Calidra backed away, keeping the Myr in her sights. She wouldn't put it past the creature to attack her if it grew bored with her defiance.

'We can give you many things you cannot obtain. We can ignore your home. Your loved ones would never be attacked by the Myr.'

The creature's words gave Calidra pause. If it spoke truthfully, it meant Fellwood would never be under threat. At least, not by the Myr. After seeing what they'd done to Foxmouth, that was a tempting offer. There wasn't much she wanted to gain, but she had plenty to lose.

The Myr smiled, fangs glinting in the shadows.

'Why?' Calidra asked.

'You proliferate.' Disgust laced his words. *'We killed you to no avail. And yet...the dragons bonded with you.'*

'They saw strength in us!' Calidra didn't care for the whim of the spirits, but she knew they could see that in people.

'No. They saw you could be a weapon. They used you for their own gain. Nothing more.'

'So are you!'

'Yes. Although we are honest about it.' The creature smiled again. *'You hurt. I see your pain. We can heal that.'*

'What do you *want* from me?' Calidra asked.

'Don't you want to get the child back? Have the ability to fight the Inquisitor?'

Calidra balled her hands into fists. She was stronger than Torsten if it came to a fight. She'd proved that, even if it had taken her by surprise. But he had more allies than she did. Including the queen. No matter how badly she wanted to get Renys back, it wasn't worth the cost of whatever the Myr wanted.

She wouldn't give herself to a dragon. The Myr were no different.

'You no longer wish to be beholden to dragon spirits? Harmed by them? Ruled by them? Neither do we. You must weaken them.'

Calidra laughed bitterly at the absurdity of the request. 'What in all of Tassar could I do against a dragon? I can't even do anything against Hassen, and he's a tiny spirit!'

'We know of the magic that bonds the iron dragon to your queen. We know how to strike at the heart of them.'

Calidra went very still. They'd spoken about that before. She remembered them talking about having magic that could sever the bond between the iron dragon and Queen Surayo. It was so difficult to think in this place, even following the conversation took most of her effort. 'You have a weapon?'

The Myr hissed. *'It was misused. There are other ways the iron dragon can be injured. We can share these with you.'*

Her head thrummed with pain. There was something *important* here, if only she could figure out the pieces. She needed to pay attention, but trying to get her thoughts straight in this place was near impossible.

Calidra considered everything it said. She could keep Fellwood safe. She wondered if they could remove Jisyel's curse, too, though the idea of these creatures anywhere near Jisyel made her feel sick.

She tried to think, tried to clear her mind and see the best way forward.

It wasn't right. None of it was.

'No! Get away from me!' Calidra pushed out, both with her hands and with her mind. Nothing good could come of whatever they promised. She'd survived so far. So had Jisyel. They'd continue to do so. 'I refuse to be beholden to any dragon spirit or Myr!'

The creature hissed, and ice crept along Calidra's skin.

Calidra woke with a gasp. Sweat dripped down the back of her neck when she sat up. She grasped her head, struggling to come to terms with the idea of the Myr inside her mind. They refused to let her go.

It took a few minutes to calm her breathing, then she reached over for Jisyel.

But her bed was empty.

Jisyel wasn't there

Calidra's breath caught, immediately taken back to when they'd been separated and Jisyel had been swept away by the river. No. That was silly. She was letting her anxious thoughts rule instead of thinking logically.

She pushed the sheets off, wincing as she swung her legs out of bed and rested her bare feet on the plush rug. Her mother's medic had removed the arrow, cleaned, dressed, and bound her thigh in thick bandages, but she couldn't put much weight on it.

Weak sunlight trickled in through the window, but the skies remained dark with smoke. She could smell the burning town even in her room, and wasn't sure that pungent odour would dissipate any time soon.

After dressing carefully—foregoing her favoured breeches and wrapping a sarong around her waist and shoulder—Calidra hobbled out of her room and down the tiled hall. Bit of the ceiling and walls had crumbled, resulting in white and grey dust covering everything.

Glad she'd slipped on some sandals before exiting her room, Calidra came to a halt by the door leading to the gardens.

Quillaja stood just outside, a shawl wrapped around her shoulders, a steaming mug of coffee held delicately in both hands. She turned at Calidra's approach, and inclined her head. 'Good morning, Miss Vantonen. You should be resting.'

Calidra didn't like the formality, but she didn't argue. 'Quillaja, have you seen Jisyel?'

'I haven't.' Quillaja took a sip of her coffee and said nothing more.

'Lady Vantonen, please!' a voice called from the right.

Calidra turned to peer through the gates at a line of townsfolk queued outside the estate. Many sported bandages or their arms in slings. Two liveried members of the household guard stood before the gates, but neither replied to the crowd or permitted them access.

'They've come for refuge. Healing. Food. Supplies. Some are just desperate for a roof over their head,' Quillaja explained. 'Sekano and his soldiers are conducting a report of the damage. Some of the griffins, too. It'll likely cost a lot to repair Fellwood. We may need to borrow money and materials from the other Lairds.'

'They'll help, won't they?'

Quillaja was too well-bred to shrug, but she let out a gentle sigh. 'It is unlikely. Kaio Ioran in particular is a thorn. He is the richest Laird by far, but I've not known him to give any support in the three years since he took over the canton. He's young. Selfish and foolhardy.'

Calidra thought back on the Myr's promises. She cast her gaze skywards, wondering if the griffin scout who'd followed Torsten had completed their duty, or if they'd been chased off by the Inquisitors. She couldn't imagine them being stupid enough to shoot at a griffin.

'Is Mother in her study?'

'She is. Though if I were you, I wouldn't distract her. Lady Vantonen is under a lot of stress during this difficult time.'

Calidra did not point out the hypocrisy in the statement. Her leg twinged in pain, and she shifted her weight, wondering how many people had lost their homes during Miroth's attack. She had seen plenty of people crossing Porsenthia in the wake of the Myr's attacks, and this brought flashbacks of those desperate faces.

Calidra turned away with a shudder. Speaking to her mother was always at the bottom of her priority list, but it was unlike Jisyel to disappear. Hesitantly, she made her way through the rooms and halls of the compound until she reached her mother's study.

The door was ajar, which usually meant Furyn was less likely to be irritated at a disturbance.

Calidra knocked.

'Enter.'

Taking a breath, Calidra walked into the room as confidently as she could, and waited on the far end of the table. 'Good morning, Mother.'

Furyn glanced up. She wore a soft green robe that covered her to her ankles, her braided hair tied high atop her head. 'Calidra.' Furyn acknowledged her with a nod.

Keeping Furyn waiting was always a bad idea, so Calidra spoke straight away. 'Have you seen Jisyel this morning? She wasn't in our room. Quillaja hasn't seen her either.'

Furyn's placid stare sharpened. 'You can't keep track of that woman, can you?'

'It's a large compound,' Calidra replied, feeling her own anger rising.

'Are you going to come to me every time you lose track of

that Porsenthian? Am I expected to traipse around Bragalia with a pack of hunting hounds?'

Calidra knew it was a mistake expecting support from Furyn. But she'd hoped her mother might have softened in light of Fellwood in pieces and her granddaughter missing. 'I only asked if you'd seen her.'

'Why would I have seen her?' Furyn got to her feet and peered behind the heavy drapes across the window.

Calidra held herself back from throwing up her hands in frustration. 'I don't know. Perhaps she wanted to help the people of Fellwood and came to you for advice? Maybe she thought she'd be a polite guest and bring you coffee?'

'Really, I don't know what you expect of me, Calidra.' Furyn remained at the window. 'You only ever come to me when you need something. Expect me to ignore my responsibilities and needs? Drop everything to help you? You have the audacity to disappear for years and come back with demands? I have lost my husband. I am trying to raise a son. Alone. In a way that prepares him to take over the Lairdship when he comes of age, seeing as you abandoned us to live your own life on that cursed Porsenthian island.'

Her mother's words stung, but Calidra held her breath. Didn't rise to them. After having the Myr in her mind, her mother seemed marginally less terrifying than usual.

Furyn turned away from the window. 'We are at war with the Myr once again. There is a rogue dragon in our skies. I don't need more problems. Especially when you should know better.'

Calidra fought to keep her voice from rising. 'Where is Paicha? I haven't seen him, either.'

Furyn's simmering anger settled, her shoulders lowering slightly. 'I sent him to Olmir to tutor under their warriors. Perhaps he'll be a griffin rider in a few years. It'll bring strength to the canton. Dragons know we need that.'

Calidra dropped her gaze. She had grown up an only

child, and hadn't given her younger brother much thought. He had only been a toddler when she'd left, and she thought more of him as a distant cousin than a sibling.

Regardless of her thoughts, Furyn was of no help. 'I apologise for disturbing you, Mother. I'll continue to look for Jisyel.' There was nothing she could say that would appease Furyn, so she decided to withdraw before anything escalated.

Calidra hobbled back down the hall, wondering where Jisyel was, and why she had left without saying anything. Perhaps she'd been too deep asleep. The Myr's words repeated in her mind, a puzzle she wanted to solve. She lingered beside the door to the gardens and stared out at the beautiful flowers and neat grass.

Coffee would help.

Just as she decided to make herself the drink, Malora approached from the gardens, her face dark as a thundercloud. Malora didn't look like she'd slept—her hair was unbound and dishevelled, dark circles hung under red eyes, and her fingers trembled.

'Mal?' Calidra hesitated.

'So stupid. Everything is so unbelievably stupid!'

Though neither of them had been home in years, Malora's voice carried the authoritative tone that made her sound so much like their mother.

'Chyram was never going to give me his blessing!'

Calidra tensed. Her sister's rage was reminiscent of Furyn. 'Mal…'

Malora looked at Calidra and blinked, as if she'd only just realised Calidra was there. 'Spirits take me, I was so stupid! I should never have left Renys with you!'

Calidra took a step back. She already blamed herself for Torsten taking Renys, but hearing her sister's anger sparked a fire inside her that had built during her talk with Furyn. 'Don't you dare say that.'

'Mother was right. You aren't good for anything!'

'Mal, I thought we'd gone past this.'

'Gone past this? I leave Renys with you and she gets kidnapped? How else am I supposed to take that?'

Calidra wanted to lash out. Hurt Malora in the same way Malora was hurting her. She also wanted to run. To get away from the vitriol and the mistakes she'd made, and get back to the Isle of Salt with Jisyel, where no one could bother them.

But none of that would help.

Whatever she did, Renys would still be gone, and Malora would still be falling apart.

Calidra shook her head. 'I fought to keep Renys with everything I had. I didn't hand her over to Torsten!'

Malora shook, jaw clenching, a vein in her neck pulsing. She stepped towards Calidra. '*If* you'd fought, I'd still have my daughter!'

Calidra stepped back, keeping distance between them. 'How do you think I got shot in the leg?' She pointed to the bandage around her thigh. 'You know me. Do you really believe Mother? Do you really think I'd *let* him take her?'

Malora gaped, gaze dropping to Calidra's leg. Tears filled her eyes.

Calidra hadn't seen her sister like this since they were in their youth. She was equal parts awed and frustrated by Malora's stubbornness and anger, though she knew she'd be exactly the same if it was Jisyel. She *had* been exactly the same, when she recalled how much she'd begged her mother to help and attempted to rally Sekano and the household guard herself when Jisyel had been lost. 'Enough is enough, Mal. I came *with* you. I followed you. Even though I didn't think getting your blessing was a good choice. It didn't matter what I thought because it was about what *you* needed. I know you're angry.'

They held each other's gaze for a long while. The air between them seemed to prickle, and Calidra braced herself. 'But I think you're angry at yourself, not me.'

Malora's shoulders slumped, some anger seeping out of her. 'Ironic, isn't it? Foxmouth was attacked by the Myr. Fellwood attacked by a dragon spirit. I've been in the middle of both.'

Calidra grasped Malora's hands. 'Yes. But you've *survived* both. That speaks to your strength.'

'Or blind luck.' Malora squeezed Calidra's hands. 'Cal, I… I don't know what to do.'

'It's okay. You don't need to have the answers.'

'I *failed* her, Cal. My own daughter. Because of that damned golden dragon!' Her voice rose again.

Calidra held her sister's chin and forced Malora to look her in the eye. 'You aren't a failure, Malora. Neither of us are.'

There was a commotion at the gate, and she glanced up, in case they were now letting the townsfolk into the estate.

Jisyel walked through the open door, and Calidra's heart leapt to her throat. 'Jisyel?'

'Where's she been?' Malora asked. She pulled away from Calidra, her eyes narrowing. 'She's wearing a gold ring.'

Calidra blinked several times, her gaze drawn to Jisyel's hand. Jisyel rarely wore jewellery, and certainly hadn't had any since they'd left the Isle of Salt. She couldn't imagine any jewellers selling in Fellwood in the wake of Miroth's attack.

'No. No. No. No! No!' Malora trembled as Jisyel approached them, a broad smile on her face. 'I don't *believe* it!'

Calidra had no idea why Malora was suddenly so upset, but she hurried over to meet Jisyel part-way. She needed to tell her about the Myr visiting her while she slept. The moment they were within touching distance, Jisyel grabbed Calidra's face in both hands, and kissed her. It was so long and caught Calidra so off-guard, that she pulled away, coughing. 'Jisyel? What…? Are you okay? Where have you been?' She looked at Jisyel's feet, in case she'd hurt herself.

'Better than I've been in years.' Jisyel beamed at her, eyes twinkling.

Calidra raised one hand to her cheek, where Jisyel had held her. Jisyel's grip had seemed stronger than usual. It pushed all thoughts of the Myr from her mind. 'You went out to get a ring?'

Jisyel raised her hand and looked at it, as if noticing it for the first time. It was bright gold and glowed faintly, though it could have simply been reflected sunlight.

Malora appeared beside them, her mouth hanging open. 'Where have you been?'

Calidra frowned at her sister's demand, then saw how much she shook. 'Mal? Are you okay?'

Malora ignored Calidra, her gaze locked on Jisyel. She pointed an accusatory finger at Jisyel's ring. 'Did you get that from Chyram?'

Jisyel's smile fell at Malora's harsh tone. 'I—It was...'

'Tell me right now, Jisyel! Did you get it from him?' Malora snapped.

'Malora! There's no need to speak to her like that!' Calidra said.

But Malora wasn't listening, her face twisted into an ugly grimace. 'Just...just tell me. Honestly.'

Jisyel looked between the two, her easy confidence shattering with the passing seconds. 'I needed to do something. I *had* to.'

Calidra suddenly understood Malora's anger. She limped forward and took Jisyel's hands in her own.

'Your hands are cold.' Jisyel raised Calidra's hands to her mouth and kissed her fingers.

'How...how can you tell they're cold?' Calidra asked, aware her voice trembled but unable to do anything about it.

'Because my curse is gone.'

Calidra didn't say anything. *Couldn't* say anything. Her breathing came out in shallow breaths.

'Chyram removed it. And...he gave me his blessing.'

38
THE PLEDGE
SELYS

Sweat trickled down Selys's neck. It had taken every scrap of concentration to speak through Neros, and she had only managed to get a handful of words out before becoming overwhelmed by the spirit's presence.

But given the look on Fenn's face, she didn't think anything more she could have said would have helped. The set in his jaw, his shadowed gaze, it all sent goosebumps along her arms.

He had the key. That was beyond question. She hadn't *seen* it, but she'd felt the Myrish magic as strongly as Neros had. And that golden light…

Neros was almost an Archon in terms of power and influence. Yet that simple key had pushed her away easily as a feather on the breeze. Neros had felt shock more than anything else. But much like her reaction to the Jade Shell, it terrified her.

The dragon spirit's fear raced through Selys, too. Things were worse than she'd imagined.

She rested her shoulder and head against the wooden walls of her cabin, breathing in time with the swell of the water below. A lantern, affixed to the ceiling, swung gently as

Wolf's Grin creaked, casting a warm yellow light that rose and fell.

'Selys?' Esto looked across the room from her bunk, rubbing sleep from her eyes. 'You okay? Do I need to get Ruka?'

Selys shivered, trying to dispel the fear that coursed through her. Fenn wasn't here. Neither was the key. 'No. No, that's not necessary. Thank you.'

Esto wasn't convinced—her frown deepened. 'You were talking in your sleep.'

Selys rubbed her face. 'I wasn't asleep. I was talking with Neros.'

Esto raised an eyebrow. 'Y'know, even if you're sticking around, I don't think I'll ever get used to that.' She swung her legs off her bunk and slipped her boots on. 'Anything you wanna share?'

'Fenn is crossing the Lasseen Ocean *right now*.' Even as she said the words, Selys struggled to believe them. Her fear was real. It was happening. Something twisted in her gut at the thought of it, and she had a sudden urge to vomit.

Esto nodded gravely. 'Well, you knew there was a good chance of it happening. It's why you rallied everyone, right?'

'I know, I know…I just…' Selys gripped the edge of her bunk, the wood digging into her palms. 'Spirits, it's bad. He has the key.'

'Sounds like Kaio should know this.'

Selys sat, mute, as Esto buttoned up her shirt and left the cabin. Selys had hoped she'd been wrong about Fenn. That she'd been overreacting to her and Neros's fear of the key. But Neros had proved he was on his way back to *Vermecio*, and all her warnings had fallen on deaf ears.

The boat he'd been travelling on hadn't been particularly large, and she definitely hadn't seen Nadja or Apollo on board. It made the slow, creeping dread more insidious. Had he killed them? Abandoned them? Were they lost somewhere in Paragos's frozen domain?

She took a few moments to catch her breath and calm her racing mind. Though she'd feared this would happen, and it wasn't a shock, the realisation had caught her off guard.

Once she'd steadied herself, Selys exited the cabin and climbed the stairs onto the deck.

It was a cloudless night, with countless stars shining brightly above. The light of the broken moon was strong, bathing the deck in ethereal, blue-white. She stared up at the stars, the cold wind of the Salt Sea chilling her face.

Wolf's Grin creaked and groaned as it shifted on the water, sails rippling.

The last time she'd sailed north across this sea, her life had changed—she'd discovered *Vermecio*, Fenn's curse had been lifted, and Neros had chosen that moment not only to acknowledge her, but bond with her. Everything had passed in a blur of fire and magic.

Now, she was sailing to the very same spot in the hopes of stopping something unspeakable.

Most of the crew were asleep, but a few footsteps crossed the deck here and there. Evarine stood by the railing, staring out at the dark waters, her hair caught in the wind. She glanced up at Selys, then headed towards her.

'You should be resting,' Selys said when Evarine approached. It wasn't quite a dismissal—she wasn't sure how she felt about this woman, exactly, but trust wasn't high on the list.

'I'm too anxious to sleep.' Evarine looked like she hadn't eaten or slept in weeks.

'Talk to Ruka. She might have something that'll help. A sleeping draught or some herbs.'

Evarine nodded, but made no move to seek out the healer.

Selys sighed. She *wanted* to like this woman. Give her the

benefit of the doubt. After all, she hadn't judged Fenn, either, and he'd been obviously afflicted by Myrish magic. But that had been before Neros. Now, any touch of the Myr set her skin crawling. 'Well, seeing as you're awake, you might as well hear what I have to say. I'm about to tell Kaio.'

She stepped carefully over coils of rope and around barrels—Fergus reclined atop one, and he blinked slowly at her. A quick glance told her Esto was up on the quarterdeck beside Kaio, and she made her way to the steps, Evarine on her heels.

Lit by moonlight, Kaio looked the spitting image of Skaru, and Selys's breath caught when he turned to greet her. The Jade Shell glinted around his neck, emitting its own soft, green light. She held back her instinct to snatch it off him and fling it overboard.

Esto had procured her hat in the few minutes since Selys had last seen her, and her silhouette was stark. Her lip curled when she spotted Evarine, but she didn't say anything.

'What's all this? Something happening?' Taran asked, jogging up the steps with an easy athleticism to join them.

There was no need to draw out the moment. 'Fenn's on his way,' Selys said, unable to meet their eyes. 'Neros told me. He's crossing the ocean as we speak.'

Kaio folded his arms, boot tapping on the deck. 'Good. Means this voyage wasn't for nothing. Know how long it'll be until he gets to the cave?'

'No, though I'll know when he leaves Neros's domain.' Selys brushed a strand of hair behind one ear. 'But…'

'But?' Kaio prompted.

'He has the key. Its magic is strong enough to keep Neros at bay.' She hoped he understood the gravity of their situation when she said that. 'He's more dangerous than I ever thought.'

'I did wonder why your dragon couldn't just, I dunno,

crush the ship. She's good at doing that,' Kaio responded, an edge to his voice.

Selys didn't rise to the barb. 'She doesn't take life without reason. And she tried with Fenn.'

'Would've saved us the trip.' Taran struck a match against the wooden rail and raised it to the cigarillo between his teeth.

'Don't you understand? Neros *couldn't* hurt him. This is bad. Very bad.' Selys hated their calm demeanour. 'I—I don't know if we can stop him.' That was her biggest fear. She'd dragged them all this way, and in the end, they couldn't do a thing.

'I don't see the problem. We'll just kill him.' Kaio folded his arms.

'Neros couldn't stand against him! You'll have no chance.'

Kaio grinned a vicious smile. 'Sure, that key might be strong. *He* isn't. We set up an ambush. Taran needs one good shot, right between the eyes. Drop him before he knows we're there. Don't give him a chance to use that key.'

A lump formed in Selys's throat. 'Kaio...'

'Taking down a stronger opponent is easy when you know how.'

'You can't kill him!' Evarine cried.

Kaio looked at her with disdain. 'I beg to differ.'

'I tried reasoning with him. Talking through Neros, but...' Selys trailed off, angry at her own weakness. 'Neros's power is too much for me. But face to face? Maybe I can get through to him.'

'And if you don't?' Esto asked softly.

'What're you talking about? *Get through to him*? We kill him on sight. End of discussion,' Kaio snapped. 'I'm just glad he's actually going to *be* there. Wasn't sure if this was a wild goose chase.'

Selys didn't know what to say. She wanted to argue for

Fenn's life, but Kaio would see that as another slight against him.

'You're the Laird of Segandis. I understand people following your word there. But we aren't in Segandis! Fenn's done nothing to you or your canton. Please don't hurt him!' Evarine pressed.

'Maybe not, but we have knowledge. I'd be letting my canton down if I didn't act. Besides, if Fenn does…whatever it is he's planning on doing, it'll affect Segandis eventually.'

'But—'

'No.' He shot her a warning look. 'I've already lost most of my family to a dragon spirit. I won't lose the rest to the Myr. We stop him now. *Wolf's Grin* is one of the fastest ships on any sea, so we get there first. Taran sets up an ambush. One shot, before he uses the key, and all our problems are over.'

Selys was torn. She was proud of Kaio stepping up, even if he didn't fully comprehend the bigger picture. He thrived when it came to fighting strategies. But on the other hand, Fenn was her friend. It wasn't *him* doing this, it was the *Myr*. 'Fenn is being manipulated, Kaio. It isn't him.'

'I'm not risking you talking to him. If he knows we're there, we lose the element of surprise,' Kaio replied flatly.

Selys didn't have an answer to that. She didn't want Fenn to die, not after she'd gone to such lengths to keep him alive.

'It could be my Fenn.' Evarine clasped her hands together. 'He's alive.'

'And working for the Myr, it seems like. Ain't *your Fenn*, in that case,' Taran said.

'Please…let me talk to him. He won't suspect you're there, surely? If I talk to him alone?' Evarine dropped to her knees and clutched the bottom of Kaio's shirt. 'I'm begging you.'

Kaio stared down at her for a long while, then raised his gaze to Selys. 'If anyone is talking to him, it'll be Selys. And I'm not risking that.'

'Then why bring me? If you're only going to rip him away

from me again?' Evarine asked, tightening her grip on the fabric of Kaio's shirt.

He stepped back, wrenching himself out of her grasp.

'If Fenn truly is your husband,' Selys said, daring to hope, 'there's a chance he'll recognise you. Maybe he could be persuaded not to use the key. You could be instrumental in stopping him.'

Evarine looked at her, eyes shining with tears. 'I'll do my best.'

'It's more important than that. Fenn is looking for you. His family. He thinks using this key is the only way he'll achieve that. But if seeing you triggers his memories? He wouldn't have to use the key because he'd have found you.' Selys desperately wanted to believe it. Fenn hadn't known anything about himself or where he'd come from, but no matter what magic the Myr had afflicted him with, surely he'd recognise his own wife?

Kaio tutted, as if annoyed she'd snatched away his chance for a fight.

'Kaio. There's no need for unnecessary bloodshed is there?'

'I don't like the risk. Taran, I want you in position regardless. You loose an arrow the second it looks like Fenn's going to make his move.'

Taran nodded.

Kaio strode away. 'Back to your posts. Selys, you tell me the moment Fenn reaches land.'

Selys let out a breath of relief. Perhaps they wouldn't be too late after all.

39
THE TRICK
FENN

Mountains pressed in on either side of the river where the fishing trawler slowly crept upstream, tacking from bank to bank as Kesi forced the boat along. The huge peaks made Fenn think of sentinels, silent and judgemental.

He hunkered down, half-hoping that hiding behind the trawler's railings would keep the iron dragon's attention off him. He wouldn't soon forget how Torsten had treated him and the other lost souls. Inquisitors and the queen were his enemy.

'This is Toriaken's domain. His shrine is close. His power is greatest here.'

Something about the words set Fenn's skin crawling, and he scratched his arms and face to rid himself of the itch.

Kesi warned him that the boat wouldn't be able to progress far upriver, especially where it narrowed and the incline increased, but Fenn didn't mind. He was finally back in Porsenthia, on the eastern side of the Nethal Mountains. A stone's throw from his destination.

They'd passed Foxmouth, though it wasn't much more than a smoking husk. Repairs were underway, and Fenn had seen scores of people walking back and forth like ants, but he'd otherwise ignored them. The river was more important, and he pushed Kesi to take them as deep into the mountains as possible.

Hunger pangs rippled through him, but the darkness pushed them away, like it did with everything unrelated to reaching *Vermecio*. It wouldn't be long before he had what he needed. Then he could rest.

The gentle thrum of the boat slowed, then stopped, and it halted it in place. 'This…this is as far as I can go,' Kesi panted. He'd shed his own heavy cloak and grasped the wheel with sweaty palms. He'd used a pole to manoeuvre along some of the trickier bends in the river, but it seemed he'd exhausted his capabilities—and the boat's.

Fenn didn't understand why the man trembled every time he spoke. He hadn't hurt him, nor tried to. He clutched the key in his pocket for the umpteenth time, reassuring himself it was still there and hadn't fallen out during the journey. 'Here will do.'

Kesi wiped his brow with the back of one hand, and carefully lowered the anchor on a chain. His eyes kept darting to Fenn's pocket, and he flinched every time the key flashed.

Fenn scowled at the sailor's caution. 'You need to watch out for Toriaken. Not me.'

'The iron dragon? Isn't he the protector of the Porsenthian Empire?'

'He might claim that title. But he's dangerous. So is the queen. I wouldn't stay here long if I were you.' Fenn gave him a brief wave as he clambered down the ship and waded across the river towards the bank, heedless of the cold water.

Kesi called after him, but Fenn didn't hear. The only sound he held onto was the one in his mind as it repeated over and over, '*Vermecio*.'

❄

HUNGRY AND TIRED, Fenn pushed himself along the rocky mountain path, grabbing hold of rocks and trees as he passed them to keep upright.

Left with only his own ragged breathing and scrambling footsteps on the path, he struggled to mark the passage of time. The sun beat down on him, but it was a cool light that didn't make him sweat as much as the steep incline did. Veins of iron filled the land here, and he saw more than one glint of grey. He made sure not to step on any of them.

The pathways were well-kept and easy to traverse—most were signposted and led to Toriaken's Shrine. He kept heading due west, avoiding the roads towards the shrine, until he left the well-travelled paths and began to crest wilder terrain. Trees grew sparsely here, leaping up wherever the land offered enough space or nutrients, and even birdsong faded to the occasional, distant call.

His throat was dry and his strides grew shorter and heavier as the day wore on. The sky shifted from clear blue to hazy purple when the sun began to set and clouds rolled in.

'*Vermecio…Vermecio…*' Fenn muttered along with the voice in his mind, though he wasn't sure if it spoke or he could only hear its echo.

He came to a stop beside a particularly large boulder and caught his breath. The heavy clouds threatened rain, or perhaps a storm, and some instinct told him to look for shelter. But overriding all thoughts, all desires, was the desperate, *vital* need to reach the cave. It itched at him, and the only way to rid himself of the constant discomfort was to keep walking.

So he continued on, trying not to stumble over loose rocks.

Rain spattered down several minutes later, and the cool droplets of water caught him on the back of his neck, trickling down between his shoulder blades. Fenn shivered, blinking rapidly.

When had he wandered into the middle of a rainstorm?

He wrapped his arms around himself and looked through the growing darkness for somewhere he could get out of the rain. There wasn't much, but a crooked conifer grew from the edge of the mountain, and Fenn hurried towards it, pulling up his cloak to cover his head as he stumbled away.

It was relatively dry under the boughs, and he sat down with a wince, his legs throbbing and feet burning. It was so cold out here, colder than he'd felt in a long while—strange considering he'd been in a blizzard not too long ago—and Fenn cupped his gloved hands together. He realised one had been torn across the palm, a thin line of blood already congealed in the cracks of his dirty skin. He hadn't had any idea he'd been injured, and the sight confused him.

'Fire?' Fenn muttered, the idea coming to him from a distant corner of his mind. 'Hassen?'

He didn't have his sword anymore—had no idea when he'd lost that—but he'd always been able to conjure the dragon's fire when he'd needed it.

Come to think of it, he couldn't remember the last time he'd done that.

He reached inside himself, but felt only the faintest ember. There was no raging fire, ready to be summoned at a moment's notice. He tried again, more desperate, to no avail.

Fenn scowled, more out of confusion than anything else. He was sure he used to be able to summon Hassen's fire with a thought. But no matter how hard he'd tried, he couldn't feel the dragon spirit.

Fenn sighed, putting the failure down to his exhaustion and confused state. The pockets of his cloak were deep, and he reached in to grab the flint he'd been carrying before, along with the last of his kindling. Gathering what leaf litter he could from under the tree, he struck the flint against a rock.

Nothing happened.

So he tried again. And again. And again, until he could hardly feel his fingers. Finally, it sparked, and the meagre fire came to life. He huddled into his furs, as close to the flames as he dared, staring into the dancing light as night crept over the land. The broken moon rose in the west, a guiding light towards his destination.

The voices were silent. No orders. No reassurances. Not even arguing, like there had been the last time he was in Porsenthia. Every muscle and joint ached after days, if not weeks, of trudging around difficult terrain on foot. If he wasn't so keen for answers, he'd be happy to sleep for a week.

So much had fallen by the wayside, but Fenn dismissed his lamentations with a shake of his head.

He couldn't tell quite how high up he was, but he could clearly see the bright lights of Toriaken's Shrine to the south, and the land as it stretched towards the dark sea he'd just crossed. Eastbrook was on the coast, where Queen Surayo held her seat.

He wondered if she could see him as he huddled on the mountain.

Fenn adjusted the layers of his cloak and buried his face in the soft comfort, one side of his body warmed by the fire, the rain gently pattering outside the tree's shelter.

It wasn't long before exhaustion took him, and he slipped into sleep.

DARKNESS. Cold. A stillness that threatened to suffocate him.

Fenn walked, stumbling along weeds and vegetation that clawed at his legs and waist. He pushed through them. He was looking for something, though he wasn't sure what it was. The weeds were slowing him down. Holding him back.

Did someone need his help? It was important he got there soon.

More vines rose up and clawed at his chest and face with sharp thorns. Fenn pushed them away, irritated. One trailing vine looped around his ankle, halting him mid-step. He swayed, careful not to lose his balance. Thorns burst from the vine's flesh and dug into his skin, pinning him in place.

Even in the dark, he saw the flash of red as they drew blood. 'Stop it!' Fenn yelled, his voice muffled by shadow. 'Let go!' He tried to yank his foot out of the vine's grip, but it had him held fast.

Awkwardly, he crouched down, grabbed the vine with both hands, and ripped it in two to free himself.

All the vegetation shrank away in response, retreating into the dark ground with a low hiss.

Fenn inspected his ankle, but the scratch didn't seem serious. He continued on, idly wondering whether the thorn had been poisonous. That had been something to fear once, hadn't it?

He rubbed his forehead, trying to clear his thoughts and recall why he was here. He was too cold to think. And it was so dark, he couldn't figure out where he needed to go.

At least the vegetation no longer pressed in on him and he could walk without being snagged on vines every handful of steps. He kept walking, not quite sure why, but with the overwhelming sense that he shouldn't stop.

Bad things would happen if he stopped.

And he was *so* cold...

Pitch black gave way to muted grey after an indeterminate amount of time, and Fenn slowed down, noting the changing light. He heard something hiss so deeply it rattled his head, and he stopped where he was, heart thumping.

Seconds ticked by, and just when he thought he was

imagining things, orange light flickered a short way ahead of him. There was no understanding, no additional knowledge, only the sense that whatever bad thing he was trying to escape was happening where that orange light was.

He ran towards it, desperate to see. Desperate for answers.

The light grew brighter and brighter, until he had to squint as he approached. Other colours drifted in. Green dominated, but there were also spots of brown and yellow. He blinked again, suddenly recognising a dragon stood before him,

It lashed its tail, fighting the shadowy mist that filled this place. It unleashed a jet of flame every so often, and the shadow would retreat, only to rush back in a few moments later. Greenery burst from the dragon's body—thorny vines wrapped around its horns, leaves sprouted from the scales atop its head and neck, and even a few mushrooms appeared near the tip of its tail.

Fenn skidded to a halt a handful of paces away. He *knew* this dragon.

Or at least, he thought he did.

His chest tightened, so cold it was as if he'd swallowed chunks of ice.

'Fenn!' Something called his name. Was it the dragon? The shadow? A twisted amalgamation of them both?

The dragon slashed out at the mist with its foreclaws—talons gouging holes in it. Turning, it unleashed more fire at the darkness creeping along the ground and blasted it away in a barrage of bright orange.

Fenn wavered, unsure whether to go to the dragon's aid or hold it down. He felt deep in his gut that he had to do *something*, but he didn't know what. And making the wrong decision would ruin everything.

Invisible forces pushed and pulled at him, trying to force him in both directions.

'Fenn!' Again, the voice cried out.

He took a hesitant step forward, towards the dragon. One shadowed tendril had grabbed its left rear leg, and held it fast. The dragon roared, whirling around to bite at the shadow, wings flapping, but another tendril wrapped itself around its neck and held it in place.

'Hassen?' Fenn whispered, though he wasn't convinced the name was correct. He took another step towards it.

'Lies!' screamed the voice in his mind, as more shadowy tendrils wrapped around the dragon. They tightened over its snout, wings, legs. Pulled it crashing down to the ground. *'This Hassen is a trick.'*

Fear flooded Fenn as he watched the dragon's furious thrashing grow quieter and less vigorous.

'We are truth. We will get you to Vermecio. We will get your family back. Your memories back.'

The shadows rippled, smothering Hassen and covering every hint of light and colour. Hassen's golden eyes stared up at him, the last thing he saw before the dragon disappeared.

Fenn collapsed to the ground, his breathing slowing.

He watched, unable to do anything—*unwilling* to do anything—and the shadows enveloped him.

FENN WOKE TO A CLEAR, cold dawn, rainwater dripping from the tree's branches above him.

He stood up, ignoring the pain in his ankle, and turned west. He left the embers of his fire, hardly aware of each step along the mountain trail.

There was nothing left for him. Only the slow but determined trudge towards *Vermecio*.

40
THE SUMMONS
TORSTEN

Bone-rattling had never been a description Torsten considered for the carriage ride from Marlrush Fortress to Eastbrook, but they seemed to hit every bump and divet—to the point where he'd looked out the window to see whether they were going across rocks instead of using marked roads.

The iron fortress of Eastbrook couldn't appear soon enough.

Torsten had never given much thought to the strain his job put on his body. Because of Miroth, he'd never needed to join the other Inquisitors and soldiers within Queen Surayo's ranks in their daily drills. Never needed to consider it.

Without Miroth, he regretted how woefully ill-equipped he was for even the most basic actions. Wearing layers of boiled armour and steel plate, a heavy uniform, cloak, boots, and lugging around a longsword took more effort than he'd ever thought possible—every muscle ached just getting to his feet after sitting for so long.

Renys travelled with them, her hands bound, and she had cried most of the way before she'd exhausted herself and slept. The carriage rattled as it was pulled through Eastbrook, horse hooves echoing loudly on the cobblestones, and she had woken with another wail.

When the horns blew to announce the carriage's arrival, despite the likely punishment that awaited him, Torsten couldn't help but let out a sigh of relief. He thought about swapping to his formal robes—anything to rid the ache in his back—then mentally berated himself. He needed to prove he remained worthy of his Master Inquisitor title.

The carriage came to a gentle halt in the front courtyard of Eastbrook castle, beside the enormous water fountain depicting Toriaken. Most of the damage from the Myrish strike had been restored during the time he'd been away, though a few buildings sported broken windows, and there was plenty of debris piled up along the streets

A young page opened the carriage door for them and stepped aside, waiting.

Torsten gestured for Halios and the other Inquisitors in the carriage to exit first, while he gathered his strength. Halios led Renys out, her crying stopping as she stared around the courtyard, eyes wide.

Once they'd flooded out, Torsten's gaze was drawn immediately to a pair of griffins that circled the palace towers, dark silhouettes against an overcast sky. His gaze lingered on them and he missed his step out of the carriage, slipping on the cobbles and only just managing to catch himself before he fell.

Torsten straightened quickly, but the page's eyes were averted. If he *had* seen, he didn't react.

Smoothing down his cloak with a grumble, Torsten turned to make his way up the stone stairway that dominated the palace courtyard. Dizziness overcame him before he took a single step, and he heaved, doubled over, and expelled bile. He leaned against the side of the carriage, one hand grasping onto the door, the other wrapped around his stomach as he spewed out green liquid.

Those gathered in the courtyard of Eastbook's castle politely averted their gaze, but the fact he was in this state before them was more painful than the retching.

It took a few minutes before the heaving stopped, and several hacking coughs brought an end to his unseemly episode. He'd stained his uniform, and wondered if this was all some cruel joke.

'Master Inquisitor? Sir?' Halios leaned around the corner of the carriage and offered Torsten a silk handkerchief, embroidered in one corner with the Iron Crown's insignia.

With nothing to do but swallow his pride, Torsten took it and dabbed at his mouth.

Two heralds in loose maroon robes hurried down the stairway, their long sleeves dragging behind them. They halted a few paces from the carriage and bowed low. The taller one said, 'Queen Surayo has been anxiously awaiting your return, Master Inquisitor. Please allow us to escort you to Her Majesty.'

Torsten wiped at the liquid staining his uniform. 'I will visit my chambers and refresh myself after the journey. Tell Her Majesty I'll be there presently.'

'I'm afraid that will not be possible, Master Inquisitor.' There was no concern in the herald's voice, though he raised a curious eyebrow at Renys, who was trying to clamber up the water fountain—Inquisitor Helios had to stand in her way to stop her. 'Inquisitor Helios and those with you may rest until called upon, but Queen Surayo has requested your immediate presence.'

'I am in no fit state to stand before the queen!' Torsten folded the kerchief and pocketed it.

The second herald looked him up and down, her lip quirking. 'Be that as it may, Her Majesty's orders were quite clear.'

Torsten couldn't believe he was being ordered around like a lowly footman. He stepped away from the puddle of bile and glared at the heralds. 'You may accompany me to my chambers if you cannot return to her side without me. But I will *not* attend Her Majesty with the dust from the road on my uniform.'

The heralds glanced at one another.

'Inquisitor Helios? Come with me. Bring Renys.'

He immediately strode towards the steps. He might not be an Inquisitor for much longer, and he was determined to draw out his last moments of control for as long as he could.

DESPITE HIS WORDS to the heralds, Torsten did not wish to push his luck with Queen Surayo. He'd already been summoned, and delaying her would not put him in a favourable light. But he could not stand before her bedraggled and covered not just in grime, but his own bile, like a filthy street urchin.

It would be deplorable.

She would know his dedication to standards had not slipped, regardless of what nonsense Varlot had spouted about him. That had to count for something.

Renys had been confined to an empty study in the lower part of his tower, partly because it was closer to Queen Surayo's chambers—and she might want to see the child—and partly because he didn't trust any of the guards in the dungeons would treat her well. Halios would have to do for now.

He'd washed as quickly as he could—though he had no time for a full bath—and changed into his formal robes of office. They were less cumbersome than the Inquisitor uniform he wore on the road, but were still appropriate when meeting his sovereign.

He held *Tinebás* for a long while, staring at the blade and the spot of rust on it that would not be removed. Miroth had touched the sword many years before, and bestowed some of his power within it so that Torsten could more easily call upon his brother.

Now, it was a dull blade that offered him nothing.

But he could not bear to part with it.

Affixing it to his hip, and deciding it was all he could do to prepare, Torsten finally allowed the heralds to lead him to the queen.

Instead of escorting him to Surayo's audience chambers, they instead took him into the depths of the palace—past Toriaken's shrine—and into the vaults. Treasures ancient and new were kept here, and Torsten desperately wished he had Miroth's protection in this place. Many artefacts were sealed in the vaults, some from the various mages across Tassar, but there were many of Myrish origin.

And that worried him.

His skin crawled at the oily feel of their magic in the air, and he pulled his collar high about his neck. It was oppressive, like a heavy blanket draped over the hall.

The heralds came to a stop beside the main door to the vault, torches burning brightly on either side. Both bowed to him, any irritation at being delayed no longer on their faces, but they didn't enter.

Torsten took a final breath, knocked once, and entered the vault.

He forced himself to straighten his back, and marched across the stone floor, hoping his legs wouldn't give way under him. Recessed alcoves on either side of the vast room bore all manner of trinkets and treasures, their shadows lengthening and moving in the flickering torchlight. Even down here, trailing plants lined the shelves and walls. They brought greenery and splashes of colour to the vault, though they didn't mask the growing sense of danger that built.

Torsten kept his gaze firmly ahead, where Queen Surayo stood before a large bookcase, two of her Iron Guards flanking her. Several large iron scales sat upon her shoulders like pauldrons, and she wore a floor-length cream dress edged in grey thread. Though her dark hair was loose and cascaded down her back, she did not wear her crown, nor did she carry her ancestral sword—the iron on her body and the solid statues with her were defence enough.

He wondered whether she feared anything in the vaults.

Neither the queen, nor the iron statues looked at him—the statues were faceless, and Surayo's attention was fixed on the books—which gave him confidence.

Torsten was about to breathe a sigh of relief when he spotted Varlot's bearskin cloak move from behind the bookcase. He gritted his teeth.

'The traitor returns,' Varlot said, his booming voice sounding twice as loud as normal in the vaulted room.

Queen Surayo silenced him with a glance, then faced Torsten as he approached. She wore a simple grey choker around her throat, unadorned save a little iron detailing. 'Master Inquisitor.'

Torsten couldn't read the emotion in her words or face. She was too good at holding her intentions beside a passive facade. He dropped to one knee. 'My queen.'

'Inquisitor Varlot has told me *he* found the artefact I sought, but you took it from him and used it on a dragon spirit to whom you were bonded. That your loyalties are misplaced, and you have carried out none of my orders.'

'I have Renys Tamlin.' Torsten rose, though Surayo had not given him leave. 'She is the daughter of Apollo Tamlin. *That* traitor will be here soon, looking for her. Isn't that treasure worth more than something the Myr created?'

Surayo's eyes flashed. 'You presume much of my desires.'

Torsten held her gaze. If he wilted before her, she would see his weakness. Pride was all he had left.

Queen Surayo said, 'You say you have Renys Tamlin imprisoned?'

'She's in my tower, under guard.'

'You lost Apollo when he was under your guard. He escaped when I wanted justice brought to him. I am not trusting you with another prisoner. Even a child.'

Torsten leaned backwards, confusion and fear rising. 'My queen...?'

'You are slipping, Torsten. Perhaps you were right to bring me a new Inquisitor. Maybe he'll replace you.' But she didn't reprimand his behaviour beyond voicing her displeasure.

'Renys will be the way we—'

'You're just trying to cover your fuck up!' Varlot stepped forward. '*I* know where there's a Myrish construct—in that cave in the Nethal Mountains. That's where Fenn was going. *That's* the problem! Queen Surayo, I'll take you there. You use your magic, see what this Myrish creation is. Find Fenn's trail. Who cares what Apollo's done? That ship has sailed.'

'Varlot. You're the reason everything has gone to shit in the first place!' Torsten knew it was beneath him to respond in such a way to Varlot, especially using such poor language, but he would not allow the man to remain unchallenged.

'This misdeed...' Queen Surayo trailed off, bringing their attention to her. She raised one hand, as though grasping for something just out of reach. It was unlike her to leave a sentence unfinished.

Torsten frowned, unsure whether or not to say something.

She pursed her lips and came back to herself a moment later. 'Torsten, this misdeed cannot be forgiven.'

Varlot shifted his weight, the smug grin on his face enough to drive Torsten to grip his sword.

'My queen. I...I did this to save you! I saw what the Myrish artefact would do, and acted on behalf of the Iron Crown.' It was a lie, but he dared not imagine what Surayo would do to punish him.

Her jaw tightened, gaze looking past Torsten as if she saw something very far away. Her brow twitched. Torsten wondered why she was so distracted, but dare not speak lest he worsened his situation. 'The bond you had was severed,' Surayo said, her voice distant.

Torsten flinched. There was no point in lying about Miroth. The mage queen had threads of farsight laid across her empire, from the ice plains to the north of the Nethal Mountains to the Olmese border in the far south-east. She could probably see every spirit if she looked hard enough. 'Yes.'

'He was feeding that lake dragon Myrish artefacts!' Varlot said.

'Hush, Inquisitor. Your decorum needs work.' One of Surayo's Iron Guard took a step closer to Varlot when she spoke, and its presence was enough for the man to hold his tongue. 'It was Miroth, correct?'

'It was.'

Queen Surayo nodded, though the gesture seemed more to herself. 'I had suspected. But Miroth had always been so weak and you so strong. I saw no issue permitting your bond. There is power in the Myr. They are spirits, after all. There is no reason dragons cannot take their magic for themselves. But *this* artefact? This was special.'

Torsten recalled the vision he'd seen when he'd touched the Topaz Hairpin. Queen Surayo without Toriaken. He'd not given it much thought at the time, but now he could see it was a vision of what that artefact was supposed to do. Sever the queen's bond with the iron dragon.

He wondered if Queen Surayo knew what it would have done when she asked them to find it.

'You have, in a way, saved me. The Porsenthian Empire, too. Were Toriaken not by my side, I could not defend the continent from the Myr. And you have been a loyal servant for many years, achieved many great things for me, Torsten.' She sounded disappointed. Bored, even.

It wasn't the blind fury he'd expected. Torsten took a shaky breath, unsure if she would punish him.

Varlot glowered at him. 'No matter how much shit you fall through, you always seem to come up smelling of roses, don't you?'

Torsten glared at Varlot, but held his tongue. He had no interest in debasing himself, especially not in front of Queen Surayo.

She froze, her eyes flashing brilliant lilac. 'The Citrine Key. It *is* here.'

Torsten held back a gasp of shock. The Citrine Key was the Myrish artefact Apollo Tamlin had been sent to destroy five years ago. 'Queen Surayo? You saw the key?'

She blinked, eyes returning to their usual brown. 'It's in Porsenthia. North of here, in the mountains.' The Iron Guard beside her shuddered and Torsten took an involuntary step backwards. 'I will not risk anyone else mistaking my orders. Toriaken and I will march out and kill the one who holds the key.'

'What if it's the Myr? Could be another attack.' Varlot asked, drawing his axe. 'Let me lead the march to battle, Queen Surayo! I'll squash this threat before it has a chance to do anything. You know my glory in war.'

'No. There are no Myr with the key. Only one man holds it.' She took a step towards the door. 'The key is…changed. It is more powerful than before. I can see it move across my lands.'

'More powerful? Are you sure you should do this yourself, your Majesty?' Torsten asked.

Queen Surayo reached out to the nearest Iron Guard and rested her palm flat against its chest. 'If Toriaken can kill the man, the key can never be used. It will be sealed here, in this vault.'

'Let me kill him for you. One man is no match for my axe.' Varlot pushed.

Queen Surayo fixed Varlot with a stare so intense even Torsten shied away from it. 'I will deal with this artefact myself. I should have known better than to trust anyone with magic of this magnitude. Inquisitor Varlot, you will hereby take over Torsten's duties. This includes the prisoner Renys Tamlin and Apollo, *if* he arrives.'

'Yes, my queen.' Varlot bowed awkwardly.

'Torsten,' Surayo turned to him.

He tried to hide his grimace at her continually dropping his title.

'You shall accompany me. After failing to bring me one artefact, perhaps you can assist me in the reclaiming of another.'

Torsten grimaced at the thought of Varlot in charge of Renys. The man was selfish and impulsive at best, and he didn't trust him in the slightest. But he knew better than to argue, especially when he'd so narrowly escaped punishment, and bowed.

The tension eased in his shoulders, relief at being taken along with Surayo. He'd been sure she'd throw him in the dungeons. If Varlot was in charge of *that*, he'd be in real trouble.

But he had a chance to redeem himself and he wasn't going to squander it.

'Once the threat has been eliminated, I shall consider how I must deal with you.' Queen Surayo strode away, towards the vault's exit.

41
THE GARDEN
CALIDRA

Calidra leaned back in her chair and winced. Sharp pain shot through her leg every time she put too much weight on it, but she hated simply sitting and doing nothing while her injury healed.

Thankfully, the formalities of her mother's household were in disarray following the attack on Fellwood, which meant any expectations of her behaviour were somewhat lessened.

Jisyel sat beside her at the large oak table that filled one side of the kitchen, an array of bowls and dishes laid out. Most of the household staff ate together here each morning, and though they were hesitant at first, soon welcomed Jisyel to sit with them. They'd explained what each dish was, and though it was now the afternoon and they were busy with their duties, Jisyel remained seated.

'This bread is the best thing on the table!' Jisyel held up a round flatbread, garlic oil dripping down her fingers. She took slow bites, closing her eyes and savouring every taste.

'Don't have too much of that or you'll be sick.' Calidra adored seeing Jisyel so happy, and didn't want that to sour. 'It's been a while since you knew how much to eat.'

'I know but…but it's just *so* good.' Jisyel picked up a spoon and reached for the pot of *shonthal*. 'And this stuff? I see why you and Mal cover everything in it!' She studied the chunky condiment, and was about to spoon a generous helping onto her bread when the silver spoon changed to gold in a flash of light. Jisyel yelped, dropping it.

Instead of clattering lightly on the wood, the solid gold spoon landed with a thud.

'That'll be something else to get used to.' Calidra sighed. She wasn't sure how she felt about Jisyel's blessing. She was glad the curse was gone, of course. But she wasn't sure the price Jisyel would pay would be worth it.

Jisyel picked up a fork and inspected it closely.

Calidra watched as the tip of Jisyel's tongue poked out, then the fork, too, shifted into gold.

Calidra said, 'I don't suppose you can turn it back, can you?'

'Maybe?' Jisyel stared at the fork.

'Does Chyram talk to you? Tell you how to do things?'

'Sort of. He's here,' Jisyel tapped her chest with her free hand, 'but he hasn't said much. Just something about spreading his glory wherever I can. And I feel a kind of… pull…in my hands when I touch things. If I think about the fire inside, it changes to gold. I don't know if it goes the other way. I'll have to talk to Malora to see if she knows.'

'Good thing my mother has plenty of silverware for you to practise on.'

Jisyel gently placed the fork on the table. 'I'm sorry, Cal. I had to do something.'

Calidra shifted in her chair, trying to find a comfortable position. Clearly, Jisyel wasn't talking about turning cutlery into gold. 'Don't apologise. You don't need permission to do what you think is right. I just hope you don't regret it.'

'I thought…because Chyram had been with Malora for a while, he wouldn't be that bad.'

'Malora probably painted a better picture of Chyram than he was. Not surprising considering how badly she wanted the blessing back.' Calidra leaned forward on the table and stared at the golden fork and spoon. 'And how similarly they behave,' she added under her breath.

'Where is Malora?'

'Last saw her in the gardens. Just staring at the sky, waiting for the griffin scout to come back, I think.' Calidra stared at the sky, too, though she was more concerned about Miroth coming back. They'd all seen what the dragon could do, and there had been no way to stop him. Even the war griffins hadn't been able to drive him away.

If he came back, he could burn the rest of the town.

'You look worried,' Jisyel said, her earlier giddiness disappearing.

Calidra sighed. 'I am worried.'

'Things will be okay, Cal.'

'Will they? Will Mal be okay? Ren? I'm worried about the Myr. I'm worried about what we'll do if Miroth comes back. Everything!'

'I understand, but...but we *aren't* defenceless anymore. I have Chyram's power! Maybe I can do something if Miroth returns,' Jisyel said, brightening a little.

Calidra rubbed her face. Jisyel had just reminded her of *another* worry. 'What did Chyram ask of you?'

Jisyel picked up a spoonful of *shonthal* and stared at it, her earlier joy flooding away. 'It doesn't matter.'

Calidra frowned. 'Of course it matters. Are you expected to go and live by his shrine? Forsake everything and everyone else? Look at how he reacted to Malora when she spoke about Renys!'

'No, no. Nothing like that. Don't worry Cal.'

Calidra worried. She *always* worried. And with the Myrish words from the night before swirling in her mind, she worried even more than usual. But Jisyel had clearly been free to walk away, to be where she wanted and use her new blessings as she chose. Her gut churned with nervous anticipation, but there was nothing she could do at this point. What was done was done. She hated things that were out of her control. It had always made her feel small and vulnerable, like a child at the mercy of everyone around her.

'You've been my legs for a long time, Cal. Let me be yours.' Jisyel grabbed Calidra's hand and squeezed—with the appropriate amount of pressure for the first time in years. 'What are you afraid of?'

Calidra chewed her lip. She'd never liked sharing her fears with Jisyel and burdening her. But given the state of the world and Jisyel's recent blessing, it was probably more pertinent now. 'After we escaped the Spindle Woods and the Myr attacked, I've been…they've been trying to talk to me.'

Jisyel immediately sat up straight, all playfulness gone.

'When I sleep, it's like I'm trapped in this…this…darkness. A space I can't get out of. And their voices are there, in my head, so it doesn't matter where I run, they don't leave.'

'What did they say? Did they hurt you?'

'I don't think they can hurt me there. They keep saying how dragon spirits are manipulative, that we shouldn't be beholden to them. Have to admit, they aren't wrong.'

'Cal…'

Calidra laughed to cover her nerves. 'They wanted me to help them fight the dragons. Said they had artefacts—weapons—that could weaken them. Toriaken, specifically. But they said this weapon had already been misused.'

Jisyel drew her hands together, picking at her nails.

'But I don't know why they didn't just kill me. Why try and get into my mind?'

'Perhaps they wrongly thought you were weak.'

'I don't know. They just said the dragons were hurting us, and wouldn't it be better if that stopped.'

Jisyel fiddled with the golden spoon, though her gaze was

on the new ring on her middle finger. 'Hassen hurt me, didn't he? Maybe they thought you'd be more likely to listen to them due to that.'

'Maybe. Why not attack you, instead? You're the one more likely to have a grudge?'

'What if Hassen's touch stopped them? The one time that curse was of any use,' Jisyel spoke bitterly.

Calidra pursed her lips, thinking back to what they'd said. She didn't like their persistence, didn't like how she was now afraid to sleep for fear they'd assault her again.

Jisyel cracked her knuckles one after the other as she thought. 'Weapon being misused...I wonder if that had anything to do with Miroth attacking Fellwood. Seems convenient they'd mention that *after* the dragon went on a rampage, doesn't it?'

'I don't like any of this. The Myr have always been a distant threat, and suddenly we're in the middle of their schemes.'

They lapsed into silence. Thoughts swirled in Calidra's mind, blocking out the pain in her thigh.

The door opened and Furyn walked through, preceded by purple-feathered Siranna and her other griffin, Artoa, with teal feathers. 'Ah, there you are.'

Calidra straightened, gritting her teeth against the pain in her thigh when she moved. 'You were looking for me?'

'And Jisyel of course.' Furyn strode in, ever graceful, and seated herself across from them. Her bandaged arm had been wrapped in a linen sling. 'Quillaja told me about your encounter with Lord Chyram. A new blessing?' Her gaze flicked down to the golden fork and spoon on the table.

Calidra braced, expecting retribution for damaging some of her fine silver.

Furyn smiled. 'Well, that makes it clear, doesn't it?'

Jisyel glanced from Furyn to Calidra, her brow furrowed. 'Yes. Chyram was...very kind.'

'You know, of course, that Lord Chyram is the patron spirit not just of the Vantonen family, but our entire canton.' Furyn helped herself to a small orange and began delicately peeling it. 'If not for Lord Chyram, we'd be at the mercy of whichever Bragalian Laird lived here before. Most are hardly better than pirates, you understand. So you can imagine what sort of life that would have been.'

Calidra caught Jisyel's eye, but she had no whispered words to explain her mother's sudden calmness. It had to be some sort of trick, and she tensed.

Furyn pulled out segments of orange and laid them on an empty plate, then reached over and added a spoonful of *shonthal* on the side with the newly golden spoon. Her smile remained when she tested the weight. 'It is wonderful to have one of Lord Chyram's Blessed with us again. It is only right, of course. He has always favoured our family. I knew it would only be a matter of time.'

Calidra's stomach sank as she realised where her mother was going with this.

Furyn dipped an orange segment into the *shonthal* and ate it in a single bite. 'I had thought since you were back, Calidra, that you both would be staying here a while. The world is unstable at the moment, and that's putting it lightly. Even Fellwood is not unscathed, and who knows when this will end?'

'I'd be happy to contribute to the repair of Fellwood. Chyram—Lord Chyram suggested that, actually,' Jisyel said, correcting herself mid-sentence.

Furyn nodded, as if she had known that all along. She ate another segment before speaking again. 'Lord Chyram's shrine is within our canton. The priests and priestesses there work for me, in a way. To help Fellwood and the other small villages within our canton. I'm sure they'll get you up to speed soon enough.'

'Jisyel doesn't work for you, Mother,' Calidra said, with as much warning in her tone as she thought she could get away with.

'Of course not,' Furyn replied, a gentle smile on her face. She ate another segment.

The door creaked open and Calidra looked up to see Quillaja enter, her arms around Malora's shoulder as she gently guided her in. 'Please have something to eat, Lady Tamlin. You need to keep your strength up.'

Malora meekly sat beside Furyn, though she made no move to take any food.

Calidra's heart bled at seeing her sister so broken. Malora had always been the better of them. The one who knew what to do, who helped everyone around her before ever thinking of herself. Who was decisive. She'd had everything ripped away, and for all her ability to help others, she had no idea how to offer herself that same compassion.

Guilt also surfaced—Jisyel had taken Malora's blessing from Chyram. The Spirit of Gold only ever bonded with one person at a time, and he hadn't chosen anyone else after Malora.

Until now.

Furyn slid her plate towards Malora, with half the orange remaining. 'Here.'

'I'm not hungry.' Malora stared into the middle distance.

'You need to eat.'

Malora pushed the plate away. 'I can't face eating right now.'

'Just a bit of fruit and some *shonthal*. It isn't much, Malora, and you—'

'Stop pushing, Mother! I'm not going to eat!'

Furyn scowled. 'Well, I never thought you would be so ungrateful. It's Apollo's influence on you, isn't it? Torsten and his Inquisitors were here looking for you, all because of him! Nothing but trouble. You leave with that Porsenthian, don't bother coming to your father's funeral, lose my granddaughter, have no chance of reclaiming your blessing, and when I extend my generosity, you push it back in my face?'

Malora turned to Furyn, eyes wide.

Calidra's stomach turned over at seeing Furyn's anger thrown at her sister, and the fear in Malora's eyes. Malora was the one who never put a foot wrong. Calidra sat, frozen, her childhood terror returning even though it wasn't directed at her.

'I'd like some fresh air. Would you show me the gardens, Mal?' Jisyel was on her feet a moment later, scooting around the table and offering her hand to Malora. She smiled at Furyn. 'I'm sure I can discuss helping restore Fellwood with you later, Lady Vantonen. Everything has been so tense, my nerves are a bit frayed!'

Her words seemed to appease Furyn, because the scowl disappeared and she leaned one elbow on the table. Siranna approached with a keening whistle, and Furyn stroked the griffin, even as she snapped her beak at one of the orange segments. 'Of course. I understand. Take all the time you need.'

Calidra pushed through the pain in her leg and limped after Jisyel and Malora, not quite able to believe how Jisyel had diffused the tension so quickly.

Calidra struggled to keep up with Jisyel and Malora, who tore down the halls and out into the bright sunshine. She followed them under an archway that led into the flower gardens.

By the time the scent of roses, lavender, and lillies reached her, Malora and Jisyel were crouched by one of the flower beds where verbena spilled onto the grass. They were surrounded by petals of yellows, oranges, and reds that had been planted in terraced layers to make the most of the afternoon and evening sunshine.

At any other time, Calidra would have admired the dedication her mother had put into the gardens. But all she could focus on was how they made Malora's devastation seem worse.

Calidra sat down on the grass when she reached them, one leg tucked, her bad leg stretched out ahead of her. She draped one arm around Malora's shoulder and pulled her in close. She didn't say anything—there was nothing she *could* say—but offered comfort while Malora sobbed, trembling in her arms.

Calidra squeezed more tightly.

Minutes dragged by. Clouds occasionally drifted across the sun, offering glimpses of shade. Calidra waited, patient, as her sister cried. She'd been through so much recently. They all had. Calidra wanted to cry herself—her eyes burning if she thought too much about what had happened—but she kept her tears at bay.

She needed to be strong for her sister.

Calidra stared into the flowers, where a pale yellow butterfly drifted from petal to petal. More joined it, and others left, flitting away. Bees and damselflies darted in and out, a chaotic dance of ever shifting movement.

She wasn't sure how long passed before Malora recovered herself, slowly quietening. Shadows were beginning to lengthen, but the air remained warm and sticky.

Malora lifted her head, but didn't pull away from the embrace.

Jisyel glanced up at the movement. 'Malora, I'm so sorry.'

'No. I'm the one who should be sorry. I...How I behaved was terrible. Stupid. So stupid.' Malora held onto Calidra's tunic.

Calidra was glad Malora had finally seen what their

mother could be like, even if she'd never wish that anger on anyone else.

'I understand what you were trying to do. We're all scared of the Myr. Chyram would be a good way to protect yourself from them,' Jisyel replied.

Malora sniffed. 'I should have brought Ren here the moment the Myr left Foxmouth. I tried to help people. Thought I could do this myself. But, Apollo was gone. He'd have told me it was a silly idea. Talked some sense into me.'

'Don't be angry with yourself. You did what you thought was best,' Calidra said.

'And look where that got us.' The bite in Malora's voice reminded Calidra of Furyn. 'I had Renys with me all this time. Now that bastard Inquisitor has her. I was so, *so* desperate to keep Renys safe that I lost…I lost what I was already holding onto. I've failed as a mother.' She began to cry again.

Calidra pulled her back in, rocking her gently where they sat. 'You haven't failed. You kept Renys safe through a Myrish attack. Trekking across half the continent!'

'But if I'd been with you! With her? Instead of obsessed with getting Chyram's favour? No wonder he wouldn't accept me. I was too much like him.' She shook her head. 'After all these years, that influence is still in me. I wish I was stronger.'

'Torsten speaks with the queen's voice. He'd have taken her even if you were there. Would have arrested you, too.' Calidra immediately regretted speaking so bluntly.

'Maybe,' Malora muttered. 'But I'd have been *with* her. Spirits take me, Ren must have been so scared. She's braver than any child ought to be, but…but, Torsten…'

'If…if Torsten took Renys because of Apollo, it means Apollo probably *hasn't* been executed. There'd have been no reason for him to take her otherwise,' Jisyel said. She sat with her back against the nearest flower bed and pulled the trailing leaves onto her lap. She brushed the delicate petals and leaves gently with her fingers. 'You have that answer now, at least.'

Malora sat up and wiped her face. 'Oh, I…I hadn't thought of that.'

'If Apollo isn't dead, he's been released?' Calidra wondered aloud.

'Released? I doubt it. If Torsten took Ren, maybe…maybe Apollo escaped.' Malora smiled, bright despite the tears.

Calidra couldn't remember the last time she'd seen that. 'Then there's hope for both Apollo and Renys. It'll be okay, Mal. It *will* be.'

A screech pierced the air. Calidra looked up in time to see a griffin sweep into view, broad feathered wings spread wide. Its feathers were pitch-dark, orange eyes glinting down at them in the evening light. Recognition dawned. 'Isn't that Hailathlyl?'

Jisyel helped Calidra to her feet, and the three of them stood back as the griffin descended in wide circles. When it was only a handful of paces from landing, Calidra spotted the griffin's rider. 'Amsel!'

'Calidra! Malora!' Amsel called to them as Hailathlyl reached the ground, sending out gusts as she navigated her mismatched paws. The Olmese warrior immediately got up from his saddle and leapt to the ground. 'Yakris be praised! We scoured Foxmouth for days, searching for you, Malora! We feared the worst after the Myr—'

'Were you the scout following Torsten?' Malora interrupted, desperation driving her.

Amsel bowed low. 'Yes. Captain Aetei sent me to follow the Master Inquisitor. We are in service to Lady Vantonen for now. But the skies are not safe with the dark dragon flying around.'

'The dragon burns the land where he flies. Attacks

anything that approaches!' Hailathlyl screeched her displeasure.

Amsel patted her on the neck. 'I know. Lucky you're faster.'

'Amsel, did you find Torsten? Do you know where Renys is?' Malora's voice hitched.

'I scented Furyn's bloodline with Torsten. We did not see inside the carriage he travelled in,' Hailathlyl answered.

'But we followed him north, into Porsenthia. He crossed the deadlands and stopped at Marlrush Fortress,' Amsel added. 'It took us a while to catch up. The dragon headed straight for us every time we took to the air.'

'Torsten is definitely at the fortress? He didn't pass by?'

Amsel nodded. 'The dragon seemed to be flying further north. We dared not fly too close—it changes direction on a whim. But the Master Inquisitor remained there. We needed to return swiftly. Captain Aetei made it clear how urgent this was. I should find him and report, actually.'

'It isn't too far,' Calidra said, trying to catch Jisyel's eye.

Malora wiped her face, smearing soot and grime across her forehead and cheeks. 'Amsel, Hailathlyl. Please. Take me to my daughter.'

42
THE CAVERN
SELYS

Selys spent the remainder of their trip staring at the Salt Sea, and her estimate that it would take them two or three days to arrive was accurate. In the afternoon of the third day, they spotted the port. The air was far colder than in southern Bragalia, and chunks of ice floated in the dark waters of the bay.

Selys shivered. She'd felt Fenn leave Neros's domain early the day before. He certainly hadn't died at sea, so it could only mean he'd reached land. Now it really was a race to the cave.

Thankfully they were on the correct side of the country, but she didn't know whether the key would speed his travels or not. He still had to make his way across the Nethal Mountains, and she dreaded arriving too late.

But she didn't want to beat him to the cave and end up confronting him, either.

She would do what needed to be done, but it didn't mean she had to like it.

Selys felt for Neros's flame and took comfort from her spirit's presence. Their bond was difficult to understand, but every day brought them a little closer.

Kaio brought *Wolf's Grin* into the bay, and the tension aboard the ship thickened. They'd sailed with as few crew as they could, leaving the bulk of their strength in Segandis. There were a dozen of them in total, most of whom wanted to see Fenn dead.

'No harbour master?' Taran asked as *Wolf's Grin* dropped anchor. He scoured the horizon with an unlit cigarillo between his teeth.

'This is more of an outpost than a trading town. Supplies come in but not much goes out. It's for Inquisitors and a score of hardy families,' Selys explained, remembering the ambush she'd walked into the last time she'd been here. Varlot had been the cause of it. Selfish, impulsive man.

She wondered where Varlot was now, and whether he regretted his betrayal.

'Selys, do we have time?' Kaio walked over to her, Fergus at his heels. 'Pushed the ship as much as I dared, but it's a risk with so much ice on the water.'

'He's in Porsenthia, that's all I know.'

'No time to rest then. We travel light.' Kaio marched along the deck, barking orders while those along for the journey's last stretch disembarked.

Nethal, the nearest town, was snow-covered and nestled against the foot of the mountains a short distance away. A mining town first and foremost, it had been wealthy many centuries before—but after sending so much iron-rich ore along the river, the capital of Eastbrook had swelled and overtaken it as the richest city in Porsenthia. Only the most desperate people lived in Nethal these days.

The wind picked up, scattering snow and ice across *Wolf's Grin*. Selys slipped on a pair of fur-lined gloves and crossed the gangplank onto the grey ground. It had rained recently, turning much of the snow into icy sludge.

'Almost like home.' Evarine held out one hand to the falling snowflakes. 'I've missed this.'

Selys desperately wanted Evarine to be right. Desperately wanted Fenn to be her husband and see their bond rekindled. It would stop whatever the Myr were trying to achieve *without* loss of life.

There was always the risk Fenn would attack her, though. Like he'd attacked Neros.

She tried not to dwell on that, and led Kaio and the rest of the crew through the sludge and into the outpost. It was hardly large enough to sustain a score of people—a handful of disorganised wooden buildings were half-buried in the snow, with several well-trodden paths weaving between thicker snowdrifts. Everything within the outpost was grey and weather-beaten, though the snow outside and towards the mountains remained white.

Retracing her steps to the cave would be easy enough, but the weight of her task grew heavier with each step. Not to mention she'd attacked two Inquisitors here. It had been a couple of weeks ago at most—she'd lost track of the days, so much had happened—but it was likely such a small place would remember her. She had no concerns if it came to another fight, but she didn't want to make things worse or draw undue attention to her brother.

Only…no one seemed to be at the outpost.

The paths had clearly been used recently, but no one was outside, and no smoke rose from any of the chimneys. Whether everyone was off duty, warming their feet somewhere more hospitable, or they were hiding inside because of the pirate ship that had just docked, Selys didn't know.

But it made their way clear and easy.

They left three aboard *Wolf's Grin*—along with Fergus, who had to be forcibly shut in a cabin to keep him from padding after Kaio—while Selys and the remaining eight crossed through the outpost. Evarine walked to her left, with Taran on her right. The rest of the crew followed, with Kaio bringing up the rear.

'I knew it was gonna be cold up here, but this is ridiculous!' Taran huffed, his breath misting the air. 'This'll freeze my bowstring!'

'Don't be silly. It'll be fine,' Selys said, though she didn't know how reassuring she sounded.

'Easy for you to say. I haven't seen snow since I was a kid. Unnatural stuff.' He scowled at it and kicked a lump of snow out of his way.

Selys laughed, grateful for the distraction.

The Myrish construct lay ahead, and her task was going to end soon—one way or another.

THEY WAITED, huddled together amongst the snow-covered rocks that littered the mountain path. Selys held onto her glaive, ready in case of any eventuality, her gaze locked on the cave.

It had been a long, cold climb, but Kaio and the others had slipped into hunting mode with heads bowed and weapons at the ready. Selys had almost forgotten what it was like to move as a single unit, each person in their place, all minds focussed on the same goal.

Even on land, and with as few of them as there were, the Ioran warband was a force to be reckoned with. Her chest swelled with pride at that realisation. Perhaps they would be capable of fending off Fenn and the key.

It had stopped snowing earlier in the day, leaving the sky crisp and blue. Visibility was excellent, and they wanted to take advantage of it for as long as it lasted. Mists were known to roll in on the higher mountain slopes, and they didn't want to be caught out if the weather turned against them.

Soft footsteps caught her attention and she turned towards the sound, keeping her own movements as small as possible. Beside her, Kaio and Esto shifted, adjusting their grips on their blades. Selys held her breath, unsure if she'd hesitate or attack blindly if Fenn appeared. Neros's flame burned fiercely in her chest, and she hoped she could rely on her dragon if nothing else.

Taran appeared at the mouth of the cave a moment later, his bow slung over one shoulder. 'It's empty. Only one way in or out from the looks of it.'

She let out a sigh of relief and followed Kaio inside, Evarine and the others on her heels. No one said a word.

Being in the tunnel again brought memories flooding back, but through her bond with Neros, Selys felt the Myr's touch in a way she'd never experienced before. It was slick and oily on her skin, a coating that tried to seep through and taint her.

She suppressed a shudder while Kaio, Evarine, and the others walked ahead.

Pressure filled the air, thick and heavy, and it drove the breath from her. Ice covered every inch of the tunnel wall, including the ceiling. Stalactites of ice hung low, threatening to pierce any who walked underneath them.

Neros writhed within her chest, flames hot and burning as the spirit announced her displeasure and fear. Selys gritted her teeth. She couldn't risk losing focus, not now. 'Neros, you will keep me protected, as you always have. Please extend that protection to my brother, too.'

'What're you whispering?' Ruka asked, the small healer staring at her.

'A small prayer to the spirits.'

'There are no spirits here. Only the Myr. I can feel them.' Ruka pulled her cloak more tightly around herself. 'This place is unholy. We shouldn't be here.'

'Don't force yourself, Ruka. You can wait outside if it's easier for you?' Selys suggested.

'I'm not leaving Chief Kaio. If anyone gets hurt, I need to be close.'

Selys didn't argue. She was glad her brother had such loyal followers, though it made Yaniv's criticism of him sting all the greater.

Their footsteps echoed as the nine of them wandered deeper into the tunnel, marred by the occasional boot slipping on ice, and muttered curse.

'There's writing.' Taran pointed at the thick ice on the walls. 'Under here.'

'Old languages. I don't know what they say,' Selys said, her voice reverberating in the tunnel.

Ruka paused as the tunnel curved around. 'This looks like an Olmese script.' She removed her gloves and followed the words with one finger. 'It…it refers to a gate. Dusk gate? No, maybe shadow? It's an old word, could mean different things.' She followed another line. 'It says something about a key needed to open it. "*Vermecio*" appears several times, too. That's the name of the construct here, isn't it?'

Selys stood beside the healer, nausea growing as Ruka translated. 'That's right. It asked Fenn for the key.'

Ruka crouched down, twisting awkwardly to read more of the script before it disappeared behind a stalagmite against the tunnel wall. 'Dragons are mentioned, too. It's the scholar's word for them, at any rate. The rest is too old for me to understand.'

Selys swallowed. 'Whatever it says, it isn't good. Not if it's something the Myr are trying to do.' She turned to find Kaio staring at her. The Jade Shell around his neck glowed, and Selys was sure it was brighter than it had been on the ship.

Kaio crouched and peered at the script. 'None of this is good, mark my words. Let's get set up, we don't know how much time we have before Fenn gets here.'

Shuddering, Selys backed away from the script, pressing

herself against the wall of the tunnel where it widened to allow plenty of room for everyone.

'Chamber is just ahead. Taran, take the two bowmen with you to higher ground. You three will have a better line of sight from there.' Kaio gestured to a ledge a short distance above them, nestled against stalactites, just before it opened into the chamber. 'Esto, you take everyone else. You'll be our second group. Keep out of sight—one of these tunnel alcoves should be good. Dark enough you can be missed as long as you keep quiet. Evarine? You're with me. We'll keep Fenn's attention on us in the main chamber. Taran? You know what needs to be done if Fenn tries anything.'

'I'm not comfortable being so far from you. And especially Evarine,' Selys protested.

'Fenn knows you and he might attack you on sight. I won't have that, so stay put. If Fenn tries to run from me, you can flank him,' Kaio replied.

She held his gaze a long moment, but there was no backing down in her brother. She conceded with a nod. 'Fine. But I'll unleash all of Neros's fury if I think you're about to be hurt.'

Kaio grinned. 'Fine by me. Let's get into position.'

Selys straightened, about to obey his instructions when a thought struck her. 'Kaio. Wait.'

'What is it?' He looked back at her.

'We…we may not have to kill Fenn.'

Kaio tutted. 'Not this again. We've been through what needs to be done, Selys.'

'I know, I know. But Fenn is on his way here to give the key to *Vermecio*, right? What if we destroyed *Vermecio before* he gets here?'

Kaio didn't say anything at first, taken aback by her suggestion.

'Beats sitting here in the cold waiting for him,' Taran said. 'Or climbing up those icy walls,' he added in a low mumble.

Kaio folded his arms but didn't say anything.

Selys pointed with the tip of her glaive. '*Vermecio* is on the far side of the chamber up ahead. Pretty sure it's made of stone. Maybe it can be damaged?'

'You really don't want to kill this guy, do you?' Kaio asked.

'There's no point in unnecessary death. If there's another way, we should take it,' Selys replied, firm in her conviction. 'I've seen how powerful the key is. What if even Evarine can't appeal to him? Why not try and destroy the construct first?'

'Won't hurt to try?' Taran said.

Selys took the lead, striding past them and into the large chamber. The tattoos on her arm lit up the moment she stepped inside, bathing the chamber in pale green light. The vast ceiling was so high she could hardly see it.

'*The Myr.*' Neros's word echoed in Selys's head, clear and resolute. Hatred flooded her, and Selys flinched under the dragon's emotion. She held herself up, tensing every muscle, so she wasn't consumed by it.

Vermecio looked exactly as she remembered, which was some relief. Nothing had changed, which meant they definitely hadn't missed Fenn. It was a creature with the maned head of a lion atop a humanoid body hunkered down on a large rock. Three pairs of feathered wings tucked against its sides, and two thick, curved horns jutted out from its chin. Its body expelled a faint, dark mist every few moments, as if it breathed.

Although it seemed to be made of stone, the surface of it rippled with ever-shifting colour. Three lidless eyes stared straight ahead—one red, one white, one gold—its lower half encased in thick ice.

It was alive in some way, she was sure, even if it was limited in what it could do.

'Chief Kaio? We shouldn't be in here,' Ruka whispered.

'Won't be here long, Ruka.' Kaio stepped into the chamber

to stand beside Selys. 'It's a lump of stone, that's all. Can't hurt you.'

Selys didn't know if her brother's claim was true—she had no recollection of *Vermecio* doing anything other than speaking in riddles—but understood Ruka's hesitation. She called upon Neros, the fire in her chest expanding and filling her limbs with strength. 'Keep back. I'll use Neros.'

She heard the draw of several bowstrings behind her, even as Neros's flames erupted from her fingertips. They shot along the shaft of her glaive, spun around the blade and poured onto *Vermecio* with a furious roar.

Ice hissed as the flames melted it, cracking the stone underneath with a jolt that shook the cavern. The jagged line ran along *Vermecio's* broad chest, but the construct did not move or speak.

Selys grinned. Neros was a force to be reckoned with, even if she'd been pushed away by the key. She kept up the assault of fire until water wept from the crack and the shadowy mist dissipated.

Snuffing out her flames and twirling her glaive to give her strike as much momentum as she could, Selys plunged the blade deep into the crack, sparks leaping into the air.

The meltwater slowed to a trickle, and the mist returned.

Gritting her teeth, Selys forced her weight against *Vermecio*, pushing her weapon deeper into the cracked stone. Neros roared again, and more fire spewed from her glaive, licking the stone and making it glow red.

Her tattoos blazed, her vision swimming with fire.

'Selys! You're going to burn up!' Kaio called.

She let out a cry of frustration, wrenching her glaive out of the stone and panting heavily. Neros's flames flickered and died, and *Vermecio* remained indifferent.

The construct turned its head slowly towards them, stone grinding against stone. '*You have the shell.*'

Kaio leapt away, sword held high and ready.

Selys's skin prickled at the construct's voice. 'Neros should have melted that rock by now. Nothing can stand against dragonfire!'

'Except whatever this is.' Kaio glanced over his shoulder. Evarine and Ruka lingered in the tunnel, watching them. 'Either of you have any ideas? Evarine, you've dealt with the Myr before, haven't you? Said you'd fought them? You see anything like this where you're from?'

Selys glowered at the construct. What in all of Tassar was *Vermecio* made of? Neros's hatred burned through her veins, and she flinched at the sensation—though a small part of her relished it.

Evarine entered the chamber cautiously, careful to avoid the growing puddle of water from all the melted ice.

Vermecio turned its massive stone head to face her, following her every step. *'Well done on completing your appointed task. The shell is where it is supposed to be.'*

Everyone froze, including Evarine, whose eyes widened. Selys stared at her brother. The Jade Shell hung around his neck, glowing faintly but not reacting otherwise. Dread filled her.

'Should've known you were in league with the Myr!' Kaio rounded on Evarine, his sword raised.

She shrank away from him, pressing against the icy wall. 'Don't hurt me!'

'Why not? What in Neros's name have you done? Dragging us all the way up here?'

Evarine seemed to gather some of her strength back. 'You're the one who dragged *me* here. Don't blame me for what you did. Selys suggested it!'

Kaio held his sword towards her. 'What a lucky coincidence for you.'

'I can help you!'

Taran stepped across the floor, arrow notched and bow

drawn. 'You wanna hear anything else she has to say? Everything she's said so far has been a twisted truth.'

'Let her speak!' Selys cried. She needed to understand what was happening. Neros thrashed around in her chest, and the raging flames made it hard to concentrate.

'Fenn is coming here. He's my husband. As soon as he's here, we're going to leave!'

'Fenn won't have the first idea who you are. He has no memory. Selys said so,' Kaio retorted.

Evarine's gaze darted between Kaio's blade and Taran's bow. 'Maybe, but I can *make* him remember. I *can*! You have to let me try. All I wanted was to keep my family safe. Just like you.'

'I don't need the Myr to do that!' Kaio pressed the tip of his sword to her throat.

Evarine flinched. 'No, don't!'

'What bargain did you have with the Myr?' Selys asked, trying to keep her rising anger in check. Dizziness made her vision dance as fire threatened to overwhelm her.

'The shell. I had to deliver the shell.' She covered her face with one arm and leant away from Kaio's blade, towards the cover of a nearby stalagmite. Her fingers scrabbled on the icy floor.

'So you never wanted to get to Queen Surayo? It was all a lie?' Kaio demanded.

'They promised me the safety of my village! Promised I'd have Fenn returned to me if I delivered their shell.' Evarine didn't cry, though she clutched at the rocks beside her. 'You never needed to know. No one did! Fenn will be here soon. If that *thing* hadn't spoken,' she glared at *Vermecio*, who continued to watch, silent, 'none of you would have known.'

'Do you have any idea what'll happen to us if a Myrish weapon is used?' Taran snarled, his fury rivalling Kaio's.

Evarine stared at him, defiant. 'You have the iron queen and her dragon to look after you! She defeated them before,

I'm sure she'll do it again. But what about *us*? No one cares about our village! No one is coming to save us! The Myr's influence is everywhere! We were being attacked by a corrupted dragon spirit. I did what I had to do to keep my loved ones safe.' She turned back to Kaio now there was some distance between herself and his sword. 'Isn't that what you're doing too, *Chief*?'

Kaio lowered his sword slightly.

Evarine looked at Selys. 'You've seen Fenn cross the ocean. He'll be here soon, and then we'll be together again. So you *can't* kill him. We'll leave. I'm so close to getting my husband back, my life back! Please!' Her voice cracked.

'I have no trouble killing the pair of you!' Kaio tapped his sword against the stalagmite Evarine huddled behind.

Selys couldn't believe how deep the Myr's manipulation ran. Overtly with Fenn. Covertly with Evarine. Taran had joked about there being a first wave, and now she thought he was on to something. Everyone had been tricked or taken advantage of—Fenn, Evarine, herself. No one was safe. The thought of it drained her anger. Left her hollow.

She couldn't trust anyone. Not when the corruption ran so deeply.

Vermecio couldn't be destroyed. And all they could do was wait for Fenn to arrive, though she held onto the faint hope that he wouldn't appear.

If he did, they had to put a stop to him and end the madness. Kaio was right. Regardless of the key, Fenn was human.

The fire in her chest flickered, and she took a deep breath, pulling strength from the Spirit of the Lasseen Ocean—Neros would guide her through this. However it ended.

43
THE CORRUPTED
TORSTEN

Every marched step reminded Torsten of his brief stint as a foot soldier. It seemed a lifetime ago, and without Miroth's strength, a worrying likely future. Thankfully, Queen Surayo respected him enough to allow him to ride a horse, for which he was extremely grateful. In his current compromised state, he wasn't sure he could march for an afternoon, let alone days on end.

Their company was led by Queen Surayo herself, astride a muscular horse large enough to rival any bear. It would have been comical, if not for the strength the animal needed to carry Surayo in her full armour. Iron scales covered her body, throat to wrists and down to her knees. Her dark brunette hair streamed behind her, iron links keeping it relatively tame in the breeze.

Already the beast frothed at the mouth, but it ploughed on obediently. It had served her the last time she rode to war, and Torsten despised the animal, prone to biting as it was.

Two of her Iron Guard marched either side of her, flanked by twenty mounted riders—of which Torsten rode on her left side. Behind them were two score footsoldiers, armed and armoured, though several carried banners. Overhead flew a small contingent of Olmese warriors atop their war griffins. There were only four of the beasts, but their ferocity and intimidating presence matched any battalion on the ground. Every so often, two would scout ahead, flying off into the distance before wheeling around and reporting anything of interest.

One had flown all the way into the mountains to search for the man who carried the key, but he had complained about poor visibility in the mists, and their scouting had been limited since.

Torsten was not privy to the Olmese individuals with them, but Queen Surayo had hand-picked each before they'd marched out of Eastbrook, and they all appeared to be highly decorated with numerous torcs around their arms.

The Myr remained a threat, though there had been no full-scale attacks since Foxmouth and Eastbrook, and no one knew when the next strike would be—or where. Queen Surayo had mostly been bolstering their defences, increasing numbers within her forces, and obtaining information.

They followed the river north towards a large patch of woodland that acted as the final natural boundary before reaching the Nethal Mountains. It was a small procession—certainly not something he would have expected if he'd been told to march for war—but he supposed the queen was simply taking down a threat herself. He and the others were there as part of *her* ceremony, rather than having the regular expectations of troops placed upon them.

At least, that's what he assumed.

Even so, it seemed a far greater expense than was necessary to deal with one man. Despite his misgivings about Varlot, sending that brute alone would probably have been adequate. But Queen Surayo had been adamant she'd personally ensure her success. Apollo had failed her in this task once, and he was fresh on his own failure with the second artefact.

Torsten rested one hand on his chest, wishing he could feel Miroth's flame, even a tiny flicker. But he was empty. It was more painful than anything he'd experienced before, and he didn't know how to cope with the loss.

If he proved himself, perhaps Queen Surayo might know of a way to restore the bond. She was a mage, after all, and was capable of twisting magical artefacts for her own use. But it was dependent on Miroth coming to his senses first, and that was the bigger worry.

Despite not having to march on foot, sitting a horse for a few hours had already made him sore, and he longed for a break to get down and stretch his legs. Torsten twisted in his saddle. Half a day's march, and Eastbrook's twisting spires of dark iron still dominated the horizon.

He hoped Varlot left Renys alone. She was his key to Apollo—and redemption—and he wouldn't put it past the man to ruin that for him as well.

When they returned to the palace, he was going to slit Varlot's throat, and be done with it. If Varlot hadn't lied about the artefact, if he'd told him the *hairpin* was what the queen wanted instead of sitting back and doing nothing, Miroth would still be bonded to him. And he wouldn't be a hair's breadth from Surayo disowning him. Or worse.

She was determined to rid Porsenthia of the Myrish key. For all his doubts about her leadership qualities and personality, he could not deny the strength of the Iron Crown. One man had no chance of surviving her wrath.

The river broke away to the west, and woodland pressed in on the north-east. Surayo led them around the trees, and Torsten adjusted his position as the ground shifted from flat plains to a gentle incline. Hills rose beyond the trees, and in the distance, the Nethal Mountains dominated.

Queen Surayo led them onwards as the day wore on, following her farsight as the Citrine Key moved through her lands. It had stopped somewhere in the Nethal Mountains—

or at least, the man carrying the key had stopped—and Surayo was keen to press their advantage. They were making good time, and she'd claimed they'd catch up with him before night fell the following day.

Torsten considered taking the man down himself. That would surely put him squarely back in Queen Surayo's good graces. He ignored the lingering doubt of his proficiency with a sword—Calidra Vantonen might have bested him, but he'd been distracted by Renys and distraught by Miroth—this man wouldn't know what was about to hit him. Such a fool.

It had rained the night before, and the ground was muddy. Though far from turning into a swamp, the occasional flick of wet mud onto his legs and horse's flanks irked Torsten. He was about to suggest an alternative—drier—path, when he heard a distant thrum, like the flapping of wings, cut across the open plains.

The air went still.

Torsten halted, one hand out to stop the Inquisitor marching beside him. 'Hold.'

The march slowed under his order, and Queen Surayo turned towards him with a frown.

A large griffin descended from the clouds—one of the scouts that had flown off some time ago—wings folded back as it dived towards the ground. 'Queen Surayo! A dragon approaches!'

Torsten looked at the river as it wound its way towards Westbrook. The spirit here was reclusive and rarely showed itself before people. Nissa, he thought her name was. He'd only glimpsed her twice in his life, and she'd not left much of an impression on him. No dragon did, compared to Miroth.

'We have no quarrel with the river spirit nor desire to cross. There is no cause for concern,' Queen Surayo replied.

The brown and black griffin alighted a short way ahead of her, the buckles on the war harness around its neck and chest clattering together. Its rider was on his feet atop the animal, breathless. 'Not a river spirit. It's as big as Lord Toriaken! Approaching from the south!'

'No spirit is the size of Toriaken,' Surayo said, an edge to her tone.

'Prepare yourselves!' cried the warrior, as he and his griffin leapt into the air again, a few wayward feathers drifting down from the creature's wings.

Torsten's heart pounded.

The Inquisitors either side of him hesitated, their horses whickering nervously while they muttered to each other—mostly doubting what the Olmese warrior had seen. It was supposed to be a straightforward march. A couple of days to catch up, then Queen Surayo and Toriaken were going to take action.

Whispers broke out across the troops, and hands went to weapons.

Queen Surayo broke away from the ranks, her dappled grey horse trotting ahead, churning up mud with each massive stride. Its black mane waved in the wind and it let out a loud, angry snort. 'Hold your positions. Shields ready!'

The whispers cut off, movement rippling across the lines as everyone braced.

Torsten stared towards the river, ready to urge his horse away the moment any threat appeared. He leaned forward in his saddle, trying to spot any sign of movement. Behind him, the queen's banners rippled, fabric flapping loudly in the quiet breeze. The horse next to him pawed at the ground.

Surayo's horse whipped its tail and shook its head, her iron scales clinking together as she adjusted her grip on the reins.

Perhaps the Olmese scout had been mistaken. Torsten relaxed, unclenching his fist.

Then Miroth crested the slope, his dark wings outstretched.

For a fleeting moment, Torsten's heart soared at the sight of his brother coming back to him. The thought was gone an instant later, as fire burst from Miroth's jaws. He strafed the plains, a column of fire preceding him as he turned everything below to ash.

Shouts of shock and fear broke out around him.

'Lord Miroth!' Torsten cried, but just like in Tonmouth and Fellwood, the dragon did not react. Did not deviate. His huge wings carried him along a meandering path, flapping slowly, lazily, and Miroth let out a guttural roar. He seemed to be flying with no purpose, no destination, save to burn whatever he came across—though Torsten wondered if Miroth had spotted the griffin and followed it.

Or if, *somehow*, Miroth was searching for his brother.

'Toriaken.' Though she was thirty or forty paces from him, Torsten heard Surayo call to her dragon spirit.

Silver-white mist erupted from the two Iron Guards with her. They crumpled, shards of light flaring out from their upper bodies. Within seconds, solid iron had faded as Toriaken formed in front of the gathered troops. Plates of iron ran along the scales on his body—an impenetrable defence—and thick horns protruded from the back of Toriaken's head, making him a formidable aggressor. He unfurled his wings and the enormous spiked club at the end of his tail gouged deep rents in the muddy ground.

Their entire company fit under one of his wings, with plenty of room to spare.

Torsten fought the urge to back away.

Suddenly under his shadow, horses snorted and stamped at the ground—several tried to break and had to be wrestled back in line by their riders. Torsten patted his own mount, trying to keep it from running.

Toriaken lowered his head and let out a furious roar.

Torsten clamped his hands over his ears as the noise shook the ground. Several horses bolted, lurching away with screams that added to the cacophony. Mud was churned up by dozens of hooves and the footsoldiers behind struggled to hold position. 'Stay in line!' Torsten yelled, trying to keep order, while his heart bled for Miroth.

Miroth veered sharply and flew towards Toriaken, answering the challenge with a bellow of his own.

The four griffins dived towards Miroth, one after another, striking out with claws while their riders unleashed arrows or attacked with long, sickle-like blades. Each attack connected, but Miroth's body gave way to shadowy mist, and their attacks passed right through him.

They wheeled around, attacking in new formations, turning and twisting in the air faster and faster. Miroth snapped at one griffin, which narrowly missed his jaws, then unleashed another flaming breath, and the griffins darted out of the line of fire. They shrieked as they escaped, retaliating immediately with more dive-bombs—to no avail.

Torsten's breath caught as Miroth swept low, gliding barely thirty feet above the ground, and headed straight for them. He tried to push his horse towards the approaching dragon so he could try and regain Miroth's senses, but the animal was unwilling and refused to budge—instead backing away, its ears flat.

'Brother!' He leapt from the horse, landing awkwardly on the soft ground, one hand raised towards Miroth. 'Stop this at once!'

But the dragon continued on course.

There was no recognition. Even Miroth's eyes were different—no longer a rich silver but a shadowed grey.

Torsten ran onwards, heedless of the danger. If he could reach Miroth, *touch* him, perhaps he could influence the spirit.

Miroth opened his jaws, and Torsten stared down the dragon's throat. Burning orange light flickered within, lighting up every fang.

A wall of iron blocked Miroth before the flames hit, accompanied by an answering snarl as Toriaken surged upwards in a torrent of force. The two dragons collided, blue so dark it was almost black, and the shifting hues of grey iron.

Torsten gasped for breath. He tilted his head backwards as the dragons fought.

They were almost of a size—something Torsten never truly believed he'd see in his lifetime—and Miroth did not submit. He broke away, sending out violent gusts with every wingbeat, and soared upwards.

Toriaken landed and held his ground, every scale on his body shifting from smooth to jagged iron spikes, and lashed his tail. '*You are tainted, Miroth. Stop now.*'

Torsten's stomach churned as the dragon spoke to Miroth in his own voice—not the queen's.

Miroth let out a thunderous roar, circling back to dive at Toriaken.

'No!' Torsten cried out. Miroth couldn't speak. Couldn't stop. It was all his fault his brother had become corrupted.

Toriaken's jaw peeled back in a vicious snarl. '*So be it.*' He bathed the diving Miroth in white-hot fire.

Torsten backed away, as did half the battalion that hadn't already retreated to safer ground. Smoke washed over him as the two dragons met in a tangle of flame and claws. He threw himself to the muddy ground, and covered the back of his head.

The world had turned mad, and nothing made sense anymore.

Dust and debris was sent flying in the wake of the dragons' wings. It scattered across the grassland, careening into the troops along with floating embers and dark smoke.

Dragons rarely met. They were bound to their domains, save Toriaken and the Archons, and the likelihood of encountering one another was mostly limited to those they bonded with as they traversed Tassar. If this was the result when they met, he wasn't sure Tassar would survive if they regularly shared space.

The snarl of the dragons lessened, and Torsten risked a glance up. Miroth and Toriaken fought in the air, biting and clawing at each other as they flew ever higher.

Someone grabbed him by the arm and hauled him to his feet. 'Master Inquisitor. Up here.'

Torsten struggled to maintain his footing. 'Helios?'

'We need to get clear of that!' Inquisitor Helios hauled him up onto his horse. 'Even Queen Surayo is falling back!'

Torsten shook his head, dazed from the sudden height. Before he'd gathered his senses, Helios whirled his horse away and they galloped across the parts of the plains that weren't on fire to join the remaining soldiers.

'Worst possible time for this! We were so close to that key!' Helios yelled.

Torsten kept his gaze skywards as Miroth and Toriaken fought, too worried for Miroth to respond to Helios's complaint. He was enraptured, too—he could not imagine Toriaken losing any battle in which he took part. Yet Miroth's newfound power was overwhelming, and neither dragon had a clear advantage.

They careened towards the ground, spitting flames, their claws raking at one another. But Toriaken's scales were iron and even Miroth could not damage them. Equally, Toriaken's claws and teeth went straight through Miroth as he shifted from corporeal to water.

As furiously as they fought, neither dragon could harm the other—though the landscape below burned. The griffins circled the two dragons warily, though they dived in to attack whenever they saw an opening.

Fire lit the sky in swathes of orange and red, and the grassland and nearby trees caught flame. Of those soldiers who hadn't fled, most hauled their gourds of water, or threw blankets down to drown the building fires. With the ground so sodden, it took time for each fire to take, and they managed to keep the worst of it under control.

Torsten knew he should help with their efforts, but he couldn't tear his gaze from the sky.

Toriaken barrelled into Miroth, looping his tail around Miroth's neck and forcing them both to the ground. They collided with a crash that sent people to their knees, huge chunks of earth and rock flung high where they landed—Miroth trapped beneath Toriaken's talons.

With a deafening snarl, Miroth again shifted into mist and water, and was free within moments.

But he did not attack again.

He took to the air, each heavy wingstroke lifting him higher. The gusts fanned the fires below, though a few were extinguished.

Toriaken leapt after him, taking to the wing and letting out a deep snarl. The dragon spirit of iron chased the lake spirit away, pushing him east towards the sea.

Torsten slowed his breathing and the ground stopped shaking. He'd been so tense throughout the battle he'd hardly realised his pounding heart or how short of breath he was. Others beside him let out audible sighs of relief as the last of the fires were put out. They'd lost all semblance of formation, and Torsten could not blame them for it.

'I am holding you personally responsible for the damage Miroth causes, Torsten.' Queen Surayo's eyes blazed with fury as she charged towards him, her mount snorting and frothing. 'Fellwood was attacked. I'm sure Westbrook and Horush are at risk now, not to mention countless smaller hamlets dotted across northern Porsenthia. If not for Toriaken, who knows whether Miroth would have stopped before Eastbrook.'

'Miroth is not himself. This destruction is not of his choosing.' Torsten wasn't sure if that was the case, but

Miroth had never been particularly aggressive. He couldn't see why the dragon spirit would rampage unless he had no control over his actions.

'It does not matter whether Miroth *chooses* to do what he does—the fact remains that my lands are burning. We have the Myr encroaching, too, if you were not too busy with your personal tasks to realise.' She dismounted and stood in front of him, meeting his gaze with lilac eyes.

Torsten trembled, and he thought he might bring up bile again. 'My queen, if there is a way Lord Miroth can be stopped, I will do everything in my power to achieve it.'

Surayo's eyes narrowed fractionally. 'There is only one way to kill a dragon spirit. Thankfully for us, Miroth is most of the way towards death already.'

Torsten tried to hide his shock. 'His…his domain?'

'If the lake dies, or is destroyed, Miroth will fade. His threat will be removed.'

Torsten swallowed. 'Is there no other way? No magic you know of that could restore our bond? If that could happen, I could speak with him and—'

'You have messed up once. You do not get a second chance.'

He sank to his knees. 'Your Majesty, please. You are bonded to Toriaken. You know what it is to share your soul with a dragon. I could not leave him to suffer any more than you could!'

'Get up, Torsten. It is most unbecoming to see you beg. You seem to have lost your sense of self-worth along with your dragon spirit. Must I throw you in irons so you can better think on your actions and how they have impacted Porsenthia?'

Torsten didn't have the strength to stand. He bowed his head.

'Miroth's appearance has not only delayed my march, but made it impossible to trek across half the country! If that key does *anything*, the inside of my dungeons will be the least of your concerns.'

Queen Surayo clambered up her horse, heedless of the mud and burnt grassland around her, and she steered her mount away. She raised one fist high, gathering her troops.

Torsten remained on his knees. He didn't hear her commands, his mind reeling, and watched them move onwards.

Slowly, his gaze drifted to the overcast sky, searching for any sign of Miroth. His body ached, the pain lighting a fire of resolve within him. 'My brother. I *will* save you. Even if you no longer see me.'

44
THE GRIFFIN
CALIDRA

It was the second time in as many weeks that Calidra had flown on a griffin. Strange it was the same griffin —Hailathlyl—though it was no less nauseating than the first experience. Thankfully, she was less fearful than before.

At least she had both Jisyel and Malora with her, rather than Varlot. Although the company was better, more things were going wrong than she'd ever imagined possible. Torsten. Renys. Chyram. The Myr.

It was as though everything that made sense in the world had been turned upside down.

Lamp lighters had been making their way from lamppost to lamppost in Fellwood when they'd left, lighting the ones that remained standing, and setting up torches where they didn't. It was a small gesture, but brought comfort.

Fellwood faded behind them, glittering like fireflies.

The sun was beginning to set by the time they'd crossed the mountains north of Fellwood, and Hailathlyl soared over the deadlands as night fell. Calidra didn't want to look down and remember that awful place where life had been stripped from the barren land, but she was compelled to sneak more than a few glances.

Jisyel leaned forward, eyes closed, face tilted into the wind, a hint of a smile playing on her lips.

Calidra hadn't considered the subtler feelings like wind upon skin. Jisyel savoured every new sensation as though it might be snatched away from her again at any moment. 'How does it feel?' Calidra asked.

'Hmm?'

'The wind.' Calidra brushed a hand along Jisyel's cheek.

'I'd forgotten.' She pressed into Calidra's hand.

Calidra had offered words of comfort and support to her sister, but Malora had dismissed most of them. Instead, Malora chewed on the tip of her thumb and stared out at the darkening sky, lost in her own thoughts. So Calidra gave her space.

She didn't think Torsten would hurt Renys, but he *had* ordered her to be shot in the leg. If it came to blows, Calidra wasn't going to be able to take him on a second time. They'd have to rely on Amsel and Hailathlyl, and even he might not want to fight the Porsenthian Empire's Master Inquisitor. Jisyel had had her blessing for less than a day, and though she was probably stronger than Calidra had ever been now she had bonded with a dragon, Calidra didn't want her involved in anything where she might get hurt.

And they'd have to sleep sooner rather than later. She wondered whether the Myr would visit her now she was with someone who had been blessed by a dragon spirit.

She was half-asleep, wondering about that, when Hailathlyl banked sharply, and the crooked fortress of half-melted stone came into view below. Calidra jolted awake and looked over the railing, grabbing hold as they turned.

Just the sight of the place made her nauseous.

She'd spent the night here once before. Back when Fenn had been with them. It was a place of death, and brought with it a deep sense of foreboding that she couldn't shake.

'Ready, Cal? Mal?' Jisyel called to the others.

Malora nodded, her eyes red-rimmed but gaze resolute.

'Hold on. Ground we're landing on is not soft,' Amsel called from his seat behind Hailathlyl's head.

Calidra tightened her grip on the railing with one hand and held onto Jisyel with the other. She closed her eyes and braced as Hailathlyl descended. She counted out her breaths while every wingbeat sent another wave of nausea through her belly, until they landed with a bump. Water or air, she wasn't comfortable unless she had both feet on solid ground.

'I'm coming, Renys,' Malora said, the first one to clamber down the harness strapped across Hailathlyl's body.

'Lady Tamlin, wait!' Amsel called. 'If the Master Inquisitor takes offence at your presence—'

'He can fuck himself,' Malora replied shortly.

Calidra's mouth dropped open. Perhaps Mother *had* been right about some of Apollo's influences on Malora.

Amsel also stuttered, grasping for words as Malora headed towards the open gates of Marlrush Fortress.

'She's angry,' Jisyel said.

'Yes, I can see that,' Calidra replied. Jisyel helped her down to the ground, and supported her as they followed Malora inside. The sooner they entered, the sooner they could leave, and Calidra didn't want to dwell on her thoughts and fears of this place.

'Renys!' Malora called, her voice echoing down the stone halls. 'Renys, darling? Where are you?'

Calidra and Jisyel loitered in the entranceway. Debris had been swept into piles, leaving several paths down the corridors and into various rooms. Though it was empty and dark, it was clear people had recently been here.

'Chyram says there are Myr here. Or...their magic lingers,' Jisyel said, tentatively touching the walls with her fingertips. 'I'm going to help Mal look.'

'Be careful,' Calidra said.

'Don't worry.' Jisyel left Calidra by the wide bannister of

the main stairway, while she, Malora, and Amsel searched rooms. Calidra hated being helpless, but she would only get in the way if she tried to hobble around on one leg. Not to mention the amount of broken weapons, glass, and crumbling stone of the place made it difficult to traverse even were she not recovering from an injury.

Her head and back ached and her eyelids grew heavy, but she forced herself to stay awake while the others searched.

'There's no one here.' Amsel placed one hand on his hip as they reconvened in the entranceway a short while later.

'Where would Torsten have gone? Back to Eastbrook?' Calidra suggested. She couldn't stand to be in the dead, dusty fortress, and Amsel helped her walk back out into the cool night. 'A fortress in disrepair doesn't seem like the usual place he'd work. There's no one here for him to annoy or walk over.' She shivered, her teeth beginning to chatter.

'I was so ready to hold Renys again.' Malora hugged herself. 'So *sure* she would be here. I'd have fought Torsten with my bare hands if I'd had to! He has no right to take her!'

Hailathlyl, who had been laying a short distance from the fortress, raised her head, one orange eye half-open. 'I was resting.'

'Sorry for the noise, Hailathlyl. Thank you for bringing us all this way.' Amsel released Calidra and stroked the griffin's sleek neck feathers affectionately.

'It's so cold. I don't know how you could sleep,' Jisyel said. 'Back to Fellwood?'

'Eastbrook,' Malora corrected. 'Whether Torsten is there or not, it's where the queen will be. I'll need to see her. Explain it's all a misunderstanding. Beg, if I have to. She's the only authority higher than Torsten, so it's the only thing I can do.'

'I must rest,' Hailathlyl said, in as close to an apologetic tone as Calidra was sure she was able.

'Yes. Rest now. You can fly in the morning.' Amsel continued to brush her feathers with the back of one hand.

'Oh! Wait!' Jisyel raced back into the fortress, kicking up a cloud of dust with each step.

Calidra shivered and waited, and when Jisyel reemerged a minute later, she had bundles of wood, rags, and papers in her arms. 'Jisyel?'

Offering them nothing but a grin, Jisyel dropped the bundle on the dry ground and pushed it together in a small pile. She sat down next to it, both hands resting on the papers at the top. She closed her eyes, her smile shifting into a frown, her eyebrows furrowing. A moment later, flames leapt from her fingertips, catching onto the materials she had brought out, and turning them into a crude campfire. 'It tickles.' Jisyel stared at one of her fingers as it burned like a candle.

Calidra grinned at the sight. Despite her misgivings of dragons, whatever gifts Chyram had bestowed upon Jisyel brought her joy. She had to accept that.

'We'll keep the fire going through the night. There's plenty of material in the fortress to feed it. And we can take turns keeping watch,' Jisyel suggested.

'Thank you.' Calidra sat down with a wince and raised her hands to the warming flames.

Malora sat opposite, her knees drawn up and arms wrapped around her legs. When she rested her chin on her knees, Calidra thought she looked very much like Renys.

The crackle of fire was comforting in a way Calidra had never noticed before. Outside the flames' light, she couldn't see the fortress—it was too dark. Her world was simply those few people around the fire, and the light and warmth it brought.

'Jisyel. I…I'm not upset. But I have to know—what was the reason for Chyram's blessing?' Malora asked, fiddling with loose strands of hair.

Calidra turned her attention to Jisyel. She'd wanted to know the same thing, too, and Jisyel had skirted around the subject. She raised an eyebrow and waited.

'It's…it's nothing, really.' Jisyel giggled.

Calidra pursed her lips. That was the giggle Jisyel always let out whenever she was nervous about something. But she didn't push. The night was long and they had hours before any of them could go anywhere.

After the minutes dragged on, and Calidra almost nodded off again, Jisyel took a deep breath. 'He…he wants to become an Archon.'

Malora almost choked. 'He wants *what*?'

'Sounds silly, doesn't it? Apparently it's possible. If he accumulates enough power.'

Malora shook her head. 'How is that supposed to happen? However much gold is in the world is already there. And whatever gold you create doesn't add to his power—not when you're using it to create the gold in the first place.'

Jisyel's gaze fell. 'More worshippers.'

'He has plenty of people fawning over him, begging for gold coins,' Calidra said.

Jisyel scratched her nose and refused to meet either Calidra or Malora's gaze. 'He…he suggested I round up others. Maybe start with those who are already blessed. We take a stand against the Myr.'

'So he wants to use you to acquire glory?' Malora asked.

'That's it. I told you, it's nothing *terrible*. I don't need to live in his shrine or anything. He actually preferred for me to go where I wanted,' Jisyel added quickly, finally looking at Calidra. 'Of course, I don't actually *know* anyone who's blessed. But Selys was a priestess of Neros, wasn't she? Maybe she knows? I was going to write to her. Ask your mother to help me with that, actually. She's from Segandis and your mother knows all the other Lairds. I thought…I thought I might start there.'

'The last time we saw Selys, she was in the Nethal Mountains with Fenn and…Varlot.' Calidra remembered the ship. The Inquisitors. Her frown deepened.

'I know. But, maybe if the letter goes to her home, someone can forward it on to wherever she is? Or she might go back there? I'll send a copy to Neros's Shrine, too. They might be able to help.'

'Will Chyram know if you *don't* do this task of his?' Calidra asked, already trying to think of ways to free Jisyel from the agreement.

'He's always here, Cal. He's not been strict with me. Not demanded anything.'

'Oh really? So he'll be fine if you don't do it? Or if you fail?'

Jisyel's smile faltered. 'He'll rescind the blessing.'

'That's not so bad.'

'And put his own curse on me.'

Calidra exhaled through her nose. She caught Malora's eye, but her sister could only shrug. Damn the dragon spirits. Whatever they did or didn't do, they were nothing but pawns to them. 'The Myr wanted me to cripple Toriaken. Said they had some sort of weapon that could sever the bond between a dragon and a person.' Calidra brushed a large pebble away, rolling it out of the firelight and into the surrounding dark. 'The Myr want me to do something. A dragon wants you to do something. It's all the same.' Bitterness laced her voice. She wondered whether a curse from Chyram would be worse than the one from Hassen.

She didn't want to find out.

Why couldn't these damned spirits leave them alone to live their lives?

They lapsed into companionable quiet for a while, only the fire offering any sound, along with the gentle snores of Hailathlyl.

Malora lifted her head from her knees. 'I am just one

woman. I don't have a blessing,' she glanced at Jisyel, 'I don't have any skill with a sword,' her gaze flicked to Calidra, 'but it doesn't matter. I'm going to Eastbrook. My daughter has been taken and I'm the only one who can do something about it. I'll crawl there if I have to.'

'Mal…' Calidra said.

'You do not have to crawl.' Amsel leaned forward, the golden torc on his arm glinting in the firelight. 'I am in service to Lady Vantonen, but I was not there for you after Foxmouth was attacked. Allow me to make it up to you, Lady Tamlin. Hailathlyl and I will take you to your queen.'

'I wouldn't ask you to. Or demand it,' Malora said in a quiet voice.

'You do not need to. You have no spirit on your side, but there are few dragons in Olmir, and we cope fine. You are the daughter of Lady Vantonen. I am a respected warrior, as is Hailathlyl. We will stand with you when you plead your case.'

Malora allowed herself a small smile. 'Thank you, Amsel.'

'Of course. You should rest. It's late. I'll take the first watch.'

❄

DARKNESS ENVELOPED CALIDRA.

She found she was getting bored of this repeated experience, and though she was nervous, the terror she'd felt during her first encounter had largely drifted away.

She had to give the Myr credit. They were persistent if nothing else. No wonder so many people bargained with them. It would be far easier to go along with what they wanted just to get the creatures out of her mind—regardless of what they offered.

'I just want to sleep.' She said it as more of an

afterthought than directing it towards the Myr, but she was tired and frustrated, and her body ached.

'We grow stronger in your lands. Creeping like mist. It won't be long now.'

'I don't care what you do.'

Chilling laughter reverberated through her mind, like blades stabbing her skull.

She grabbed her head against the pain of it.

'We will reach Fellwood. Even the Isle of Salt. Don't you want your loved ones to be safe? Dragons have hurt them already. Let us take that hurt away and offer protection insead.'

Calidra fumed at their words. The thought of the shadowy creatures of death watching her and her loved ones was enough to make her gut churn. 'I am *not* a pawn to be used. Not by dragons or you.'

She wasn't entirely sure, but it felt like the cold wind receded. So she kept going. Kept pushing. 'I am not going to be part of your scheme! So kill me if you must. Otherwise, get out of my head and leave me alone!' She wished she had her sword. Had the strength in both legs to fight against whatever the Myr threw at her. That would show them.

The cold receded again. *'Fellwood will not be safe. When we rend bone from flesh. When your people are left to die. Know this is your decision.'*

'You'd do that regardless of what I choose!' Calidra didn't care about their words and promises. The Myr had been killing people for centuries. They were creatures of death. It followed in their wake. It was the natural way of the world.

'You could have protected them. You failed.'

Calidra balled her hands. Her heart pounded as sudden fear threatened to billow up and consume her. She sank to her knees and screamed.

'We will cover the land. Returning everything to ash and bone and dust.'

She couldn't speak. Couldn't move. Hatred and panic kept

her rooted to the spot as the Myr's words rushed around her like a gale.

Then, Jisyel was there—a shining, golden light that pushed away the dark mist.

'Jisyel?' Calidra called, her words snatched away by the freezing wind. She reached out with both hands, fumbling in the dark towards the silhouette of her partner, illuminated in gold. Her light pulsed, brighter than the sun.

The Myrish voices disappeared, fading along with the darkness.

The intense, burning cold released its hold on her mind, blown away like dust in the breeze.

And she was surrounded by warm light.

Calidra breathed deeply. The darkness evaporated. She fell into restful sleep.

DAWN WOKE Calidra with tendrils of warmth.

She rubbed away sleep from her eyes. Their small fire burned beside her, but it was a gentle, low flame. It had consumed most of Jisyel's haphazard kindling and left sooty smears on the cracked ground.

Hailathlyl was awake, standing a short distance away, flexing her wings and preening the fur and feathers on her body. Occasionally, she'd pause and fluff up her plumage, only to shake her head and resume preening.

Calidra sat up. Amsel walked out of the fortress, a sack carried over one shoulder. When he spotted her looking, he shrugged. 'Extra supplies are always needed. No one is here to use it except us.'

It was a good idea. Perhaps a few days before, she'd have panicked that Torsten or other Inquisitors would be back here. That they'd get in trouble for taking things that belonged to the queen. But Jisyel had been blessed by a spirit.

And they had a war griffin. The balance of power had shifted, and Torsten would be very foolish indeed to challenge them over a few supplies.

Malora stood to the side, staring up at the fortress, her hair bound back. 'She was here. All alone.'

In the pale morning light, the fortress seemed less unsettling and more…tragic. Calidra got to her feet and limped over to her sister. She hugged Malora tight. 'I know. It'll be okay. If she's half as brave as her mother, she'll be fine. Probably giving Torsten a hard time!'

Malora looked at her feet. Her lip quirked into a half-smile. 'Cal. You came with me this far. It wasn't something I asked of you, but I'm grateful you were with me. You helped show me the right path, even when I was lost in the weeds and struggled to see it myself. You don't have to come with me to face the queen. You should be with Jisyel.'

Amsel stared at the sky. It was clear blue, with only a few wisps of clouds here and there. 'We should leave. Miroth makes the skies unsafe, and visibility is clear. Will you come with Lady Tamlin? Or go back to Fellwood?' He attached the bag of supplies to Hailathlyl's harness, looping it through metal rings with a leather strap to keep it secure.

Jisyel stretched her arms wide. 'I have Chyram's blessing, Cal. Don't worry about me. You can go with your sister. Get your niece back safely.'

Calidra frowned. 'Jisyel, you don't know how to fight.'

'I don't need to. If any Myr try anything, Chyram's fire will keep them away. Fellwood isn't far, and I'm stronger than I've been in years.'

Calidra looked back at Malora, already heading over to Hailathlyl and Amsel.

She was torn.

Her partner was going to gather strength to defend Fellwood—her home—while working with her mother and Chyram. Her sister was going after the Master Inquisitor to get her daughter back—the family Calidra had only recently learned of.

She'd be letting *someone* down, whichever decision she made, even if they didn't say it.

Despite the uncertainty, she felt very little of her usual anxiety. No racing thoughts, no angry voices in her mind of how badly she was messing things up or how she was making things worse. How stupid she was being. She hadn't realised how many of those voices belonged to her mother.

Regardless of where she went, she had her sister back. Malora was no longer acting out of desperation, and she had Amsel and a war griffin to defend her. Jisyel had finally lost her curse—she could experience the delights of the world once again, and with Chyram's blessing in addition.

Calidra would no longer hold her back.

She took a deep breath, enjoying the growing warmth of the early morning sun on her face, and let her heart guide her.

45
THE SHADOW GATE
FENN

Snow gave way to barren stone. No more trees lined the path, no more birds soared overhead. There were no animals crawling past or moss clinging to rocks.

It was peaceful.

As it should be.

Without noise. Without movement.

It was cold, too. No fires to burn and blacken the landscape. Not much colour, either.

'Wouldn't it be so much better if everything was like this?'

Fenn nodded, absently. There was a deep ache in his left foot, but it was hardly worth spending any thought on. He trudged onwards, safe in the knowledge his journey was almost over.

He was dimly aware of movement, though he couldn't tell where it was. A slight flutter, like a butterfly. A hint of silver glowing in the dark. Some part of him reached inward for it, but it slipped through his grasp.

Without thinking, he reached into his pocket and clutched the key. It was all that mattered. Not butterflies or pains.

A deep roar echoed faintly in the distance, and he turned

his head towards the noise. So high up, he could see for leagues into Porsenthia—parts of it were blackened and smoking. But aside from smudges of colour here and there, he couldn't make out any details. Certainly nothing responsible for that guttural roar.

Fenn returned his attention to the path. He hadn't stopped to sleep or eat—didn't feel the need to—even though each step grew heavier and harder than the one before. It wouldn't be long now.

Soon, everything would be over.

THERE WERE footsteps in the snow surrounding the cave. Noise, light, and movement, too.

It irritated him for reasons he couldn't explain.

He followed the path to the cave mouth, some tension easing away when he stepped into the dark tunnel. It was familiar in a way he couldn't describe—like coming home. Ice covered the rocky walls and ceiling, and he had to be careful not to slip. It took several moments for his eyes to adjust to the dim light, not that he *needed* to see with much clarity. The invisible pull on his body had been all he'd needed to find his way.

Fenn grasped the stalagmites with his free hand as he walked past them, more to ensure he didn't walk into them than for support. Water dripped somewhere ahead, and he slowed his pace to listen. There was plenty of ice here, but it was so cold, he couldn't think how any of it could melt.

He continued down the tunnel, wary. It was bathed heavily in shadow, though he could just make out where it opened up ahead, widening into the chamber where *Vermecio* waited. Recognising that made him giddy.

A silhouette appeared in front of him. Beads rattled together as the person moved.

Fenn halted in the middle of the tunnel, one hand on a nearby stalagmite, the other pressed against the icy wall. Joy shifted to irritation. 'Who's there?'

'I hoped you wouldn't come here,' replied the voice. It was somewhat distorted in the tunnel, but he recognised it. She sounded tired. Resigned.

It took him another few seconds to add a name to the recognition. 'Selys?'

'The betrayer.'

'Selys, don't talk to him!' Cried a male voice from deeper in the tunnel—perhaps the chamber itself.

Selys ignored it and stared at him, not breaking eye contact. He shifted, uncomfortable under her gaze. 'Fenn. I have a ship docked nearby. Let's go to it. We can sail anywhere you want. I've heard you might be from Ma-Rai, might have family there. Isn't that great?' She stepped forward, her features appearing more clearly as she drew closer. 'There's no need for the key if we have answers, is there?'

Fenn wavered.

Selys had betrayed him. Had spoken to him through Neros. And now he was moments from getting his memories back, she was trying another trick to get him to stop. Anger bubbled up. 'I thought you were my friend.' He hadn't spoken since getting off the boat, and his voice didn't sound like his own. It grated.

'I am your friend, Fenn! I have *always* been your friend!'

'But you're trying to stop me.'

Selys took another step closer. 'I'm trying to help you. The key is Myrish. They're the enemy. Have you forgotten what I told you?' She reached for him with one hand, the other holding onto her glaive.

He stared at the wicked-looking blade. She could easily disembowel him with that.

'Don't do this, Fenn. Don't!' Selys pleaded.

He took a shuddering breath. The voice in his head and the pull on his body were insistent on dragging him towards *Vermecio*. Selys didn't understand what he'd been through, nor what he was trying to do. 'You are a liar.' Something in him wanted to grab the key, to blast her away like he'd done with Neros, but he refused to let it. He didn't want to give her any more reason to hate him.

Selys had stood by him when everyone else had been afraid and mistrustful. She was scared now, and he didn't want to punish her for that. 'Get out of my way, Selys. Go to your ship and leave.' Fenn pushed past her.

She tried to bar his path with the glaive, then caught his gaze. Whatever she saw was enough to get her to back off, and Fenn continued unhindered into the wide chamber, where cold water pooled up to his ankles.

Two people stood in the far corner, a man who bore a striking resemblance to Selys—he wore a curious, faintly glowing shell around his neck—and a woman.

The man raised a short, curved sword towards him. 'Fenn. Stop right there.'

Fenn ignored him—the key was stronger than any blade—and looked at the woman. She had pale skin and black hair, but her eyes…he couldn't make out her features. Her face was obscured by darkness, a shadow that shifted continually like writhing mist.

Something in his chest pulled him towards her, not *Vermecio*.

'An imposter.'

Fenn nodded, and the pull disappeared. Everything made sense when he listened to the voice.

'Fenn? Fenn, it's me!' The pale woman stepped towards him, only to be held back at the last moment as the man grabbed her arm.

'Not too close.' The warning was evident in his tone, even though his pale blue eyes were locked on Fenn.

There was something about the man, or perhaps it was the shell—

'Fenn, it's Evarine! Don't you know me? Selys said you'd forgotten so much! I can't believe it's really you! You're alive! You're *here*! They said you would be!'

Fenn remembered Sanis had mentioned Evarine's name. It had been floating around in his mind, gone in an instant, only to reappear again hours later, like petals on the wind. 'You…you use that name against me? Is this another trick of yours, Selys? How dare you sink so low.' He turned around to face Selys, who lingered in the mouth of the tunnel, both hands on her glaive.

'Fenn…' Selys shook her head.

Frustrated, he returned his attention to the chamber.

Vermecio sat beside the two people, a statue of stone and ice—though most of the ice seemed to have melted into the pool that filled the cavern. It watched him with three eyes. '*Our time is now.*'

The voice in his head echoed *Vermecio's* words.

This was it. The end of his journey. What he had been fighting so hard to achieve.

'Fenn. Not another step.'

He barely glanced at the man who'd spoken with such authority. Not too long ago, and he'd have cowered before anyone who raised their voice at him. Now, with the key, on the cusp of regaining everything he'd lost, Fenn had nothing to fear. 'Stand aside. I'm going to find out who I am.'

Fenn waited for the man to move, but neither he or the woman with him so much as shifted their weight. He walked towards them, water splashing as he crossed the pool.

A thin wisp of smoke passed across his face, acrid and burning. It tickled his nose and made his eyes water.

'No!' Evarine cried.

Fenn ducked, moving by some hidden instinct, as an arrow whistled past his head and embedded itself in the ice-covered wall. Shocked, he threw himself to the ground as a second arrow sliced through his cheek. Blood splattered into the water. He wiped his face, fingers coming away red.

Someone swore behind and above him, and he rolled onto his back, heedless of the freezing water. It was too dark to make out the people on the ledge, but there was nowhere else the arrows could have been fired from.

Fenn grabbed the key and pulled it from his pocket, filling the chamber with vivid yellow light.

Everyone around him screamed.

Selys disappeared down the tunnel, and the man and woman in the chamber sank to their knees, covering their eyes and faces with cries of agony.

'A sliver of gold. A blade you cannot fight with. A bow from which an arrow cannot fire,' Vermecio's grating voice rumbled around the chamber.

'The Citrine Key,' Fenn pulled himself to his feet, water trickling down his arms and legs in cold rivulets. 'You said if I brought it to you, you'd have the power to restore my memories.' He took several panting breaths, hands shaking.

The butterfly thrashed in his chest.

Vermecio's mouth opened with the grinding of stone, dust scattering to the icy ground. The movement seemed to suck all breath from the air. A keyhole appeared within its parted stone jaws.

Another arrow whizzed past. Fenn wondered if they were so desperate to keep him from his family they were shooting blindly into the chamber.

But it didn't matter.

It was over.

He took the last few steps through the pool, ripples shivering across the water, until he stood before the construct. It did not speak, did not move, simply stared at him with three lidless eyes, its body shifting from grey to black to purple to yellow and back again.

Fenn pushed the Citrine Key deep into *Vermecio's* open jaws, his arm half-swallowed by the rock.

Something heavy crunched, dust and pebbles skittering down *Vermecio's* body and splashing into the water. Colours flickered across the surface of *Vermecio*, shifting through the spectrum too fast to follow, before settling on the deepest grey. Each of *Vermecio's* eyes turned black before brightening slowly to amber. Then it spoke.

'Time has come to tear the veil,
When key and gate collide,
Our shadows cover land and sea,
Your forces stand allied.'

Dark mist poured from the construct, a waterfall cascading down its body. More appeared every second, until a deluge careened into Fenn with such force, it knocked him backwards.

Fenn yelped and landed heavily in the water. Mist covered him, creeping up his arms, legs, across his chest. He let out a cry of shock as it snaked up his neck and over his face. He squeezed his eyes shut, expecting pain.

But there was nothing.

When he opened his eyes, the shadows were gone from him—though they continued to pour from *Vermecio*, slowly covering the chamber floor—and he saw and *felt* his body with devastating clarity. He'd twisted his ankle at some point, though hadn't truly felt the pain until now. He was exhausted, hungry, and so thirsty his throat ached. Bruises littered his body, the skin on the soles of his feet scraped raw.

Hassen's fury rose like a torrent—threatening to overwhelm his senses. The dragon roared, butterflies bursting from his scales and filling his mind with violent thrashing.

The shadowy mist bubbling from *Vermecio* reached the cavern walls and stretched upwards, slowly blackening the roof of the cave. Thick plumes of mist filled every inch of the chamber, bubbling and swirling against the walls like a caged animal trying to break free.

The roof cracked, and a thin stream of weak sunlight filtered in.

Still, the darkness grew. It swelled and writhed like a living creature, and more dark mist poured out from the construct every second. Suddenly, with a deafening explosion that sent Fenn reeling, the chamber blasted open. Chunks of stone and ice were flung in all directions, crashing into the water around him. Above him, the smoke coalesced into a pillar that shot into the sky.

Fenn tilted his head back as far as he could, mouth falling open at the incomprehensible sight.

'Fenn!' someone shouted at him—Selys or Evarine, or both, he couldn't tell—but he was transfixed and couldn't tear his gaze away.

What remained of the grey, overcast day transformed before his eyes. The top of the shadowy pillar stretched outwards, swirling in a circular vortex. Wisps of shadow broke off and snaked away, jumping down the pillar like fish leaping from a river. Every moment that passed, the vortex grew wider, until a circle of darkness filled the sky far above the mountain.

'You fool!' Hassen roared, fire streaking through Fenn's mind. *'I fought against the Myr inside you. But you stopped fighting! You let them suppress me! You believed their tricks and lies!'*

Fenn trembled, looking away from the shadows above. 'Their... lies?'

'You were so afraid of the harder path that you blocked me out. I should curse you for this!' More flames roiled within Fenn. *'But you've cursed all of Tassar, so it makes no difference.'*

He didn't want to believe it, but the fog of confusion that had been present in his mind since meeting *Vermecio* that first time finally lifted. Fenn could see Hassen in all his glory, a green dragon in his mind, with plants, vegetation, and thorns protruding from his scales and fire in his jaws.

He looked at the woman standing close to *Vermecio* and saw not an imposter—her face marred by shadow, eyes sunken and lost—but Evarine. *Evarine.* His Evarine.

Whom he'd spent close to a decade of his life with.

Saw them walking hand in hand along the snowy banks of the river behind their village. Saw them hand-feeding their goats, ready for a difficult winter. Saw them curled up beside a fire, surrounded by the quiet of night and starlight overhead.

Saw the corrupted river spirit, Manori, burning through Ma-Rai. It had burned Evarine, too.

He...

He'd...

Evarine's eyes brimmed with tears. 'I waited for you, Fenn. All through the night. In the freezing snow. And you never came! You *left* me!'

Fenn swallowed hard. The Myr had swept through Ma-Rai like a plague, and he'd taken up arms against the creatures of death. He remembered them, saw them as vividly as if they were standing in front of him right now. Hunched creatures with skin like tar and amber eyes that glinted. The same fear he'd felt then flooded him again, even with Hassen's presence. No one had stood a chance against the creatures of death, but they'd tried anyway. The Myr had rushed forward, a flood of magic and shadow, sweeping through everyone who'd fought them.

They'd spoken of Manori's attack. How Evarine had been burned and left for dead, along with scores of others from Ma-Rai. They'd offered a path to take vengeance. A way to fight the dragons who had hurt them.

The only way to fight back.

He'd wanted to keep Evarine safe. Protect everyone else in Ma-Rai from Manori's rampage.

Their words had filled him, consumed him, as they'd dragged his body—and countless others—to the freezing cliffs far to the north of Meneos.

'What belonged to thine,

Now stolen as mine.

Memories, once crystal clear,

Are lost, leaving only fear.'

Everything he knew of himself and his life had been stripped away. Where he lived. His friends and families. Hopes and dreams. He'd clutched onto his name, the very essence of himself, as everything else was peeled away in a roaring storm of mist and shadow. A gust whipped him, pulling away more and more of himself, piece by piece, as a bladed whip might rip away chunks of flesh, until there was nothing but a shadow of himself left.

'Hope gone and dreams broken,

Scattered in the wind, unspoken.

Smother iron's endless sight,

Restore our voices unto light.'

They'd wanted to break Toriaken. The one true threat against the Myr. The force that had driven them away before. Fenn had been ordered to help in this. To act *against* the Iron Crown. He'd had any loyalties removed so he'd be willing to obey.

More of the Myr's magic had flooded him after they'd stolen his life, burning his veins and breath.

'Open soon will the gate,

Your suffering within do'eth await.

Revenge is our key to start,

And life's fate shall be Death's art.'

The Myrish curse branded itself onto him, pressing deep into his skin, his bones, his mind. More and more magic flooded through him, pushing out all else but the curse, but *their* desires. His heart pounded at the invading force, his muscles taut as he'd tried to push them out.

Then there had been the cold snap of the sea as he'd been pushed in and left adrift as the Myr's magic shredded his mind. Ripping it apart and stitching it back together, over and over, forcing out everything except their goals.

The iron dragon blinded.

The key, the start of their revenge. To open the gate. To allow death's art to reign.

To enable their revenge against Tassar.

Fenn sank to his knees as his memories returned to him, one by one, each a burn on his mind for what he'd done, and who he'd done it for. For every ignored warning, every question pushed aside in favour of the easier path.

Apollo and Nadja, whom he'd left to die in the Moonlight Palace without a thought.

More stone shook free in the tremors, chunks of rubble collapsing from the ceiling and walls. Stalactites fell with a piercing shriek, spearing the ground below. Part of the cave wall crumbled, sending splinters of ice and rock splashing into the pool on the chamber floor.

'Everyone get clear!' yelled the man with the shell.

'Fenn! We have to get out of here!' Evarine shouted. She ran to him and grabbed him by the shoulders.

But the man hesitated, glaring at *Vermecio*, his face pulled into an ugly grimace.

'Kaio! Get out of there!' Selys cried.

Fenn was too dazed to move, his legs weak and shaky. He held onto Evarine, but his grip was weak.

Kaio leapt forward and plunged his arm into *Vermecio's* open jaws.

'What are you doing?' Selys half-stepped into the chamber, using her glaive to bat away falling rocks and bits of ice.

'Key started this! Trying to get it out of there!' Kaio yelled back, adjusting his grip despite the mist pouring from *Vermecio* and adding to the growing pillar overhead. More stone crumbled around them, shaking the ground. The muscles in Kaio's arms bunched as he heaved.

'Kaio!' More people shouted for him.

Fenn wondered who this man was to inspire such loyalty in others. Evarine crouched in the water beside Fenn, squeezing him tightly.

With a final wrench, Kaio pulled his arm out—skin blackened like charcoal around his empty fingers—and hissed in pain. He clutched his arm with his good hand and stepped back, panting. 'Fucking Myr. Was worth a try.' Dark mist wreathed his forearm where he'd touched *Vermecio*—or the key—and stuck to his skin like oil. He shook his head and ran across the chamber, back into the tunnel, ignoring Fenn and Evarine where they huddled together.

Fenn watched him go. Selys was gone from the tunnel's mouth. So were the archers. Everyone who'd been there waiting for him—save Evarine.

'Fenn, please!' Evarine begged.

He trembled. He'd ruined everything. He'd worked so hard to gain what he'd lost that he hadn't seen what was right in front of him. The Myr's voices had tricked him from the beginning, fooled him into thinking he was listening to Hassen.

Even the dragon said nothing now his fury had been unleashed.

'I don't want to die here, Fenn.'

He brought her hands to his lips and kissed them. 'Go with them. Get away from here. From…from me. Trust Selys. Listen to her. I'm sorry. I'm so sorry, Evarine. For everything. You deserve better.'

She held on tight, refusing to go. 'Fenn.'

Something screamed, an otherworldly shriek that set his teeth on edge. Fenn looked up, following the pillar of darkness to the vortex swirling far above. It pulsed, more mist spilling down it like a waterfall. Wisps of shadow darted in and out.

Abruptly, the vortex stopped expanding. The rushing wind slowed to a gentle breeze. His breath caught, and it felt as if the entire world did the same.

Then, just as he dared to exhale shakily, everything shifted.

Rolling darkness swept down the pillar—dozens, hundreds of shadowed creatures leaping and falling in a wave large enough to rival anything Neros could make. Claws and wings, muzzles and tails, skulls and horns. They careened down the pillar and flowed along the mountainside, falling beyond sight, covering everything they touched in shadow.

The bastion spoke again. Its voice grew stronger with every word, until its booming filled the shaking, mist-filled cavern.

'Rolling darkness, spirits live,
Your people left to die,
And once we rend bone from flesh,
Dragons will ne'er again arise.'

END

EPILOGUE

APOLLO

Stinging cold seeped into Apollo, both muscle and bone. It numbed every limb, gently sapping away his pain like a lover leaving tender kisses across his skin.

It was comforting. Peaceful, almost. Apt that he was going to die here—in the vast, quiet palace, in a desolate landscape, where death reigned.

Accepting it took away his fear. His fight.

He wished he could see Malora one last time. Tell her how much she meant to him, how much he loved her. How she'd made him a better person.

Renys's face flashed in his mind, along with the knowledge she was trapped by Torsten. Apollo forced his eyes back open. He *couldn't* give up. Not while that bastard had her. Not while he had breath left—even if that wasn't to be for much longer.

With effort, he turned towards Nadja. The woman was slumped forward, eyes shut, holding her elbow. It had stopped bleeding, but she'd drifted into unconsciousness some time ago, and hadn't moved in a while. Her chest rose and fell with occasional breaths, but even they were slowing down.

They were finished.

Even if Torsten had passed Nadja's message to Queen Surayo—or anyone else who was willing to help—they were days away at best. And they had to get past Paragos.

He fell forward, catching himself on his forearms. He'd only slumped over from a sitting position, but the stone floors were so hard and cold, the sudden contact jolted him. A worrying thud and splatter accompanied the movement, and he looked underneath himself to see more blood oozing from the deep wound across his belly.

He turned away. Better to not look.

Then he realised something else shone underneath him. With great effort, he reached down, fingers catching the side of something sharp as he pulled it towards his face.

Malora's dagger.

Even in the gloom, the bright ogee pattern was unmistakable. Emotion writhed in his gut. Love. Terror. Anger.

'Fuck…this…' Apollo gasped, eyes rolling back when he tried to stand up. 'I can't…can't die here. I have…have to…get…Renys.'

There was only one thing he could do.

Apollo crawled.

He pulled himself forward inch by inch, blood trailing on the blue floor behind him. Every movement was agony, the muscles in his arms burning by the time he reached the door, but he no longer felt the pain in his belly. He didn't know how much time he had left.

Apollo gritted his teeth and continued on, dragging himself along the dark corridor, only the pulsing blue light in the walls for company, until he reached the top of the stairs. Faint chewing noises drifted up from below, and he almost threw up at the sound of it.

He wasn't sure how long he and Nadja had spent in that room. Minutes? Hours? Days?

No, couldn't have been days. They'd be dead already if that was the case.

He kept talking himself through what he'd done, what he'd seen, what he'd felt. As long as he kept his mind alert, he would be fine. He'd manage.

Every step down sent another jolt of pain along his arms, but he continued, half pulling, half rolling down the staircase. His vision swam, mixing blue stone and red blood, or maybe that was because he'd rolled down the last few steps. He landed with a thud, the breath pushed from his lungs.

His head pounded and he grew dizzy. Had he just fallen down the front steps of *The Grumpy Fisherman*? He couldn't remember the last time he'd had that much ale that he'd tripped over. Malora would help him to his feet, then she'd laugh at him for being so silly. Tell him he needed to go to bed and sleep off the worst of it.

Renys would want to try a sip of his ale, and when Malora wasn't looking, he'd let her drink the froth on top, bubbles coating her face.

Apollo blinked.

Everything grew dim, and a faint pulse of blue light drew his attention.

Fuck.

He wasn't at home.

He was in the Moonlight Palace, lying in a pool of his own blood.

Silence surrounded him—the chewing had stopped. There were no footsteps approaching, no breath of the creature down here. He tried to gather what strength he had left to speak. 'You here…Myr? I…I dunno your…name.'

'You are almost dead.' Came a disembodied voice.

Apollo closed his eyes, it took too much concentration to focus on what little he could see in the darkness. 'Not yet.'

'Soon enough. You are on the edge of the spirit world. You will be ours soon.'

'Got a request...if you don't mind...' Why was talking so difficult? His breathing grew laboured, a pressure on his lung stopping him from taking more than a shallow gasp of air.

'A request?'

'Can you...save eating my legs...until last...Kinda need them to...walk out...of here.'

Laughter resounded, the noise so sharp it hurt his ears. *'You will not be walking out of here. You cannot stand. Soon you will not live.'*

'You sure?'

'We are of death. I see you more clearly in the spirit world than in this one.'

Apollo coughed, groaning at the effort and resulting pain. 'A bargain, then. If...if I'm to be yours...anyway. Why not... help me? You'll have...me soon enough. And I...I get one last thing.'

The creature moved around him.

Apollo felt the air shift as it considered. 'Don't have... much time... '

'You have nothing I want. I desire flesh. You have provided this.'

'Nothing in...all of Tassar...you want? More than...a meal?' Apollo coughed again, felt himself drool. Or perhaps it was blood dripping down his lips. He didn't have the ability to even wipe his face. 'Save me. Save Nadja. And...I'll...help you.'

'Why? You fought me. Tried to stop the key being taken.'

'My...daughter. I need...to save her.'

'Ah. You would give your life for hers. You creatures care so much for your fleeting time here.'

Apollo couldn't speak anymore. He'd made his last attempt to bargain. He couldn't lift his head, couldn't feel anything.

The creature touched him—something sharp pressed against his forehead. Its voice hissed in his ear and mind at the same time. *'You will destroy Queen Surayo's sword, forged centuries ago, into which Toriaken's soul is bound.'*

'A sword?' There was nothing but darkness in all directions. He couldn't feel the floor under him, but equally, couldn't feel any more pain. He had no body to move.

'Yes. The sword,' replied the Myr.

'What happens if it's destroyed? Will it kill the spirit of iron?'

'No. Toriaken will be free.'

Apollo was confused, which wasn't surprising considering he was caught somewhere between life and death, while bargaining for his life. It reminded him of how vulnerable he'd felt with Nestol peeling back his mind and sorting through his thoughts. He wanted to recoil, but the Myr was offering him a final thread to hold onto. So he reached for it.

'If Toriaken is free, won't he be more deadly? I thought the Myr were driven away by him?'

'He has been a slave to humanity for generations. I would think he would be angry. Leave them. The Iron Crown will be no more.'

Apollo didn't see how it could help the Myr. But he wasn't one of them and didn't pay much attention to the magic in the world. Things that didn't impact his life had never been worth knowing.

And yet the bargain was simple. So very, very simple.

It was a second chance. He could free Renys. Ensure Malora was safe. Maybe throw Torsten off a bridge if he had the chance before the Myr claimed him.

If he stayed here and died, everything was for nothing.

With the Myr's help, he'd be able to do right by his family. Maybe even leave his mark on the world.

'Destroy the sword. This is our bargain.'

'Nadja is not part of this bargain. She has to do nothing for you. But I need her to get away. My life for hers. You don't touch Nadja. Malora. Renys.'

'Our bargain,' the Myr repeated.

The power was a terrible beauty.

'Our bargain.'

The *Dragon Spirits* trilogy concludes in Book Three:
The Broken Sword